W9-ANJ-674

VINTAGE
INTERNATIONAL

BOOKS BY *Vladimir Nabokov*

NOVELS

Mary
King, Queen, Knave
The Defense
The Eye
Glory
Laughter in the Dark
Despair
Invitation to a Beheading
The Gift
The Real Life of Sebastian Knight
Bend Sinister
Lolita
Pnin
Pale Fire
Ada or Ardor: A Family Chronicle
Transparent Things
Look at the Harlequins!

SHORT FICTION

Nabokov's Dozen
A Russian Beauty and Other Stories
Tyrants Destroyed and Other Stories
Details of a Sunset and Other Stories
The Enchanter

DRAMA

The Waltz Invention
Lolita: A Screenplay
The Man from the USSR and Other Plays

AUTOBIOGRAPHY AND INTERVIEWS

Speak, Memory: An Autobiography Revisited

Strong Opinions

BIOGRAPHY AND CRITICISM

Nikolai Gogol

Lectures on Literature

Lectures on Russian Literature

Lectures on Don Quixote

TRANSLATIONS

Three Russian Poets: Translations of Pushkin, Lermontov, and Tiutchev

A Hero of Our Time (Mikhail Lermontov)

The Song of Igor's Campaign (Anon.)

Eugene Onegin (Alexander Pushkin)

LETTERS

The Nabokov-Wilson Letters: Correspondence between Vladimir Nabokov and Edmund Wilson, 1940–1971

Vladimir Nabokov: Selected Letters: 1940–1977

MISCELLANOUS

Poems and Problems

The Annotated Lolita

THE GIFT

THE GIFT

A NOVEL BY

Vladimir Nabokov

Translated from the Russian by Michael Scammell with the collaboration of the author

VINTAGE INTERNATIONAL
VINTAGE BOOKS
A DIVISION OF RANDOM HOUSE, INC.
NEW YORK

FIRST VINTAGE INTERNATIONAL EDITION, MAY 1991

Copyright © 1963 by Article 3C Trust
Under the Will of Vladimir Nabokov

All rights reserved under International and Pan-American Copyright Conventions. Published in the United States by Vintage Books, a division of Random House, Inc., New York, and distributed in Canada by Random House of Canada Limited, Toronto. This translation originally published by G. P. Putnam's Sons in 1963. This edition published by arrangement with the Estate of Vladimir Nabokov.

Portions of this book first appeared in English in *The New Yorker*. © 1963 by The New Yorker Magazine, Inc.

Library of Congress Cataloging-in-Publication Data
Nabokov, Vladimir Vladimirovich, 1899–1977.
[Dar. English]
The gift: a novel/by Vladimir Nabokov; translated from the Russian by Michael Scammell with the collaboration of the author.–
1st Vintage international ed.
p. cm.–(Vintage international)
ISBN 0-679-72725-6 (pbk.)
I. Title.
PG3476.N3D313 1991
891.73′42–dc20 90-50624
CIP

Manufactured in the United States of America
10 9 8 7 6 5 4 3 2 1

TO VÉRA

Foreword

THE greater part of *The Gift* (in Russian, *Dar*) was written in 1935–1937, in Berlin; its last chapter was completed in 1937 on the French Riviera. The leading émigré magazine *Sovremennye Zapiski*, conducted in Paris by a group of former members of the Social Revolutionary party, published the novel serially (63–67, 1937–8), omitting, however, Chapter Four, which was rejected for the same reasons that the biography it contains was rejected by Vasiliev in Chapter Three (p. 219): a pretty example of life finding itself obliged to imitate the very art it condemns. Only in 1952, almost twenty years after it was begun, did there appear an entire edition of the novel brought out by that Samaritan organization, the Chekhov Publishing House, New York. It is fascinating to imagine the regime under which *Dar* may be read in Russia.

I had been living in Berlin since 1922, thus synchronously with the young man of the book; but neither this fact, nor my sharing some of his interests, such as literature and lepidoptera, should make one say "aha" and identify the designer with the design. I am not, and never was, Fyodor Godunov-Cherdyntsev; my father is not the explorer of Central Asia that I still may become some day; I never wooed Zina Mertz, and never worried about the poet Koncheyev or any other writer. In fact, it is rather in Koncheyev, as well as in another incidental character, the novelist Vladimirov, that I distinguish odds and ends of myself as I was circa 1925.

In the days I worked on this book, I did not have the knack of recreating Berlin and its colony of expatriates as radically and ruthlessly as I have done in regard to certain environments in my later, English, fiction. Here and there history shows through artistry. Fyodor's attitude toward Germany reflects too typically perhaps the crude and irrational contempt that Russian émigrés had for the "natives" (in Berlin, Paris or Prague). My young man is moreover influenced by the rise of a nauseous dictatorship belonging to the period when the novel was written and not to the one it patchily reflects.

The tremendous outflow of intellectuals that formed such a prominent part of the general exodus from Soviet Russia in the first years of the Bolshevist Revolution seems today like the wanderings of some mythical tribe whose bird-signs and moon-signs I now retrieve from the desert dust. We remained unknown to American intellectuals (who, bewitched by Communist propaganda, saw us merely as villainous generals, oil magnates, and gaunt ladies with lorgnettes). That world is now gone. Gone are Bunin, Aldanov, Remizov. Gone is Vladislav Khodasevich, the greatest Russian poet that the twentieth century has yet produced. The old intellectuals are now dying out and have not found successors in the so-called Displaced Persons of the last two decades who have carried abroad the provincialism and Philistinism of their Soviet homeland.

The world of *The Gift* being at present as much of a phantasm as most of my other worlds, I can speak of this book with a certain degree of detachment. It is the last novel I wrote, or ever shall write, in Russian. Its heroine is not Zina, but Russian Literature. The plot of Chapter One centers in Fyodor's poems. Chapter Two is a surge toward Pushkin in Fyodor's literary progress and contains his attempt to describe his father's zoological explorations. Chapter Three shifts to Gogol, but its real hub is the love poem dedicated to Zina. Fyodor's book on Chernyshevski, a spiral within a sonnet, takes care of Chapter Four. The last chapter combines all the preceding themes and adumbrates the book Fyodor dreams of writing some day: *The Gift*. I wonder how far the imagination of the reader will follow the young lovers after they have been dismissed.

The participation of so many Russian muses within the orchestration of the novel makes its translation especially hard. My son Dmitri Nabokov completed the first chapter in English, but was prevented from continuing by the exigencies of his career. The four other chapters were translated by Michael Scammell. In the winter of 1961, at Montreux, I carefully revised the translation of all five chapters. I am responsible for the versions of the various poems and bits of poems scattered throughout the book. The epigraph is not a fabrication. The epilogic poem mimicks an Onegin stanza.

VLADIMIR NABOKOV

Montreux, March 28, 1962

THE GIFT

An oak is a tree. A rose is a flower. A deer is an animal. A sparrow is a bird. Russia is our fatherland. Death is inevitable.

P. SMIRNOVSKI, *A Textbook of Russian Grammar.*

Chapter One

ONE cloudy but luminous day, towards four in the afternoon on April the first, 192– (a foreign critic once remarked that while many novels, most German ones for example, begin with a date, it is only Russian authors who, in keeping with the honesty peculiar to our literature, omit the final digit) a moving van, very long and very yellow, hitched to a tractor that was also yellow, with hypertrophied rear wheels and a shamelessly exposed anatomy, pulled up in front of Number Seven Tannenberg Street, in the west part of Berlin. The van's forehead bore a star-shaped ventilator. Running along its entire side was the name of the moving company in yard-high blue letters, each of which (including a square dot) was shaded laterally with black paint: a dishonest attempt to climb into the next dimension. On the sidewalk, before the house (in which I too shall dwell), stood two people who had obviously come out to meet their furniture (in *my* suitcase there are more manuscripts than shirts). The man, arrayed in a rough greenish-brown overcoat to which the wind imparted a ripple of life, was tall, beetle-browed and old, with the gray of his whiskers turning to russet in the area of the mouth, in which he insensitively held a cold, half-defoliated cigar butt. The woman, thickset and no longer young, with bowlegs and a rather attractive pseudo-Chinese face, wore an astrakhan jacket; the wind, having rounded her, brought a whiff of rather good but slightly stale perfume. They both stood motionless and watched fixedly, with such attentiveness that one might think they were about to be short-changed, as three red-necked husky fellows in blue aprons wrestled with their furniture.

Some day, he thought, I must use such a scene to start a good, thick old-fashioned novel. The fleeting thought was touched with a careless irony; an irony, however, that was quite unnecessary, because somebody within him, on his behalf, independently from him, had absorbed all this, recorded it, and filed it away. He himself had only moved in today, and now, for the first time, in the still unaccustomed state of local resident, he had run out to buy a few things. He knew the street and indeed the whole neighborhood: the boardinghouse from which he had moved was not far; until now, however, the street had revolved and glided this way and that, without any connection with him; today it had suddenly stopped; henceforth it would settle down as an extension of his new domicile.

Lined with lindens of medium size, with hanging droplets of rain distributed among their intricate black twigs according to the future arrangement of leaves (tomorrow each drop would contain a green pupil); complete with a smooth tarred surface some thirty feet across and variegated sidewalks (hand-built, and flattering to the feet), it rose at a barely perceptible angle, beginning with a post office and ending with a church, like an epistolary novel. With a practiced eye he searched it for something that would become a daily sore spot, a daily torture for his senses, but there seemed to be nothing of that sort in the offing, and the diffuse light of the gray spring day was not only above suspicion but even promised to mollify any trifle that in more brilliant weather would not fail to crop up; this could be anything: the color of a building, for instance, that immediately provoked an unpleasant taste in the mouth, a smack of oatmeal, or even halvah; an architectural detail that effusively caught one's attention every time one passed by; the irritating sham of a caryatid, a hanger-on and not a support, which, even under a lighter burden, would crumble into plaster dust; or, on a tree trunk, fastened to it by a rusty thumbtack, a pointless but perpetually preserved corner of a notice in longhand (runny ink, blue runaway dog) that had outlived its usefulness but had not been fully torn off; or else an object in a shop window, or a smell that refused at the last moment to yield a memory it had seemed ready to shout, and remained instead on its street corner, a mystery withdrawn into itself. No, there was nothing like that (not yet in any case); it would be a good idea, he thought, some time at leisure to study the sequence of three or four kinds of shops and see if he were right in conjecturing that such a sequence followed its own law of composition, so that, having found the most frequent arrangement, one could deduce the average cycle for the streets of a given city, for example: tobacco shop, pharmacy, greengrocery. On Tannenberg Street these three were dissociated, occurring on different corners; perhaps, however, the rhythmic swarming had not yet established itself, and in the future, yielding to that counterpoint (as the proprietors either went broke or moved) they would gradually begin to gather according to the proper pattern: the greengrocery, with a glance over its shoulder, would cross the street, so as to be at first seven and then three doors away from the pharmacy—in somewhat the same way as the jumbled letters find their places in a film commercial; and at the end there is always one that does a kind of flip, and then hastily assumes its position (a comic character, the inevitable Jack the Sack among the new recruits); and thus they will wait until an adjacent place becomes vacant, whereupon they will both wink across at the tobacco shop, as if to say: "Quick, over here"; and before you know it they are all in a row, forming a typical line. God, how I hate all this—the things in the shop windows, the obtuse face of merchandise, and, above all, the ceremonial of transaction, the exchange of cloying compliments before and after! And those lowered lashes of modest price . . . the nobility of the discount . . . the altruism of advertisements . . . all of this nasty imitation of good, which has a strange way of drawing in good people: Alexandra Yakovlevna, for example, confessed to me that when she goes shopping in familiar stores she is morally transplanted to a special world where she grows intoxicated from the wine of honesty, from the sweetness of mutual favors, and replies to the salesman's incarnadine smile with a smile of radiant rapture.

The type of Berlin store that he entered can adequately be determined by the presence in a corner of a small table holding a telephone, a directory, narcissi in a vase, and a large ashtray. This shop did not carry the Russian tipped cigarettes that he preferred, and he would have left empty-handed if it had not been for the tobacconist's speckled vest with mother-of-pearl buttons and his pumpkin-colored bald spot. Yes, all my life I shall be getting that extra little payment in kind to compensate my regular overpayment for merchandise foisted on me.

As he crossed toward the pharmacy at the corner he involuntarily turned his head because of a burst of light that had ricocheted from his temple, and saw, with that quick smile with which we greet a rainbow or a rose, a blindingly white parallelogram of sky being unloaded from the van—a dresser with mirror across which, as across a cinema screen, passed a flawlessly clear reflection of boughs sliding and swaying not arboreally, but with a human vacillation, produced by the nature of those who were carrying this sky, these boughs, this gliding façade.

He walked on toward the shop, but what he had just seen—whether because it had given him a kindred pleasure, or because it had taken him unawares and jolted him (as children in the hayloft fall into the resilient darkness)—released in him that pleasant something which for several days now had been at the murky bottom of his every thought, taking possession of him at the slightest provocation: my collection of poems has been published; and when, as now, his mind tumbled like this, that is, when he recalled the fifty-odd poems that had just come out, he would skim in an instant the entire book, so that in the instantaneous mist of its madly accelerated music one could not make any readable sense of the flicking lines—the familiar words would rush past, swirling amid violent foam (whose seething was transformed into a mighty flowing motion if one fixed one's eyes on it, as we used to do long ago, looking down at it from a vibrating mill bridge until the bridge turned into a ship's stern: farewell!)—and this foam, and this flickering, and a separate verse that rushed past all alone, shouting in wild ecstasy from afar, probably calling him home, all of this, together with the creamy white of the cover, was merged in a blissful feeling of exceptional purity. . . . What am I doing! he thought, abruptly coming to his senses and realizing that the first thing he had done upon entering the next shop was to dump the change he had received at the tobacconist's onto the rubber islet in the middle of the glass counter, through which he glimpsed the submerged treasure of flasked perfumes, while the salesgirl's gaze, condescending toward his odd behavior, followed with curiosity this absentminded hand paying for a purchase that had not yet been named.

"A cake of almond soap, please," he said with dignity.

Thereupon he returned with the same springy step to the house. The sidewalk before it was now empty save for three blue chairs that looked as if they had been placed together by children. Within the van a small brown piano lay supine, tied up so that it could not rise, and with its two little metal soles up in the air. On the stairs he met the movers pounding down, knees turned out, and, as he was ringing the doorbell of his new abode, he heard voices and hammering upstairs. His landlady let him in and said that she had left his keys in his room. This large, predatory German woman had a funny name: Klara Stoboy—which to a Russian's ear sounded with sentimental firmness as "Klara is with thee (*s toboy*)."

And here is the oblong room, and the patiently waiting suitcase . . . and at this point his carefree mood changed to revulsion: God forbid that anyone know the awful, degrading boredom, the recurrent refusal to accept the vile yoke of recurrent new quarters, the impossibility of living face-to-face with totally strange objects, the inevitability of insomnia on that daybed!

For some time he stood by the window. In the curds-and-whey sky opaline pits now and then formed where the blind sun circulated, and, in response, on the gray convex roof of the van, the slender shadows of linden branches hastened headlong toward substantiation, but dissolved without having materialized. The house directly across the way was half enclosed in scaffolding, while the sound part of its brick façade was overgrown with window-invading ivy. At the far end of the path that cut through its front yard he could make out the black sign of a coal cellar.

Taken by itself, all this was a view, just as the room was itself a separate entity; but now a middleman had appeared, and now that view became the view from this room and no other. The gift of sight which it now had received did not improve it. It would be hard, he mused, to transform the wallpaper (pale yellow, with bluish tulips) into a distant steppe. The desert of the desk would have to be tilled for a long time before it could sprout its first rhymes. And much cigarette ash would have to fall under the armchair and into its folds before it would become suitable for traveling.

The landlady came to call him to the telephone, and he, politely stooping his shoulders, followed her into the dining room. "In the first place, my dear sir," said Alexander Yakovlevich Chernyshevski, "why are they so reluctant at your old boardinghouse to divulge your new number? Left there with a bang, didn't you? In the second place, I want to congratulate you. . . . What, you haven't heard yet? Honestly?" ("He hasn't heard anything about it yet," said Alexander Yakovlevich, turning the other side of his voice toward someone out of the range of the telephone). "Well, in that case get a firm grip on yourself and listen to this—I'm going to read it to you: 'The newly published collection of poems by the hitherto unknown author Fyodor Godunov-Cherdyntsev strikes one as such a brilliant phenomenon, and the poetic talent of the author is so indisputable. . . .' You know what, I shan't go on, but you come over to our place tonight. Then you will get the whole article. No, Fyodor Konstantinovich, my good friend, I won't tell you anything now, neither who wrote this review, nor in what émigré Russian-language paper it appeared, but if you want my personal opinion, then don't be offended, but I think the fellow is treating you much too kindly. So you'll come? Excellent. We'll be expecting you."

As he hung up the receiver Fyodor nearly knocked the stand with flexible steel rod and attached pencil off the table; he tried to catch it, and it was then that he did knock it off; then he bumped his hip against the corner of the sideboard; then he dropped a cigarette that he was pulling out of the pack as he walked; and finally he miscalculated the swing of the door which flew open so resonantly that Frau Stoboy, just then passing along the corridor with a saucer of milk in her hand, uttered an icy "Oops!" He wanted to tell her that her pale yellow dress with bluish tulips was beautiful, that the parting in her frizzled hair and the quivering bags of her cheeks endowed her with a George-Sandesque regality; that her dining room was the height of perfection; but he limited himself to a beaming smile and nearly tripped over the tiger stripes which had not kept up with the cat as it jumped aside; after all, though, he had never doubted that it would be this way, that the world, in the person of a few hundred lovers of literature who had left St. Petersburg, Moscow and Kiev, would immediately appreciate his gift.

We have before us a thin volume entitled *Poems* (a plain swallow-tailed livery, which in recent years has become just as much *de rigueur* as the braiding of not long ago—from "Lunar Reveries" to symbolic Latin), containing about fifty twelve-line poems all devoted to a single theme: childhood. In fervently composing them, the author sought on the one hand to generalize reminiscenses by selecting elements typical of any successful childhood—hence their seeming obviousness; and on the other hand he has allowed only his genuine quiddity to penetrate into his poems—hence their seeming fastidiousness. At the same time he had to take great pains not to lose either his control of the game, or the viewpoint of the plaything. The strategy of inspiration and the tactics of the mind, the flesh of poetry and the specter of translucent prose—these are the epithets that seem to us to characterize with sufficient accuracy the art of this young poet. . . . And, having locked his door, he took out his book and threw himself on the couch—he had to reread it right away, before the excitement had time to cool, in order to check the superior quality of the poems and fore-fancy all the details of the high approbation given them by the intelligent, delightful, as yet unnamed reviewer. And now, as he sampled and tested them, he was doing the exact opposite of what he had done a short time ago, when he had skimmed over the book in one instantaneous thought. Now he read in three dimensions, as it were, carefully exploring each poem, lifted out like a cube from among the rest and bathed from all sides in that wonderful, fluffy country air after which one is always so tired in the evening. In other words, as he read, he again made use of all the materials already once gathered by his memory for the extraction of the present poems, and reconstructed everything, absolutely everything, as a returning traveler sees in an orphan's eyes not only the smile of its mother, whom he had known in his youth, but also an avenue ending in a burst of yellow light and that auburn leaf on the bench, and everything, everything. The collection opened with the poem "The Lost Ball," and one felt it was beginning to rain. One of those evenings, heavy with clouds, that go so well with our northern firs, had condensed around the house. The avenue had returned from the park for the night, and its entrance was shrouded in dusk. Now the unfolding white shutters separate the room from the exterior darkness, whither the brighter portions of various household objects have already crossed to take up tentative positions on different levels of the helplessly black garden. Bedtime is now at hand.

Games grow halfhearted and somewhat callous. She is old and she groans painfully as she kneels in three laborious stages.

> My ball has rolled under Nurse's commode.
> On the floor a candle
> Tugs at the ends of the shadows
> This way and that, but the ball is gone.
> Then comes the crooked poker.
> It potters and clatters in vain,
> Knocks out a button
> And then half a zwieback.
> Suddenly out darts the ball
> Into the quivering darkness,
> Crosses the whole room and promptly goes under
> The impregnable sofa.

Why doesn't the epithet "quivering" quite satisfy me? Or does the puppeteer's colossal hand appear here for an instant among the creatures whose size the eye had come to accept (so that the spectator's first reaction at the end of the show is "How big I have grown!")? After all the room really *was* quivering, and that flickering, carrousel-like movement of shadows across the wall when the light is being carried away, or the shadowy camel on the ceiling with its monstrous humps heaving when Nurse wrestles with the bulky and unstable reed screen (whose expansion is inversely proportional to its degree of equilibrium)—these are all my very earliest memories, the ones closest to the original source. My probing thought often turns toward that original source, toward that reverse nothingness. Thus the nebulous state of the infant always seems to me to be a slow convalescence after a dreadful illness, and the receding from primal nonexistence becomes an approach to it when I strain my memory to the very limit so as to taste of that darkness and use its lessons to prepare myself for the darkness to come; but, as I turn my life upside down so that birth becomes death, I fail to see at the verge of this dying-in-reverse anything that would correspond to the boundless terror that even a centenarian is said to experience when he faces the positive end; nothing, except perhaps the aforementioned shadows, which, rising from somewhere below when the candle takes off to leave the room (while the shadow of the left brass knob at the foot of my bed sweeps past like a black head swelling as it moves), assume their accustomed places above my nursery cot,

> And in their corners grow brazen
> Bearing only a casual likeness
> To their natural models.

In a whole set of poems, disarming by their sincerity . . . no, that's nonsense—Why must one "disarm" the reader? Is he dangerous? In a whole set of excellent . . . or, to put it even more strongly, remarkable poems the author sings not only of these frightening shadows, but of brighter moments as well. Nonsense, I say! He does not write like that, my nameless, unknown eulogist, and it was only for his sake that I poetized the memory of two precious, and, I think, ancient toys. The first was an ample painted flowerpot containing an artificial plant from a sunny land, on which was perched a stuffed tropical songbird, so astonishingly lifelike that it seemed about to take wing, with black plumage and an amethyst breast; and, when the big key had been wheedled from the housekeeper Yvonna Ivanovna, inserted in the side of the pot and given several tight, vivifying turns, the little Malayan nightingale would open its beak . . . no, it would not even open its beak, for something odd had happened to the clockworn mechanism, to some spring or other, which, however, stored up its action for later: the bird would not sing then, but if one forgot about it and a week later happened to walk past its lofty wardrobe-top perch, then some mysterious tremor would suddenly make it emit its magical warbling—and how marvelously, how long it would trill, puffing out its ruffled little breast; it would finish; then, on your way out, you would tread on another floorboard and in special response it would utter a final whistle, and grow silent halfway through the note. The other of the poetized toys, which was in another room, also on a high shelf, behaved in similar fashion, but with a zany suggestion of imitation—as the spirit of parody always goes along with genuine poetry. This was a clown in satin plus fours who was propping himself on two whitewashed parallel bars and who would be set in motion by an accidental jolt,

To the sound of a miniature music
With a comical pronunciation

tinkling somewhere beneath his little platform, as he lifted his legs in white stockings and with pompons on the shoes, higher and higher with barely perceptible jerks—and abruptly everything stopped and he froze in an angular attitude. And perhaps it is the same with my poems? But the truthfulness of juxtapositions and deductions is sometimes better preserved on the near side of the verbal fence.

From the accumulating poetical pieces in the book we gradually obtain the image of an extremely receptive boy, living in extremely favorable surroundings. Our poet was born on July 12, 1900, in the Leshino manor, which for generations had been the country estate of the Godunov-Cherdyntsevs. Even before he reached school age the boy read through a considerable number of books from his father's library. In his interesting reminiscences so-and-so recalls how enthusiastically little Fedya and his sister Tanya, who was two years his elder, engaged in amateur theatricals, and how they would even write plays themselves for their performances. . . . That, my good man, may be true of other poets but in my case it is a lie. I have always been indifferent to the theater; although I remember that we did have a puppet theater with cardboard trees and a crenellated castle with celluloid windows the color of raspberry jelly through which painted flames like those on Vereshchagin's picture of the Moscow Fire flickered when a candle was lighted inside—and it was this candle which, not without our participation, eventually caused the conflagration of the entire building. Oh, but Tanya and I were fastidious when it came to toys! From indifferent givers on the outside we would often receive quite wretched things. Anything that came in a flat carton with an illustrated cover boded ill. To one such cover I tried to devote my stipulated twelve lines, but somehow the poem did not rise. A family, seated around a circular table illuminated by a lamp: the boy is dressed in an impossible sailor suit with a red tie, the girl wears laced boots, also red; both, with expressions of sensuous delectation, are stringing beads of various colors on straw-like rods, making little baskets, birdcages and boxes; and, with similar enthusiasm, their half-witted parents take part in the same pastime—the father with a prize growth on his pleased face, the mother with her imposing bosom; the dog is also looking at the table, and envious Grandma can be seen ensconced in the background. Those same children have now grown up and I often run across them in advertisements: he, with his glossy, sleekly tanned cheeks, is puffing voluptuously on a cigarette or holding in his brawny hand, with a carnivorous grin, a sandwich containing something red ("eat more meat!"); she is smiling at a stocking she herself is wearing, or, with depraved delight, pouring artificial cream on canned fruit; and in time they will become sprightly, rosy, gormandizing oldsters—and still have ahead of them the infernal black beauty of oaken caskets in a palm-decked display window. . . . Thus a world of handsome demons develops side by side with us, in a cheerfully sinister relationship to our everyday existence; but in the handsome demon there is always some secret flaw, a shameful wart on the behind of this semblance of perfection: the glamorous glutton of the advertisement, gorging himself on gelatin, can never know the quiet joys of the gourmet, and his fashions (lingering on the billboard while we move onward) are always just a little behind those of real life. Some day I shall come back to a discussion of this nemesis, which finds a soft spot for its blow exactly where the whole sense and power of the creature it strikes seem to lie.

In general Tanya and I preferred sweaty games to quiet ones—running, hide-and-seek, battles. How remarkably the word "battle" *(srazhenie)* suggests the sound of springy compression when one rammed into the toy gun its projectile—a six-inch stick of colored wood, deprived of its rubber suction cup in order to increase the impact with which it struck the gilt tin of a breastplate (worn by a cross between a cuirassier and a redskin), making in it a respectable little dent.

> . . . You reload to the bottom the barrel,
> With a creaking of springs
> Resiliently pressing it down on the floor,
> And you see, half concealed by the door,
> That your double has stopped in the mirror,
> Rainbow feathers in head band
> Standing on end.

The author had occasion to hide (we are now in the Godunov-Cherdyntsevs' mansion on the English Quay of the Neva, where it stands even today) among draperies, under tables, behind the upright cushions of silk divans, in a wardrobe, where moth crystals crunched under one's feet (and whence one could observe unseen a slowly passing manservant, who would seem strangely different, alive, ethereal, smelling of apples and tea) and also

> Under a helical staircase,
> Or behind a lonely buffet
> Forgotten in a bare room

on whose dusty shelves vegetated such objects as: a necklace made of wolf's teeth; a small bare-bellied idol of almatolite; another, of porcelain, its black tongue stuck out in national greeting; a chess set with camels instead of bishops; an articulated wooden dragon; a Soyot snuffbox of clouded glass; ditto, of agate; a shaman's tambourine and the rabbit's foot going with it; a boot of wapiti leather with an innersole made from the bark of the blue honeysuckle; an ensiform Tibetan coin; a cup of Kara jade; a silver brooch with turquoises; a lama's lampad; and a lot of similar junk which—like dust, like the postcard from a German spa with its mother-of-pearl "Gruss"—my father, who could not stomach ethnography, somehow happened to bring back from his fabulous travels. The real treasures—his butterfly collection, his museum—were preserved in three locked halls; but the present book of poems contains nothing about that: a special intuition forewarned the young author that some day he would want to speak in quite another way, not in miniature verse with charms and chimes but in very, very different, manly words about his famous father.

Again something has gone wrong, and one hears the flippantly flat little voice of the reviewer (perhaps even of the female sex). With warm affection the poet recalls the rooms of the family house where it (his childhood) was spent. He has been able to imbue with much lyricism the poetic descriptions of objects among which it was spent. When you listen closely. . . We all, attentively and piously . . . The strains of the past. . . Thus, for instance, he depicts lampshades, lithographs on the walls, his schoolroom desk, the weekly visit of the floor-polishers (who leave behind an odor compounded of "frost, sweat, and mastic"), and the checking of the clocks:

On Thursdays there comes from the clock shop
A courteous old man who proceeds
To wind with a leisurely hand
All the clocks in the house.
He steals at his own watch a glance
And sets the clock on the wall.
He stands on a chair, and he waits
For the clock to discharge its noon
Completely. Then, having done well
His agreeable task,
He soundlessly puts back the chair,
And with a slight whir the clock ticks.

Giving an occasional tongue clack with its pendulum and making a strange pause, as if to gather its strength, before striking. Its ticking, like an unrolled tape divided by stripes into inches, served as an endless measure of my insomnias. It was just as hard for me to fall asleep as to sneeze without having tickled with something the inside of a nostril, or to commit suicide by resorting to means at the body's disposal (swallowing my tongue, or something like that). At the beginning of the agonizing night I could still play for time by subsisting on conversations with Tanya, whose bed stood in the next room; despite rules, we would open the door slightly, and then, when we heard our governess going to her own room, which was adjacent to Tanya's, one of us would gently shut it: a lightning barefoot sprint and then a dive into bed. While the door was ajar we would exchange conundrums from room to room, every now and then lapsing into silence (I can still hear the tone of this twin silence in the dark), she to guess mine, I to think of another. Mine were always on the fantastic and silly side, while Tanya adhered to classical models:

mon premier est un métal précieux,
mon second est un habitant des cieux,
et mon tout est un fruit délicieux.

Sometimes she would fall asleep while I waited patiently, thinking that she was struggling with my riddle, and neither my pleading nor my imprecations would succeed in reviving her. After this I would voyage for more than an hour through the dark of my bed, arching the bedclothes over myself, so as to form a cavern, at whose distant exit I glimpsed a bit of oblique bluish light that had nothing in common with my bedroom, with the Neva night, with the rich, darkly translucent flounces of the window curtains. The cave I was exploring held in its folds and fissures such a dreamy reality, brimmed with such oppressive mystery, that a throbbing, as of a muted drum, would begin in my chest and in my ears; in there, in its depths, where my father had discovered a new species of bat, I could make out the high cheekbones of an idol hewn from the rock; and, when I finally dozed off, a dozen strong hands would overturn me and, with an awful silk-ripping sound, someone would unstitch me from top to bottom, after which an agile hand would slip inside me and powerfully squeeze my heart. Or else I would be turned into a horse, screaming in a Mongolian voice: shamans yanked at its hocks with lassos, so that its legs would break with a crunch and collapse at right angles to the body—my body—which lay with its chest pressed against the yellow ground, and, as a sign of extreme agony, the horse's tail would rise fountain-like; it dropped back, and I awoke.

Time to get up. The stove-heater pats
The glistening facings
Of the stove to determine
If the fire has grown to the top.
It has. And to its hot hum
The morning responds with the silence of snow,
Pink-shaded azure,
And immaculate whiteness.

It is strange how a memory will grow into a wax figure, how the cherub grows suspiciously prettier as its frame darkens with age—strange, strange are the mishaps of memory. I emigrated seven years ago; this foreign land has by now lost its aura of abroadness just as my own ceased to be a geographic habit. The Year Seven. The wandering ghost of an empire immediately adopted this system of reckoning, akin to the one formerly introduced by the ardent French citizen in honor of newborn liberty. But the years roll on, and honor is no consolation; recollections either melt away, or else acquire a deathly gloss, so that instead of marvelous apparitions we are left with a fan of picture postcards. Nothing can help here, no poetry, no stereoscope—that gadget which in ominous bug-eyed silence used to endow a cupola with such convexity and surround mug-carrying Karlsbad promenaders with such a diabolical semblance of space that I was tormented by nightmares after this optical diversion far more than after tales of Mongolian tortures. The particular stereo camera I remember adorned the waiting room of our dentist, an American named Lawson, whose French mistress Mme. Ducamp, a gray-haired harpy, seated at her desk among vials of blood-red Lawson mouthwash, pursed her lips and nervously scratched her scalp as she tried to find an appointment for Tanya and me, and finally, with an effort and a screech, managed to push her spitting pen between la Princesse Toumanoff, with a blot at the end, and Monsieur Danzas, with a blot at the beginning. Here is the description of a drive to this dentist, who had warned the day before that "this one will have to come out." . . .

> What will it be like to be sitting
> Half an hour from now in this brougham?
> With what eyes shall I look at these snowflakes
> And black branches of trees?
> How shall I follow again with my gaze
> That conical curbstone
> In its cottonwool cap? How recall
> On my way back my way there?
> (While with revulsion and tenderness
> Constantly feeling the handkerchief
> Wherein carefully folded is something
> Like an ivory watch charm.)

That "cottonwool cap" is not only ambiguous but does not even begin to express what I meant—namely, the snow piled caplike on granite cones joined by a chain somewhere in the vicinity of the statue of Peter the Great. Somewhere! Alas, it is already difficult for me to gather all the parts of the past; already I am beginning to forget relationships and connections between objects that still thrive in my memory, objects I thereby condemn to extinction. If so, what insulting mockery to affirm smugly that

> Thus a former impression keeps living
> Within harmony's ice.

What, then, compels me to compose poems about my childhood if in spite of everything, my words go wide of the mark, or else slay both the pard and the hart with the exploding bullet of an "accurate" epithet? But let us not despair. The man says I am a real poet—which means that the hunt was not in vain.

Here is another twelve-line poem about boyhood torments. It deals with the ordeals of winter in town when, for example, ribbed stockings chafe behind the knees, or when the shopgirl pulls an impossibly flat kid glove onto your hand, laid on the counter as if on an executioner's block. There is more: the hook's double pinch (the first time it slipped off) while you stand with outspread arms to have your fur collar fastened; but in compensation for this, what an amusing change in acoustics, how rounded all sounds become when the collar is raised; and since we have touched upon ears, how unforgettable the silky, taut, buzzing music while the strings of your cap's earflaps are being tied (raise your chin).

Merrily, to coin a phrase, youngsters romp on a frosty day. At the entrance to the public park we have the balloon vendor; above his head, three times his size, an enormous rustling cluster. Look, children, how they billow and rub against each other, all full of God's sunshine, in red, blue and green shades. A beautiful sight! Please, Uncle, I want the biggest (the white one with the rooster painted on it and the red embryo floating inside, which, when its mother is destroyed, will escape up to the ceiling and a day later will come down, all wrinkled and quite tame). Now the happy children have bought their ruble balloon and the kindly hawker has pulled it out of the jostling bunch. Just a minute, my lad, don't grab, let me cut the string. After which he puts on his mittens again, checks the string around his waist, from which his scissors dangle, and pushing off with his heel, slowly begins to rise in an upright position, higher and higher into the blue sky: look, his cluster is no larger now than a bunch of grapes, while beneath him lies hazy, gilded, berimed St. Petersburg, a little restored here and there, alas, according to the best pictures of our national painters.

But joking aside, it really was all very beautiful, very quiet. The trees in the park mimed their own ghosts and the whole effect revealed immense talent. Tanya and I would make fun of the sleds of our coevals, especially if they were covered with fringed, carpet-like stuff and had a high seat (equipped even with a back) and reins that the rider held as he braked with his felt boots. This kind never made it all the way to the final snowdrift, but instead went off course almost immediately and began to spin helplessly while continuing to descend, carrying a pallid, intent child who was obliged, when the sled's momentum was spent, to work with his feet in order to reach the end of the icy run. Tanya and I had weighty belly sleds from Sangalli's: such a sled consisted simply of a rectangular velvet cushion on iron runners curved at each end. You did not have to pull it on the way to the slide—it glided with so little effort and so impatiently along the snow, sanded in vain, that it bumped against your heels. Here we are at the hill.

One climbed up a sparkle-splashed platform. . . . (Water carried up in buckets to pour on the slide had *splashed* over the wooden steps so that they were coated with *sparkling* ice, but the well-meaning alliteration had not been able to get all this in.)

One climbed a sparkle-splashed platform,
One dashingly fell belly first
On the sled, and it rattled
Down the blueness; and then
When the scene underwent a grim change,
And there somberly burned in the nursery
Scarlet fever on Christmas,
Or, on Easter, diphtheria,
One rocketed down the bright, brittle,
Exaggerated ice hill
In a kind of half-tropical,
Half-Tavricheski park

where, by the power of delirium, General Nikolai Mihailovich Przhevalski was transferred, together with his stone camel, from the Alexandrovski park near us, and where he immediately turned into a statue of my father who was at that moment somewhere between Kokand and Ashkhabad, for example, or else on a slope of the Tsinin Range. What illnesses Tanya and I went through! Now together, now by turns; and how I would suffer when I heard, between the slam of a distant door and the restrained quiet sound of another one, her footfall and laughter bursting through, sounding celestially indifferent to me, unaware of me, infinitely distant from my fat compress with its tawny oilcloth filling, my aching legs, my bodily heaviness and constriction; but if it was she who was sick, how earthly and real, how like a crisp soccer ball I felt when I saw her lying in bed with an air of remoteness about her as if she had turned toward the other world, with only the limp lining of her being toward me! Let us describe the last stand before the capitulation when, not yet having stepped out of the normal course of the day, concealing from your own self the fever, the ache in your joints, and wrapping yourself up Mexican fashion, you disguise the claims of fever's chill as the demands of the game; and when, a half hour later, you have surrendered and ended up in bed, your body no longer believes that just a short time ago it was playing, crawling on all fours along the floor of the hall, along the parquet, along the quarpet. Let us describe Mother's questioning smile of alarm when she has just put the thermometer in my armpit (a task she would not entrust either to the valet or to the governess). "Well, you've got yourself into a nice fix, haven't you?" says she, still trying to joke about it. Then a minute later: "I knew it yesterday, I knew you had a fever, you can't fool me." And after another minute: "How much do you think you have?" And finally: "I think we can take it out now." She brings the incandescent glass tube close to the light and, drawing together her lovely sealskin eyebrows—which Tanya has inherited—she looks for a long time . . . and then without saying anything she unhurriedly shakes the thermometer and slips it back into its case, looking at me as if not quite recognizing me, while my father rides his horse at a walk across a vernal plain all blue with irises; let us describe also the delirious state in which one feels huge numbers grow, inflating one's brain, accompanied by someone's incessant patter quite unrelated to you, as if in the dark garden adjoining the madhouse of the book-of-sums several of its characters, half out (or more precisely, fifty-seven one-hundred-and-elevenths out) of their terrible world of increasing interests, appeared in their stock parts of apple-woman, four ditchdiggers and a Certain Person who has bequeathed his children a caravan of fractions, and chatted, to the accompaniment of the nocturnal sough of trees, about something extremely domestic and silly, but therefore all the more awful, all the more doomed to turn into those very numbers, into that mathematical universe expanding endlessly (an expansion which for me sheds an odd light on the macrocosmic theories of today's physicists). Let us describe finally the recovery, when there is no longer any point in shaking the mercury down, and the thermometer is carelessly left lying on the bedtable, where an assembly of books that has come to congratulate you and a few playthings (idle onlookers) are crowding out the half-empty bottles of turbid potions.

A writing case with my note paper
Is what I most vividly see:
The leaves are adorned with a horseshoe
And my monogram. I had become
Quite an expert in twisted initials,
Intaglio seals, dry flattened flowers
(Which a little girl sent me from Nice)
And sealing wax, red and bronze-gleaming.

None of the poems in the book alludes to a certain extraordinary thing that happened to me as I was recovering from a particularly severe case of pneumonia. When everyone had moved into the drawing room (to use a Victorian cliché), one of the guests who (to go on with it) had been silent all evening. . . . The fever had ebbed away during the night and I had finally scrambled ashore. I was, let me tell you, weak, capricious and transparent—as transparent as a cut-glass egg. Mother had gone to buy me—I did not know what exactly—one of those freakish things that from time to time I coveted with the greed of a pregnant woman, afterwards forgetting them completely; but my mother made lists of these desiderata. As I lay flat in bed among bluish layers of indoor twilight I felt myself evolving an incredible lucidity, as when a distant stripe of radiantly pale sky stretches between long vesperal clouds and you can make out the cape and shallows of God knows what far-off islands—and it seems that if you release your volatile glance just a little further you will discern a shining boat drawn up on the damp sand and receding footsteps filled with bright water. In that minute, I think, I attained the highest limit of human health: my mind had been dipped and rinsed only recently in a dangerous, supernaturally clean blackness; and now, lying still and not even shutting my eyes, I mentally saw my mother, in chinchilla coat and black-dotted veil, getting into the sleigh (which always seemed in old Russia so small compared to the tremendous stuffed bottom of the coachman) and holding her dove-gray fluffy muff to her face as she sped behind a pair of black horses covered with a blue net. Street after street unfolded without any effort on my part; lumps of coffee-colored snow pounded against the sleigh's front. Now it has stopped. Vasiliy the footman steps down from his footboard, in the same motion unfastening the bearskin lap robe, and my mother walks briskly toward a shop whose name and display I do not have time to identify, since just at that instant my uncle, her brother, passes by and hails her (but she has already disappeared), and for several steps I involuntarily accompany him, trying to make out the face of the gentleman with whom he is chatting as they both walk away, but catching myself, I turn back and hastily flow, as it were, into the store, where my mother is already paying ten rubles for a perfectly ordinary green Faber pencil, which is then lovingly wrapped in brown paper by two clerks and handed to Vasiliy, who is already carrying it behind my mother to the sleigh, which now speeds along anonymous streets back to our house, now advancing to meet it; but here the crystalline course of my clairvoyance was interrupted by Yvonna Ivanovna's arrival with broth and toast. I needed her help to sit up in bed. She gave the pillow a swat and placed the bed tray (with its midget feet and a perpetually sticky area near its southwestern corner) across the animated blanket before me. Suddenly the door opened and Mother came in, smiling and holding a long, brown paper package like a halberd. From it emerged a Faber pencil a yard long and of corresponding thickness: a display giant that had hung horizontally in the window as an advertisement and had once happened to arouse my whimsical greed. I must still have been in that blissful state when any oddity descends among us like a demigod to mingle unrecognized with the Sunday crowd, since at that moment I felt no amazement at what had happened to me, but only remarked to myself in passing how I had been mistaken in regard to the object's size; but later, when I had grown stronger and plugged up certain chinks with bread, I would ponder with superstitious pangs about my clairvoyant spell (the only one I ever experienced), of which I was so ashamed that I concealed it even from Tanya; and I nearly burst into tears from embarrassment when we happened to meet, on my very first trip outdoors, a distant relative of Mother's, one Gaydukov, who said to her: "Your brother and I saw you the other day near Treumann's."

Meanwhile the air in the poems has grown warmer and we are preparing to return to the country, where we might move as early as April in the years before I began school (I began it only at the age of twelve).

The snow, gone from the slopes, lurks in ravines,
And the Petersburg spring
Is full of excitement and of anemones
And of the first butterflies.
But I don't need last year's Vanessas,
Those bleached hibernators,
Or those utterly battered Brimstones,
Through transparent woods flying.
I shall not fail, though, to detect
The four lovely gauze wings
Of the softest Geometrid moth in the world
Spread flat on a mottled pale birchtrunk.

This poem is the author's own favorite, but he did not include it in the collection because, once again, the theme is connected with that of his father and economy of art advised him not to touch that theme before the right time came. Instead he reproduced such spring impressions as the first sensation immediately upon walking out of the station: the softness of the ground, its kindred proximity to your foot, and around your head the totally unrestrained flow of air. Vying with each other, furiously lavishing invitations, standing up on their boxes, flourishing their free hand and mingling their uproar with exaggerated "whoas," the droshky drivers called to the early arrivals. A little way off an open motorcar, crimson both inside and out, awaited us: the idea of speed had already given a slant to the steering wheel (sea-cliff trees will understand what I mean), while its general appearance still retained—out of a false sense of propriety, I suppose—a servile link with the shape of a victoria; but if this was indeed an attempt at mimicry then it was totally destroyed by the roar of the motor with the muffler bypass opened, a roar so ferocious that long before we came in sight a peasant on a hay wagon coming the other way would jump off and try to hood his horse with a sack—after which he and his cart would often end up in the ditch or even in the field; where, a minute later, having already forgotten us and our dust, the rural stillness would collect again, cool and tender, with only the tiniest aperture left for the song of a skylark.

Perhaps one day, on foreign-made soles with heels long since worn down, feeling myself a ghost despite the idiotic substantiality of the insulators, I shall again come out of that station and without visible companions walk along the footpath that accompanies the highway the ten or so versts to Leshino. One after another the telegraph poles will hum at my approach. A crow will settle on a boulder—settle and straighten a wing that has folded wrong. The day will probably be on the grayish side. Changes in the appearance of the surrounding landscape that I cannot imagine, as well as some of the oldest landmarks that somehow I have forgotten, will greet me alternately, even mingling from time to time. I think that as I walk I shall utter something like a moan, in tune with the poles. When I reach the sites where I grew up and see this and that—or else, because of fires, rebuilding, lumbering operations or the negligence of nature, see neither this nor that (but still make out something infinitely and unwaveringly faithful to me, if only because my eyes are, in the long run, made of the same stuff as the grayness, the clarity, the dampness of those sites), then, after all the excitement, I shall experience a certain satiation of suffering—perhaps on the mountain pass to a kind of happiness which it is too early for me to know (I know only that when I reach it, it will be with pen in hand). But there is one thing I shall definitely not find there awaiting me—the thing which, indeed, made the whole business of exile worth cultivating: my childhood and the fruits of my childhood. Its fruits—here they are, today, already ripe; while my childhood itself has disappeared into a distance even more remote than that of our Russian North.

The author has found effective words to describe sensations experienced upon making the transition to the countryside. How much fun it is, says he, when

No longer one needs to put on
A cap, or change one's light shoes,
In order to run out again in the spring
On the brick-colored sand of the garden.

At the age of ten a new diversion was added. We were still in the city when the marvel rolled in. For quite a time I led it around by its ram horns from room to room; with what bashful grace it moved along the parquet floor until it impaled itself on a thumbtack! Compared to my old, rattling and pitiful little tricycle, whose wheels were so thin that it would get stuck even in the sand of the garden terrace, the newcomer possessed a heavenly lightness of movement. This is well expressed by the poet in the following lines:

Oh that first bicycle!
Its splendor, its height,
"Dux" or "*Pobéda*" inscribed on its frame,
The quietness of its tight tire!
The wavers and weavers in the green avenue
Where sun macules glide up one's wrists
And where molehills loom black
And threaten one's downfall!
But next day one skims over them,
And support as in dreamland is lacking,
And trusting in this dream simplicity,
The bicycle does not collapse.

And the day after that there inevitably come thoughts of "freewheeling"—a word which to this day I cannot hear without seeing a strip of smooth, sloping, sticky ground glide past, accompanied by a barely audible murmur of rubber and an ever-so-gentle lisp of steel. Bicycling and riding, boating and bathing, tennis and croquet; picnicking under the pines; the lure of the water mill and the hayloft—this is a general list of the themes that move our author. What about his poems from the point of view of form? These, of course, are miniatures, but they are executed with a phenomenally delicate mastery that brings out clearly every hair, not because everything is delineated with an excessively selective touch, but because the presence of the smallest features is involuntarily conveyed to the reader by the integrity and reliability of a talent that assures the author's observance of all the articles of the artistic covenant. One can argue whether it is worth while to revive album-type poetry, but one certainly cannot deny that within the limits he has set himself Godunov-Cherdyntsev has solved his prosodic problem correctly. Each of his poems iridesces with harlequin colors. Whoever is fond of the picturesque genre will appreciate this little volume. To the blind man at the church door it would have nothing to say. What vision the author has! Awaking early in the morning he knew what kind of a day it would be by looking at a chink in the shutter, which

> Showed a blue that was bluer than blue
> And was hardly inferior in blueness
> To my present remembrance of it.

And in the evening he gazes with the same screwed-up eyes at the field, one side of which is already in shadow, while the other, farther one

> Is illumed, from its central big boulder
> To the edge of the forest beyond it
> And is bright as by day.

It would seem to us that perhaps it was really not literature but painting for which he was destined from childhood, and while we know nothing of the author's present condition, we can nevertheless clearly picture a straw-hatted boy, sitting very uncomfortably on a garden bench with his watercolor paraphernalia and painting the world bequeathed him by his forebears:

Cells of white porcelain
Contain blue, green, red honey.
First, out of pencil lines,
On rough paper a garden is formed.
The birches, the balcony of the outbuilding,
All is spotted with sunlight. I soak
And twirl tight the tip of my paintbrush
In rich orange yellow;
And, meantime, within the full goblet,
In the radiance of its cut glass,
What colors have blazed,
What rapture has bloomed!

This, then, is Godunov-Cherdyntsev's little volume. In conclusion let us add . . . What else? What else? Imagination, do prompt me! Can it be true that all the enchantingly throbbing things of which I have dreamt and still dream through my poems have not been lost in them and have been noticed by the reader whose review I shall see before the day is over? Can it really be that he has understood everything in them, understood that besides the good old "picturesqueness" they also contain special poetic meaning (when one's mind, after going around itself in the subliminal labyrinth, returns with newfound music that alone makes poems what they should be)? As he read them, did he read them not only as words but as chinks between words, as one should do when reading poetry? Or did he simply skim over them, like them and praise them, calling attention to the significance of their sequence, a feature fashionable in our time, when time is in fashion: if a collection opens with a poem about "A Lost Ball," it must close with "The Found Ball."

Only pictures and ikons remained
In their places that year
When childhood was ended, and something
Happened to the old house: in a hurry
All the rooms with each other
Were exchanging their furniture,
Cupboards and screens, and a host

Of unwieldy big things:
And it was then that from under a sofa,
On the suddenly unmasked parquet,
Alive, and incredibly dear,
It was revealed in a corner.

The book's exterior appearance is pleasing.

Having squeezed the final drop of sweetness from it, Fyodor stretched and got up from his couch. He felt very hungry. The hands of his watch had lately begun to misbehave, now and then starting to move counterclockwise, so that he could not depend on them; to judge by the light, however, the day, about to leave on a journey, had sat down with its family for a pensive pause. When Fyodor went outside he felt immersed in a damp chill (it's a good thing I put that on): while he had been musing over his poems, rain had lacquered the street from end to end. The van had gone and in the spot where its tractor had recently stood, there remained next to the sidewalk a rainbow of oil, with the purple predominant and a plumelike twist. Asphalt's parakeet. And what had been the name of the moving company? Max Lux. Mac's luck.

Did I take the keys? Fyodor suddenly thought, stopping and thrusting his hand into his raincoat pocket. There he located a clinking handful, weighty and reassuring. When, three years ago, still during his existence here as a student, his mother had moved to Paris to live with Tanya, she had written that she just could not get used to being liberated from the perpetual fetters that chain a Berliner to the door lock. He imagined her joy upon reading the article about him and for an instant he felt maternal pride toward himself; not only that but a maternal tear burned the edge of his eyelids.

But what do I care whether or not I receive attention during my lifetime, if I am not certain that the world will remember me until its last darkest winter, marveling like Ronsard's old woman? And yet . . . I am still a long way from thirty, and here today I am already noticed. Noticed! Thank you, my land, for this remotest . . . A lyric possibility flitted past, singing quite close to his ear. Thank you, my land, for your most precious . . . I no longer need the sound "oticed": the rhyme has kindled life, but the rhyme itself is abandoned. And maddest gift my thanks are due . . . I suppose "meshes" waits in the wings. Did not have time to make out my third line in that burst of light. Pity. All gone now, missed my cue.

He bought some piroshki (one with meat, another with cabbage, a third with tapioca, a fourth with rice, a fifth . . . could not afford a fifth) in a Russian foodshop, which was a kind of wax museum of the old country's cuisine, and quickly finished them off on a damp bench in a small public garden.

The rain began coming down faster: someone had suddenly tilted the sky. He had to take cover in the circular shelter at the streetcar stop. There on the bench two Germans with briefcases were discussing a deal and endowing it with such dialectic details that the nature of the merchandise was lost, as when you are looking through an article in Brockhaus' Encyclopedia and lose its subject, indicated in the text only by its initial letter. Shaking her bobbed hair a girl entered the shelter with a small, wheezing, toadlike bulldog. Now this is odd: "remotest" and "noticed" are together again and a certain combination is ringing persistently. I will not be tempted.

The shower ended. With perfect simplicity—no dramatics, no tricks—all the streetlamps came on. He decided he could already set off for the Chernyshevskis' so as to be there towards nine, Rhine, fine, cline. As happens with drunks, something preserved him when he crossed streets in this state. Illuminated by a streetlamp's humid ray, a car stood at the curb with its motor running: every single drop on its hood was trembling. Who could have written it? Fyodor could not make a final choice among several émigré critics. This one was scrupulous but untalented; that one, dishonest but gifted; a third wrote only about prose; a fourth only about his friends; a fifth . . . and Fyodor's imagination conjured up this fifth one: a man the same age as he or even, he thought, a year younger, who had published during those same years in those same émigré papers and magazines, no more than he (a poem here, an article there), but who in some incomprehensible manner, which seemed as physically natural as some kind of emanation, had unobtrusively clothed himself in an aura of indefinable fame, so that his name was uttered not necessarily especially often, but quite differently from all the other young names; a man whose every new searing line he, Fyodor, despising himself, quickly and avidly devoured in a corner, trying by the very act of reading to destroy the marvel of it—after which for two days or so he could not rid himself either of what he had read or of his own feeling of debility or of a secret ache, as if while wrestling with another he had injured his own innermost, sacrosanct particle; a lonely, unpleasant, myopic man, with some kind of unpleasant defect in the reciprocal position of his shoulder blades. But I shall forgive everything if it is you.

He thought he was keeping his pace to a dawdle, yet the clocks that he came across on the way (the emergent giants of watchmakers' shops) advanced even more slowly and when, almost at his destination, he overtook in one stride Lyubov Markovna, who was going to the same place, he understood that he had been borne along throughout his journey by his impatience, as by an escalator that transforms even a motionless man into a runner.

Why did this flabby, unloved, elderly woman still make up her eyes when she already wore a pince-nez? The lenses exaggerated the unsteadiness and crudity of the amateurish ornamentation and as a result, her perfectly innocent gaze became so ambiguous that one could not break away from it: the hypnosis of error. In fact nearly everything about her seemed based on an unfortunate misunderstanding—and one wondered if it was not even a form of insanity when she thought that she spoke German like a native, that Galsworthy was a great writer, or that Georgiy Ivanovich Vasiliev was pathologically attracted to her. She was one of the most faithful frequenters of the literary parties that the Chernyshevskis, together with Vasiliev, a fat old journalist, organized every other Saturday; today was only Tuesday; and Lyubov Markovna was still living on her impressions from the previous Saturday, sharing them generously. Men fatally became absentminded boors in her company. Fyodor himself felt he was slipping too, but fortunately they were coming to the front door and there the Chernyshevskis' maid already stood waiting, keys in hand; actually, she had been sent to meet Vasiliev, who suffered from an extremely rare disease of the heart valves—he had, in fact, made a hobby of it and sometimes arrived at the home of friends with an anatomical model of the heart and demonstrated everything very clearly and lovingly. "*We* don't need the elevator," said Lyubov Markovna and started up the stairs with a strong plodding gait which turned to a curiously smooth and silent swing on the landings; Fyodor had to zigzag behind her at a reduced pace, as you sometimes see a dog do, weaving and shoving its nose past its master's heel now on the right, now on the left.

They were admitted by Alexandra Yakovlevna herself. Fyodor had scarcely time to notice her unusual expression (as if she disapproved of something or wanted to avert something quickly), when her husband darted into the hallway on his short plump legs, waving a newspaper as he ran.

"Here it is," he shouted, the corner of his mouth violently jerking downward (a tic acquired since the death of his son). "Look, here it is!"

"When I married him," observed Mme. Chernyshevski, "I expected his humor to be more subtle."

Fyodor saw with surprise that the paper he uncertainly took from his host was a German one.

"The date!" shouted Chernyshevski. "Go ahead, look at the date, young man!"

"April 1," said Fyodor with a sigh, and unconsciously he folded up the paper. "Yes, of course, I should have remembered."

Chernyshevski began to guffaw ferociously.

"Don't be cross with him, please," said his wife in an indolently sorrowful tone, slightly rolling her hips and gently taking the young man by the wrist.

Lyubov Markovna clicked her purse shut and sailed off toward the parlor.

It was a smallish, rather tastelessly furnished, badly lighted room with a shadow lingering in one corner and a pseudo-Tanagra vase standing on an unattainable shelf, and when at last the final guest had arrived and Mme. Chernyshevski, becoming for a moment—as usually happens—remarkably similar to her own (blue, gleaming) teapot, began to pour tea, the cramped quarters assumed the guise of a certain touching, provincial coziness. On the sofa, among cushions of various hue—all of them unappetizing and blurry—a silk doll with an angel's limp legs and a Persian's almond-shaped eyes was being squeezed alternately by two comfortably settled persons: Vasiliev, huge, bearded, wearing prewar socks arrowed above the ankle; and a fragile, charmingly debilitated girl with pink eyelids, in general appearance rather like a white mouse; her first name was Tamara (which would have better suited the doll), and her last was reminiscent of one of those German mountain landscapes that hang in picture-framing shops. Fyodor sat by the bookshelf and tried to simulate good spirits, despite the lump in his throat. Kern, a civil engineer, who prided himself on having been a close acquaintance of the late Alexander Blok (the celebrated poet), was producing a gluey sound as he extracted a date from an oblong carton. Lyubov Markovna carefully examined the pastries on a large plate with a poorly pictured bumblebee and, suddenly botching her investigation, contented herself with a bun—the sugar-powdered kind that always bears an anonymous fingerprint. The host was telling an ancient story about a medical student's April Fool's prank in Kiev. . . . But the most interesting person in the room sat a little distance apart, by the writing desk, and did not take part in the general conversation—which, however, he followed with quiet attention. He was a youth somewhat resembling Fyodor—not so much in facial features (which at that moment were difficult to distinguish) but in the tonality of his general appearance: the dunnish auburn shade of the round head which was closely cropped (a style which, according to the rules of latter-day St. Petersburg romanticism, was more becoming to a poet than shaggy locks); the transparency of the large, tender, slightly protruding ears; the slenderness of the neck with the shadow of a hollow at its nape. He sat in the same pose Fyodor sometimes assumed—head slightly lowered, legs crossed, arms not so much crossed as hugging each other, as if he felt chilled, so that the repose of the body was expressed more by angular projections (knee, elbow, thin shoulder) and the contraction of all the members rather than by the general softening of the frame when a person is relaxing and listening. The shadows of two volumes standing on the desk mimicked a cuff and the corner of a lapel, while the shadow of a third volume, which was leaning against the others, might have passed for a necktie. He was about five years younger than Fyodor and, as far as the face itself was concerned, if one judged by the photographs on the walls of the room and in the adjacent bedroom (on the little table between twin beds that wept at night), there was perhaps no resemblance at all, if you discounted a certain elongation of outline combined with prominent frontal bones and the dark depth of the eye sockets—Pascal-like, according to the physiognomists—and also there might have been something in common in the breadth of the eyebrows . . . but no, it was not a matter of ordinary resemblance, but of generic spiritual similarity between two angular and sensitive boys, each odd in his own way. This youth sat with downcast eyes and a trace of mockery on his lips, in a modest, not very comfortable position, on a chair along whose seat copper tacks glinted, to the left of the dictionary-cluttered desk; and Alexander Yakovlevich Chernyshevski, with a convulsive effort, as if regaining lost balance, would tear his gaze away from that shadowy youth, as he went on with the jaunty banter behind which he tried to conceal his mental sickness.

"Don't worry, there'll be reviews," he said to Fyodor, winking involuntarily. "You can be sure the critics will squeeze out your blackheads."

"By the way," asked his wife, "what do those 'weavers and wavers' mean exactly—in the poem about the bicycle?"

Fyodor explained, relying more on gestures than on words: "You know, when you are learning to ride a bike and you sort of swerve from side to side."

"Doubtful expression," remarked Vasiliev.

"My favorite is the one about children's diseases, yes," said Alexandra Yakovlevna, nodding to herself, "that's good: Christmastime scarlet fever and Eastertime diphtheria."

"Why not the other way around?" inquired Tamara.

Oh, how the boy had loved poetry! The glass-doored bookcase in the bedroom was full of his books: Gumilyov and Hérédia, Blok and Rilke—and how much he knew by heart! And the notebooks. . . . One day she and I will have to sit down and go through it all. She has the strength to do it, I don't. Strange how one keeps postponing things. One would think it would be a pleasure—the only, the bitter pleasure—to go through the belongings of the dead, yet his stuff goes on lying there, untouched (the provident laziness of one's soul?); it is unthinkable that a stranger should touch it, but what a relief it would be if an accidental fire were to destroy that precious little cabinet. Chernyshevski abruptly got up and, as if by chance, moved the chair by the desk in such a way that neither it nor the shadows of the books could serve as a theme for the phantom.

By then the talk had shifted to some unlamented Soviet politician who had fallen from power after Lenin's death. "Oh, in the years I knew him he was at the 'height of glory and good deeds,'" the journalist Vasiliev was saying, professionally misquoting Pushkin (who has "hope," not "height").

The boy who looked like Fyodor (to whom the Chernyshevskis had become so attached for this very reason) was now by the door, where he paused before leaving the room, half turning toward his father—and, despite his purely imaginary nature, how much more substantial he was than all those sitting in the room! The sofa could be seen through Vasiliev and the pale girl! Kern, the engineer, was represented only by the glint of his pince-nez; so was Lyubov Markovna; and Fyodor himself existed only because of a vague congruity with the deceased—while Yasha was perfectly real and live, and only the instinct of self-preservation prevented one from taking a good look at his features.

But perhaps, thought Fyodor, perhaps, this is all wrong, perhaps he [Alexander Yakovlevich Chernyshevski] is not imagining his dead son at all right now as I imagine him doing. He may be really occupied with the conversation and if his eyes are wandering it may be only because he has always been fidgety, poor soul. I am unhappy, I am bored, nothing rings true here and I don't know why I keep sitting here, listening to nonsense.

However he still continued to sit there and smoke and gently swing the toe of his foot—and while the others talked on and he talked on himself, he tried as he did everywhere and always to imagine the inner, transparent motion of this or that other person.

He would carefully seat himself inside the interlocutor as in an armchair, so that the other's elbows would serve as armrests for him, and his soul would fit snugly into the other's soul—and then the lighting of the world would suddenly change and for a minute he would actually become Alexander Chernyshevski, or Lyubov Markovna, or Vasiliev. Sometimes a sporting excitement would be added to the seltzerlike effervescence of the transformation, and he felt flattered when a chance word aptly confirmed the train of thought he was divining in the other. He, to whom so-called politics (that ridiculous sequence of pacts, conflicts, aggravations, frictions, discords, collapses, and the transformation of perfectly innocent little towns into the names of international treaties) meant nothing, would sometimes immerse himself with a thrill of curiosity and revulsion into the vast bowels of Vasiliev and live for an instant actuated by his, Vasiliev's, inner mechanism, where next to the "Locarno" button there was one for "Lockout" and where a pseudo-clever, pseudo-entertaining game was conducted by such ill-matched symbols as "The Five Kremlin Rulers," or "The Kurd Rebellion," or individual surnames that had lost all human connotations: Hindenburg, Marx, Painlevé, Herriot (whose macrocephalic initial in Russian, the reverse E, had become so autonomous in the columns of Vasiliev's *Gazeta* as to threaten a complete rift with the original Frenchman); this was a world of prophetic utterances, presentiments, mysterious combinations; a world that was in fact a hundredfold more spectral than the most abstract dream. And when Fyodor moved over into Mme. Chernyshevski he found himself within a soul where not everything was alien to him, but where he marveled at many things, as a prim traveler might marvel at the customs in a distant land: the bazaar at sunrise, the naked children, the din, the monstrous size of fruit. This forty-five-year-old, plain, indolent woman, who two years ago had lost her only son, had suddenly come alive: mourning had given her wings and tears had rejuvenated her—or at any rate so said those who had known her before. The memory of her son, which in her husband had become an illness, burned in her with a quickening fervor. It would be incorrect to say that this fervor filled her completely; no, it far exceeded the confines of her soul, seeming even to ennoble the absurdity of these two rented rooms into which, after the tragedy, she and her husband had moved from the large In den Zelten apartment (where her brother had lived with his family back in the years before the war). Now she regarded all her friends only in the light of their receptivity toward her loss, and also, for greater precision, recalled or imagined Yasha's opinion of this or that individual with whom she had to keep up acquaintance. She was seized with the fever of activity, with the thirst for an abundant response; her child grew within her and struggled to issue forth; the literary circle newly founded by her husband jointly with Vasiliev, in order to give himself and her something to do, seemed to her the best possible posthumous honor for her poet son. It was just at that time that I first saw her and was more than a little perplexed when suddenly this plump, terribly animated little woman with dazzling blue eyes burst into tears in the midst of her first conversation with me, as if a brimful crystal vessel had broken for no apparent reason, and, without taking her dancing gaze off me, laughing and sobbing, started saying over and over "Goodness, how you remind me of him!" The frankness with which, during our subsequent meetings, she spoke about her son, about all the details of his death and about the way she now dreamed of him (as if big with him and as translucent as a bubble) seemed to me vulgar and shameless; it irked me even more when I learned indirectly that she was "a little hurt" that I did not answer her with corresponding vibrations but instead only changed the subject the moment she mentioned my own grief, my own loss. Very soon, however, I noticed that this rapture of sorrow in which she managed to live without dying of a ruptured aorta was beginning somehow to draw me in and make demands on me. You know that characteristic movement when someone hands you a treasured photograph and watches you in anticipation . . . and you, having lengthily and piously gazed at the face in the snapshot, which smiles innocently and without a thought of death, feign to delay its return, feign to retard your own hand, while with a lingering glance you give back the picture, as if it would have been impolite to part with it sooner. This sequence of movements she and I repeated endlessly. Her husband would sit at his brightly lit desk in the corner, working and occasionally clearing his throat: he was compiling his dictionary of Russian technical terms, commissioned by a German publisher. All was quiet and wrong. The remains of cherry jam mingled with cigarette ash in my saucer. The more she continued to tell about Yasha, the less attractive he grew: oh no, he and I bore little resemblance to each other (far less than she supposed, projecting inward the coincidental similarity of external features, of which, moreover, she found additional ones that did not exist—in reality, the little there was within us corresponded to the little there was without), and I doubt we would have become friends if he and I had ever met. His somberness, interrupted by the sudden shrill gaiety characteristic of humorless people; the sentimentality of his intellectual enthusiasms; his purity, which would have strongly suggested timidity of the senses were it not for the morbid over-refinement of their interpretation; his feeling for Germany; his tasteless spiritual throes ("For a whole week," he said, "I was in a daze"—after reading Spengler!); and finally his poetry . . . in short, everything that to his mother was filled with enchantment only repelled me. As a poet he was, in my opinion, very feeble; he did not create, he merely dabbled in poetry, just as thousands of intelligent youths of his type did; but if they did not meet with some kind of more or less heroic death—having nothing to do with Russian letters, which, however, they knew meticulously (oh, those notebooks of Yasha's, filled with prosodic diagrams expressing modulations of rhythm in the tetrameter!)—they subsequently abandoned literature altogether; and if they exhibited talent in some field, it would be in science or administration, or else simply in a well-ordered life. His poems, replete with fashionable clichés, exalted his "grievous" love of Russia—autumn scenes à la Esenin, the smoky blue of Blok-ish bogs, the powder snow upon the wooden paving blocks of Mandelshtam's neoclassicism, and the Neva's granite parapet on which one can scarcely discern today the imprint of Pushkin's elbow. His mother would read them to me, stumbling in her agitation, with an awkward schoolgirl intonation which did not at all suit those tragically scudded iambics; Yasha himself must have recited them in an oblivious singsong, dilating his nostrils and swaying in the bizarre blaze of a kind of lyric pride, after which he would immediately sink back, again becoming humble, limp and withdrawn. The sonorous epithets that lived in his throat—*neveroyatnyy* (incredible), *hladnyy* (cold), *prekrasnyy* (beautiful)—epithets avidly employed by the young poets of his generation under the delusion that archaisms, prosaisms, or simply destitute words, having completed their life cycle, now, when used in poems, gained a kind of unexpected freshness, returning from the opposite direction—these words in Mme. Chernyshevski's stumbling diction made, as it were, another half cycle, faded away again, and again revealed their decrepit poverty—thus exposing the deception of style. Besides patriotic elegies, Yasha had poems about the low haunts of adventurous sailors, about gin and jazz (which he pronounced, in the German way, as "yatz"), and poems about Berlin, in which he attempted to endow German proper names with a lyric voice in the same way, for instance, as Italian street names resound in Russian poetry with a suspiciously euphonious contralto; he also had poems dedicated to friendship, without rhyme and without meter, full of muddled, hazy and timid emotions, of some internal spiritual bickerings, and apostrophes to a male friend in the polite form (the Russian "*vy*"), as a sick Frenchman addresses God, or a young Russian poetress her favorite gentleman. And all this was expressed in a pale, haphazard manner, with many vulgarisms and incorrect word accents peculiar to his provincial middle-class set. Misled by its augmentative suffix, he assumed that "*pozharishche*" (the site of a recent fire) meant a "big fire," and I also remember a rather pathetic reference to "Vrublyov's frescoes"—an amusing cross between two Russian painters (Rublyov and Vrubel) that only served to prove our dissimilarity: no, he could not have loved painting as I do. My true opinion of his poetry I concealed from his mother, while the forced sounds of inarticulate approbation that I politely made were construed by her as signs of incoherent rapture. For my birthday she gave me, beaming through her tears, Yasha's best necktie, an old-fashioned affair of watered silk, freshly ironed, with, still discernible, the label of a well-known but not elegant shop: I hardly think Yasha himself ever wore it; and in exchange for everything which she had shared with me, for her giving me a complete and detailed image of her late son, with his poetry, his neurasthenia, his enthusiasms, his death, Mme. Chernyshevski imperiously demanded from me a certain amount of creative collaboration. Her husband, who was proud of his century-old name and spent hours entertaining guests with its history (his grandfather had been baptized in the reign of Nicholas I—in Volsk, I believe—by the father of the famous political writer Chernyshevski, a stout, energetic Greek Orthodox priest who liked to do missionary work among the Jews, and who, on top of the spiritual benison, would bestow upon converts the added bonus of his last name), said to me on numerous occasions, "Look, you ought to write a little book in the form of a *biographie romancée* about our great man of the sixties—Now, now, stop frowning, I can foresee all your objections, but believe me, there are, after all, cases where the fascinating beauty of a good man's dedicated life fully redeems the falsity of his literary views, and Nikolay Chernyshevski was indeed a heroic soul. If you should decide to describe his life, there are many curious things I could tell you." I had no desire at all to write about the great man of the sixties and even less to write about Yasha, as his mother persistently counseled for her part (so that, taken together, here was an order for a complete history of their family). But, while I was both amused and irritated by these efforts of theirs to channel my muse, I nevertheless felt that before long Mme. Chernyshevski would have me cornered and, just as I was compelled to put on Yasha's necktie on my visits to her (until it occurred to me to say I was saving it for special occasions), I would have to undertake writing a long short story depicting Yasha's fate. At one time I was even weak enough (or bold enough, perhaps) to ponder how I might tackle the subject, if by any chance . . . Any corny man of ideas, any "serious" novelist in horn-rimmed glasses—the family doctor of Europe and the seismographer of its social tremors—would no doubt have found in this story something highly characteristic of the "frame of mind of young people in the postwar years"—a combination of words which in itself (even apart from the "general idea" it conveyed) made me speechless with scorn. I used to feel a cloying nausea when I heard or read the latest drivel, vulgar and humorless drivel, about the "symptoms of the age" and the "tragedy of youth." And, since I could not be kindled by Yasha's tragedy (though his mother did think I was afire), I would have become enmired involuntarily in a "deep" social-interest novel with a disgusting Freudian reek. My heart stood still as I exercised my imagination, probing with my toe, as it were, the mica-thin ice over the puddle; I would go so far as to picture myself making a fair copy of my work and bringing it to Mme. Chernyshevski, seating myself in such a way that the lamp would illuminate my fatal road from the left (thank you, I can see fine this way), and after a brief foreword about how difficult it had been, about the sense of responsibility I felt . . . but here everything would be obscured by the crimson mist of shame. Fortunately I did not fulfill the order—I am not sure exactly what saved me: for one thing, I kept putting it off too long; for another, certain blessed intervals occurred between our meetings; and then perhaps Mme. Chernyshevski herself grew a little bored with me as a listener; be that as it may, the story remained unused by the writer—a story that was in fact very simple and sad.

Yasha and I had entered Berlin University at almost exactly the same time, but I did not know him although we must have passed each other many times. Diversity of subjects—he took philosophy, I studied infusoria—diminished the possibility of our association. If I were to return now into that past, enriched in but one respect—awareness of the present day—and retrace exactly all my interlooping steps, then I would certainly notice his face, now so familiar to me through snapshots. It is a funny thing, when you imagine yourself returning into the past with the contraband of the present, how weird it would be to encounter there, in unexpected places, the prototypes of today's acquaintances, so young and fresh, who in a kind of lucid lunacy do not recognize you; thus a woman, for instance, whom one loves since yesterday, appears as a young girl, standing practically next to one in a crowded train, while the chance passerby who fifteen years ago asked you the way in the street now works in the same office as you. Among this throng of the past only a dozen or so faces would acquire this anachronistic importance: low cards transfigured by the radiance of the trump.

And then how confidently one could . . . But alas, even when you do happen, in a dream, to make such a return journey, then, at the border of the past your present intellect is completely invalidated, and amid the surroundings of a classroom hastily assembled by the nightmare's clumsy property man, you again do not know your lesson—with all the forgotten shades of those school throes of old.

At the university Yasha made close friends with two fellow students, Rudolf Baumann, a German, and Olya G., a compatriot—the Russian-language papers did not print her name in full. She was a girl of his age and set, even, I think, from the same town as he. Their families, however, were not acquainted. Only once did I have a chance to see her, at a literary soirée about two years after Yasha's death—I remember her remarkably broad and clear forehead, her aquamarine eyes and her large red mouth with black fuzz over the upper lip and a plump mole at the wick; she stood with her arms folded across her soft bosom, at once arousing in me all the proper literary associations, such as the dust of a fair summer evening and the threshold of a highway tavern, and a bored girl's observant gaze. As for Rudolf, I never saw him myself and can conclude only from the words of others that he had pale blond hair brushed back, was swift in his movements and handsome—in a hard, sinewy way, remindful of a gundog. Thus I use a different method to study each of the three individuals, which affects both their substance and their coloration, until, at the last minute, the rays of a sun that is my own and yet is incomprehensible to me, strike them and equalize them in the same burst of light.

Yasha kept a diary and in those notes he neatly defined the mutual relationship between him, Rudolf and Olya as "a triangle inscribed in a circle." The circle represented the normal, simple, "Euclidian" (as he put it) friendship that united all three, so that if it alone had existed their union would have remained happy, carefree and unbroken. But the triangle inscribed within it was a different system of relationships, complex, agonizing and slow in forming, which had an existence of its own, quite independent of its common enclosure of uniform friendship. This was the banal triangle of tragedy, formed within an idyllic circle, and the mere presence of such a suspiciously neat structure, to say nothing of the fashionable counterpoint of its development, would never have permitted me to make it into a short story or novel.

"I am fiercely in love with the soul of Rudolf," wrote Yasha in his agitated, neoromantic style. "I love its harmonious proportions, its health, the joy it has in living. I am fiercely in love with this naked, suntanned, lithe soul, which has an answer to everything and proceeds through life as a self-confident woman does across a ballroom floor. I can imagine only in the most complex, abstract manner, next to which Kant and Hegel are child's play, the fierce ecstasy I would experience if only . . . If only what? What can I do with his soul? This is what kills me—this yearning for some most mysterious tool (thus Albrecht Koch yearned for "golden logic" in the world of madmen). My blood throbs, my hands grow icy like a schoolgirl's when I remain alone with him, and he knows this and I become repulsive to him and he does not conceal his disgust. I am fiercely in love with his soul—and this is just as fruitless as falling in love with the moon."

Rudolf's squeamishness is understandable, but if one looks at the matter more closely, one suspects that Yasha's passion was perhaps not so abnormal after all, that his excitement was after all very much akin to that of many a Russian youth in the middle of last century, trembling with happiness when, raising his silky eyelashes, his pale-browed teacher, a future leader, a future martyr, would turn to him; and I would have refused to see in Yasha's case an incorrigible deviation had Rudolf been to the least degree a teacher, a martyr, or a leader; and not what he really was, a so-called "Bursch," a German "regular guy," notwithstanding a certain propensity for obscure poetry, lame music, lopsided art—which did not affect in him that fundamental soundness by which Yasha was captivated, or thought he was.

The son of a respectable fool of a professor and a civil servant's daughter, he had grown up in wonderful bourgeois surroundings, between a cathedral-like sideboard and the backs of dormant books. He was good-natured although not good; sociable, and yet a little skittish; impulsive, and at the same time calculating. He fell in love with Olya conclusively after a bicycle ride with her and Yasha in the Black Forest, a tour which, as he later testified at the inquest, "was an eye-opener for all three of us"; he fell in love with her on the lowest level, primitively and impatiently, but from her he received a sharp rebuff, made all the stronger by the fact that Olya, an indolent, grasping, morosely freakish girl, had in her turn (in those same fir woods, by the same round, black lake) "realized she had fallen for" Yasha, who was just as oppressed by this as Rudolf was by Yasha's ardor, and as she herself was by the ardor of Rudolf, so that the geometric relationship of their inscribed feelings was complete, reminding one of the traditional and somewhat mysterious interconnections in the *dramatis personae* of eighteenth-century French playwrights where X is the *amante* of Y ("the one in love with Y") and Y is the *amant* of Z ("the one in love with Z").

By winter, the second winter of their friendship, they had become clearly aware of the situation; the winter was spent in studying its hopelessness. On the surface everything seemed to be fine: Yasha read incessantly; Rudolf played hockey, masterfully speeding the puck across the ice; Olya studied the history of art (which, in the context of the epoch, sounds—as does the tone of the entire drama in question—like an unbearably typical, and therefore false, note); within, however, a hidden agonizing torment was growing, which became formidably destructive the moment that these unfortunate young people began to find some pleasure in their threefold torture.

For a long time they abided by a tacit agreement (each knowing, shamelessly and hopelessly, everything about the others) never to mention their feelings when the three of them were together; but whenever one of them was absent, the other two would inevitably set to discussing his passion and his suffering. For some reason they celebrated New Year's Eve in the restaurant of one of the Berlin railroad stations—perhaps because at railroad stations the armament of time is particularly impressive—and then they went slouching through the varicolored slush of grim festive streets, and Rudolf ironically proposed a toast to the exposure of their friendship—and since that time, at first discreetly, but soon with all the rapture of frankness, they would jointly discuss their feelings with all three present. It was then that the triangle began to erode its circumference.

The elder Chernyshevskis, as well as Rudolf's parents and Olya's mother (a sculptress, obese, black-eyed, and still handsome, with a low voice, who had buried two husbands and used to wear long necklaces that looked like bronze chains), not only did not sense that something doomful was growing, but would have confidently replied (should an aimless questioner have turned up among the angels already converging, already swarming and fussing professionally around the cradle where lay a dark little newborn revolver) that everything was all right, that everybody was happy. Afterwards, though, when everything had happened, their cheated memories made every effort to find in the routine past course of identically tinted days, traces and evidence of what was to come—and, surprisingly, they would find them. Thus Mme. G., paying a call of condolence on Mme. Chernyshevski, fully believed what she was saying when she insisted she had had presentiments of the tragedy for a long time—since the very day when she had come into the half-dark drawing room where, in motionless poses on a couch, in the various sorrowful inclinations of allegories on tombstone bas-reliefs, Olya and her two friends were sitting in silence; this was but a fleeting momentary harmony of shadows, but Mme. G. professed to have noticed that moment, or, more likely, she had set it aside in order to return to it a few months later.

By spring the revolver had grown. It belonged to Rudolf, but for a long time passed inconspicuously from one to the other, like a warm ring sliding on a string in a parlor game, or a playing card with Black Mary. Strange as it may seem, the idea of disappearing, all three together, in order that—already in a different world—an ideal and flawless circle might be restored, was being developed most actively by Olya, although now it is hard to determine who first proposed it and when. The role of poet in this enterprise was taken by Yasha—his position seemed the most hopeless since, after all, it was the most abstract; there are, however, sorrows that one does not cure by death, since they can be treated much more simply by life and its changing yearnings: a material bullet is powerless against them, while on the other hand, it copes perfectly well with the coarser passions of hearts like Rudolf's and Olya's.

A solution had now been found and discussions of it became especially fascinating. In mid-April, at the flat the Chernyshevskis then had, something happened that apparently served as the final impulse for the *dénouement*. Yasha's parents had peacefully left for the cinema across the street. Rudolf unexpectedly got drunk and let himself go, Yasha dragged him away from Olya and all this happened in the bathroom, and presently Rudolf, in tears, was picking up the money that had somehow fallen out of his trouser pockets, and what oppression all three felt, what shame, and how tempting was the relief offered by the finale scheduled for the next day.

After dinner on Thursday the eighteenth, which was also the eighteenth anniversary of the death of Olya's father, they equipped themselves with the revolver, which had become by now quite burly and independent, and in light, flimsy weather (with a damp west wind and the violet rust of pansies in every garden) set off on streetcar fifty-seven for the Grunewald where they planned to find a lonely spot and shoot themselves one after the other. They stood on the rear platform of the tram, all three wearing raincoats, with pale puffy faces—and Yasha's big-peaked cap, which he had not worn for about four years and had for some reason put on today, gave him an oddly plebeian look; Rudolf was hatless and the wind ruffled his blond hair, thrown back from the temples; Olya stood leaning against the rear railing, gripping the black stang with a white, firm hand that had a prominent ring on its index finger—and gazed with narrowed eyes at the streets flicking by, and all the time kept stepping by mistake on the treadle of the gentle little bell in the floor (intended for the huge, stonelike foot of the motorman when the rear of the car became the front). This group was noticed from inside the car, through the door, by Yuliy Filippovich Posner, former tutor of a cousin of Yasha's. Leaning out quickly—he was an alert, self-confident person—he beckoned to Yasha, who, recognizing him, went inside.

"Good thing I ran across you," said Posner, and after he had explained in detail that he was going with his five-year-old daughter (sitting separately by a window with her rubber-soft nose pressed against the glass) to visit his wife in a maternity ward, he produced his wallet and from the wallet his calling card, and then, taking advantage of an accidental stop made by the car (the trolley had come off the wire on a curve), crossed out his old address with a fountain pen and wrote the new one above it. "Here," he said, "give this to your cousin as soon as he comes back from Basel and remind him, please, that he still has several of my books which I need, which I need very much."

The tramcar was speeding along the Hohenzollerndamm and on its rear platform Olya and Rudolf continued to stand just as sternly as before in the wind, but a certain mysterious change had occurred: by the act of leaving them alone, although only for a minute (Posner and his daughter got off very soon), Yasha had, as it were, broken the alliance and had initiated his separation from them, so that when he rejoined them on the platform he was, though as much unaware of it as they were, already on his own and the invisible crack, in keeping with the law governing all cracks, continued irresistibly to creep and widen.

In the solitude of the spring forest where the wet, dun birches, particularly the smaller ones, stood around blankly with all their attention turned inside themselves; not far from the dove-gray lake (on whose vast shore there was not a soul except for a little man who was tossing a stick into the water at the request of his dog) they easily found a convenient lonely spot and right away got down to business; to be more exact, Yasha got down to business: he had that honesty of spirit that imparts to the most reckless act an almost everyday simplicity. He said he would shoot himself first by right of seniority (he was a year older than Rudolf and a month older than Olya) and this simple remark rendered unnecessary the stroke of drawn lots, which, in its coarse blindness, would probably have fallen on him anyway; and throwing off his raincoat and without bidding his friends farewell (which was only natural in view of their identical destination), silently, with clumsy haste, he walked down the slippery, pine-covered slope into a ravine heavily overgrown with scrub oak and bramble bushes, which, despite April's limpidity, completely concealed him from the others.

These two stood for a long time waiting for the shot. They had no cigarettes with them, but Rudolf was clever enough to feel in the pocket of Yasha's raincoat where he found an unopened pack. The sky had grown overcast, the pines were rustling cautiously and it seemed from below that their blind branches were groping for something. High above and fabulously fast, their long necks extended, two wild ducks flew past, one slightly behind the other. Afterwards Yasha's mother used to show the visiting card, DIPL. ING. JULIUS POSNER, on the reverse of which Yasha had written in pencil, *Mummy, Daddy, I am still alive, I am very scared, forgive me.* Finally Rudolf could stand it no longer and climbed down to see what was the matter with him. Yasha was sitting on a log among last year's still unanswered leaves, but he did not turn; he only said: "I'll be ready in a minute." There was something tense about his back, as if he were controlling an acute pain. Rudolf rejoined Olya, but no sooner had he reached her than both of them heard the dull pop of the shot, while in Yasha's room life went on for a few more hours as if nothing had happened—the cast-off banana skin on a plate, the volume of Annenski's poems *The Cypress Chest* and that of Khodasevich's *The Heavy Lyre* on the chair by the bed, the ping-pong bat on the couch; he was killed outright; to revive him, however, Rudolf and Olya dragged him through the bushes to the reeds and there desperately sprinkled him and rubbed him, so that he was all smudged with earth, blood and silt when the police later found the body. Then the two began calling for help, but nobody came: architect Ferdinand Stockschmeisser had long since left with his wet setter.

They returned to the place where they had waited for the shot and here dusk begins to fall on the story. The one clear thing is that Rudolf, whether because a certain terrestrial vacancy had opened for him or because he was simply a coward, lost all desire to shoot himself, and Olya, even if she had persisted in her intention, could do nothing since he had immediately hidden the revolver. In the woods, where it had grown cold and dark, with a blind drizzle crepitating around, they remained for a long time until a stupidly late hour. Rumor has it that it was then that they became lovers, but this would be really too flat. At about midnight, at the corner of a street poetically named Lilac Lane, a police sergeant listened skeptically to their horrible, voluble tale. There is a kind of hysterical state that assumes the semblance of childish swaggering.

If Mme. Chernyshevski had met Olya immediately after the event then perhaps some kind of sentimental sense would have come of it for them both. Unfortunately the meeting occurred only several months later, because, in the first place, Olya went away, and in the second, Mme. Chernyshevski's grief did not immediately take on that industrious, and even enraptured, form that Fyodor found when he came on the scene. Olya was in a certain sense unlucky: it so happened that Olya had come back for her stepbrother's engagement party and the house was full of guests; and when Mme. Chernyshevski arrived without warning, beneath a heavy mourning veil, with a choice selection from her sorrowful archives (photographs, letters) in her handbag, all prepared for the rapture of shared tears, she was met by a morosely polite, morosely impatient young woman in a semitransparent dress, with blood-red lips and a fat white-powdered nose, and one could hear from the little side room where she took her guest the wailing of a phonograph, and of course no communion of souls came of it. "All I did was to take a long look at her," recounted Mme. Chernyshevski—after which she carefully snipped off, on many little snapshots, both Olya and Rudolf; the latter, however, had visited her at once and had rolled at her feet and pounded his head on the soft corner of the divan, and then had walked off with his wonderful bouncy stride down the Kurfürstendamm, which glistened after a spring shower.

Yasha's death had its most painful effect on his father. He had to spend the whole summer in a sanatorium and he never really recovered: the partition dividing the room temperature of reason from the infinitely ugly, cold ghostly world into which Yasha had passed suddenly crumbled, and to restore it was impossible, so that the gap had to be draped in makeshift fashion and one tried not to look at the stirring folds. Ever since that day the other world began to seep into his life; but there was no way of resolving this constant intercourse with Yasha's spirit and he finally told his wife about it, in the vain hope that he might thus render harmless a phantom that secrecy had nurtured: the secrecy must have grown back, for soon he again had to seek the tedious, essentially mortal, glass-and-rubber help of doctors. Thus he lived only half in our world, at which he grasped the more greedily and desperately, and when one listened to his sprightly speech and looked at his regular features, it was difficult to imagine the unearthly experiences of this healthy-looking, plump little man, with his bald spot and the thin hair on either side, but then all the more strange was the convulsion that suddenly disfigured him; also the fact that sometimes for weeks on end he wore a gray cloth glove on his right hand (he suffered from eczema) hinted eerily at a mystery, as if, repelled by life's unclean touch, or burned by another life, he was reserving his bare handclasp for inhuman, hardly imaginable meetings. Meanwhile nothing stopped with Yasha's death and many interesting things were happening: in Russia one observed the spread of abortions and the revival of summer houses; in England there were strikes of some kind or other; Lenin met a sloppy end; Duse, Puccini and Anatole France died; Mallory and Irvine perished near the summit of Everest; and old Prince Dolgorukiy, in shoes of plaited leather thong, secretly visited Russia to see again the buckwheat in bloom; while in Berlin three-wheeled taxis appeared, only to disappear again shortly afterwards, and the first dirigible slowly stepped across the ocean and papers spoke a great deal about Coué, Chang Tso-lin and Tutankhamen, and one Sunday a young Berlin merchant with his locksmith friend set out on a trip to the country in a large, four-wheel cart with only the slightest smell of blood, rented from his neighbor, a butcher: two fat servant maids and the merchant's two small children sat in plush chairs set on the wagon, the children cried, the merchant and his pal guzzled beer and drove the horses hard, the weather was beautiful so that, in their high spirits, they deliberately hit a cleverly cornered cyclist, beat him up violently in the ditch, tore his portfolio to bits (he was an artist) and rolled on, very happy, and when he had come to his senses, the artist overtook them in a tavern garden, but the policeman who tried to establish their identities was also beaten up, after which they very happily rolled on along the highway, and when they saw that police motorcycles were gaining on them, they opened fire with revolvers and in the ensuing gunplay a bullet killed the merry merchant's three-year-old son.

"Listen, we ought to change the subject," Mme. Chernyshevski said softly. "I am afraid to have my husband listen to things like that. You do have a new poem, don't you? Fyodor Konstantinovich is going to read us a poem," she proclaimed loudly, but Vasiliev, half reclining, having in one hand a monumental cigarette holder with a nicotineless cigarette, and with the other absentmindedly tousling the doll, which was executing all kinds of emotional evolutions in his lap, nevertheless went on for a good half minute about how that gay incident had been investigated in court the previous day.

"I haven't got anything with me, and I don't know anything by heart," Fyodor repeated several times.

Chernyshevski quickly turned to him and put his small hairy hand on his sleeve. "I have a feeling you are still cross with me. You're not? Word of honor? I realized afterwards what a cruel joke it was. You don't look well. How are things going? You never really did explain to me why you changed your lodgings."

He explained: at the boardinghouse where he had lived for a year and a half people he knew had suddenly moved in, very kind, innocently intrusive bores who kept "dropping in for a chat." Their room was near his and before long Fyodor had the feeling that the wall between them had crumbled and he was defenseless. Of course, in the case of Yasha's father no change of residence could possibly have helped.

Vasiliev had got up. Whistling softly, his huge back bent slightly, he was examining the books on the shelves; he pulled one out, opened it, stopped whistling and, wheezing instead, began reading the first page to himself. His place on the couch was taken by Lyubov Markovna and her large purse: now that her tired eyes were naked, her expression grew softer, as with a seldom humored hand she stroked the golden back of Tamara's head.

"Yes!" Vasiliev said abruptly, slamming the book shut and cramming it into the first available opening. "All things in the world must end, comrades. As for me, I must get up at seven tomorrow."

Engineer Kern took a look at his wrist.

"Oh, stay a while longer," said Mme. Chernyshevski, her blue eyes beaming imploringly, and turning to the engineer, who had risen and stood behind his empty chair which he slightly moved to one side (thus a Russian merchant who has drunk his fill of tea might turn his glass upside down on its saucer), she started talking about the lecture he had agreed to deliver at the next Saturday meeting—its title was "Alexander Blok in the War."

"I put 'Blok and War' on the announcements by mistake," she said, "but it doesn't make any difference, does it?"

"On the contrary, it certainly does make a difference," replied Kern with a smile on his thin lips, but with murder behind his thick eyeglasses, without unclasping his hands which were joined on his abdomen. " 'Blok in the War' conveys the proper meaning—the personal nature of the speaker's own observations, while 'Blok and War,' if you will excuse me, is philosophy."

And now they all began gradually to grow less distinct, to ripple with the random agitation of a fog, and then to vanish altogether; their outlines, weaving in figure-eight patterns, were evaporating, though here and there a bright point still glowed—the cordial glint in an eye, the gleam of a bracelet; there was also a momentary reappearance of the intently furrowed forehead of Vasiliev, who was shaking somebody's already dissolving hand, and at the very last there was a floating glimpse of pistachio-colored straw, decorated with silk roses (Lyubov Markovna's hat), and now everything was gone, and into the smoky parlor, without a sound, in his bedroom slippers, came Yasha, thinking that his father had already retired, and with a magic tinkling, by the light of crimson lanterns, dim beings were repairing the pavement at the corner of the square, and Fyodor, who did not have money for the streetcar, was walking home. He had forgotten to borrow from the Chernyshevskis those two or three marks that would have tided him over until he got paid for a lesson or translation: this thought alone would not have disturbed him had he not been possessed by a general feeling of wretchedness consisting of that rotten disappointment (he had imagined so vividly the success of his book), and a chill leak in his left shoe, and fear of the imminent night in a new place. He was tired, he was dissatisfied with himself for wasting the tender beginning of the night, and he was tormented by the feeling that there was some line of thought he had not pursued to its conclusion that day and now could never finish.

He was walking along streets that had already long since insinuated themselves into his acquaintance—and as if that were not enough, they expected affection; they had even purchased in advance, in his future memories, space next to St. Petersburg, an adjacent grave; he walked along these dark, glossy streets and the blind houses retreated, backing or sidling into the brown sky of the Berlin night, which, nevertheless, had its soft spots here and there, spots that would melt under one's gaze, allowing it to obtain a few stars. Here at last is the square where we dined and the tall brick church and the still quite transparent poplar, resembling the nervous system of a giant; here, also, is the public toilet, reminiscent of Baba Yaga's gingerbread cottage. In the gloom of the small public garden crossed obliquely by the faint light of a streetlamp, the beautiful girl who for the last eight years had kept refusing to be incarnated (so vivid was the memory of his first love), was sitting on a cinder-gray bench, but when he got closer he saw that only the bent shadow of the poplar trunk was sitting there. He turned into his street, plunging in it as in cold water—he was so loath to go back, such melancholy was promised him by that room, that malevolent wardrobe, that daybed. He located his front door (disguised by darkness) and pulled out his keys. None of them would open the door.

"What's this . . ." he muttered crossly, looking at the key bit, and then furiously began jamming it in again. "What the hell!" he exclaimed and retreated one step in order to throw back his head and make out the house number. Yes, it was the right house. He was just about to bend over the lock once more when a sudden truth dawned upon him: these were, of course, the boardinghouse keys, which he had carried away in his raincoat pocket by mistake when he moved today, and the new ones must have remained in the room that he now wanted to get into much more than a moment ago.

In those days Berlin janitors were for the most part opulent bullies who had corpulent wives and belonged, out of petty bourgeois considerations, to the Communist Party. White Russian tenants quailed before them: accustomed to subjection, we everywhere appoint over ourselves the shadow of supervision. Fyodor understood perfectly well how stupid it was to be afraid of an old fool with a bobbing Adam's apple, but still he could not bring himself to wake him up after midnight, to summon him up out of his giant featherbed, to perform the act of pushing the button (even though it was more than likely that no one would answer, squeeze as he might); he could not bring himself to do it, especially because he did not have that ten-pfennig coin without which it was unthinkable to walk past the palm, grimly cupped at hip level, confident of receiving its tribute.

"What a mess, what a mess" he whispered, stepping away and feeling, from behind, the weight of a sleepless night settling on him from head to heels, a leaden twin whom he must carry somewhere or other. "How stupid, *kak glupo*," he added, pronouncing the Russian *glupo* with a soft French "l" as his father used to do in a mildly jocular absentminded way, when perplexed.

He wondered what to do next. Wait for somebody to come out? Try to find the black-caped night watchman who looked after door locks on residential streets? Force himself after all to blow up the house by ringing the bell? Fyodor began pacing the sidewalk to the corner and back. The street was echoic and completely empty. High above it milk-white lamps were suspended, each on its own transverse wire; beneath the closest one a ghostly circle swung with the breeze across the wet asphalt. And this swinging motion, which had no apparent relation to him, with a sonorous tambourine-like sound nevertheless nudged something off the brink of his soul where that something had been resting, and now, no longer with the former distant call but reverberating loudly and close by, rang out "Thank you, my land, for your remotest . . ." and immediately, on a returning wave, "most cruel mist my thanks are due. . . ." And again, flying off in search of an answer: ". . . by you unnoticed. . . ." He was somnambulistically talking to himself as he paced a nonexistent sidewalk; his feet were guided by local consciousness, while the principal Fyodor Konstantinovich, and in fact the only Fyodor Konstantinovich that mattered, was already peering into the next shadowy strophe, which was swinging some yards away and which was destined to resolve itself in a yet-unknown but specifically promised harmony. "Thank you, my land . . ." he began again, aloud, gathering momentum afresh, but suddenly the sidewalk turned back to stone under his feet, everything around him began speaking at once, and, instantly sobered, he hurried to the door of his house, for now there was a light behind it.

A middle-aged woman with high cheekbones, a karakul jacket over her shoulders, was letting a man out and had paused together with him at the door. "So don't forget to do it, dear," she was saying in a drab, everyday voice, when Fyodor arrived grinning and immediately recognized her: that morning she and her husband had been meeting their furniture. But he also recognized the visitor who was being let out—it was the young painter Romanov, whom he had run into a couple of times at the editorial offices of the *Free Word.* With an expression of surprise on his delicate face, whose Hellenic purity was spoiled by dull, crooked teeth, he greeted Fyodor; the latter awkwardly bowed to the lady, who was rearranging the jacket slipping from her shoulder, and then bounded up the stairs with enormous strides, tripped horribly at the bend and climbed on holding the banister. Bleary-eyed Frau Stoboy in her dressing gown was awesome, but that did not last long. In his room he groped for the light and found it with difficulty. On the table he saw the glistening keys and the white book. That's already all over, he thought. Such a short time ago he had been giving copies to friends with pretentious or platitudinous inscriptions and now he was ashamed to recall those dedications and how all these last few days he had been nurtured by the joy of his book. But after all, nothing much had happened: today's deception did not exclude a reward tomorrow or after tomorrow; somehow, however, the dream had begun to cloy and now the book lay on the table, completely enclosed within itself, delimited and concluded, and no longer did it radiate those former powerful, glad rays.

A moment later, in bed, just as his thoughts had begun to settle down for the night and his heart to sink in the snow of slumber (he always had palpitations when falling asleep), Fyodor ventured imprudently to repeat to himself the unfinished poem—simply to enjoy it once more before the separation by sleep; but he was weak, and it was strong, twitching with avid life, so that in a moment it had conquered him, covered his skin with goose pimples, filled his head with a heavenly buzz, and so he again turned on the light, lit a cigarette, and lying supine, the sheet pulled up to his chin and his feet protruding, like Antokolski's Socrates (one toe lost to Lugano's damp), abandoned himself to all the demands of inspiration. This was a conversation with a thousand interlocutors, only one of whom was genuine, and this genuine one must be caught and kept within hearing distance. How difficult this is, and how wonderful. . . . And in these talks between tamtambles, tamtam my spirit hardly knows. . . .

After some three hours of concentration and ardor dangerous to life, he finally cleared up the whole thing, to the last word, and decided that tomorrow he would write it down. In parting with it he tried reciting softly the good, warm, farm-fresh lines:

> Thank you, my land; for your remotest
> Most cruel mist my thanks are due.
> By you possessed, by you unnoticed,
> Unto myself I speak of you.
> And in these talks between somnambules
> My inmost being hardly knows
> If it's my demency that rambles
> Or your own melody that grows.

And realizing only now that this contained a certain meaning, he followed it through with interest and approved it. Exhausted, happy, with ice-cold soles (the statue lies half-naked in a gloomy park), still believing in the goodness and importance of what he had performed, he got up to turn off the light. In his torn nightshirt, with his skinny chest and long turquoise-veined, hairy legs exposed, he dawdled by the mirror, still with that same solemn curiosity examining and not quite recognizing himself, those broad eyebrows, that forehead with its projecting point of close-cropped hair. A small vessel had burst in his left eye and the crimson invading it from the canthus imparted a certain gypsy quality to the dark glimmer of the pupil. Goodness, what a growth on those hollow cheeks after a few nocturnal hours, as if the moist heat of composition had stimulated the hair as well! He turned the switch, but most of the night had dissolved and all the pale and chilled objects in the room stood like people come to meet someone on a smoky railroad platform.

For a long time he could not fall asleep: discarded word-shells obstructed and chafed his brain and prickled his temples and there was no way he could get rid of them. Meanwhile the room had grown quite light and somewhere—most likely in the ivy—crazy sparrows, all together, not listening to each other, shrilled deafeningly: big recess in a little school.

Thus began his life in his new hole. His landlady could not get used to his habits of sleeping till noon, lunching none knew how or where, and dining off greasy wrapping paper. His book of poems did not get any reviews after all (somehow he had assumed it would happen automatically and had not even taken the trouble of sending out review copies), except for a brief note in Vasiliev's *Gazeta,* signed by the financial correspondent, who expressed an optimistic view of his literary future and quoted one stanza with a deadly misprint. He came to know Tannenberg Street better and it yielded him all its fondest secrets: such as the fact that next door in the basement lived an old shoemaker by the name of Kanarienvogel and there actually was a bird cage, although minus its yellow captive, in his purblind window, among samples of repaired footwear; but as for Fyodor's shoes, the cobbler looked at him over the top of the steel-rimmed spectacles of his guild and refused to repair them; so Fyodor started thinking of buying a new pair. He also learned the name of the upstairs tenants: having zoomed one day by mistake to the top landing, he read on a brass nameplate *Carl Lorentz, Geschichtsmaler,* and one day Romanov, whom he met at a street corner and who shared a studio in another part of the city with the *Geschichtsmaler,* told Fyodor a few things about him: he was a toiler, a misanthrope and a conservative, who had spent his whole life painting parades, battles, the imperial phantom with his star and ribbon, haunting the Sans-Souci park—and who now, in the uniformless republic, was impoverished and begloomed. He had enjoyed before 1914 a distinguished reputation, had visited Russia to paint the Kaiser's meeting with the Tsar, and while wintering in St. Petersburg had met his present wife, Margarita Lvovna, who was at the time a young and enchanting dilettante who dabbled in all the arts. His alliance in Berlin with the Russian émigré painter had begun by accident, as a result of a newspaper advertisement. This Romanov was of quite a different cut. Lorentz developed a sullen attachment to him, but since the day of Romanov's first exhibition (in which he showed his portrait of Countess d'X, stark naked with corset marks on her stomach, holding her own self diminished to one-third life-size) had considered him a madman and a swindler. Many, however, were captivated by the young artist's bold and original gift; extraordinary successes were predicted for him and some even saw in him the originator of a neonaturalist school: after passing through all the trials of so-called modernism, he was said to have arrived at a renovated, interesting and somewhat cold narrative art. In his early works a certain trace of the cartoonist's style was still evident—for example, in that thing of his called "Coincidence," where, on an advertising post, among the vivid, remarkably harmonious colors of playbills, astral names of cinemas and other transparent motley, one could read a notice about a lost diamond necklace (with a reward to the finder), which necklace lay right there on the sidewalk, at the very foot of the post, its innocent fire sparkling. In his "Autumn," though, the black tailor's dummy with its ripped side, dumped in a ditch among magnificent maple leaves, was already expressiveness of a purer quality; connoisseurs found in it an abyss of sadness. But his best work to date remained one that had been acquired by a discerning tycoon and had already been extensively reproduced, called "Four Citizens Catching a Canary"; all four were in black, broad-shouldered, tophatted (although for some reason one of them was barefoot), and placed in odd, exultant and at the same time wary poses beneath the strikingly sunny foliage of a squarely trimmed linden tree in which hid the bird, perhaps the one that had escaped from my shoemaker's cage. I was obscurely thrilled by Romanov's strange, beautiful, yet venomous art; I perceived in it both a forestalling and a forewarning: having far outdistanced my own art, it simultaneously illuminated for it the dangers of the way. As for the man himself, I found him boring to the point of revulsion—I could not stand his extremely rapid, extremely lisping speech, accompanied by a totally irrelevant, automatic rolling of his shining eyes. "Listen," he said, spitting at my chin, "why don't you let me introduce you to Margarita Lorentz—she has told me to bring you over some night—do come, we hold little soirées at the studio—you know, with music, sandwiches, red lampshades—a lot of young people come—the Polonski girl, the Shidlovski brothers, Zina Mertz. . . ."

These names were unknown to me; I felt no desire to spend evenings in the company of Vsevolod Romanov, nor did Lorentz's pug-faced wife interest me in any way—so not only did I not accept the invitation, but since that time I began avoiding the artist.

In the morning the potato-hawker's cry *"Prima Kartoffel!"* rang out in the street, in a high, disciplined singsong (but how the young vegetable's heart throbs!) or else a sepulchral bass proclaimed *"Blumenerde!"* The thump of rugs being beaten was sometimes joined by a hurdy-gurdy, which was painted brown and mounted on squalid cart wheels, with a circular design on its front depicting an idyllic brook; and cranking now with his right hand, now with his left, the sharp-eyed organ-grinder pumped out a thick "O sole mio." That sun was already inviting me into the square. In its garden a young chestnut tree, still unable to walk alone and therefore supported by a stake, suddenly came out with a flower bigger than itself. The lilacs, however, did not bloom for a long time; but when they finally made up their mind, then, within one night, which left a considerable number of cigarette butts under the benches, they encircled the garden with ruffled richness. In a quiet lane behind the church the locust trees shed their petals on a gray June day, and the dark asphalt next to the sidewalk looked as if cream of wheat had been spilled on it. In the rose beds around the statue of a bronze runner the Dutch Glory disengaged the corners of its red petals and was followed by General Arnold Janssen. One happy and cloudless day in July, a very successful ant flight was staged: the females would take to the air, and the sparrows, also taking to the air, would devour them; and in places where nobody bothered them they kept crawling along the gravel and shedding their feeble prop-room wings. From Denmark the papers reported that as a result of a heat wave there, numerous cases of insanity were being observed: people were tearing off their clothes and jumping into the canals. Male gypsy moths dashed about in wild zigzags. The lindens went through all their involved, aromatic, messy metamorphoses.

Fyodor, in his shirt-sleeves and with sneakers on his sockless feet, would spend the greater part of the day on an indigo bench in the public garden, a book in his long tanned fingers; and when the sun beat down too hard, he would lean his head on the hot back of the bench and shut his eyes for long periods; the ghostly wheels of the city day revolved through the interior bottomless scarlet, and the sparks of children's voices darted past, and the book, open in his lap, became ever heavier and more unbooklike; but now the scarlet darkened under a passing cloud, and lifting his sweaty neck, he would open his eyes and once again see the park, the lawn with its marguerites, the freshly watered gravel, the little girl playing hopscotch with herself, the pram with the baby consisting of two eyes and a pink rattle, and the journey of the blinded, breathing, radiant disk through the cloud—then everything would blaze once again and along the dappled street, lined with restless trees, a coal truck would thunder by with the grimy driver on his high, bumpy seat, clenching the stalk of an emerald-bright leaf in his teeth.

In the late afternoon he would go to give a lesson—to a businessman with sandy eyelashes, who looked at him with a dull gaze of malevolent perplexity as Fyodor unconcernedly read him Shakespeare; or to a schoolgirl in a black jumper, whom he sometimes felt like kissing on her bent yellowish nape; or to a jolly thickset fellow who had served in the imperial navy, who said *est'* (aye-

aye) and *obmozgovat'* (to dope it out), and was preparing *dat' drapu* (to blow) to Mexico, escaping secretly from his mistress, a two-hundred-pound, passionate and doleful old woman who had happened to flee to Finland in the same sleigh as he and since then, in perpetual jealous despair, had been feeding him meat pies, cream pudding, pickled mushrooms. . . . Besides these English lessons there were lucrative commercial translations—reports on the low sound conductivity of tile floors or treatises about ball bearings; and finally, a modest but particularly precious income came from his lyrical poems, which he composed in a kind of drunken trance, and always with that same nostalgic, patriotic fervor; some of them did not materialize in final form, dissolving instead, fertilizing the innermost depths, while others, completely polished and equipped with all their commas, were taken to the newspaper office—first via a subway train with glinting reflections rapidly ascending its vertical stangs of brass, then in the strange emptiness of an enormous elevator to the ninth floor, where at the end of a corridor the color of gray modeling clay, in a narrow little room smelling of "the decaying corpse of actuality" (as the number one office comic used to crack), sat the secretary, a moon-like, phlegmatic person, ageless and virtually sexless, who had more than once saved the day when, angered by some item in Vasiliev's liberal paper, menacing rowdies would come, German Trotskyists hired locally, or some robust Russian Fascist, a rogue and a mystic.

The telephone jangled; ripply proofs breezed past; the theater critic kept on reading a stray Russian newspaper from Vilna. "Why, do we owe you money? Nothing of the kind," the secretary would say. When the door to the room on the right opened, one could hear the juicily dictating voice of Getz, or Stupishin clearing his throat, and among the clatter of several typewriters one could make out the swift rat-tat-tat of Tamara.

At the left was Vasiliev's office; his lustrine jacket grew tight across his plump shoulders as, standing before the lectern he used as a writing table and puffing like some powerful machine, he wrote the leading article in his untidy handwriting with its school-room blots, headed: "No Improvement in Sight," or "The Situation in China." Suddenly stopping, lost in thought, he made a noise like a metal scraper as he scratched his large bearded cheek with one finger and narrowed his eye, overhung by a raffish black brow without a single gray hair in it—remembered in Russia to this day. By the window (outside which there was a similar multi-office building, with repairs going on so high in the sky that it seemed as though they might as well do something about the ragged rent in the gray cloud bank) stood a bowl with an orange and a half and an appetizing jar of yogurt, and in the bookcase, in its locked bottom compartment, forbidden cigars and a large blue-and-red heart were preserved. A table was cluttered with the old trash of Soviet newspapers, cheap books with lurid covers, letters—requesting, reminding, rebuking—the squeezed-out half of an orange, a newspaper page with a window cut out and a portrait photograph of Vasiliev's daughter, who lived in Paris, a young woman with a charming bare shoulder and smoky hair: she was an unsuccessful actress and there was frequent mention of her in the cinema column of the *Gazeta*: ". . . our talented compatriot Silvina Lee . . ."—although no one had ever heard of the compatriot.

Vasiliev would good-humoredly accept Fyodor's poems and print them, not because he liked them (generally he did not even read them) but because it was absolutely immaterial to him what adorned the nonpolitical part of his paper. Having ascertained once for all the level of literacy below which a given contributor by nature could not fall, Vasiliev gave him a free hand, even if the given level barely rose above zero. And poems, since they were mere trifles, passed almost entirely without control, trickling through openings where rubbish of greater weight and volume would have got stuck. But what joyful, exciting squealing arose in all the peacock coops of our émigré poetry from Latvia to the Riviera! They've printed mine! And mine! Fyodor himself, who felt he had only one rival—Koncheyev (who, by the way, was not a contributor to the *Gazeta*)—did not concern himself with his neighbors in print and rejoiced over his poems no less than the others. There were times when he could not wait for the evening mail that brought his copy and instead would buy one half an hour earlier in the street, and shamelessly, scarcely having left the newsstand, catching the reddish light near the fruitstands where mountains of oranges glowed in the blue of early twilight, would unfold the paper—and sometimes find nothing: something else had squeezed it out; but if he found it, he would gather the pages more conveniently and, resuming his progress along the sidewalk, read his poem over several times, varying the inner intonations; that is, imagining one by one the various mental ways the poem would be read, perhaps was now being read, by those whose opinion he considered important—and with each of these different incarnations he would almost physically feel a change in the color of his eyes, and also in the color behind his eyes, and in the taste in his mouth, and the more he liked the chef-d'oeuvre du jour, the more perfectly and succulently he could read it through the eyes of others.

Having thus dawdled away the summer, having given birth to, raised, and stopped loving forever some two dozen poems, he went out one clear and cool day, a Saturday (tonight is the meeting), to make an important purchase. The fallen leaves lay not flat on the sidewalk but warped and stiffly crumpled so that from under each protruded a blue corner of shadow. Carrying a broom, the little old woman in a clean apron, with a small sharp face and disproportionately large feet, came out of her gingerbread cottage with its candy windows. Yes, it was autumn! He walked happily; everything was fine: morning had brought a letter from his mother, who was planning to come and visit him at Christmas, and through his deteriorating summer footwear he felt the ground with extraordinary sensitivity when he walked across an unpaved section, next to deserted vegetable-garden plots with their faint burnt odor, between houses which turned the sliced-off blackness of their outer walls toward them, and there, in front of lacy bowers, grew cabbages beaded with large bright drops, and the bluish stalks of withered carnations, and sunflowers, their heavy bulldog faces bowed. For a long time he had wanted to express somehow that it was in his feet that he had the feeling of Russia, that he could touch and recognize all of her with his soles, as a blind man feels with his palms. And it was a pity when he reached the end of that stretch of rich brown earth and once again had to step along the resonant sidewalk.

A young woman in a black dress, with a shiny forehead and quick, wandering eyes, sat down at his feet for the eighth time, sideways on a stool, nimbly extracted a narrow shoe from the rustling interior of its box, spread her elbows apart as she slackened the edges, glanced abstractedly aside as she loosened the laces, and then, producing a shoehorn from her bosom, addressed Fyodor's large, shy, poorly darned foot. Miraculously the foot fitted inside, but having done so, went completely blind: the wiggling of toes inside had no effect on the exterior smoothness of the taut black leather. With phenomenal speed the salesgirl tied the lace ends and touched the tip of the shoe with two fingers. "Just right," she said. "New shoes are always a little . . ." she went on rapidly, raising her brown eyes. "Of course if you wish, we can make some adjustments. But they fit perfectly, see for yourself!" And she led him to the X-ray gadget and showed him where to place his foot. Looking down in the glass aperture he saw, against a luminous background, his own dark, neatly separated phalanges. With this, with this I'll step ashore. From Charon's ferry. Putting on the other shoe as well, he walked along the carpet the length of the store and back, glancing sideways at the ankle-high mirror which reflected his beautified step and his trouser leg, now looking twice its age. "Yes, they're fine," he said cravenly. When he was a child they used to scrape the glossy black sole with a buttonhook so it would not be slippery. He carried them off to his lesson under his arm, came home, ate, put them on, admiring them apprehensively, and left for the meeting. They do seem all right after all—for an agonizing beginning.

The meeting was at the smallish, pathetically ornate flat of some relatives of Lyubov Markovna's. A red-haired girl in a green dress that ended above her knees was helping the Estonian maid (who was conversing with her in a loud whisper) to serve the tea. Among the familiar crowd, which contained few new faces, Fyodor at once descried Koncheyev, who was attending for the first time. He looked at the round-shouldered, almost humpbacked figure of this unpleasantly quiet man whose mysteriously growing talent could have been checked only by a ringful of poison in a glass of wine—this all-comprehending man with whom he had never yet had a chance to have the good talk he dreamt of having some day and in whose presence he, writhing, burning and hopelessly summoning his own poems to come to his aid, felt himself a mere contemporary. That young face was of the Central-Russian type and seemed a little common, common in a kind of oddly old-fashioned way; it was bounded above by wavy hair and below by starched collar wings, and at first in the presence of this man, Fyodor experienced a glum discomfort. . . . But three ladies were smiling at him from the sofa, Chernyshevski was salaaming to him from afar, Getz was raising like a banner a magazine he had brought for him, which contained Koncheyev's "Beginning of a Long Poem" and an article by Christopher Mortus entitled "The Voice of Pushkin's Mary in Contemporary Poetry." Behind him somebody pronounced with the intonation of an explanatory response, "Godunov-Cherdyntsev." Never mind, never mind, Fyodor thought rapidly, smiling to himself, looking around and tapping the end of a cigarette against his eagle-emblazoned cigarette case, never mind, we'll still clink eggs some day, he and I, and we'll see whose will crack.

Tamara was indicating a vacant chair to him, and as he made his way to it he again thought he heard the sonorous ring of his name. When young people of his age, lovers of poetry, followed him on occasion with that special gaze that glides like a swallow across a poet's mirrory heart, he would feel inside him the chill of a quickening, bracing pride; it was the forerunner of his future fame; but there was also another, earthly fame—the faithful echo of the past: he was proud of the attention of his young coevals, but no less proud of the curiosity of older people, who saw in him the son of a great explorer, a courageous eccentric who had discovered new animals in Tibet, the Pamirs and other blue lands.

"Here," said Mme. Chernyshevski with her dewy smile, "I want you to meet. . . ." She introduced him to one Skvortsov, who had recently escaped from Moscow; he was a friendly fellow, had raylike lines around his eyes, a pear-shaped nose, a thin beard and a dapper, youthful, melodiously talkative little wife in a silk shawl—in short, a couple of that more or less academic type that was so familiar to Fyodor through his memory of the people who used to flicker around his father. Skvortsov in courteous and correct terms began by expressing his amazement at the total lack of information abroad about the circumstances surrounding the death of Konstantin Kirillovich: "We'd thought," his wife put in, "that if nobody knew anything back home, that was to be expected." "Yes," Skvortsov continued, "I recall terribly clearly how one day I happened to be present at a dinner in honor of your father, and how Kozlov—Pyotr Kuzmich—the explorer, remarked wittily that Godunov-Cherdyntsev looked upon Central Asia as his private game reserve. Yes . . . That was quite a time ago, I don't think you were born then."

At this point Fyodor suddenly noticed that Mme. Chernyshevski was directing a sorrowful, meaningful, sympathy-laden gaze at him. Curtly interrupting Skvortsov, he began questioning him, without much interest, about Russia. "How shall I put it . . ." replied the latter. "You see it's like this . . ."

"Hello, hello, dear Fyodor Konstantinovich!" A fat lawyer who resembled an overfed turtle shouted this over Fyodor's head, although already shaking his hand while pushing through the crowd, and by now he was already greeting someone else. Then Vasiliev rose from his seat and leaning lightly on the table for a moment with splayed fingers, in a position peculiar to shopkeepers and orators, announced that the meeting was opened. "Mr. Busch," he added, "will now read us his new, philosophical tragedy."

Herman Ivanovich Busch, an elderly, shy, solidly built, likable gentleman from Riga, with a head that looked like Beethoven's, seated himself at the little Empire table, emitted a throaty rumble and unfolded his manuscript; his hands trembled perceptibly and continued to tremble throughout the reading.

From the very beginning it was apparent that the road led to disaster. The Rigan's farcical accent and bizarre solecisms were incompatible with the obscurity of his meaning. When, already in the Prologue, there appeared a "Lone Companion" (*odinokiy sputnik* instead of *odinokiy putnik*, lone wayfarer) walking along that road, Fyodor still hoped against hope that this was a metaphysical paradox and not a traitorous *lapsus*. The Chief of the Town Guard, not admitting the traveler, repeated several times that he "would not pass definitely" (rhyming with "nightly"). The town was a coastal one (the lone companion was coming from the Hinterland) and the crew of a Greek vessel was carousing there. This conversation went on in the Street of Sin:

FIRST PROSTITUTE

All is water. That is what my client Thales says.

SECOND PROSTITUTE

All is air, young Anaximenes told me.

THIRD PROSTITUTE

All is number. My bald Pythagoras cannot be wrong.

FOURTH PROSTITUTE

Heraclitus caresses me whispering "All is fire."

LONE COMPANION (*enters*)

All is fate.

There were also two choruses, one of which somehow managed to represent the de Broglie's waves and the logic of history, while the other chorus, the good one, argued with it. "First Sailor, Second Sailor, Third Sailor," continued Busch, enumerating the conversing characters in his nervous bass voice edged with moisture. There also appeared three flower vendors: a "Lilies' Woman," a "Violets' Woman" and a "Woman of Different Flowers." Suddenly something gave: little landslides began among the audience.

Before long, certain power lines formed in various directions all across the room—a network of exchanged glances between three or four, then five or six, then ten people, which represented a third of the gathering. Koncheyev slowly and carefully took a large volume from the bookshelf near which he was sitting (Fyodor noticed that it was an album of Persian miniatures), and just as slowly turning it this way and that in his lap, he began to glance through it with myopic eyes. Mme. Chernyshevski wore a surprised and hurt expression, but in keeping with her secret ethics, somehow tied up with the memory of her son, she was forcing herself to listen. Busch was reading rapidly, his glossy jowls gyrated, the horseshoe in his black tie sparkled, while beneath the table his feet stood pigeon-toed—and as the idiotic symbolism of the tragedy became ever deeper, more involved and less comprehensible, the painfully repressed, subterraneously raging hilarity more and more desperately needed an outlet, and many were already bending over, afraid to look, and when the Dance of the Maskers began in the square, someone—Getz it was—coughed, and together with the cough there issued a certain additional whoop, whereupon Getz covered his face with his hands and after a while emerged again with a senselessly bright countenance and humid, bald head, while on the couch Tamara had simply lain down and was rocking as if in the throes of labor, while Fyodor, who was deprived of protection, shed floods of tears, tortured by the forced noiselessness of what was going on inside him. Unexpectedly Vasiliev turned in his chair so ponderously that a leg collapsed with a crack and Vasiliev lurched forward with a changed expression, but did not fall, and this event, not funny in itself, served as a pretext for an elemental, orgiastic explosion to interrupt the reading, and while Vasiliev was transferring his bulk to another chair, Herman Ivanovich Busch, knitting his magnificent but quite unfruitful brow, jotted something on the manuscript with a pencil stub, and in the relieved calm an unidentified woman uttered something in a separate final moan, but Busch was already going on:

LILIES' WOMAN

You're all upset about something today, sister.

WOMAN OF DIFFERENT FLOWERS

Yes, the fortuneteller told me that my daughter would
marry yesterday's passerby.

DAUGHTER

Oh, I did not even notice him.

LILIES' WOMAN

And he did not notice her.

"Hear, hear!" chimed in the Chorus, as in the British Parliament. Again there was a slight commotion: an empty cigarette box, on which the fat lawyer had written something, began a journey across the whole room, and everybody followed the stages of its trip; something extremely funny must have been written on it, but no one read it and it was passed dutifully from hand to hand, destined for Fyodor, and when it finally reached him, he read on it: *Later I want to discuss a certain little affair with you.*

The last act was nearing its conclusion. The god of laughter imperceptibly forsook Fyodor and he gazed meditatively at the shine of his shoe. Onto the cold shore from the ferry. The right one pinched more than the left. Koncheyev, his mouth half open, was leafing through the final pages of the album. "*Zanaves* [curtain]," exclaimed Busch, accenting the last syllable instead of the first.

Vasiliev announced that there would be an intermission. Most of the audience had a rumpled and wilted look, as after a night in a third-class coach. Busch had rolled his tragedy into a thick tube and was standing in a far corner, and it seemed to him that in the din of voices there formed and spread constant ripples of admiration; Lyubov Markovna offered him some tea and then his powerful face suddenly assumed a defenseless, gentle expression, and blissfully licking his lips, he bent toward the glass that had been handed him. Fyodor observed this from afar with a certain feeling of awe, while behind him he heard the following:

"Please give me some explanation!" (The angry voice of Mme. Chernyshevski.)

"Well, you know, such things do happen . . ." (guiltily debonair Vasiliev).

"I ask you for an explanation."

"But, my dear lady, what can I do now?"

"Well, didn't you read it beforehand? Didn't he bring it to you at the office? I thought you said it was a serious, interesting work. A significant work."

"Yes, that's true, a first impression you know, when I skimmed it—I did not take into consideration how it would sound—I was fooled! It's really baffling. But go over to him, Alexandra Yakovlevna, say something to him."

The lawyer grasped Fyodor above the elbow. "You're just the

person I'm looking for. It suddenly occurred to me that there is something for you here. A client of mine came to me—he requires a German translation of some papers of his, for a divorce case, don't you see? The Germans who are handling the affair for him have a Russian girl in their office but apparently she will be able to do only part of it, and they need someone to help her out with the rest. Would you undertake this? Here, let me take your telephone number. *Gemacht.*"

"Ladies and gentlemen, be seated please," rang out Vasiliev's voice. "Now we shall have a discussion of the work that has been read. Those who wish to participate please sign up."

Just then Fyodor saw that Koncheyev, stooping and with his hand behind his lapel, was making a serpentine course toward the exit. Fyodor followed, nearly forgetting his magazine in the process. In the anteroom they were joined by old Stupishin; he frequently moved from one rented room to another but lived always so far from the center of the city that these changes, important and complicated for him, seemed to others to happen in an ethereal world, beyond the horizon of human worries. Draping a skimpy, gray-striped scarf around his neck, he held it in place with his chin in the Russian manner while, also in the Russian manner, he got into his overcoat by means of several dorsal jerks.

"Well, he certainly gave us a treat," he said as they descended, accompanied by the maid with the front door key.

"I confess I didn't listen very carefully," commented Koncheyev.

Stupishin went to wait for a rare, almost legendary streetcar, while Godunov-Cherdyntsev and Koncheyev set out in the opposite direction, to walk as far as the corner.

"What nasty weather," said Godunov-Cherdyntsev.

"Yes, it's quite cold," agreed Koncheyev.

"Rotten—And in what part do you live?"

"Charlottenburg."

"Well, well, that's quite a way. You're walking?"

"Oh yes, walking. I think that here I must . . ."

"Yes, you turn right, I go straight."

They said good-by. "Brr, what a wind!"

"Wait, wait a minute though—I'll see you home. Surely you're a night owl like me and I don't have to expound to you on the black enchantment of stone promenades. So you didn't listen to our poor lecturer?"

"Only at the beginning, and then only with half an ear. However, I don't think it was quite as bad as that."

"You were examining Persian miniatures in a book. Did you not notice one—an amazing resemblance!—from the collection of the St. Petersburg Public Library—done, I think, by Riza Abbasi, say about three hundred years ago: that man kneeling, struggling with baby dragons, big-nosed, mustachioed—Stalin!"

"Yes, I think *that* one is the strongest of the lot. By the way, I've read your very remarkable collection of poems. Actually, of course, they are but the models of your future novels."

"Yes, some day I'm going to produce prose in which 'thought and music are conjoined as are the folds of life in sleep.' "

"Thanks for the courteous quotation. You have a genuine love of literature, don't you?"

"I believe so. You see, the way I look at it, there are only two kinds of books: bedside and wastebasket. Either I love a writer fervently, or throw him out entirely."

"A bit severe, isn't it? And a bit dangerous. Don't forget that the whole of Russian literature is the literature of one century and, after the most lenient eliminations, takes up no more than three to three and a half thousand printed sheets, and scarcely one-half of this is worthy of the bookshelf, to say nothing of the bedside table. With such quantitative scantiness we must resign ourselves to the fact that our Pegasus is piebald, that not everything about a bad writer is bad, and not all about a good one good."

"Perhaps you will give me some examples so that I can refute them."

"Certainly: if you open Goncharov or—"

"Stop right there! Don't tell me you have a kind word for Oblomov—that first 'Ilyich' who was the ruin of Russia—and the joy of social critics? Or you want to discuss the miserable hygienic conditions of Victorian seductions? Crinoline and damp garden bench? Or perhaps the style? What about his 'Precipice' where Rayski at moments of pensiveness is shown with 'rosy moisture shimmering between his lips'?—which reminds me somehow of Pisemski's protagonists, each of whom under the stress of violent emotion 'massages his chest with his hand!' "

"Here I shall trap you. Aren't there some good things in the same Pisemski? For example, those footmen in the vestibule, during a ball, who play catch with a lady's velveteen boot, horribly muddy and worn. Aha! And since we are speaking of second-rank authors, what do you think of Leskov?"

"Well, let me see. . . . Amusing Anglicisms crop up in his style, such as '*eto byla durnaya veshch*' [this was a bad thing] instead of simply '*plokho delo*.' As to his contrived punning distortions—No, spare me, I don't find them funny. And his verbosity—Good God! His 'Soboryane' could easily be condensed to two newspaper *feuilletons*. And I don't know which is worse—his virtuous Britishers or his virtuous clerics."

"And yet . . . how about his image of Jesus 'the ghostly Galilean, cool and gentle, in a robe the color of ripening plum'? Or his description of a yawning dog's mouth with 'its bluish palate as if smeared with pomade'? Or that lightning of his that at night illumines the room in detail, even to the magnesium oxide left on a silver spoon?"

"Yes, I grant you he has a Latin feeling for blueness: *lividus*. Lyov Tolstoy, on the other hand, preferred violet shades and the bliss of stepping barefoot with the rooks upon the rich dark soil of plowed fields! Of course, I should never have bought them."

"You're right, they pinch unbearably. But we have moved up to the first rank. Don't tell me you can't find weak spots there too? In such stories as 'The Blizzard'—

"Leave Pushkin alone: he is the gold reserve of our literature. And over there is Chekhov's hamper, which contains enough food for years to come, and a whimpering puppy, and a bottle of Crimean wine."

"Wait, let's go back to the forebears. Gogol? I think we can accept his 'entire organism.' Turgenev? Dostoevski?"

"Bedlam turned back into Bethlehem—that's Dostoevski for you. 'With one reservation,' as our friend Mortus says. In the 'Karamazovs' there is somewhere a circular mark left by a wet wine glass on an outdoor table. That's worth saving if one uses your approach."

"But don't tell me all is well with Turgenev? Remember those inept tête-à-têtes in acacia arbors? The growling and quivering of Bazarov? His highly unconvincing fussing with those frogs? And in general, I don't know if you can stand the particular intonation of the Turgenevian row of dots at the close of a 'fading phrase' and the maudlin endings of his chapters. Or should we forgive all his sins because of the gray sheen of Mme. Odintsev's black silks and the outstretched hind legs of some of his graceful sentences, those rabbitlike postures assumed by his resting hounds?"

"My father used to find all kinds of howlers in Turgenev's and Tolstoy's hunting scenes and descriptions of nature, and as for the wretched Aksakov, let's not even discuss his disgraceful blunders in that field."

"Now that the dead bodies have been removed we might, perhaps, proceed to the poets? All right. By the way, speaking of dead bodies, has it ever occurred to you that in Lermontov's most famous short poem the 'familiar corpse' at the end is extremely funny? What he really wanted to say was 'corpse of the man she once knew.' The posthumous acquaintance is unjustified and meaningless."

"Of late it's Tyutchev who shares my night lodgings most often."

"A worthy house guest. And how do you feel about Nekrasov's iambics—or don't you have a taste for him?"

"Oh, I do. There is, in his best verse, a certain guitar twang, a sob and a gasp, which for instance Fet, a more refined artist, somehow lacks."

"I have a feeling that Fet's secret weakness is his rationality and stress on antitheses—This hasn't escaped you, has it?"

"Our oafish school-of-social-intent writers criticized him for the wrong reasons. No, I can forgive him everything for 'rang out in the darkening meadow,' for 'dew-tears of rapture shed the night,' for the wing-fanning, 'breathing' butterfly."

"And so we move on to the next century: mind the step. You and I began to rave about poetry in our boyhood, didn't we? Refresh my memory—how did it go?—'how the rims of the clouds palpitate' . . . Poor old Balmont!"

"Or, illuminated from Blok's side, 'Clouds of chimerical solace.' Oh, but it would have been a crime to be choosy here. My mind in those days accepted ecstatically, gratefully, completely, without critical carpings, all of the five poets whose names began with 'B'—the five senses of the new Russian poetry."

"I'd be interested to know which of the five represents taste. Yes, yes, I know—there are aphorisms that, like airplanes, stay up only while they are in motion. But we were talking about the dawn. How did it begin with you?"

"When my eyes opened to the alphabet. Sorry, that sounds pretentious, but the fact is, since childhood I have been afflicted with the most intense and elaborate *audition colorée*."

"So that you too, like Rimbaud, could have—"

"Written not a mere sonnet but a fat opus, with auditive hues he never dreamt of. For instance, the various numerous '*a*'s of the four languages which I speak differ for me in tinge, going from lacquered-black to splintery-gray—like different sorts of wood. I recommend to you my pink flannel '*m*.' I don't know if you remember the insulating cotton wool which was removed with the storm windows in spring? Well, that is my Russian '*y*,' or rather 'ugh,' so grubby and dull that words are ashamed to begin with it. If I had some paints handy I would mix burnt-sienna and sepia for you so as to match the color of a gutta-percha '*ch*' sound; and you would appreciate my radiant '*s*' if I could pour into your cupped hands some of those luminous sapphires that I touched as a child, trembling and not understanding when my mother, dressed for a ball, uncontrollably sobbing, allowed her perfectly celestial treasures to flow out of their abyss into her palm, out of their cases onto black velvet, and then suddenly locked everything up and did not go anywhere after all, in spite of the impassioned persuasions of her brother, who kept pacing up and down the rooms giving fillips to the furniture and shrugging his epaulets, and if one turned the curtain slightly on the side window of the oriel, one could see, along the receding riverfront, façades in the blue-blackness of the night, the motionless magic of an imperial illumination, the ominous blaze of diamond monograms, colored bulbs in coronal designs . . ."

"*Buchstaben von Feuer*, in short . . . Yes, I know what is coming. Shall I finish this banal and soul-rending tale for you? How you delighted in any poem that happened along. How at ten you were writing dramas, and at fifteen elegies—and all about sunsets, sunsets . . . Blok's 'Incognita' who 'passed slowly in between the drunkards.' By the way, who was she?"

"A young married woman. It lasted a little less than two years, until my escape from Russia. She was lovely and sweet—you know, with large eyes and slightly bony hands—and somehow I have remained faithful to her even to this day. Her taste in poetry was limited to fashionable gypsy lyrics, she adored poker and she died of typhus—God knows where, God knows how."

"And what comes now? Would you say it's worth going on writing verse?"

"Oh, decidedly! To the very end. Even at this moment I am happy, in spite of the degrading pain in my pinched toes. To tell the truth, I again feel that turbulence, that excitement. . . . Once again I shall spend the whole night . . ."

"Show me. Let's see how it works: It is with *this*, that from the slow black ferry . . . No, try again: Through snow that falls on water never freezing . . . Keep trying: Under the vertical slow snow in gray-enjambment-Lethean weather, in the usual season, with *this* I'll step upon the shore some day. That's better but be careful not to squander the excitement."

"Oh that's all right. My point is that one cannot help being happy with this tingling sensation in the skin of your brow. . . ."

". . . as from an excess of vinegar in chopped beet. Do you know what has just occurred to me? That river is not the Lethe but rather the Styx. Never mind. Let's proceed: And now a crooked bough looms near the ferry, and Charon with his boathook, in the dark, reaches for it, and catches it, and very . . ."

". . . slowly the bark revolves, the silent bark. Homeward, homeward! I feel tonight like composing with pen in hand. What a moon! What a black smell of leaves and earth from behind those railings."

"And what a pity no one has overheard the brilliant colloquy that I would have liked so much to hold with you."

Never mind, it won't be wasted. In fact, I'm glad it turned out this way. Whose business is it that actually we parted at the very first corner, and that I have been reciting a fictitious dialogue with myself as supplied by a self-teaching handbook of literary inspiration?

Chapter Two

The rain still fell lightly, but with the elusive suddenness of an angel, a rainbow had already appeared. In languorous self-wonder, pinkish-green with a purplish suffusion along its inner edge, it hung suspended over the reaped field, above and before a distant wood, one tremulous portion of which showed through it. Stray arrows of rain that had lost both rhythm and weight and the ability to make any sound, flashed at random, this way and that, in the sun. Up the rain-washed sky, from behind a raven cloud, a cloud of ravishing whiteness was extricating itself and shining with all the detail of a monstrously complicated molding.

"Well, well, it's over," he said in a low voice and emerged from under the shelter of aspens that crowded where the greasy, clayey *zemskaya* (rural district) road—and what a bump in this designation!—descended into a hollow, gathering there all its ruts into an oblong pit, full to the brim with thick café crème.

My darling! Pattern of Elysian hues! Once in Ordos my father, climbing a hill after a storm, inadvertently entered the base of a rainbow—the rarest occurrence!—and found himself in colored air, in a play of light as if in paradise. He took one more step—and left paradise.

The rainbow was already fading. The rain had quite stopped, it was scorching hot, a horsefly with satiny eyes settled on his sleeve.

A cuckoo began to call in a copse, listlessly, almost questioningly: the sound swelled like a cupule, and again, like a cupule, unable to find a solution. The poor, fat bird probably flew further away, for everything was repeated from the beginning in the manner of a reduced reflection (it sought, who knows, a place for the best, the saddest effect). A huge butterfly, flat in flight, bluish-black with a white band, described a supernaturally smooth arc, settled on the damp earth, closed its wings and with that disappeared. This is the kind that now and then a panting peasant lad brings one, cramming it with both hands into his cap. This is the kind that soars up from under the mincing hooves of the doctor's well-behaved little pony, when the doctor, holding the almost superfluous reins in his lap or else simply tying them to the front board, pensively drives along the shady road to the hospital. But on occasion you find four black-and-white wings with brick-colored undersides scattered like playing cards over a forest footpath: the rest, eaten by an unknown bird.

He jumped a puddle where two dung-beetles had fastened onto a straw, getting in each other's way, and printed his sole on the edge of the road: a highly significant footprint, ever looking upward and ever seeing him who has vanished. Walking through a field, alone, beneath the magnificently rushing clouds, he remembered how, with his first cigarettes in his first cigarette case, he had approached an old reaper here and asked for a light; the peasant had taken out a box from his gaunt breast and given it to him unsmilingly, but the wind was blowing, match after match went out before it had hardly flared and after every one he grew more ashamed, while the man watched with a kind of detached curiosity the impatient fingers of the wasteful young squire.

He went deeper into the wood; planks had been laid along the path, black and slimy, with reddish-brown aments and leaves that had stuck to them. Who was this had dropped a russula, breaking open its white fan? In reply came the sound of hallooing: girls were gathering mushrooms and bilberries, the latter seeming so much darker in the basket than on their stalks! Among the birches there was an old acquaintance, with a double trunk, a birch-lyre, and beside it an old post with a board on it; nothing could be made out on it except bullet marks; a Browning had once been fired at it by his English tutor—also Browning—and then Father had taken the pistol, swiftly and dexterously ramming bullets into the clip, and knocked out a smooth *K* with seven shots.

Farther on, a bog orchis bloomed unceremoniously in a patch of marshy ground, behind which he had to cross a back road, and off to the right a white wicket gate gleamed: the entrance to the park. Trimmed with ferns outside, luxuriantly lined with jasmine and honeysuckle inside, in places darkened by fir needles, in others lightened by birch leaves, this huge, dense and multipathed park stood poised in an equilibrium of sun and shadow, which formed from night to night a variable, but in its variability a uniquely characteristic harmony. If circles of warm light palpitated underfoot in the avenue, then a thick velvet stripe was sure to stretch across in the distance, behind it again came that tawny sieve, while further, at the bottom, there deepened a rich blackness that, transferred to paper, would satisfy the water colorist only as long as the paint remained wet, so that he would have to put on layer after layer to retain its beauty—which would immediately fade. All paths led to the house, but geometry notwithstanding, it seemed the quickest way was not by the straight avenue, slim and sleek with a sensitive shadow (rising like a blind woman to meet you and touch your face) and with a burst of emerald sunlight at the very end, but by any of its tortuous and unweeded neighbors. He walked along his favorite one toward the still invisible house, past the bench on which according to established tradition his parents used to sit on the eve of his father's regular departures on his travels: Father, knees apart, twirling his spectacles or a carnation in his hands, had his head lowered, with a boater tipped onto the back of it and with a taciturn almost mocking smile around his puckered eyes and in the soft corners of his mouth, somewhere in the very roots of his trimmed beard; and Mother was telling him something, from the side, from below, from beneath her large, trembling white hat; or was pressing out crunchy little holes in the dumb sand with the tip of her parasol. He walked past a boulder with rowan saplings clambering onto it (one had turned to offer a hand to the younger), past a small grass-grown plat which had been a pond in Grandfather's time and past some shortish fir trees which used to become quite round in winter under their burden of snow: the snow used to fall straight and slow, it could fall like that for three days, five months, nine years—and already, ahead, in a clear space traversed by white specks, one glimpsed a dim yellow blotch approaching, which suddenly came into focus, shuddered, thickened and turned into a tramcar, and the wet snow drifted slantingly, plastering over the left face of a pillar of glass, the tram stop, while the asphalt remained black and bare, as if incapable by nature of accepting anything white, and among the signs over chemists' shops, stationers' and grocers', which swam before the eyes and, at first, were even incomprehensible, only one could still appear to be written in Russian: Kakao. Meanwhile, around him everything that had just been imagined with such pictorial clarity (which in itself was suspicious, like the vividness of dreams at the wrong time of day or after a soporific) paled, corroded, disintegrated, and if one looked around, then (as in a fairy tale the stairs disappear behind the back of whoever is mounting them) everything collapsed and disappeared, a farewell configuration of trees, standing like people come to see someone off and already swept away, a scrap of rainbow faded in the wash, the path, of which there remained only the gesture of a turn, a butterfly on a pin with only three wings and no abdomen, a carnation in the sand, by the shade of the bench, the very last most persistent odds and ends, and in another moment all this yielded Fyodor without a struggle to his present, and straight out of his reminiscence (swift and senseless, visiting him like an attack of a fatal illness at any hour, in any place), straight from the hothouse paradise of the past, he stepped onto a Berlin tramcar.

He was going to a lesson, was late as usual, and as usual there grew in him a vague, evil, heavy hatred for the clumsy sluggishness of this least gifted of all methods of transport, for the hopelessly familiar, hopelessly ugly streets going by the wet window, and most of all for the feet, sides and necks of the native passengers. His reason knew that they could also include genuine, completely human individuals with unselfish passions, pure sorrows, even with memories shining through life, but for some reason he got the impression that all these cold, slippery eyes, looking at him as if he were carrying an illegal treasure (which his gift was, essentially), belonged only to malicious hags and crooked hucksters. The Russian conviction that the German is in small numbers vulgar and in large numbers—unbearably vulgar was, he knew, a conviction unworthy of an artist; but nonetheless he was seized with a trembling, and only the gloomy conductor with hunted eyes and a plaster on his finger, eternally and painfully seeking equilibrium and room to pass amidst the convulsive jolts of the car and the cattle-like crowding of standing passengers, seemed outwardly, if not a human being, then at least a poor relation to a human being. At the second stop a lean man in a short coat with a fox-fur collar, wearing a green hat and frayed spats, sat down in front of Fyodor. In settling down he bumped him with his knee and with the corner of a fat briefcase with a leather handle, and this trivial thing turned his irritation into a kind of pure fury, so that, staring fixedly at the sitter, reading his features, he instantly concentrated on him all his sinful hatred (for this poor, pitiful, expiring nation) and knew precisely why he hated him: for that low forehead, for those pale eyes; for *Vollmilch* and *Extrastark*, implying the lawful existence of the diluted and the artificial; for the Punchinello-like system of gestures (threatening children not as we do—with an upright finger, a standing reminder of Divine Judgment—but with a horizontal digit imitating a waving stick); for a love of fences, rows, mediocrity; for the cult of the office; for the fact that if you listen to his inner voice (or to any conversation on the street) you will inevitably hear figures, money; for the lavatory humor and crude laughter; for the fatness of the backsides of both sexes, even if the rest of the subject is not fat; for the lack of fastidiousness; for the visibility of cleanliness—the gleam of saucepan bottoms in the kitchen and the barbaric filth of the bathrooms; for the weakness for dirty little tricks, for taking pains with dirty tricks, for the abominable object stuck carefully on the railings of the public gardens; for someone else's live cat, pierced through with wire as revenge on a neighbor, and the wire cleverly twisted at one end; for cruelty in everything, self-satisfied, taken for granted; for the unexpected, rapturous helpfulness with which five passersby help you to pick up some dropped farthings; for. . . . Thus he threaded the points of his biased indictment, looking at the man who sat opposite him—until the latter took a copy of Vasiliev's newspaper from his pocket and coughed unconcernedly with a Russian intonation.

That's wonderful, thought Fyodor, almost smiling with delight. How clever, how gracefully sly and how essentially good life is! Now he made out in the newspaper reader's features such a compatriotic softness—in the corners of the eyes, large nostrils, a Russian-cut mustache—that it became at once both funny and incomprehensible how anyone could have been deceived. His thoughts were cheered by this unexpected respite and had already taken a different turn. The pupil he was visiting was a scantily educated but inquisitive old Jew who the previous year had conceived a sudden desire to learn how to "chat in French," which seemed to the old man both more attainable and more becoming to his years, character, and experience of life than the dry study of the grammar of a language. Invariably at the beginning of the lesson, groaning and mixing a multitude of Russian and German words with a pinch of French, he described his exhaustion after the day's work (he was manager of a sizable paper factory), and went from these lengthy complaints to a discussion—in French!—landing immediately up to the ears in hopeless darkness, of international politics, and with this demanded miracles: that all this wild, viscous and ponderous stuff, comparable to the transportation of stones over a washed-out road, should turn suddenly into filigreed speech. Entirely lacking in the ability to remember words (and liking to talk of this not as a shortcoming but as an interesting characteristic of his nature), he not only made no progress but even managed in a year of studying to forget those few French phrases with which Fyodor had found him, and on the basis of which the old man had thought to construct in three or four evenings his own animated, light, portable Paris. Alas, the time passed fruitlessly, proving the futility of the effort and the impossibility of the dream—and then the instructor turned out to be inexperienced, completely lost when the unfortunate factory manager suddenly needed exact information (what's "dandy roll" in French?) which, out of delicacy, the questioner immediately renounced, and both were momentarily embarrassed, like an innocent youth and maiden in some old idyll who inadvertently touch one another. It gradually became unendurable. Since the pupil referred more and more despondently to the tiredness of his brain and more and more often postponed the lessons (his secretary's heavenly voice on the telephone was the melody of happiness!), it seemed to Fyodor that the latter had finally become convinced of his teacher's ineptitude, but that he was prolonging the mutual torment out of pity for his worn trousers, and would continue to do so to the grave.

And now, sitting in the tramcar, he saw with ineffable vividness how in seven or eight minutes he would enter the familiar study, furnished in Berliner animal luxury, would settle in the deep leather armchair beside the low, metal table with its glass cigarette box opened for him, and its lamp fashioned like a terrestrial globe, would light a cigarette, cross his legs with cheap gaiety and come face to face with the agonized, submissive gaze of his hopeless pupil, would hear so clearly his sigh and the ineradicable "*Nu, voui*" with which he interlarded his answers; but suddenly the unpleasant feeling of lateness was replaced in Fyodor's soul by a distinct and somehow outrageously joyful decision not to appear at all for the lesson—to get off at the next stop and return home to his half-read book, to his unworldly cares, to the blissful mist in which his real life floated, to the complex, happy, devout work which had occupied him for about a year already. He knew that today he would receive payment for several lessons, knew that otherwise he would have to smoke and eat again on credit, but he was quite reconciled to this for the sake of that energetic idleness (everything is here, in this combination), for the sake of the lofty truancy he was allowing himself. And he was allowing it not for the first time. Shy and exacting, living always uphill, spending all his strength in pursuit of the innumerable beings that flashed inside him, as if at dawn in a mythological grove, he could no longer force himself to mix with people either for money or for pleasure, and therefore he was poor and solitary. And, as if to spite common fate, it was pleasant to recall how once in the summer he had not gone to a party in a "suburban villa" solely because the Chernyshevskis had warned him that a man would be there who "perhaps could help him"; or how the previous autumn he had not found time to communicate with a divorce bureau which needed a translator—because he was composing a verse drama, because the lawyer promising him this income was importunate and stupid, because, finally, he put it off too long and then was unable to make up his mind.

He worked his way out onto the car's platform. Just then the wind searched him cruelly after which Fyodor drew the belt of his mackintosh tighter and adjusted his scarf, but the small amount of tram warmth had already been taken away from him. The snow had ceased falling, but where it went no one knew; there remained only a ubiquitous dampness which was evidenced both in the swishing sound of motor tires and in the piglike sharpness of the ear-torturing, ragged squeal of car horns, and in the darkness of the day, shivering with cold, with sadness, with loathing for itself, and in the particular shade of yellow of the already lighted shop windows, in the reflections and refractions, in the liquid lights, in all this sick irretention of electric light. The tram came out on the square and, braking excruciatingly, stopped, but it was only a preliminary stop, because in front, by the stone island crowded with people standing by to board, two other trams had got stuck, both with cars coupled on, and this inert agglomeration was also evidence somehow of the disastrous imperfection of the world in which Fyodor still continued to reside. He could stand it no longer, he jumped out and strode across the slippery square to another tramline on which, by cheating, he could return to his own district on the same ticket—good for one transfer but not at all for a return journey; but the honest, official calculation that a passenger would travel in one direction only was undermined in certain cases by the fact that, knowing the routes, one could turn a straight journey imperceptibly into an arc, bending back to the point of departure. This clever system (pleasant evidence of a certain purely German flaw in the planning of tram routes) was willingly followed by Fyodor; from absentmindedness however, from an incapacity to cherish a material advantage for any length of time, and already thinking of something else, he paid automatically for the new ticket he had intended to save on. And even then the cheat prospered, even then not he but the city transport department proved to be out of pocket, and furthermore for a much, much greater sum (the price of a Nord Express ticket!) than could have been expected: crossing the square and turning into a side street, he walked toward the tram stop through a small, at first glance, thicket of fir trees, gathered here for sale on account of the approach of Christmas; they formed between them a kind of small avenue; swinging his arms as he walked he brushed his fingertips against the wet needles; but soon the tiny avenue broadened out, the sun burst forth and he emerged onto a garden terrace where on the soft red sand one could make out the sigla of a summer day: the imprints of a dog's paws, the beaded tracks of a wagtail, the Dunlop stripe left by Tanya's bicycle, dividing into two waves at the turn, and a heel dent where with a light, mute movement containing perhaps a quarter of a pirouette she had slid off it to one side and started walking, keeping hold of the handlebars. An old wooden house in the so-called "abietineous" style, painted a pale green, with like-colored drainpipes, carved designs under the roof and a high stone foundation (where in the gray putty one could fancy one saw the round pink cruppers of walled-up horses), a large, sturdy and extraordinarily expressive house, with balconies on a level with the lime branches, and verandas decorated with precious glass, sailed forward to meet him in a cloud of swallows, with a full spread of awnings, its lightning conductor cleaving through the blue sky and the bright white clouds extending an endless embrace. Sitting on the stone steps of the foremost veranda, illuminated squarely by the sun, are: Father, obviously just back from a swim, turbaned in a shaggy towel so that one cannot see—and how one would like to!—his dark crop, streaked with gray and tapering to a peak on his forehead; Mother, all in white, staring straight in front of her and somehow so youthfully hugging her knees; next to her—Tanya, in an ample blouse, the end of her black braid lying on her collarbone, her smooth parting lowered, holding in her arms a fox terrier whose mouth is creased in a wide smile from the heat; higher up—Yvonna Ivanovna, who for some reason has not come out, her features blurred but her slim waist, her belt and her watch chain clearly visible; to one side, lower down, reclining and resting his head in the lap of the round-faced girl (velvet neck-ribbon, silk bows) who gave Tanya music lessons, his father's brother, a stout army doctor, a joker and a very handsome man; lower still, two sour little glowering schoolboys, Fyodor's cousins: one in a school cap, the other without—the one without to be killed seven years later in the battle of Melitopol; at the very bottom, on the sand, in exactly the same pose as his mother—Fyodor himself, as he was then, though he had changed little since that time, white teeth, black brows, short hair, wearing an open shirt. One forgot who had taken it, but this transient, faded and generally insignificant (how many others and better were there) photograph, unsuitable even for copying, had alone been saved by a miracle and had become priceless, reaching Paris among his mother's belongings and brought by her to Berlin last Christmas; for now, choosing her son a present, she was guided not by what was most costly to get but by what was most difficult to part with.

She had come to him for two weeks, after a three-year separation, and in the first moment when, powdered to a deathly pallor, wearing black gloves and black stockings and an old sealskin coat thrown open, she had descended the iron steps of the coach, glancing with equal quickness first at him and then at what was underfoot, and the next moment, her face twisted with the pain of happiness, was clinging to him, blissfully moaning, kissing him anywhere—ear, neck—it had seemed to him that the beauty of which he had been so proud had faded, but as his vision adjusted itself to the twilight of the present, so different at first from the distantly receding light of memory, he again recognized in her everything that he had loved: the pure outline of her face, narrowing down to the chin, the changeful play of those green, brown, yellow, entrancing eyes under their velvet brows, the long, light stance, the avidity with which she lit a cigarette in the taxi, the attention with which she suddenly looked—unblinded, therefore, by the excitement of the meeting, as any other would have been—at the grotesque scene noticed by both of them: an imperturbable motorcyclist carrying a bust of Wagner in his sidecar; and already by the time they were coming up to the house the light of the past had overtaken the present, had soaked it to saturation point, and everything became the same as it had been in this very Berlin three years previously, as it had once been in Russia, as it had been, and would be, forever.

A spare room was found at Frau Stoboy's place and there, on the first evening (an opened dressing case, rings taken off and laid on the marble washstand), lying on the sofa and ever so quickly eating raisins, without which she could not pass a single day, she spoke of what she had constantly returned to for almost nine years now, repeating over again—incoherently, gloomily, ashamedly, turning her eyes away, as if confessing to something secret and terrible—that she believed more and more that Fyodor's father was alive, that her mourning was ridiculous, that the vague news of his death had never been confirmed by anyone, that he was somewhere in Tibet, in China, in captivity, in prison, in some desperate quagmire of troubles and privations, that he was convalescing after some long, long illness—and suddenly, flinging open the door noisily, stamping on the step, he would enter. And to an even greater degree than before these words made Fyodor feel both happier and more frightened. Accustomed willy-nilly to consider his father dead all these years, he sensed something grotesque in the possibility of his return. Was it admissible that life could perform not only miracles, but miracles necessarily deprived (otherwise they would be unbearable) of even the tiniest hint of the supernatural? The miracle of this return would consist in its earthly nature, in its compatibility with reason, in the swift introduction of an incredible event into the accepted and comprehensible linkage of ordinary days; but the more the necessity for such naturalness grew with the years, the more difficult it became for life to meet it, and now what frightened him was not simply the imagining of a ghost, but the imagining of one that would not be frightening. There were days when it seemed to Fyodor that suddenly on the street (in Berlin there are little cul-de-sacs where at dusk the soul seems to dissolve) he would be approached by an old man of seventy, in fairy-tale rags, shrouded to the eyes in beard, who would wink and say, as he had once been wont to: "Hello, Son!" His father often appeared to him in dreams, as if just returned from some monstrous penal servitude, having experienced physical tortures which it was forbidden to mention, now changed into clean linen—it was impossible to think of the body underneath—and with a completely uncharacteristic expression of unpleasant, momentous sullenness, with a sweaty brow and slightly bared teeth, sitting at table in the circle of his hushed family. But when, overcoming his sensation of the spuriousness of the very style foisted on fate, he nevertheless forced himself to imagine the arrival of a live father, aged but undoubtedly his, and the most complete, most convincing possible explanation of his silent absence, he was seized, not by happiness, but by a sickening terror—which, however, immediately disappeared and yielded to a feeling of satisfied harmony when he removed this meeting beyond the boundary of earthly life.

But on the other hand. . . . It happens that over a long period you are promised a great success, in which from the very start you do not believe, so dissimilar is it from the rest of fate's offerings, and if from time to time you do think of it, then you do so as it were to indulge your fantasy—but when, at last, on a very ordinary day with a west wind blowing, the news comes—simply, instantaneously and decisively destroying any hope in it—then you are suddenly amazed to find that although you did not believe in it, you had been living with it all this time, not realizing the constant, close presence of the dream, which had long since grown fat and independent, so that now you cannot get it out of your life without making a hole in that life. Thus had Fyodor, in spite of all logic and not daring to envision its realization, lived with the familiar dream of his father's return, a dream which had mysteriously embellished his life and somehow lifted it above the level of surrounding lives, so that he could see all sorts of distant and interesting things, just as, when a little boy, his father used to lift him by his elbows thus enabling him to see what was interesting over a fence.

After the first evening, when she had renewed her hope and become convinced that the same hope was alive in her son, Elizaveta Pavlovna no longer referred to it in words, but as usual, it was taken for granted in all their conversations, especially since they did not converse much aloud: frequently, after several minutes of animated silence, Fyodor would suddenly notice that the whole time they both knew very well what it was about, this double, almost subgramineal speech which emerged as a single stream, as a word understood to both of them. And sometimes they would play like this: sitting side by side and silently imagining to themselves that each was taking the same Leshino walk, they went out of the park, took the path along the field (there was a river to the left behind the alders), across the shady graveyard where sun-flecked crosses were measuring something terribly large with their arms and where it was somehow awkward to pick the raspberries, across the river, upwards again, through the wood, to another bend of the river, to the Pont des Vaches and farther, through the pines and along the Chemin du Pendu—familiar nicknames, not grating to their Russian ears but thought up when their grandfathers had been children. And suddenly, in the middle of this silent walk being performed by two minds, using according to the rules of the game the rate of a human footstep (although they could have flown over their whole domains in a single instant), both stopped and said where they had got to, and when it turned out, as it often did, that neither one had outpaced the other, having halted in the same coppice, the same smile flashed upon mother and son and shone through their common tear.

Very soon they again got into their inner rhythm of intercourse, for there was little new that they did not know already from letters. She told him in great detail about the recent wedding of Tanya, who had now gone off to Belgium until January with a husband still unknown to Fyodor, an agreeable, quiet, very polite and completely unremarkable gentleman "working in the field of radio"; and that when they returned she would move into a new flat with them in an enormous house near one of the Paris gates: she was glad to be leaving the small hotel with the steep dark staircase, where she had been living with Tanya in a tiny but many-cornered room completely swallowed up by a mirror and visited by bedbugs of various caliber—from transparent pink baby ones to leathery brown fatties—which congregated first behind the wall calendar with a Russian landscape by Levitan on it and then closer to the field of action, in the inside pocket of the torn wallpaper, directly above the double bed; but the pleasant prospect of a new home was not unmixed with dread: she had an antipathy to her son-in-law and there was something forced in Tanya's brisk, showy happiness—"You see, he's not quite our set," she confessed, stressing this with a certain tightening of the jaws and a downward look; but that was not all, and anyway Fyodor had already heard about that other man whom Tanya loved but who did not love her.

They went out quite often; as always Elizaveta Pavlovna seemed to be looking for something, rapidly spanning the world with a skimming glance of her shimmery eyes. The German holiday proved wet, puddles made the sidewalks seem full of holes, the Christmas tree lights burned dully in the windows, and here and there at street corners a commercial Santa Claus in a red stormcoat and with hungry eyes was distributing handbills. In the windows of a department store some villain had had the idea of setting up dummy skiers on artificial snow beneath the Star of Bethlehem. Once, they saw a modest Communist procession walking through the slush—with wet flags—most of the marchers battered by life, some crookbacked, others lame or sickly, a lot of plain-looking women and several sedate petty-bourgeois. Fyodor and his mother went to have a look at the apartment house where the three of them had lived for two years, but the janitor had already changed, the former proprietor had died, strange curtains hung in the familiar windows, and somehow there was nothing their hearts could recognize. They visited a cinema where a Russian film was being shown which conveyed with particular *brio* the globules of sweat rolling down the glistening faces of the factory workers—while the factory owner smoked a cigar all the time. And of course he took her to see Mme. Chernyshevski.

The introduction was not altogether a success. Mme. Chernyshevski met her guest with a doleful tenderness meant to show that the experience of grief had linked them long and closely; but Elizaveta Pavlovna was most of all interested in what the other woman thought of Fyodor's verses and in why no one was writing about them. "May I embrace you before you go?" asked Mme. Chernyshevski, preparatorily rising on tiptoe—she was a head shorter than Elizaveta Pavlovna, who bent down toward her with an innocent and radiant smile which quite destroyed the meaning of the embrace. "It's all right, one must be brave," said the lady, letting them out onto the stairs and covering her chin with the end of the downy shawl in which she was wrapped. "One must be brave; I've learned to be so brave that I could give lessons in endurance, but I think you've also come well through this school."

"You know," said Elizaveta Pavlovna, stepping lightly but cautiously down the stairs and not turning her lowered head toward her son, "I think I'll just buy cigarette papers and tobacco, otherwise it comes out so dear," and immediately she added in the same voice: "Goodness, how sorry I am for her." And indeed, it was impossible not to pity Mme. Chernyshevski. Her husband had been kept over three months already in an institute for the mentally ailing, in "the semi-loony bin" as he himself playfully expressed it in moments of lucidity. As long ago as October Fyodor had once visited him there. In the sensibly furnished ward sat a fatter, rosier, beautifully shaven and completely insane Chernyshevski, in rubber slippers and a waterproof cloak with a hood. "Why, are you dead?" was the first thing he asked, more discontent than surprised. In his capacity as "Chairman of the Society for Struggle With the Other World" he was continually devising methods to prevent permeation by ghosts (his doctor, employing a new system of "logical connivance," did not oppose this) and now, probably on the basis of its nonconductive quality in another sphere, he was trying out rubber, but evidently the results achieved so far were mainly negative since, when Fyodor was about to take a chair for himself which was standing to one side, Chernyshevski said irritably: "Leave it alone, you see very well there are two sitting on it already," and this "two," and the rustling cloak which plashed up with every movement, and the wordless presence of the attendant, as if this had been a meeting in prison, and the whole of the patient's conversation seemed to Fyodor an unbearable, caricatured vulgarization of that complex, transparent and still noble though half-insane state of mind in which Chernyshevski had so recently communicated with his lost son. With the broad-comedy inflections he had formerly reserved for jokes—but which he now used in earnest—he launched into extensive lamentations, all for some reason in German, over the fact that people were wasting money to invent antiaircraft guns and poison gases and not caring at all about the conduct of another, million times more important, struggle. Fyodor had a healed-over scrape on the side of his temple —that morning he had knocked it against one of the ribs of a radiator in hastily recovering the top of a toothpaste tube which had rolled underneath it. Suddenly breaking off his speech, Chernyshevski pointed squeamishly and anxiously at his temple. "*Was haben Sie da?*" he asked, with a grimace of pain, and then smiled unpleasantly, and growing more and more angry and agitated, began to say that you could not get by him—he had recognized right away, he said, a recent suicide. The attendant came up to Fyodor and asked him to leave. And walking through the funereally luxuriant garden, past unctuous beds in which bass-toned, dark crimson dahlias were blooming in blessed sleep and eternal repose, toward the bench where he was awaited by Mme. Chernyshevski (who never went in to her husband but spent whole days in the immediate vicinity of his quarters, preoccupied, brisk, always with packages)—walking over the variegated gravel between myrtle shrubs resembling furniture and taking the visitors he passed for paranoiacs, troubled Fyodor kept pondering over the fact that the misfortune of the Chernyshevskis appeared to be a kind of mocking variation on the theme of his own hope-suffused grief, and only much later did he understand the full refinement of the corollary and all the irreproachable compositional balance with which these collateral sounds had been included in his own life.

Three days before his mother's departure, in a large hall which was well known to Berlin Russians and which belonged to a society of dentists, judging by the portraits of venerable tooth doctors that looked down from the walls, an open literary evening was held in which Fyodor Konstantinovich also took part. Few people had turned up and it was cold; by the doors the same a thousand times seen representatives of the local Russian intelligentsia stood around smoking, and as usual, catching sight of some familiar, friendly face, Fyodor hurried toward it with sincere pleasure, only to have it replaced by boredom after the first burst of conversation. Elizaveta Pavlovna was joined in the first row by Mme. Chernyshevski; and from the fact that his mother occasionally turned her head this way and that while adjusting her hairdo from behind, Fyodor, hovering about the hall, concluded that she was little interested in the society of her neighbor. At last the program began. First to read was a name writer who in his time had appeared in all the Russian reviews, a gray-haired, clean-shaven old man rather resembling a hoopoe, with eyes which were too good-natured for literature; in a sensibly everyday kind of voice he read a tale of Petersburg life on the eve of the revolution, with an ether-sniffing vamp, chic spies, champagne, Rasputin and apocalyptically apoplectic sunsets over the Neva. After him a certain Kron, writing under the pseudonym of Rostislav Strannyy (Rostislav the Strange), gladdened us with a long story about a romantic adventure in the town of a hundred eyes, beneath skies unknown; for the sake of beauty his epithets were placed after the nouns, his verbs had also flown off somewhere or other and for some reason the word *storozhko*, "warily," was repeated about a dozen times. ("She warily let fall a smile"; "The chestnuts broke warily into blossom.") After the interval poets came thick and fast: a tall youth with a buttonlike face, another, shortish but with a large nose, an elderly lady wearing pince-nez, another, younger, one—and finally Koncheyev, who, in contrast to the triumphant precision and polish of the others, muttered his verses in a low tired voice; but there dwelt independently in them such music, in the seemingly dark verse such a chasm of meaning yawned at one's feet, so convincing were the sounds and so unexpectedly, out of the very same words every poet was stringing together, there sprang up, played, and slipped away without ever quenching one's thirst a unique perfection, bearing no resemblance to words and in no need of words, that for the first time that evening the applause was not feigned. Last to appear was Godunov-Cherdyntsev. From the poems written during the summer he read those which Elizaveta Pavlovna liked so much—on Russia:

> The yellow birches, mute in the blue sky . . .

and on Berlin, beginning with the stanza:

Things here are in a sorry state;
Even the moon is much too rough
Though it is rumored to come straight
From Hamburg where they make the stuff . . .

and the one which moved her most of all, although she did not think to connect it with the memory of a young woman, long dead, whom Fyodor had loved when sixteen:

One night between sunset and river
On the old bridge we stood, you and I.
Will you ever forget it, I queried,
—That particular swift that went by?
And you answered, so earnestly: Never!

And what sobs made us suddenly shiver,
What a cry life emitted in flight!
Till we die, till tomorrow, for ever,
You and I on the old bridge one night.

But it was getting late, many people were moving toward the exit, one lady was putting on her coat with her back to the platform, the applause was sparse. . . . The damp night gleamed black on the street, with a raging wind: never, never will we reach home. But nonetheless a tram came, and hanging on a strap in the gangway over his mother sitting by the window, Fyodor thought with heavy revulsion of the verses he had written that day, of word-fissures, of the leakage of poetry, and at the same time, with proud, joyous energy, with passionate impatience, he was already looking for the creation of something new, something still unknown, genuine, corresponding fully to the gift which he felt like a burden inside himself.

On the eve of her departure they both sat up late in his room, she, in the armchair, easily and skillfully (whereas formerly she could not sew a button on) darning and mending his pitiful things, while he, on the sofa, biting his nails, was reading a thick battered book; earlier, in his youth, he had skipped some of the pages —"Angelo," "Journey to Arzrum"—but lately it was precisely in these that he had found particular pleasure. He had only just got to the words: "The frontier held something mysterious for me; to travel had been my favorite dream since childhood," when suddenly he felt a sweet, strong stab from somewhere. Still not understanding, he put the book to one side and slipped blind fingers into a boxful of homemade cigarettes. At that moment his mother said without raising her head: "What did I just remember! Those funny rhymes about butterflies and moths which you and he composed together when we were out walking, you remember. 'Your blue stripe, Catocalid, shows from under its gray lid.' " "Yes," replied Fyodor, "some were downright epics: 'A dead leaf is not hoarier than a newborn *arborea.*' " (What a surprise it had been! Father had only just brought back the very first specimen from his travels, having found it during the initial trek through Siberia—he had not even had time to describe it yet—and on the first day after his return, in the Leshino park, two paces from the house, with no thought of lepidoptera, while strolling with his wife and children, throwing a tennis ball for the fox terriers, basking in his return, in the balmy weather and the health and gaiety of his family, but unconsciously noting with the experienced eye of a hunter every insect along his path, he had suddenly pointed out to Fyodor with the tip of his cane a plump reddish-gray *Epicnaptera* moth, with sinuate margins, of the leaf-mimicking kind, hanging asleep from a stalk under a bush; he had been about to walk on (the members of this genus look very much alike) but then squatted down, wrinkled his forehead, inspected his find and suddenly said in a bright voice: "*Well, I'm damned!* I need not have gone so far!" "I always said so," interposed his wife with a laugh. The furry little monster in his hand belonged to the new species he had just brought back—and now it had cropped up here, in the Province of St. Petersburg, whose fauna had been so well investigated! But, as often happens, the momentum of mighty coincidence did not stop there, it was good for one more stage: only a few days later his father learned that this new moth had just been described from St. Petersburg specimens by a fellow scientist, and Fyodor cried all night long: they had beaten Father to it!

And now Elizaveta Pavlovna was about to return to Paris. They stood for a long time on the narrow platform waiting for the train, next to the luggage elevator, while on the other lines the sad city trains stopped for a moment, hastily banging their doors. The Paris express rushed in. His mother boarded and immediately thrust her head through the window, smiling. By the neighboring opulent sleeping car, seeing off an unpretentious old lady, stood a couple: a pale, red-lipped beauty in a black silk coat with a high fur collar, and a famous stunt flyer; everyone was staring at him, at his muffler, at his back, as if expecting to find wings on it.

"I have a suggestion to make," said his mother gaily as they parted. "I have about seventy marks left which are quite useless to me, and you must eat better. I can't look at you, you're so thin. Here, take them." "*Avec joie,*" he replied, instantly envisioning a year's pass to the state library, milk chocolate and some mercenary young German girl whom, in his baser moments, he kept planning to get for himself.

Pensive, abstracted, vaguely tormented by the thought that somehow in his talks with his mother he had left the main thing untold, Fyodor returned home, took off his shoes, broke off the corner of a chocolate bar together with its silver paper, moved the book left open on the sofa closer. . . . "The harvest rippled, awaiting the sickle." Again that divine stab! And how it called, how it *prompted* him, the sentence about the Terek ("In faith, the river was awesome!") or—even more fitly, more intimately—about the Tartar women: "They were sitting on horseback, swathed in yashmaks: all one could see were their eyes and the heels of their shoes."

Thus did he hearken to the purest sound from Pushkin's tuning fork—and he already knew exactly what this sound required of him. Two weeks after his mother's departure he wrote her about what he had conceived, what he had been helped to conceive by the transparent rhythm of "Arzrum," and she replied as if she had already known about it:

> It is a long time since I have been as happy as I was with you in Berlin, but watch out, this is no easy undertaking. I feel in my heart that you will accomplish it wonderfully, but remember that you need a great deal of exact information and very little family

sentimentality. If you need anything I'll tell you all I can, but take care of the special research where you are, and this is most important, take all his books and those of Grigoriy Efimovich, and those of the Grand Duke, and lots more; of course you know how to obtain all this, and be sure to get into touch with Vasiliy Germanovich Krüger, search him out if he's still in Berlin, they once traveled together, I remember, and approach other people, you know whom better than I, write to Avinov, to Verity, write to that German who used to visit us before the war, Benhaas? Banhaas? Write to Stuttgart, to London, to Tring, in Oxford, everywhere, *débrouille-toi* because I know nothing of these matters and all these names merely sing in my ears, but how certain I am that you will manage, my darling.

He continued, however, to wait—the planned work was a wafture of bliss, and he was afraid to spoil that bliss by haste and moreover the complex responsibility of the work frightened him, he was not ready for it yet. Continuing his training program during the whole of spring, he fed on Pushkin, inhaled Pushkin (the reader of Pushkin has the capacity of his lungs enlarged). He studied the accuracy of the words and the absolute purity of their conjunction; he carried the transparency of prose to the limits of blank verse and then mastered it: in this he was served by a living example in the prose of Pushkin's *History of the Pugachyov Rebellion:*

God help us not to see a Russian riot
Senseless and merciless . . .

To strengthen the muscles of his muse he took on his rambles whole pages of *Pugachyov* learned by heart as a man using an iron bar instead of a walking stick. Toward him out of a Pushkin tale came Karolina Schmidt, "a girl heavily rouged, of meek and modest appearance," who acquired the bed in which Schoning died. Beyond Grunewald forest a postmaster who resembled Simeon Vyrin (from another tale) was lighting his pipe by the window, and there also stood pots with balsam flowers. The sky-blue *sarafan* of the Damsel turned Peasant could be glimpsed among the alder bushes. He was in that state of feeling and mind "when reality, giving way to fancies, blends with them in the nebulous visions of first sleep."

Pushkin entered his blood. With Pushkin's voice merged the voice of his father. He kissed Pushkin's hot little hand, taking it for another, large hand smelling of the breakfast *kalach* (a blond roll). He remembered that his and Tanya's nurse hailed from the same place that Pushkin's Arina came from—namely Suyda, just beyond Gatchina: this had been within an hour's ride of their area —and she had also spoken "singsong like." He heard his father on a fresh summer morning as they walked down to the river bathhouse, on whose plank wall shimmered the golden reflection of the water, repeating with classic fervor what he considered to be the most beautiful not only of Pushkin's lines but of all the verses ever written in the world: *"Tut Apollon-ideal, tam Niobeya-pechal'"* (Here is Apollo-ideal, there is Niobe-grief) and the russet wing and mother-of-pearl of a Niobe fritillary flashed over the scabiosas of the riverside meadow, where, during the first days of June, there occurred sparsely the small Black Apollo.

Indefatigably, in ecstasy, he was really preparing his work now (in Berlin with an adjustment of thirteen days it was also the first days of June), collected material, read until dawn, studied maps, wrote letters and met with the necessary people. From Pushkin's prose he had passed to his life, so that in the beginning the rhythm of Pushkin's era commingled with the rhythm of his father's life. Scientific books (with the Berlin Library's stamp always on the ninety-ninth page), such as the familiar volumes of *The Travels of a Naturalist* in unfamiliar black and green bindings, lay side by side with the old Russian journals in which he sought Pushkin's reflected light. There, one day, he stumbled over the remarkable *Memoirs of the Past* of A. N. Suhoshchokov, in which there were among other things two or three pages concerning his grandfather, Kirill Ilyich (his father had once referred to them—with displeasure), and the fact that the writer of these memoirs mentioned him incidentally in connection with his thoughts on Pushkin now seemed somehow to have particular significance, even though he portrayed Kirill Ilyich as a gay dog and a good-for-nothing.

Suhoshchokov wrote:

They say that a man whose leg is cut off at the hip can feel it for a long time, moving nonexistent toes and flexing nonexistent muscles. Thus will Russia long continue to feel the living presence of Pushkin. There is something seductive, like an abyss, in his fatal destiny, and indeed, he himself felt that he had had, and would have, a special reckoning with fate. In addition to the poet's extracting poetry out of his past, he also found it in tragic thoughts about the future. The triple formula of human existence: irrevocability, unrealizability, inevitability—was well known to him. But how he wanted to live! In the above-mentioned album of my "academic" aunt he personally wrote a poem which I can remember to this day, both mentally and visually, so that I can even see its position on the page:

Oh no, my life has not grown tedious,
I want it still, I love it still.
My soul, although its youth has vanished,
Has not become completely chill.
Fate will yet comfort me; a novel
Of genius I shall yet enjoy,
I'll see yet a mature Mickiéwicz,
With something I myself may toy.

I do not think one could find any other poet who peered so often —now in jest, now superstitiously, or with inspired seriousness—into the future. Right to this day there lives in the Province of Kursk, topping the hundred mark, an old man whom I remember as being already elderly, stupid and malicious—but Pushkin is no longer with us. Meeting in the course of my long life with remarkable talents and living through remarkable events, I have often meditated on how he would have reacted to this and that: why, he could have seen the emancipation of the serfs and could have read *Anna Karenin!* . . . Returning now to these reveries of mine I recall that once in my youth I had something in the nature of a vision. This psychological episode is closely linked with the recollection of a personage still thriving to this very day, whom I shall call Ch.—I trust he will not blame me for this revival of a distant past. We were acquainted through our families—my grandfather had once been friendly with his father. In 1836, while abroad, this Ch. who was then quite young—barely seventeen —quarreled with his family (and in so doing hastened, so they say, the decease of his sire, a hero of the Napoleonic War), and in the company of some Hamburg merchants sailed nonchalantly off to

Boston, from there landing in Texas where he successfully took up cattle breeding. In that manner twenty years passed. The fortune he had made he lost playing écarté on a Mississippi keel-boat, won it back in the gaming houses of New Orleans, blued it all over again, and after one of those scandalously prolonged, noisy, smoky duels on closed premises which were then fashionable in Louisiana—and after many other adventures—he became homesick for Russia where, conveniently, a demesne was awaiting him, and with the same carefree easiness with which he had left it, he returned to Europe. Once, on a winter's day in 1858, he visited us unexpectedly at our house on the Moyka, in St. Petersburg; Father was away and the guest was received by us youngsters. As we looked at this outlandish fop in his soft black hat and black clothes, the romantic gloom of which caused his silk shirt with its sumptuous pleats, and his blue, lilac and pink waistcoat with diamond buttons to stand out particularly dazzlingly, my brother and I could hardly contain our laughter and decided there and then to take advantage of the fact that during all these years he had heard absolutely nothing of his homeland, as if it had fallen through some trap door, so that now, like a forty-year-old Rip van Winkle waking up in a transformed St. Petersburg, Ch. was hungry for any news, the which we undertook to give him plenty of, mixed with our outrageous fabrications. To the question, for instance, was Pushkin alive and what was he writing, I blasphemously replied, "Why, he came out with a new poem the other day." That night we took our guest to the theater. It did not turn out too well, however. Instead of treating him to a new Russian comedy we showed him *Othello* with the famous black tragedian Aldridge. At first our American planter seemed to be highly amused by the appearance of a genuine Negro on the stage. But he remained indifferent to the marvelous power of his acting and was more taken up with examining the audience, especially our St. Petersburg ladies (one of whom he soon afterwards married), who were devoured at that moment with envy for Desdemona.

"Look who's sitting next to us," my brother suddenly said to Ch. in a low voice, "There, to our right."

In the neighboring box there sat an old man. . . . Of shortish stature, in a worn tailcoat, with a sallow and swarthy complexion, disheveled ashen side-whiskers, and sparse, gray-streaked tousled hair, he was taking a most eccentric delight in the acting of the African: his thick lips twitched, his nostrils were dilated, and at certain bits he even jumped up and down in his seat and banged with delight on the parapet, his rings flashing.

"Who's that?" asked Ch.

"What, don't you recognize him? Look closer."

"I don't recognize him."

Then my brother made big eyes and whispered, "Why, that's Pushkin!"

Ch. looked again . . . and after a minute became interested by something else. It seems funny now to recall what a strange mood came upon me then: the prank, as happens from time to time, rebounded, and this frivolously summoned ghost did not want to disappear: I was quite incapable of tearing myself away from the neighboring box; I looked at those harsh wrinkles, that broad nose, those large ears . . . shivers ran down my back, and not all of Othello's jealousy was able to drag me away. What if this is indeed Pushkin, I mused, Pushkin at sixty, Pushkin spared two decades ago by the bullet of the fatal coxcomb, Pushkin in the rich autumn of his genius. . . . This is he; this yellow hand grasping those lady's opera glasses wrote *Anchar, Graf Nulin, The Egyptian Nights*. . . . The act finished; applause thundered. Gray-haired Pushkin stood up abruptly, and still smiling, with a bright sparkle in his youthful eyes, quickly left his box.

Suhoshchokov errs in depicting my grandfather as an empty-headed rake. It was simply that the latter's interests were situated on a different plane from the intellectual habitus of a young dilettante, member of the St. Petersburg literary set which our memoirist was then. Even if Kirill Ilyich had been pretty wild in his youth, once married he not only settled down but also entered government service, simultaneously doubling his inherited fortune by successful operations and later retiring to his country place, where he manifested extraordinary skill in farming, produced a new sort of apple on the side, left a curious "Discours" (the fruit of winter leisure) on the "Equality Before the Law in the Animal Kingdom" plus a proposal for a clever reform under the kind of intricate title that was fashionable then, "Visions of an Egyptian Bureaucrat," and as an old man accepted an important consular post, in London. He was kind, brave and truthful, and had his quirks and passions—what more could be needed? A tradition has subsisted in the family that, having sworn not to game, he was physically incapable of remaining in a room where there was a pack of cards. An ancient Colt revolver that had served him well and a medallion with the portrait of a mysterious lady attracted indescribably my boyhood dreams. His life, which had retained to the end the freshness of its stormy beginning, ended peacefully. He returned to Russia in 1883, no longer a Louisiana duelist but a Russian dignitary, and on a July day, on the leather sofa in the little blue corner room where I later kept my collection of butterflies, he expired without suffering, talking all the while in his deathbed delirium about a big river and the music and lights.

My father was born in 1860. A love of lepidoptera was inculcated into him by his German tutor. (By the way: what has happened to those originals who used to teach natural history to Russian children—green net, tin box on a sling, hat stuck with pinned butterflies, long, learned nose, candid eyes behind spectacles—where are they all, where are their frail skeletons—or was this a special breed of Germans, for export to Russia, or am I not looking properly?) After completing early (in 1876) his schooling in St. Petersburg, he received his university education in England, at Cambridge, where he studied biology under Professor Bright. His first journey, around the world, he made while my grandfather was still alive, and from then until 1918 his whole life consisted of traveling and the writing of scientific works. The main ones among them are: *Lepidoptera Asiatica* (8 volumes published in parts from 1890 to 1917), *The Butterflies and Moths of the Russian Empire* (the first four out of six proposed volumes came out 1912–1916) and, best known to the general public, *The Travels of a Naturalist* (7 volumes 1892–1912). These works were unanimously recognized as classics and he was still a young man when his name occupied one of the first places in the study of the Russo-Asiatic fauna, side by side with the names of its pioneers, Fischer von Waldheim, Menetriés, Eversmann.

He worked in close touch with his remarkable Russian contemporaries. Kholodkovski calls him "the conquistador of Russian entomology." He collaborated with Charles Oberthur, Grand Duke Nikolai Mihailovich, Leech and Seitz. Scattered throughout entomological journals are hundreds of his papers, of which the first —"On the peculiarities of the occurrence of certain butterflies in the Province of St. Petersburg" (Horae Soc. Ent. Ross.)—is dated 1877, and the last—"*Austautia simonoides* n. sp., a Geometrid Moth Mimicking a Small Parnassius" (Trans. Ent. Soc. London)—is dated 1916. He conducted a weighty and acrimonious polemic with Staudinger, author of the notorious *Katalog*. He was vice-president of the Russian Entomological Society, Full Member of the Moscow Soc. of Investigators of Nature, Member of the Imperial Russian Geographical Soc., and Honorary Member of a multitude of learned societies abroad.

Between 1885 and 1918 he covered an incredible amount of territory, making surveys of his route on a three-mile scale for a distance of many thousands of miles and forming astounding collections. During these years he completed eight major expeditions which in all lasted eighteen years; but between them there was also a multitude of minor journeys, "diversions" as he called them, considering as part of these minutiae not only his trips to the less-well-investigated countries of Europe but also the journey around the world he had made in his youth. Tackling Asia in earnest he investigated Eastern Siberia, Altai, Fergana, the Pamirs, Western China, "the islands of the Gobi Sea and its coasts," Mongolia, and "the incorrigible continent" of Tibet—and described his travels in precise, weighty words.

Such is the general scheme of my father's life, copied out of an encyclopedia. It still does not sing, but I can already hear a living voice within it. It remains to be said that in 1898, at thirty-eight years of age, he married Elizaveta Pavlovna Vezhin, the twenty-year-old daughter of a well-known statesman; that he had two children by her; that in the intervals between his journeys. . . .

An agonizing, somehow sacrilegious question, hardly expressible in words: was her life with him happy, together and apart? Shall we disturb this inner world or shall we limit ourselves to a mere description of routes—*arida quaedam viarum descripto?* "Dear Mamma, I now have a great favor to ask of you. Today is the 8th of July, his birthday. On any other day I could never bring myself to ask you. Tell me something about you and him. Not the sort of thing I can find in our shared memories but the sort of thing you alone have gone through and preserved." And here is part of the reply:

. . . imagine—a honeymoon trip, the Pyrenees, the divine bliss of everything, of the sun, the brooks, the flowers, the snowy summits, even the flies in the hotels—and of being every moment together. And then, one morning, I had a headache or something, or the heat was too much for me. He said he would go for a half hour's stroll before lunch. With odd clearness I remember sitting on a hotel balcony (around me peace, the mountains, the wonderful cliffs of Gavarnie) and reading for the first time a book not intended for young girls, *Une Vie* by Maupassant. I remember I liked it very much at the time. I look at my little watch and I see that it is already lunchtime, more than an hour has passed since he left. I wait. At first I am a little cross, then I begin to worry. Lunch is served on the terrace and I am unable to eat. I go out onto the lawn in front of the hotel, I return to my room, I go outside again. In another hour I was in an indescribable state of terror, agitation, God knows what. I was traveling for the first time, I was inexperienced and easily frightened, and then there was *Une Vie*. . . . I decided that he had abandoned me, the most stupid and terrible thoughts kept getting into my head, the day was passing, it seemed to me that the servants were gloating at me—oh, I cannot convey to you what it was like! I had even begun to thrust some dresses into a suitcase in order to return immediately to Russia, and then I suddenly decided he was dead, I ran out and began to babble something crazy and to send for the police. Suddenly I saw him walking across the lawn, his face more cheerful than I had ever seen it before, although he had been cheerful the whole time; there he came, waving his hand to me as if nothing had happened, and his light trousers had wet green spots on them, his panama had gone, his jacket was torn on one side. . . . I expect you have already guessed what had happened. Thank God at least that he finally caught it after all—in his handkerchief, on a sheer cliff—if not he would have spent the night in the mountains, as he coolly explained to me. . . . But now I want to tell you about something else, from a slightly later period, when I already knew what a really good separation could be. You were quite small then, coming up to three, you can't remember. That spring he went off to Tashkent. From there he was due to set off on a journey on the first of June and to be away for not less than two years.

That was already the second big absence during our time together. I often think now that if all the years he spent without me from the day of our wedding were added together they would amount in all to no more than his present absence. And I also think of the fact that it sometimes seemed to me then that I was unhappy, but now I know that I was always happy, that that unhappiness was one of the colors of happiness. In short, I don't know what came over me that spring, I had always been sort of batty when he went away, but that time I was quite disgracefully so. I suddenly decided that I would catch up with him and travel with him at least till autumn. Secretly I gathered a thousand things together; I had absolutely no idea what was needed, but it seemed to me that I was stocking up everything well and properly. I remember binoculars, and an alpenstock, and a camp-bed, and a sun helmet, and a hareskin coat straight out of *The Captain's Daughter,* and a little mother-of-pearl revolver, and some great tarpaulin affair that I was afraid of, and a complicated water bottle that I couldn't unscrew. In short, think of the equipment of Tartarin de Tarascon: How I managed to leave you little ones, how I said good-by to you—that's in a kind of mist, and I don't remember any more how I slipped out from Uncle Oleg's surveillance, how I got to the station. But I was both frightened and cheerful, I felt myself a heroine, and on the stations everyone looked at my English traveling costume with its short (*entendons-nous:* to the ankle) checked skirt, with the binoculars over one shoulder and a kind of purse over the other. That's how I looked when I jumped out of the tarantass in a settlement just outside of Tashkent, when in the brilliant sunlight, I shall never forget it, I caught sight of your father within a hundred yards of the road: he was standing with one foot resting on a white stone, one elbow on a fence, and talking to two Cossacks. I ran across the gravel, shouting and laughing; he turned slowly, and when I suddenly stopped in front of him like a fool, he looked me all over, slit his eyes, and in a horribly unexpected voice spoke three words: "You go home." And I immediately turned, and went back to my carriage, and got in it, and saw he had put his foot in exactly the same place and had again propped his elbow, continuing his conversation with the Cossacks. And now I was driving back, in a trance, petrified, and only somewhere deep within me preparations had started for a storm of tears. But then after a couple of miles [and here a smile broke through the written line] he overtook me, in a cloud of dust, on a white horse, and we parted this time quite differently, so that I resumed my way to St. Petersburg almost as cheerfully as I had left it, only that I kept worrying about you two, wondering how you were, but no matter, you were in good health.

No—somehow it seems to me that I do remember all this, perhaps because it was subsequently often mentioned. In general our whole daily life was permeated with stories about Father, with worry about him, expectations of his return, the hidden sorrow of farewells and the wild joy of welcomings. His passion was reflected in all of us, colored in different ways, apprehended in different ways, but permanent and habitual. His home museum, in which stood rows of oak cabinets with glassed drawers, full of crucified butterflies (the rest—the plants, beetles, birds, rodents and reptiles—he gave to his colleagues to study), where it smelled as it probably smells in Paradise, and where the laboratory assistants worked at tables along the one-piece windows, was a kind of mysterious central hearth, illuminating from inside the whole of our St. Petersburg house—and only the noonday roar of the Petropavlovsk cannon could invade its quiet. Our relatives, non-entomological friends, the servants and the meekly touchy Yvonna Ivanovna talked of butterflies not as of something really existing but as of a certain attribute of my father, which existed only insofar as he existed, or as of an ailment with which everybody had long since got used to coping, so that with us entomology turned into some sort of routinary hallucination, like a harmless domestic ghost that sits down, no longer surprising anyone, every evening by the fireside. At the same time, none of our countless uncles and aunts took any interest in his science and had hardly even read his popular work, read and reread by dozens of thousands of cultured Russians. Of course Tanya and I had learned to appreciate Father from earliest childhood and he seemed even more enchanting to us than, say, that Harold about whom he told stories to us, Harold who fought with the lions in the Byzantine arena, who pursued brigands in Syria, bathed in the Jordan, took eighty fortresses by storm in Africa, "the Blue Land," saved the Icelanders from starvation—and was famed from Norway to Sicily, from Yorkshire to Novgorod. Then, when I fell under the spell of butterflies, something unfolded in my soul and I relived all my father's journeys, as if I myself had made them: in my dreams I saw the winding road, the caravan, the many-hued mountains, and envied my father madly, agonizingly, to the point of tears—hot and violent tears that would suddenly gush out of me at table as we discussed his letters from the road or even at the simple mention of a far, far place. Every year, with the approach of spring, before moving to the country, I would feel within me a pitiful fraction of what I would have felt before departing for Tibet. On the Nevski Avenue, during the last days of March, when the wooden blocks of the spacious street pavements gleamed dark blue from the damp and the sun, one might see, flying high over the carriages, along the façades of the houses, past the city hall, past the lindens in the square, past the statue of Catherine, the first yellow butterfly. In the classroom the large window was open, sparrows perched on the windowsill and teachers let lessons go by, leaving in their stead squares of blue sky, with footballs falling down out of the blueness. For some reason I always had bad marks in geography and what an expression our geography teacher would have when he used to mention my father's name, how the inquisitive eyes of my comrades turned on me at this point and how within me the blood rose and fell from suppressed rapture and from fear of expressing that rapture—and now I think of how little I know, how easy it is for me to make some idiotic blunder in describing my father's researches.

At the beginning of April, to open the season, the members of the Russian Entomological Society used to make a traditional trip to the other side of Black River, in a suburb of St. Petersburg, where in a birch grove which was still naked and wet, still showing patches of holey snow, there occurred on the trunks, its feeble transparent wings pressed flat against the papery bark, our favorite rarity, a specialty of the province. Once or twice they took me with them too. Among these elderly family men cautiously, tensely practicing sorcery in an April wood, there was an old theater critic, a gynecologist, a professor of international law and a general—for some reason I can recall especially clearly the figure of this general (X. B. Lambovski—there was something Paschal about him), his fat back bending low, with one arm placed behind it, next to the figure of my father, who had sunk on his haunches with a kind of Oriental ease—both were carefully examining in search of pupae a handful of reddish earth dug up with a trowel—and even to this day I am wondering what the coachmen waiting on the road made of all this.

Sometimes, in the country, Grandmother would sail into our schoolroom, Olga Ivanovna Vezhin, plump, fresh-complexioned, in mittens and lace: "*Bonjour les enfants,*" she would sing out sonorously and then, heavily accenting the prepositions, she informed us: "*Je viens de voir* DANS *le jardin,* PRÈS *du cèdre,* SUR *une rose un papillon de toute beauté: il était bleu, vert, pourpre, doré—et grand comme ça.*" "Quickly take your net," she continued, turning to me, "and go into the garden. Perhaps you can still catch it." And she sailed out, completely oblivious to the fact that if such a fabulous insect were to come my way (it was not even worth a guess as to what banal garden visitor her imagination had so adorned), I would have died of heartbreak. Sometimes, to give me special pleasure, our French governess would choose a certain fable of Florian's for me to learn by heart, about another impossibly gaudy *petit-maître* butterfly. Sometimes some aunt or other would give me a book by Fabre, whose popular works, full of chitchat, inaccurate observations and downright mistakes, my father treated with scorn. I also remember this: one day, upon missing my net I went out to look for it on the veranda and met my uncle's orderly returning from somewhere with it on his shoulder, all flushed and with a kindly and shy smile on his rosy lips: "Just see what I've caught for you," he proclaimed in a satisfied voice, dumping the net on the floor; the mesh was secured near the frame by a bit of string, so that a bag was formed in which a variety of live matter swarmed and rustled—and good heavens, what rubbish there was in it: thirty-odd grasshoppers, the head of a daisy, a couple of dragonflies, ears of wheat, some sand, a cabbage butterfly crushed out of all recognition, and finally, an edible toadstool noticed on the way and added just in case. The Russian common people know and love their country's nature. How many jeers, how many conjectures and questions have I had occasion to hear when, overcoming my embarrassment, I walked through the village with my net! "Well, that's nothing," said my father, "you should have seen the faces of the Chinese when I was collecting once on some holy mountain, or the look the progressive schoolmistress in a Volga town gave me when I explained to her what I was doing in that ravine."

How to describe the bliss of our walks with Father through the woods, the fields and the peat bogs, or the constant summer thought of him if he was away, the eternal dream of making some discovery and of meeting him with this discovery—How to describe the feeling I experienced when he showed me all the spots where in his own childhood he had caught this and that—the beam of a half-rotted little bridge where he had caught his first peacock butterfly in '71, the slope of the road down to the river where he had once fallen on his knees, weeping and praying (he had bungled his stroke, it had flown for ever!). And what fascination there was in his words, in the kind of special fluency and grace of his style when he spoke about his subject, what affectionate precision in the movements of his fingers turning the screw of a spreading board or a miscroscope, what a truly enchanting world was unfolded in his lessons! Yes, I know this is not the way to write—these exclamations won't take me very deep—but my pen is not yet accustomed to following the outlines of his image, and I myself abominate these accessory curlicues. Oh, don't look at me, my childhood, with such big, frightened eyes.

The sweetness of the lessons! On a warm evening he would take me to a certain small pond to watch the aspen hawk moth swing over the very water, dipping in it the tip of its body. He showed me how to prepare genital armatures to determine species which were externally indistinguishable. With a special smile he brought to my attention the black Ringlet butterflies in our park which with mysterious and elegant unexpectedness appeared only in even years. He mixed beer with treacle for me on a dreadfully cold, dreadfully rainy autumn night in order to catch at the smeared tree trunks that glistened in the light of a kerosene lamp a multitude of large, banded moths, silently diving and hurrying toward the bait. He variously warmed and cooled the golden chrysalids of my tortoiseshells so that I was able to get from them Corsican, arctic and entirely unusual forms looking as if they had been dipped in tar and had silky fuzz sticking to them. He taught me how to take apart an ant-hill and find the caterpillar of a Blue which had concluded a barbaric pact with its inhabitants, and I saw how an ant, greedily tickling a hind segment of that caterpillar's clumsy, sluglike little body, forced it to excrete a drop of intoxicant juice, which it swallowed immediately. In compensation it offered its own larvae as food; it was as if cows gave us Chartreuse and we gave them our infants to eat. But the strong caterpillar of one exotic species of Blue will not stoop to this exchange, brazenly devouring the infant ants and then turning into an impenetrable chrysalis which finally, at the time of hatching, is surrounded by ants (those failures in the school of experience) awaiting the emergence of the helplessly crumpled butterfly in order to attack it; they attack—and nevertheless she does not perish: "I have never laughed so much," said my father, "as when I realized that nature had supplied her with a sticky substance which caused the feelers and feet of those zealous ants to get stuck together, so that they rolled and writhed all around her while she herself, calm and invulnerable, let her wings strengthen and dry."

He told me about the odors of butterflies—musk and vanilla; about the voices of butterflies; about the piercing sound given out by the monstrous caterpillar of a Malayan hawkmoth, an improvement on the mouselike squeak of our Death's Head moth; about the small resonant tympanum of certain tiger moths; about the cunning butterfly in the Brazilian forest which imitates the whir of a local bird. He told me about the incredible artistic wit of mimetic disguise, which was not explainable by the struggle for existence (the rough haste of evolution's unskilled forces), was too refined for the mere deceiving of accidental predators, feathered, scaled and otherwise (not very fastidious, but then not too fond of butterflies), and seemed to have been invented by some waggish artist precisely for the intelligent eyes of man (a hypothesis that may lead far an evolutionist who observes apes feeding on butterflies); he told me about these magic masks of mimicry; about the enormous moth which in a state of repose assumes the image of a snake looking at you; of a tropical geometrid colored in perfect imitation of a species of butterfly infinitely removed from it in nature's system, the illusion of the orange abdomen possessed by one being humorously reproduced in the other by the orange-colored inner margins of the secondaries; and about the curious harem of that famous African swallowtail, whose variously disguised females copy in color, shape and even flight half a dozen different species (apparently inedible), which are also the models of numerous other mimics. He told me about migrations, about the long cloud consisting of myriads of white pierids that moves through the sky, indifferent to the direction of the wind, always at the same level above the ground, rising softly and smoothly over hills and sinking again into valleys, meeting perhaps another cloud of butterflies, yellow, filtering through it without stopping and without soiling its own whiteness—and floating further, to settle on trees toward nighttime which stand until morning as if bestrewn with snow—and then taking off again to continue their journey—whither? Why? A tale not yet finished by nature or else forgotten. "Our thistle butterfly," he said, "the 'painted lady' of the English, the '*belle dame*' of the French, does not hibernate in Europe as related species do; it is born on the African plains; there, at dawn, the lucky traveler may hear the whole steppe, glistening in the first rays, crackle with an incalculable number of hatching chrysalids." From there, without delay it begins its journey north, reaching the shores of Europe in early spring, suddenly enlivening the gardens of the Crimea and the terraces of the Riviera; without lingering, but leaving individuals everywhere for summer breeding, it proceeds further north and by the end of May, by now in single specimens, it reaches Scotland, Heligoland, our parts and even the extreme north of the earth: it has been caught in Iceland! With a strange crazy flight unlike anything else the bleached, hardly recognizable butterfly, choosing a dry glade, "wheels" in and out of the Leshino firs, and by the end of the summer, on thistleheads, on asters, its lovely pink-flushed offspring is already reveling in life. "Most moving of all," added my father, "is that on the first cold days a reverse phenomenon is observed, the ebb: the butterfly hastens southward, for the winter, but of course it perishes before it reaches the warmth."

Simultaneously with the Englishman Tutt, who observed the same thing in the Swiss Alps as he in the Pamirs, my father discovered the true nature of the corneal formation appearing beneath the abdomen in the impregnated females of Parnassians, and explained how her mate, working with a pair of spatulate appendages, places and molds on her a chastity belt of his own manufacture, shaped differently in every species of this genus, being sometimes a little boat, sometimes a helical shell, sometimes—as in the case of the exceptionally rare dark-cinder gray *orpheus* Godunov—a replica of a tiny lyre. And as a frontispiece to my present work I think I would like to display precisely this butterfly—for I can hear him talk about it, can see the way he took the six specimens he had brought back out of their six thick triangular envelopes, the way he lowered his eyes with the field magnifier close to the abdomen of the only female—and how reverently his laboratory assistant relaxed in a damp jar the dry, glossy, tightly folded wings in order later to drive a pin smoothly through the insect's thorax, stick it in the cork groove of the spreading board, hold down flat upon it by means of broad strips of semitransparent paper its open, defenseless, gracefully expanded beauty, then slip a bit of cotton wool under its abdomen and straighten its black antennae—so that it dried that way forever. Forever? In the Berlin museum there are many of my father's captures and these are as fresh today as they were in the eighties and nineties. Butterflies from Linnaeus' collection now in London have subsisted since the eighteenth century. In the Prague museum one can see that same example of the showy Atlas moth that Catherine the Great admired. Why then do I feel so sad?

His captures, his observations, the sound of his voice in scientific words, all this, I think, I will preserve. But that is still so little. With the same relative permanence I would like to retain what it was, perhaps, that I loved most of all about him: his live masculinity, inflexibility and independence, the chill and the warmth of his personality, his power over everything that he undertook. As if playing a game, as if wishing in passing to imprint his force on everything, he would pick out here and there something from a field outside entomology and thus he left his mark upon almost all branches of natural science: there is only one plant described by him out of all those he collected, but that one is a spectacular species of birch; one bird—a most fabulous pheasant; one bat—but the biggest one in the world. And in all parts of nature our name echoes a countless number of times, for other naturalists gave his name either to a spider, or to a rhododendron, or to a mountain ridge—the latter, by the way, made him angry: "To ascertain and preserve the ancient native name of a pass," he wrote, "is always both more scientific and more noble than to saddle it with the name of a good acquaintance."

I liked—I only now understood how much I liked it—that special easy knack he showed in dealing with a horse, a dog, a gun, a bird or a peasant boy with a two-inch splinter in his back—he was constantly being brought people who were wounded, maimed, even infirm, even pregnant women, who probably took his mysterious occupation for voodoo practice. I liked the fact that, in contradistinction to the majority of non-Russian travelers, Sven Hedin for example, he never changed his clothes for Chinese ones on his wanderings; in general he kept aloof, was severe and resolute in the extreme in his relations with the natives, showing no indulgence to mandarins and lamas; and in camp he practiced shooting, which served as an excellent precaution against any importuning. He was entirely uninterested in ethnography, a fact that for some reason greatly irritated certain geographers, and his great friend, the Orientalist Krivtsov, almost wept when reproaching him: "If only you had brought back one wedding song, Konstantin Kirillovich, had described one local dress!" There was one professor at Kazan who attacked him especially; proceeding from some sort of humanitarian-liberal premises he convicted him of scientific aristocratism, of a haughty contempt for Man, of disregard for the reader's interests, of dangerous eccentricity—and of much more. And once at an international banquet in London (and this episode pleases me most of all), Sven Hedin, sitting next to my father, asked him how it had happened that, traveling with unprecedented freedom over the forbidden parts of Tibet, in the immediate vicinity of Lhasa, he had not gone to look at it, to which my father replied that he had not wanted to sacrifice even one hour's collecting for the sake of visiting "one more filthy little town"—and I can see so clearly how his eyes must have narrowed as he spoke.

He was endowed with an even temper, self-control, strong willpower and a vivid sense of humor; but when he became angry his wrath was like a sudden stroke of frost (Grandmother said behind his back: "All the clocks in the house stopped"), and I can well remember those sudden silences at table and the kind of absent-minded look that immediately appeared on Mother's face (ill-wishers among our female kin maintained that she "trembled before Kostya"), and how one of the governesses at the end of the table would hastily place her palm on a glass which was on the point of tinkling. The cause of his wrath could be a blunder by someone, a miscomputation by the steward (Father was well versed in the estate affairs), a flippant remark made about an intimate of his, trite political sentiments in the spirit of soapbox patriotism brought out by some ill-starred guest, or finally some misdemeanor or other of mine. He who in his time had slaughtered countless multitudes of birds, he who had once brought the newly wed botanist Berg the *complete* vegetable covering of a motley little mountain meadow in one piece, the size of a room in area (I imagined it rolled up in a case like a Persian carpet), which he had found somewhere at some fantastic height among bare cliffs and snow—he could not forgive me a Leshino sparrow wantonly shot down with a Montecristo rifle or the young pondside aspen I had slashed with a sword. He could not stand procrastination, hesitation, the blinking eyes of a lie, could not stand hypocrisy or syrupiness—and I am sure that had he caught me out in physical cowardice he would have laid a curse on me.

I have not said everything yet; I am coming up to what is perhaps most important. In and around my father, around this clear and direct strength, there was something difficult to convey in words, a haze, a mystery, an enigmatic reserve which made itself felt sometimes more, sometimes less. It was as if this genuine, very genuine man possessed an aura of something still unknown but which was perhaps the most genuine of all. It had no direct connection either with us, or with my mother, or with the externals of life, or even with butterflies (the closest of all to him, I daresay); it was neither pensiveness nor melancholy—and I have no means of explaining the impression his face made on me when

I looked through his study window from outside and saw how, having suddenly forgotten his work (I could feel inside me how he had forgotten it—as if something had fallen through or trailed off), his large wise head turned slightly away from the desk and resting on his fist, so that a wide crease was raised from his cheek to his temple, he sat for a minute without moving. It sometimes seems to me nowadays that—who knows—he might go off on his journeys not so much to seek something as to flee something, and that on returning, he would realize that it was still with him, inside him, unriddable, inexhaustible. I cannot track down a name for his secret, but I only know that that was the source of that special—neither glad nor morose, having indeed no connection with the outward appearance of human emotions—solitude to which neither my mother nor all the entomologists of the world had any admittance. And strange: perhaps the estate watchman, a crooked old man who had twice been singed by night lightning, the sole person among our rural retainers who had learned without my father's help (who had taught it to a whole regiment of Asian hunters) to catch and kill a butterfly without mangling it (which, of course, did not stop him advising me with a businesslike air not to be in a hurry to catch small butterflies, "tiddlers" as he expressed it, in spring, but to wait till summer when they would have grown up), namely he, who frankly and with no fear or surprise considered that my father knew a thing or two that nobody else knew, was in his own way right.

However that may have been, I am convinced now that our life then really was imbued with a magic unknown in other families. From conversations with my father, from daydreams in his absence, from the neighborhood of thousands of books full of drawings of animals, from the precious shimmer of the collections, from the maps, from all the heraldry of nature and the cabbalism of Latin names, life took on a kind of bewitching lightness that made me feel as if my own travels were about to begin. Thence, I borrow my wings today. Among the old, tranquil, velvet-framed family photographs in my father's study there hung a copy of the picture: Marco Polo leaving Venice. She was rosy, this Venice, and the water of her lagoon was azure, with swans twice the size of the boats, into one of which tiny violet men were descending by way of a plank, in order to board a ship which was waiting a little way off with sails furled—and I cannot tear myself away from this mysterious beauty, these ancient colors which swim before the eyes as if seeking new shapes, when I now imagine the outfitting of my father's caravan in Przhevalsk, where he used to go with post-horses from Tashkent, having dispatched in advance by slow convoy a store of supplies for three years. His Cossacks went round the neighboring villages buying horses, mules and camels; they prepared the pack boxes and pouches (what was there not in these Sartish yagtans and leather bags tried by centuries, from cognac to pulverized peas, from ingots of silver to nails for horseshoes); and after a requiem on the shore of the lake by the burial rock of the explorer Przhevalski, crowned with a bronze eagle—around which the intrepid local pheasants were wont to roost—the caravan took the road.

After that I see the caravan, before it gets drawn into the mountains, winding among hills of a paradisean green shade, depending both on their grassy raiment and on the apple-bright epidotic rock, of which they are composed. The compact, sturdy Kalmuk ponies walk in single file forming echelons: the paired packloads of equal weight are seized twice with lariats so that nothing can shift and a Cossack leads every echelon by the bridle. In front of the caravan, a Berdan rifle over his shoulder and a butterfly net at the ready, wearing spectacles and a nankin blouse, Father rides on his white trotter accompanied by a native horseman. Closing the detachment comes the geodesist Kunitsyn (this is the way I see it), a majestic old man who has spent half a lifetime in imperturable wanderings, with his instruments in cases—chronometers, surveying compasses, an artifical horizon—and when he stops to take a bearing or to note down azimuths in his journal, his horse is held by an assistant, a small anemic German, Ivan Ivanovich Viskott, formerly chemist at Gatchina, whom my father had once taught to prepare bird skins and who took part from then on in all the expeditions, until he died of gangrene in the summer of 1903 in Dyn-Kou.

Further I see the mountains: the Tyan-Shan range. In search of passes (marked on the map according to oral data but first explored by my father) the caravan ascended over steep slopes and narrow ledges, slipped down to the north, to the steppe teeming with saigas, ascended again to the south, here fording torrents, there trying to get across high water—and up, up, along almost impassable trails. How the sunlight played! The dryness of the air produced an amazing contrast between light and shadow: in the light there were such flashes, such a wealth of brilliance, that at times it became impossible to look at a rock, at a stream; and in the shadow a darkness which absorbed all detail, so that every color lived a magically multiplied life and the coats of the horses changed as they entered the cool of the poplars.

The boom of water in the gorge was enough to stun a man; head and breast filled with an electric agitation; the water rushed with awesome force—as smooth, however, as molten lead—then suddenly swelled out monstrously as it reached the rapids, its varicolored waves piling up and falling over the lustrous brows of the stones with a furious roar; and then, crashing from a height of twenty feet, out of a rainbow and into darkness, it ran further, now changed: seething, smoke-blue and snowlike from the foam, it struck first one side and then the other of the conglomeratic canyon in such a way that it seemed the reverberating mountain fastness could never withstand it; on its banks, meanwhile, in blissful quiet, the irises were in bloom—and suddenly a herd of marals dashed out of a black firwood onto a dazzling Alpine meadow and halted, quivering. No, it was only the air quivering . . . they had already vanished.

I can conjure up with particular clarity—in this transparent and changeable setting—my father's principal and constant occupation, the occupation for whose only sake he undertook these tremendous journeys. I see him leaning down from the saddle amid a clatter of sliding stones to sweep in with a swing of his net on the end of its long handle (a twist of the wrist causing the end of the muslin bag, full of rustling and throbbing, to flip across the ring, thus preventing escape) some royal relative of our Apollos, which had been skimming with a ranging flight over the dangerous screes; and not only he but also the other riders (the Cossack corporal Semyon Zharkoy, for example, or the Buryat Buyantuyev, or else that representative of mine whom I sent in the wake of my father throughout my boyhood) work their way fearlessly up the rocks, in pursuit of the white, richly ocellated butterfly which they catch at last; and here it is in my father's fingers, dead, its hairy yellowish incurved body resembling a willow catkin, and the glazy underside of its crisp folded wings showing the blood-red maculation at their roots.

He avoided dawdling in Chinese roadhouses, especially overnight, because he disliked them for their "bustle devoid of feeling" that consisted solely of shouting without the slightest hint of laughter; but strangely enough, in his memory later the smell of these inns, that special air belonging to any place where Chinese dwell—a rancid mixture of kitchen fumes, smoke from burned manure, opium and the stable—spoke more to him of his beloved hunting than the recollected fragrancy of mountain meadows.

Moving across the Tyan-Shan with the caravan I can now see evening approaching, drawing a shadow over the mountain slopes. Postponing until the morning a difficult crossing (a ramshackle bridge has been thrown across the turbulent river, consisting of stone slabs on top of brushwood, but the way up on the other side is steepish, and, moreover, as smooth as glass), the caravan settles down for the night. While the colors of sunset still linger in the aerial tiers of the sky, and supper is being prepared, the Cossacks, having first taken off the animals' sweatcloths and felt underblankets, wash the wounds made by the packs. In the darkling air the clear ring of shoeing resounds above the ample noise of water. It has grown quite dark. Father has climbed a rock looking for a place to suit his calcium lamp for catching moths. Thence one can see in Chinese perspective (from above), in a deep gully, the redness, transparent in the darkness, of the campfire; through the edges of its breathing flame seem to float the broad-shouldered shadows of men, endlessly changing their outlines, and a red reflection trembles, without moving from the spot, on the seething water of the river. But above, all is quiet and dark, only rarely does a bell tinkle: the horses, who have already stood to receive their portion of dry fodder, are now roaming among the granite debris. Overhead, frighteningly and entrancingly close, the stars have come out, each conspicuous, each a live orbicle, clearly revealing its globular essence. Moths begin to come to the lure of the lamp: they describe crazy circles around it, hitting the reflector with a ping; they fall, they crawl over the spread sheet into the circle of light, gray, with eyes like burning coals, vibrating, flying up and falling again—and a large, brightly illumined, unhurriedly skillful hand, with almond-shaped fingernails, rakes noctuid after noctuid into the killing jar.

Sometimes he was quite alone, without even this nearness of men sleeping in camp tents, on felt mattresses, around the camel bedded down on the campfire ashes. Taking advantage of lengthy halts in places with abundant food for the caravan animals, Father would go away for several days on reconnaissance, and in doing so, carried away by some new pierid, more than once ignored the rule of mountain hunting: never to follow a path of no return. And now I continually ask myself what did he use to think about in the solitary night: I try fervently in the darkness to divine the current of his thoughts, and I have much less success with this than with my mental visits to places which I have never seen. What did he think about? About a recent catch? About my mother, about us? About the innate strangeness of human life, a sense of which he mysteriously transmitted to me? Or perhaps I am wrong in retrospectively forcing upon him the secret which he carries now, when newly gloomy and preoccupied, concealing the pain of an unknown wound, concealing death as something shameful, he appears in my dreams, but which then he did not have—but simply was happy in that incompletely named world in which at every step he named the nameless.

After spending the whole summer in the mountains (not one summer but several, in different years, which are superimposed one on another in translucent layers) our caravan moved east through a gulch into a stony desert. We saw gradually disappear both the bed of the stream as it split and fanned out, and those plants that to the last remain faithful to travelers: stunted ammodendrons, lasiagrostis, and ephedras. Having loaded the camels with water we plunged into spectral wilds where here and there big pebbles covered completely the yielding, reddish-brown clay of the desert, in places mottled with crusts of dirty snow and outcrops of salt, which we took in the distance for the walls of the town we sought. The way was dangerous as a result of the terrible storms, during which at midday everything was blanketed in a salty brown fog; the wind roared, granules of gravel lashed one's face, the camels lay down and our tarpaulin tent was torn to shreds. Because of these storms the surface of the land has changed unbelievably, presenting the fantastic outlines of castles, colonnades and staircases; or else the hurricane would scour out a hollow—as if here in this desert the elemental forces that had fashioned the world were still furiously in action. But there were also days of a wonderful lull, when horned larks (Father aptly called them "gigglers") poured forth their mimetic trills and flocks of ordinary sparrows accompanied our emaciated animals. On occasion we would pass the day in isolated settlements consisting of two or three homesteads and a ruined temple. At other times we would be attacked by Tanguts in sheepskin coats and red-and-blue woolen boots: a brief colorful episode on the way. And then there were the mirages—the mirages where nature, that exquisite cheat, achieved absolute miracles: visions of water were so clear that they reflected the *real* rocks nearby!

Further came the quiet sands of the Gobi, dune after dune went by like waves revealing short ocher horizons, and all that was audible in the velvet air was the labored, quickened breathing of the camels and the scrape of their broad feet. The caravan went onward, now ascending to the crest of a dune now plunging downward, and by the evening its shadow had attained gigantic proportions. The five-carat diamond of Venus disappeared in the west together with the glow of the sunset, which distorted everything in its blanched, orange and violet light. And Father loved to recall how once at such a sunset, in 1893, in the dead heart of the Gobi desert he had met with—taking them at first for phantoms projected by the prismatic rays—two cyclists in Chinese sandals and round felt hats, who turned out to be the Americans Sachtleben and Allen, riding all across Asia to Peking for fun.

Spring awaited us in the mountains of Nan-Shan. Everything foretold it: the babbling of the water in the brooks, the distant thunder of the rivers, the whistle of the creepers which lived in holes on the slippery wet hillsides, the delightful singing of the local larks, and "a mass of noises whose origins are hard to explain" (a phrase from the notes of a friend of my father's, Grigoriy Efimovich Grum-Grzhimaylo, which is fixed in my mind forever and full of the amazing music of truth because written not by an ignorant poet but by a naturalist of genius). On the southern slopes we had already met our first interesting butterfly—Potanin's subspecies of Butler's pierid—and in the valley to which we descended by way of a torrent bed we found real summer. All the slopes were studded with anemones and primulae. Przhevalski's gazelle and Strauch's pheasant tempted the hunters. And what sunrises there were! Only in China is the early mist so enchanting, causing everything to vibrate, the fantastic outlines of hovels, the dawning crags. As into an abyss, the river runs into the murk of the prematutinal twilight that still hangs in the gorges, while higher up, along flowing waters, all glimmers and scintillates, and quite a company of blue magpies has already awakened in the willows by the mill.

Escorted by fifteen Chinese foot soldiers armed with halberds and carrying enormous, absurdly bright banners, we crossed passes through the ridge a number of times. In spite of it being the middle of summer, night frosts were so bad there that in the morning the flowers were filmed with rime and had become so brittle that they snapped underfoot with a surprising, gentle tinkle; but two hours later, just as soon as the sun began to be warm, the wonderful Alpine flora again resplended, again scented the air with resin and honey. Clinging to steep banks we made our way under the hot blue sky; grasshoppers shot from under our feet, the dogs ran with their tongues hanging out, seeking refuge from the heat in the short shadows thrown by the horses. The water in the wells smelled of gunpowder. The trees seemed to be a botanist's delirium: a white rowan with alabaster berries or a birch with red bark!

Placing one foot on a fragment of rock and leaning slightly on the handle of his net, my father looks down from a high spur, from the glacier boulders of Tanegma, at the lake Kuka-Nor—a huge spread of dark blue water. There down below on the golden steppes a herd of kiangs rushes past, and the shadow of an eagle flicks across the cliffs; overhead there is perfect peace, silence, transparency . . . and again I ask myself what Father is thinking about when he is not busy collecting and stands there like that, quite still . . . appearing as it were on the crest of my recollection, torturing me, enrapturing me—to the point of pain, to an insanity of tenderness, envy and love, tormenting my soul with his inscrutable solitariness.

There were the times when going up the Yellow River and its tributaries, on some splendid September morning, in the lily thickets and hollows on the banks, he and I would take Elwes' Swallowtail —a black wonder with tails in the shape of hooves. On inclement evenings, before sleeping, he would read Horace, Montaigne, and Pushkin—the three books he had brought with him. One winter when crossing the ice of a river I noticed in the distance a line of dark objects strung across it, the large horns of twenty wild yaks which had been caught in crossing by the suddenly forming ice; through its thick crystal the immobilization of their bodies in a swimming attitude was clearly visible; the beautiful heads lifted above the ice would have seemed alive if the birds had not already pecked out their eyes; and for some reason I recalled the tyrant Shiusin, who used to cut open pregnant women out of curiosity and who, one cold morning, seeing some porters fording a stream, ordered their legs to be amputated at the shin in order to inspect the condition of the marrow in their bones.

In Chang during a fire (some wood prepared for the construction of a Catholic mission was burning) I saw an elderly Chinese at a safe distance from the fire throwing water assiduously, determinedly and without tiring over the *reflection* of the flames on the walls of his dwelling; convinced of the impossibility of proving to him that his house was not burning we abandoned him to his fruitless occupation.

Frequently we had to push our way through, ignoring Chinese intimidation and interdictions: good marksmanship is the best passport. In Tatsien-Lu shaven-headed lamas roamed about the crooked, narrow streets spreading the rumor that I was catching children in order to brew their eyes into a potion for the belly of my Kodak. There on the slopes of a snowy range, which were drowned in the rich, rosy foam of great rhododendrons (we used their branches at night for our campfires), I looked in May for the slate-gray, orange-spotted larvae of the Imperatorial Apollo and for its chrysalis, fastened by means of a silk thread to the underside of a stone. That same day, I remember, we glimpsed a white Tibetan bear and discovered a new snake: it fed on mice, and the mouse I extracted from its stomach also turned out to be an undescribed species. From the rhododendrons and from the pines draped in lacy lichen came a heady smell of resin. In my vicinity some witch doctors with the wary and crafty look of competitors were collecting for their mercenary needs Chinese rhubarb, whose root bears an extraordinary resemblance to a caterpillar, right down to its prolegs and spiracles—while I, in the meantime, found under a stone the caterpillar of an unknown moth, which represented not in a general way but with absolute concreteness a copy of that root, so that it was not quite clear which was impersonating which—or why.

Everyone tells lies in Tibet: it was devilishly hard to obtain the exact names of places or directions for the right roads; involuntarily I too deceived them: since they were unable to distinguish a light-haired European from a white-haired one they took me, a young chap with hair bleached in the sun, for an ancient old man. Everywhere on the masses of granite one could read the "mystic formula," a shamanic jumble of words which certain poetic travelers "translate" prettily as: oh, jewel in the lotus, oh! Some kind of officials were sent out to me from Lhasa who conjured me not to do something and threatened to do something to me—I paid little attention to them; however, I remember one idiot, particularly tiresome, in yellow silk under a red umbrella; he was sitting astride a mule whose natural dolefulness was doubled by the presence under its eyes of thick icicles formed from frozen tears.

From a great height I saw a dark marshy depression all trembling from the play of innumerable springs, which recalled the night sky with stars scattered over it—and that is what it was called: the Starry Steppe. The passes ascended beyond the clouds, marches were tough. We rubbed the pack animals' wounds with a mixture of iodoform and vaseline. On occasion, having camped in a completely deserted spot, I would suddenly see in the morning that around us during the night a wide circle of brigands' tents had grown up like black toadstools—which, however, very quickly disappeared.

Having explored the uplands of Tibet I headed for Lob-Nor in order to return from there to Russia. The Tarym, overcome by the desert, exhausted, forms with its last waters an extensive reedy swamp, the present-day Kara-Koshuk-Kul, Przhevalski's Lob-Nor—and Lob-Nor at the time of the Khans, whatever Ritthofen might say. It is fringed with salt marshes but the water is salt only at the edges—for those rushes would not grow around a salt lake. One spring I was five days going round it. There in twenty-foot-high reeds I had the luck to discover a remarkable semi-aquatic moth with a rudimentary system of veins. The bunchy salt marsh was strewn with the shells of mollusks. In the evenings the harmonious, melodic sounds of swan flights reverberated through the silence; the yellow of the rushes distinctly brought out the lusterless white of the birds. In 1862, sixty Russian Old-Believers with their wives and children lived for half a year in these parts, after which they went to Turfan, and where they went thence nobody knows.

Further on comes the desert of Lob: a stony plain, tiers of clay precipices, glassy salt ponds; that pale fleck in the gray air is a lone individual of Roborovski's White, carried away by the wind. In this desert are preserved traces of an ancient road along which Marco Polo passed six centuries before I did: its markers are piles of stones. Just as I had heard in a Tibetan gorge the interesting drum-like roar which had frightened our first pilgrims, so in the desert during the sandstorms I also saw and heard the same as Marco Polo: "the whisper of spirits calling you aside" and the queer flicker of the air, an endless progression of whirlwinds, caravans and armies of phantoms coming to meet you, thousands of spectral faces in their incorporeal way pressing upon you, through you, and suddenly dispersing. In the twenties of the fourteenth century when the great explorer was dying, his friends gathered by his bedside and implored him to reject what in his book had seemed incredible to them—to water down its miracles by means of judicious deletions; but he responded that he had not recounted even a half of what he had in fact seen.

All this lingered bewitchingly, full of color and air, with lively movement in the foreground and a convincing backdrop; then, like smoke from a breeze, it shifted and dispersed—and Fyodor saw again the dead and impossible tulips of his wallpaper, the crumbling mound of cigarette butts in the ashtray, and the lamp's reflection in the black windowpane. He threw open the window. The written-up sheets of paper on his desk started; one folded over, another glided onto the floor. The room immediately turned damp and cold. Down below, an automobile went slowly along the dark empty street—and, strangely enough, this very slowness reminded Fyodor of a host of petty, unpleasant things—the day just past, the missed lesson—and when he thought that next morning he would have to phone the deceived old man, his heart was oppressed by an abominable despondency. But once the window was closed again, already feeling the void between his bunched fingers, he turned to the patiently waiting lamp, to the scattered first drafts, to the still-warm pen which now quietly slipped back into his fingers (explaining the void and filling it) and returned at once to that world which was as natural to him as snow to the white hare or water to Ophelia.

He remembered with incredible vividness, as if he had preserved that sunny day in a velvet case, his father's last return, in July 1912. Elizaveta Pavlovna had already gone the six miles to the station to meet her husband: she always met him alone and it always happened that no one knew with any clearness which side they would return on, to the right or left of the house, since there were two roads, one longer and smoother—along the highway and through the village; the other shorter and bumpier—through Peshchanka. Fyodor put on his riding breeches just in case and ordered his horse saddled, but nonetheless he could not make up his mind to ride out and meet his father because he was afraid of missing him. He tried vainly to come to terms with inflated, exaggerated time. A rare butterfly taken a day or two before among the blueberries of a peat bog had not yet dried on the spreading board: he kept touching its abdomen with the end of a pin—alas it was still soft, and this meant it was impossible to take off the paper strips completely covering the wings which he was so keen to show his father in all their beauty. He loafed about the manor, feeling the weight and pain of his agitation, and envying the way the others got through these big, empty minutes. From the river came the desperately ecstatic shrieks of the village boys bathing, and this hubbub, playing constantly in the depths of the summer day, sounded like distant ovations. Tanya was swinging enthusiastically and powerfully on the swing in the garden, standing on the seat; the violet shadow of the foliage swept over her flying white skirt in variegations that made one blink, and her blouse now lagged behind, now clung to her back, designating the hollow between her drawn-back shoulders; beneath her, one fox terrier was barking at her, another was chasing a wagtail; the ropes creaked joyfuly and it seemed that Tanya was soaring up like that in order to see over the trees into the road. Our French governess, under her moiré parasol, with rare politeness was sharing her misgivings ("the train was two hours late or else would not come at all") with Mr. Browning, whom she hated, while the latter stood slapping his gaiters with a riding stick—he was no polyglot. Yvonna Ivanovna kept visiting first one and then the other veranda with that discontented expression on her small face with which she greeted all joyful events. Around the outbuildings there was especial animation: servants pumped water, hacked firewood, and the gardener came bringing two oblong, red-stained baskets of strawberries. Zhaksybay, an elderly Kirghiz, thickset, fat-faced, with intricate wrinkles around his eyes, who had saved Konstantin Kirillovich's life in '92 (he had shot a she-bear that was mauling him) and who now lived in peace, nursing his hernia, in their Leshino house, had put on his blue *beshmet* with half-moon pockets, polished boots, red skullcap with spangles and silk, tasseled sash, and settled down on a bench near the kitchen porch, where by now he had been sitting for quite a time sunning himself, a silver watch chain gleaming on his chest, in quiet and festive expectation.

Suddenly, running heavily up the curved path which led down to the river, there appeared out of deep shadow, with a wild glint in his eyes and with a mouth that was already shaped for a shout though still silent, the old, gray, side-whiskered footman Kazimir:

he was running with the news that beyond the nearest bend, the sound of hooves had been heard on the bridge (a swift wooden drumming which was immediately cut off)—a guarantee that the victoria was about to come bowling next minute along the dirt road parallel to the park. Fyodor rushed in that direction—between the tree trunks, over the moss and bilberries—and there beyond the marginal path one could see, as they skimmed above the level of the young firs, the driver's head and indigo sleeves sweeping by with the impetuosity of a vision. He dashed back—and the abandoned swing was still quivering in the garden, while by the porch stood the empty victoria with its crumpled traveling rug; his mother was walking up the steps, trailing behind her a smoke-colored scarf—and Tanya was hanging on the neck of her father, who had taken a watch from his pocket with his free hand and was looking at it, for he always liked to know how fast he had got home from the station.

The following year, busy with scientific work, he did not go anywhere, but by the spring of 1914 he had already begun to prepare for a new expedition to Tibet together with the ornithologist Petrov and the English botanist Ross. War with Germany suddenly canceled all this.

He looked upon the war as a tiresome obstacle which became more and more tiresome as time went on. His kinsfolk were for some reason certain that Konstantin Kirillovich would volunteer and set off right away at the head of a detachment: they considered him an eccentric, but a manly eccentric. Actually, Konstantin Kirillovich, who was now over fifty but had retained untapped reserves of health, agility, freshness and strength—and perhaps was even more ready than before to overcome mountains, Tanguts, bad weather and a thousand other dangers undreamt of by stay-at-homes—now not only stayed at home but tried not to notice the war, and if he ever spoke about it, he did so only with angry contempt. "My father," wrote Fyodor, recalling that time, "not only taught me a great deal but also trained my very thoughts, as a voice or hand is trained, according to the rules of his school. Thus I was rather indifferent to the cruelty of war; I even conceded that one could take a certain delight in the accuracy of a shot, in the danger of a reconnaissance or in the delicacy of a maneuver; but these little pleasures (which are better represented moreover in other special branches of sport, such as: tiger hunting, noughts and crosses, professional boxing) in no way compensated for that touch of dismal idiocy which is inherent in any war."

However, in spite of "Kostya's unpatriotic position" as Aunt Ksenia expressed it (solidly and skillfully using "high connections" to hide her officer-husband away in the shadows of the rear) the house was penetrated by the cares of war. Elizaveta Pavlovna was drawn into Red Cross work, which had people comment that her energy "was making up for her husband's idleness," he being "more concerned with Asian bugs than with the glory of Russian arms" as was actually pointed out, by the way, in one jaunty newspaper. Phonograph records revolved with the words of the love song "The Sea Gull" reclad in khaki (. . . here's a young ensign with an infantry section . . .); coy nurses appeared in the house with little curls peeping out from under their regulation headdress and a deft way of tapping cigarettes on their cigarette cases before lighting up; the doorkeeper's son ran away to the front and Konstantin Kirillovich was asked to assist his return; Tanya began visiting her mother's military hospital to give Russian grammar lessons to a placid, bearded Oriental whose leg was being cut off ever higher in an attempt to overtake the gangrene; Yvonna Ivanovna knit woolen wrist-warmers; on holidays the variety artist Feona entertained the soldiers with vaudeville songs; the hospital staff staged *Vova Makes the Best of It*, a play on draft dodgers; and the newspapers printed versicles dedicated to the war:

Today thou art Fate's scourge o'er our dear land,
But with bright joy the Russian's gaze will shine
When he sees Time dispassionately brand
The German Attila with Shame's own sign!

In the spring of 1915, instead of getting ready to move from St. Petersburg to Leshino, which always seemed as natural and unshakable as the succession of months in the calendar, we went for the summer to our Crimean estate—on the coast between Yalta and Alupka. On the sloping lawns of the heavenly-green garden, his face distorted with anguish, his hands trembling with happiness, Fyodor boxed southern butterflies; but the genuine Crimean rarities were to be found not here among the myrtles, wax shrubs, and magnolias but much higher, in the mountains, among the rocks of Ai-Petri and on the grassy plateau of the Yayla; more than once that summer his father accompanied him up a trail through the pinewoods in order to show him, with a smile of condescension for this European trifle, the Satyrid recently described by Kuznetsov, which was flitting from stone to stone in the very place where some vulgar daredevil had carved his name in the sheer rock. These walks were Konstantin Kirillovich's only distraction. It was not that he was gloomy or irritable (these limited epithets did not tally with his spiritual style) but that, putting it simply, he was fretting—and Elizaveta Pavlovna and the children were perfectly aware of what it was he wanted. Suddenly in August he went away for a short time; where he went no one except those closest to him knew; he covered up his journey so thoroughly as to excite the envy of any traveling terrorist; it was funny and frightening to imagine how Russian public opinion would have wrung its little hands had it learned that at the height of the war Godunov-Cherdyntsev had traveled to Geneva to meet a fat, bald, extraordinarily jovial German professor (a third conspirator was also present, an old Englishman wearing thin-rimmed spectacles and a roomy gray suit), that they had come together there in a small room in a modest hotel for a scientific consultation, and that having discussed what was necessary (the subject was a work of many volumes, stubbornly continuing publication in Stuttgart with longstanding cooperation of foreign specialists on separate groups of butterflies) they peaceably parted—each in his own direction. But this trip did not cheer him up; on the contrary, the constant dream weighing on him even increased its secret pressure. In the autumn they returned to St. Petersburg; he worked strenuously on the fifth volume of *Butterflies and Moths of the Russian Empire,* went out rarely and—fuming more at his opponent's blunders than at his own—played chess with the recently widowed botanist Berg. He would look through the daily papers with an ironical smile; he would take Tanya on his knees, then lapse into pensiveness, and his hand on Tanya's round shoulder would grow pensive too. Once in November he was given a telegram at table; he unsealed it, read it to himself, read it again to judge by the second movement of his eyes, laid it aside, took a sip of port wine from a ladle-shaped goblet of gold, and imperturbably continued his conversation with a poor relative of ours, a little old man with freckles all over his skull who came to dinner twice a month and invariably brought Tanya soft, sticky toffees—*tyanushki*. When the guests had departed he sank into an armchair, took off his glasses, passed his palm from top to bottom over his face and announced in an even voice that Uncle Oleg had been dangerously wounded in the stomach by a grenade fragment (while working at a first-aid post under fire)—and immediately there stood out in Fyodor's soul, tearing it with its sharp edges, one of those numberless deliberately grotesque dialogues that the brothers had still so recently indulged in at table:

UNCLE OLEG (*in a bantering tone*)
Well, tell me, Kostya, did you ever happen to see on the Wie reservation the little bird So-was?

FATHER (*curtly*)
I'm afraid I did not.

UNCLE OLEG (*warming up*)
And Kostya, did you never see Popovski's horse stung by Popov's fly?

FATHER (*even more curtly*)
Never.

UNCLE OLEG (*completely ecstatic*)
And have you never had occasion, for example, to observe the diagonal motion of entoptic swarms?

FATHER (*looking him straight in the eye*)
I have.

That same night he set out for Galicia to get him, brought him back extremely quickly and comfortably, obtained the best of the best doctors, Gershenzon, Yezhov, Miller-Melnitski, and himself attended two protracted operations. By Christmas his brother was well. And then something suddenly changed in Konstantin Kirillovich's mood: his eyes came to life and softened, one again heard that musical humming which he used to emit on the move when he was particularly pleased about something, he went off somewhere, certain boxes arrived and departed and in the house, around all this mysterious gaiety of the master's, one could sense a growing feeling of indefinite, expectant perplexity—and once when Fyodor happened to be passing through the gilt reception hall, bathed in spring sunshine, he suddenly noticed the brass handle of the white door leading into Father's study jiggle but not turn, as if someone was limply fingering it without opening the door; but then it quietly opened and Mother came out with a vague meek smile on her tear-stained face, making an odd gesture of helplessness as she went past Fyodor. He knocked on his father's door and entered the study. "What do you want?" asked Konstantin Kirillovich without looking up or stopping writing. "Take me with you," said Fyodor.

The fact that at the most alarming time, when Russia's borders were crumbling and her inner flesh was being eaten away, Konstantin Kirillovich suddenly planned to abandon his family for two years for the sake of a scientific expedition into a remote country, struck most people as a wild caprice, a monstrous frivolity. There was even talk that the government "would not permit purchase of provision," that "the madman" would get neither traveling companions nor pack animals. But no further away than in Turkestan the peculiar smell of the epoch was hardly perceptible; practically the only reminder of it was a reception organized by some district administrators to which the guests brought gifts to aid the war (a little later a rebellion broke out among the Kirghiz and the Cossacks in connection with the summons to do war work). Just before his departure in June 1916, Godunov-Cherdyntsev came from town to Leshino to bid his family farewell. Until the very last minute Fyodor dreamed that his father would take him with him—once he had said he would do so as soon as his son was fifteen—"At any other time I would take you," he said now, as if forgetting that for him time was always *another* one.

In itself this last farewell was in no way different from preceding ones. After the orderly succession of embraces worked out by family custom, both parents, donning identical amber goggles with suede blinkers, settled themselves in a red touring car; all around stood the servants; leaning on his stick, the old watchman remained at a distance by the lightning-split poplar; the driver, a short, fat, round little man in velveteen livery and orange gaiters—with a carroty nape and a topaze on his pudgy hand—straining horribly, jerked, jerked again, started the engine (Mother and Father began to vibrate in their seats), got quickly behind the steering wheel, shifted a lever on it, pulled on his gauntlets, and turned his head. Konstantin Kirillovich gave him a pensive nod and the car moved off; the fox terrier choked with barking as it squirmed wildly in Tanya's arms, turning over onto its back and twisting its head over her shoulder; the red back of the car disappeared round the bend and then, from behind the fir trees, on top of a rising whine there sounded the sharp change of gears, followed by a comfortably receding murmur; all was still, but a few moments later, from the village beyond the river came again the triumphant roar of the engine, which gradually faded away—forever. Yvonna Ivanovna, weeping profusely, went for some milk for the cat. Tanya, affecting to sing, returned to the cool, resonant, empty house. The shade of Zhaksybay, who had died the preceding autumn, slipped off the porch bench and went back to its quiet, handsome paradise, rich in roses and sheep.

Fyodor walked across the park, opened the tuneful wicket gate and cut across the road where the thick tires had just imprinted their tracks. A familiar black-and-white beauty rose smoothly off the ground and described a wide circle, also taking part in the seeing-off. He turned into the trees and came by way of a shady path, where golden flies hung aquiver in transversal sunbeams, to his favorite clearing, boggy, blooming, moistly glistening in the hot sun. The divine meaning of this wood meadow was expressed in its butterflies. Everyone might have found something here. The holidaymaker might have rested on a stump. The artist might have screwed up his eyes. But its truth would have been probed somewhat deeper by knowledge-amplified love: by its "wide-open orbs" —to paraphrase Pushkin.

Freshly emerged and because of their fresh, almost orange coloration, merry-looking Selene Fritillaries floated with a kind of enchanting demureness on outstretched wings, flashing ever so rarely, like the fins on a goldfish. An already rather bedraggled but still powerful Swallowtail, minus one spur and flapping its panoply, descended on a camomile, took off as if backing from it, and the flower it left straightened up and started to sway. A few Black-veined Whites flew about lazily; one or two were spattered with bloodlike pupal discharge (spots of which on the white walls of cities predicted to our ancestors the fall of Troy, plagues, earthquakes). The first chocolate *Aphantopus* Ringlets were already fluttering, with a bouncy, unsteady motion over the grass, and pale micros rose from it, immediately falling again. A blue-and-red Burnet moth with blue antennae, resembling a beetle in fancy dress, was settled on a scabiosa in company with a midge. Hastily abandoning the meadow to alight on an alder leaf, a female cabbage butterfly by means of an odd upturn of her abdomen and the flat spread of her wings (somewhat reminiscent of flattened-back ears), informed her badly rubbed pursuer that she was already impregnated. Two violet-tinged Coppers (*their* females were not yet out) tangled in lightning-swift flight in midair, zoomed, spinning one around the other, scrapping furiously, ascending ever higher and higher—and suddenly shot apart, returning to the flowers. An Amandus Blue in passing annoyed a bee. A dusky Freya Fritillary flicked by among the Selenas. A small hummingbird moth with a bumblebee's body and glasslike wings, beating invisibly, tried from the air a flower with its long proboscis, darted to another and then to a third. All this fascinating life, by whose present blend one could infallibly tell both the age of the summer (with an accuracy almost to within one day), the geographical location of the area, and the vegetal composition of the clearing—all this that was living, genuine and eternally dear to him, Fyodor perceived in a flash, with one penetrating and experienced glance. Suddenly he placed a fist against the trunk of a birch tree and leaning on it, burst into tears.

Although his father had no liking for folklore, he used to cite one remarkable Kirghiz fairy tale. The only son of a great khan, having lost his way during a hunt (thus begin the best fairy tales and thus end the best lives), caught sight among the trees of something sparkling. Coming closer he saw it was a girl gathering brushwood, in a dress made of fish-scales; however, he could not decide what precisely was sparkling so much, the girl's face or her clothing. Going with her to her old mother, the young prince offered to give her as bride-money a nugget of gold the size of a horse's head. "No," said the girl, "but here, take this tiny bag—it's little bigger than a thimble as you can see—go and fill it." The prince, laughing ("Not even one," he said, "will go in"), threw in a coin, threw in another, a third, and then all that he had with him. Extremely puzzled, he went off to consult his father.

> All his treasures gathering,
> public funds and everything,
> in the bag the good khan threw;
> shook, and listened, shook anew;
> threw in twice as much again:
> just a dingle in the drain!

They summoned the old woman. "That," she said, "is a human eye—it wants to encompass everything in the world"; then she took a pinch of earth and filled up the bag immediately.

The last reliable evidence concerning my father (not counting his own letters) I found in some notes by the French missionary (and learned botanist) Barraud, who in the summer of 1917 chanced to meet him in the mountains of Tibet, near the village of Chetu. "I was amazed to see," writes Barraud (*Exploration catholique* for 1923), "a saddled white horse grazing in a mountain meadow. Presently a man in European dress appeared, descending from the rocks; he greeted me in French and turned out to be the famous Russian traveler Godunov. I had not seen a European for over eight years. We passed several delightful minutes on the sward in the shade of a rock, discussing a fine nomenclatorial point in connection with the scientific name of a tiny, light blue iris which grew in the vicinity, and then, exchanging an amicable farewell, we parted, he to his companions calling him from a ravine and I to Father Martin, dying in a remote hostelry."

Beyond this there is fog. Judging by my father's last letter, brief as usual but unusually alarmed, which was delivered to us by a miracle at the beginning of 1918, he was preparing soon after he met Barraud to make the return journey. Having heard of the revolution he asked us in it to move to Finland, where our aunt had a country house, and he wrote that according to his calculations he would be home "with the maximum haste" by the summer. We waited two summers for him, until the winter of 1919. We lived some of the time in Finland and some in St. Petersburg. Our house had long since been plundered but Father's museum, the heart of the house, as if retaining the invulnerability inherent in sacred objects, survived whole (later coming under the jurisdiction of the Academy of Sciences), and this joy completely compensated for the demise of chairs and tables familiar since childhood. We lived in St. Petersburg in two rooms in Grandmother's flat. For some reason or other she was twice taken off for questioning. She caught cold and died. A few days after that, on one of those terrible winter evenings, hungry and hopeless, which played such an ominously close part in the civil disorder, an unknown youth visited me, in pince-nez, unprepossessing and uncommunicative, and asked me to call immediately on his uncle, the geographer Berezovski. He did not know or did not want to say what for, but suddenly everything somehow crumbled inside me and I began to live mechanically. Nowadays, several years later, I sometimes meet this Misha in the Russian bookshop in Berlin where he works—and every time I see him, although we talk little, I feel a hot shiver run down the whole of my spinal column and my whole being relives our brief road together. My mother was not there when this Misha came (this name I shall also remember forever) but we met her on our way downstairs; not knowing my companion she anxiously asked where I was going. I replied I was going for some hair clippers of which we had happened to be speaking a few days beforehand. Later I often dreamed about them, those nonexistent clippers, which took the most unexpected forms—mountains, landing stages, coffins, hand organs—but I always knew with a dreamer's instinct that it was clippers. "Wait," cried Mother, but we were already downstairs. We walked along the street quickly and silently, he slightly ahead of me. I looked at the masks of the houses, at the humps of the snowdrifts, and I tried to outwit fate by imagining to myself (and thus destroying its possibility in advance) the still uncomprehended, black, fresh grief which I would carry back home. We entered a room which I recall as being completely yellow, and there an old man with a pointed beard, wearing a field jacket and jackboots, informed me without preamble that according to still unverified information my father was no longer living. Mother was waiting for me below, on the street.

During the next six months (until Uncle Oleg almost forcibly took us abroad) we tried to find out how, and where, he had perished—and indeed whether he had perished at all. Apart from the fact that it happened in Siberia (Siberia is a big place!) on the return journey from Central Asia, we found out nothing at all. Can it be that they hid from us the place and circumstances of his mysterious death and have continued to hide them to this day? (His biography in the Soviet Encyclopaedia ends simply with the words: *He died in 1919.*) Or did the contradictoriness of the vague evidence truly rule out any explicitness in their answers? Once in Berlin we learned one or two supplementary things from various sources and from various people, but these supplements turned out to be nothing but new layers of uncertainty rather than glimpses through it. Two shaky versions, both more or less of a deductive nature (and telling us nothing, moreover, about the most important point: how exactly did he die—if he died), were entangled in one another and mutually contradictory. According to one of them, news of his death was brought to Semipalatinsk by a Kirghiz; according to the other, it was brought by a Cossack to Ak-Bulat. What was my father's route? Was he going from Semirechie to Omsk (by way of the feather-grass steppe, with the guide on a piebald pony) or from the Pamirs to Orenburg through the Turgay region (by way of the sandy steppe, with the guide on a camel, he himself on a horse, birchbark-stirruped, from well to well, avoiding villages and railway lines)? How did he pass through the storm of the peasant war, how did he steer clear of the Reds? I cannot make anything out. And then, what kind of *shapka-nevidimka*, "invisible-making cap," could have fitted him, who would have worn even that at a rakish angle? Did he hide in fishermen's huts (as Krüger supposes) at the post "Aralskoye more" among the stolid Urals Old-Believers? And if he died, how did he die? "What is your profession?" Pugachyov asked the astronomer Lowitz. "Counting the stars." Whereupon they hanged him so he could be nearer the stars. Oh, how did he die? From illness? From exposure? From thirst? By the hand of man? And if—by somebody's hand, can that hand be still living, taking bread, raising a glass, chasing flies, stirring, pointing, beckoning, lying motionless, shaking other hands? Did he return their fire for a long time? Did he save a last bullet for himself? Was he taken alive? Did they bring him to the parlor car at the railway headquarters of some punitive detachment (I can see its hideous locomotive stoked with dried fish), having suspected him of being a White spy (and not without reason: he knew well the White general, Lavr Kornilov, with whom once in his youth he had traveled over the Steppe of Despair and whom in later years he had seen in China)? Did they shoot him in the ladies' room of some godforsaken station (broken looking glass, tattered plush), or did they lead him out into some kitchen garden one dark night and wait for the moon to peep out? How did he wait with them in the dark? With a smile of disdain? And if a whitish moth had hovered among the shadowy burdocks he would, even at that moment, I *know*, have followed it with that same glance of encouragement with which, on occasion, after evening tea, smoking his pipe in our Leshino garden, he used to greet the pink hawks sampling our lilacs.

But sometimes I get the impression that all this is a rubbishy rumor, a tired legend, that it has been created out of those same suspicious granules of approximate knowledge that I use myself when my dreams muddle through regions known to me only by hearsay or out of books, so that the first knowledgeable person who has really seen at the time the places referred to will refuse to recognize them, will make fun of the exoticism of my thoughts, the hills of my sorrow, the precipices of my imagination, and will find in my conjectures just as many topographical errors as he will anachronisms. So much the better. Once the rumor of my father's death is a fiction, must it not then be conceded that his very journey out of Asia is merely attached in the shape of a tail to this fiction (like that kite which in Pushkin's story young Grinyov fashioned out of a map), and that perhaps, if my father even did set out on this return journey (and was not dashed to pieces in an abyss, not held in captivity by Buddhist monks) he chose a completely different road? I have even had occasion to hear surmises (sounding like belated advice) that he could well have proceeded west to Ladakh in order to go south into India, or why could he not have pushed on to China and from there, on any ship to any port in the world?

"Whether it was this way or that, Mother, all material connected with his life is now collected at my place. Out of swarms of drafts, long manuscript extracts from books, indecipherable jottings on miscellaneous sheets of paper, penciled remarks straggling over the margins of other writings of mine; out of half-crossed-out sentences, unfinished words, and improvidently abbreviated, already forgotten names, hiding from full view among my papers; out of the fragile staticism of irredeemable information, already destroyed in places by a too swift movement of thought, which in turn dissolved into nothingness; out of all this I must now make a lucid, orderly book. At times I feel that somewhere it has already been written by me, that it is here, hiding in this inky jungle, that I have only to free it part by part from the darkness and the parts will fall together of themselves. . . . But what is the use of that to me when this labor of liberation now seems to me so difficult and complicated and when I am so much afraid I might dirty it with a flashy phrase, or wear it out in the course of transfer onto paper, that I already doubt whether the book will be written at all. You yourself wrote to me of the demands which in such a task should be presupposed. But now I am of the opinion that I would fulfill them badly. Do not scold me for weakness and cowardice. Sometime I shall read you at random disjointed and inchoate extracts from what I have written: how little it resembles my statuesque dream! All these months while I was making my research, taking notes, recollecting and thinking, I was blissfully happy: I was certain that something unprecedentedly beautiful was being created, that my notes were merely small props for the work, trail-marks, pegs, and that the most important thing was developing and being created of itself, but now I see, like waking up on the floor, that besides these pitiful notes there is nothing. What shall I do? You know, when I read his or Grum's books and I hear their entrancing rhythm, when I study the position of the words that can neither be replaced nor rearranged, it seems to me a sacrilege to take all this and dilute it with myself. If you like I'll admit it: I myself am a mere seeker of verbal adventures, and forgive me if I refuse to hunt down my fancies on my father's own collecting ground. I have realized, you see, the impossibility of having the imagery of his travels germinate without contaminating them with a kind of secondary poetization, which keeps departing further and further from that real poetry with which the live experience of these receptive, knowledgeable and chaste naturalists endowed their research."

"Of course I understand and sympathize," answered his mother. "It is a pity you cannot manage it, but of course you must not force yourself. On the other hand I am convinced that you are exaggerating a little. I am convinced that, if you thought less about style, about difficulties, about the poetaster's cliché that 'with a kiss starts the death of romance,' etc., you would produce something very good, very true and very interesting. Only if you imagine him reading your book and you feel it grates upon him, and makes you ashamed, then, of course, give it up, give it up. But I know this cannot be, I know he would tell you: well done. Even more: I am convinced that some day you shall yet write this book."

The external stimulus to the cancel of his work was provided for Fyodor by his removal to another lodging. To his landlady's credit it must be said that she had put up with him for a very long time, for two years. But when she was offered the chance of obtaining an ideal roomer in April—an elderly spinster rising at seven thirty, working in an office till six, dining at her sister's and retiring at ten—Frau Stoboy requested Fyodor to find himself another roof within the month. He continually postponed his inquiries, not only out of laziness and an optimistic tendency to endow a stretch of granted time with the rounded shape of eternity, but also because he found it unbearably nasty to invade alien worlds for the purpose of discovering a place for himself. Mme. Chernyshevski, however, promised him her assistance. March was drawing to an end when, one evening, she said to him:

"I think I have something for you. You once saw here Tamara Grigorievna, the Armenian lady. She has had a room in the flat of a Russian family but now wants to turn it over to somebody."

"Which means it's a bad room if she wants to get rid of it," remarked Fyodor carelessly.

"No, it's simply that she's going back to her husband. However, if you don't like it in advance then I won't do anything about it."

"I didn't mean to offend you," said Fyodor. "I like the idea very much, really I do."

"Naturally, there's no guarantee the room is not already disposed of, but still I would advise you to give her a ring."

"Oh, of course," said Fyodor.

"Since I know you," continued Mme. Chernyshevski, already leafing through a black notebook, "and since I know you'll never ring yourself . . ."

"I'll do it first thing tomorrow," said Fyodor.

". . . since you will never do it—Uhland forty-eight thirty-one—I'll do it myself. I'll get her right now and you can ask her everything."

"Stop, wait a minute," said Fyodor anxiously. "I have no idea what I have to ask."

"Don't worry, she'll tell you herself." And Mme. Chernyshevski, rapidly repeating the number under her breath, stretched her hand toward the little table with the telephone.

As soon as she put the receiver to her ear her body assumed its usual telephone posture on the sofa; from a sitting attitude she slipped into a reclining one, adjusted her skirt without looking, and her blue eyes wandered here and there as she waited to be connected. "It would be nice—" she began, but then the girl answered and Mme. Chernyshevski said the number with a kind of abstract exhortation in her tone and a special rhythm in her pronunciation of the figures—as if 48 was the thesis and 31 the antithesis—adding in the shape of a synthesis: *ja wohl.*

"It would be nice," she re-addressed Fyodor, "if she went there with you. I'm sure you've never in your life . . ." Suddenly, with a smile, dropping her eyes, moving a plump shoulder and slightly crossing her outstretched legs: "Tamara Grigorievna?" she asked in a new voice, suave and inviting. She laughed softly as she listened, pinching a fold in her skirt. "Yes, it's me, you're right. I thought that as always you wouldn't recognize me. All right—let's say often." Settling her tone even more comfortably: "Well, what's new?" She listened to what was new, blinking; as if in parenthesis she pushed a box of fruit-paste bonbons in Fyodor's direction; then the toes of her small feet in their shabby velvet slippers began to rub gently against one another; they stopped. "Yes, so I've heard, but I thought he had a permanent practice." She continued to listen. One could make out in the silence the infinitely small drumming of the voice from another world. "Well, that's ridiculous," said Alexandra Yakovlevna, "oh, that's ridiculous." . . . "So that's how things are with you," she drawled after a moment, and then, to a quick question which sounded to Fyodor like a microscopic bark, she replied with a sigh: "Yes, more or less, nothing new. Alexander Yakovlevich is well, keeps himself busy, he's at a concert now, and I have nothing to report, nothing special. Right now I have here . . . Well, of course, it amuses him, but you can't imagine how I sometimes dream of going away somewhere with him, even if only for a month. What's that? Oh, anywhere. Generally speaking, things get a little depressing at times, but otherwise there's nothing new." She slowly inspected her palm and remained like that with her hand before her. "Tamara Grigorievna, I have Godunov-Cherdyntsev here. By the way, he's looking for a room. Do those people of yours. . . . Oh, that's wonderful. Wait a minute, I'm passing him the receiver."

"How do you do?" said Fyodor, bowing to the telephone. "I've been told by Alexandra Yakovlevna—"

Loudly, so that it even tickled his middle ear, an extraordinarily nimble and distinct voice took over the conversation. "The room's not yet rented," began the almost unknown Tamara Grigorievna, "and as it happens they would very much like to have a Russian boarder. I'll tell you right away who they are. The name is Shchyogolev, that tells you nothing, but in Russia he was a public prosecutor, a very, very cultured and pleasant gentleman. . . . Then there is his wife, who is also extremely nice, and a daughter from the first marriage. Now listen: they live at 15 Agamemnonstrasse, a wonderful district, in a small flat but *hoch-modern*, central heating, bath—in short, everything you could wish for. The room you'll live in is delightful, but [with a retractive intonation] it looks out onto the yard, that of course is a small minus. I'll tell you how much I paid for it, I paid thirty-five marks a month. It is quiet and has a fine daybed. Well, there we are. What else can I tell you? I had my meals there and I must confess the food was excellent, excellent, but you must ask them the price yourself. I was on a diet. Here's what we'll do now. I have to be there in any case tomorrow morning, about half past eleven, I'm very punctual, so you come there too."

"Wait a second," said Fyodor (for whom to rise at ten was the equivalent of rising at five for anyone else). "Wait a second. I'm afraid that tomorrow . . . Perhaps it might be better if I. . ."

He wanted to say: "give you a ring," but Mme. Chernyshevski, who was sitting nearby, made such eyes that with a gulp he instantly corrected himself: "Yes, I think on the whole I can," he said without animation, "thank you, I'll come."

"Well then [in a narrative tone], it's 15, Agamemnonstrasse, third floor, with an elevator. So that's what we'll do. Until tomorrow then, I shall be very glad to see you."

"Good-by" said Fyodor Konstantinovich.

"Wait," cried Alexandra Yakovlevna, "please don't ring off."

The next morning when he arrived at the stipulated address—in an irritable mood, with a woolly brain and with only half of him functioning (as if the other half of him had still not opened on account of the earliness of the hour)—it turned out that Tamara Grigorievna not only was not there but had rung to say she could not come. He was received by Shchyogolev himself (no-one else was at home), who turned out to be a bulky, chubby man whose outline reminded one of a carp, about fifty years old, with one of those open Russian faces whose openness is almost indecent. It was a fairly full face of oval cut, with a tiny black tuft just under the lower lip. He had a remarkable hair style that was also somehow indecent: thin black hair evenly smoothed down and divided by a parting which was not quite in the middle of the head and yet not quite to one side either. Big ears, simple male eyes, a thick yellowish nose and a moist smile completed the general pleasant impression. "Godunov-Cherdyntsev," he repeated, "of course, of course, an extremely well-known name. I once knew . . . let me see—isn't your father Oleg Kirillovich? Aha, uncle. Where's he living now? In Philadelphia? Hm, that's quite a way. Just look where we émigrés get to! Amazing. And are you in touch with him? I see, I see. Well, never put off to tomorrow what you have already done—ha-ha! Come. I'll show you your quarters."

To the right of the hallway there was a short passage immediately turning right again at a right-angle to become another embryo corridor that terminated in the half-open door of the kitchen. The left wall had two doors, the first of which, with an energetic intake of breath, Shchyogolev threw back. Turning its head, there froze before us a small oblong room with ochered walls, a table by the window, a couch along one wall and a wardrobe by the other. To Fyodor, it seemed repellent, hostile, completely "unhandy" in regard to his life, as if positioned several fateful degrees out of true (with a dusty sunbeam representing the dotted line that marks the bias of a geometric figure when it is revolved) in relation to that imaginary rectangle within whose limits he might be able to sleep, read and think; but even if by a miracle he had been able to adjust his life to fit the angle of this deviant box, nevertheless its furniture, color, view onto the asphalt yard—everything about it was unendurable, and he decided at once that he would not take it.

"Well, here it is," said Shchyogolev jauntily, "and here's the bathroom next door. It needs a little cleaning up in here. Now, if you don't mind . . ." He bumped violently into Fyodor in turning around in the narrow corridor and uttering an apologetic "Och!" grasped him by the shoulder. They returned to the entrance hall. "Here is my daughter's room, here is ours," he said, pointing to two doors on the left and right. "And here's the dining room," and opening a door in the depths, he held it in that position for several seconds, as if taking a time exposure. Fyodor passed his eyes over the table, a bowl of nuts, a sideboard. . . . By the far window, near a small bamboo table, stood a high-backed armchair: across its arms there lay in airy repose a gauze dress, pale bluish and very short (as was worn then at dances), and on the little table gleamed a silvery flower and a pair of scissors.

"That's all," said Shchyogolev, carefully closing the door, "you see—cozy, homely; everything we have is small, but we do have everything. If you wish to have your grub with us you're very welcome, we'll talk to my missus about that; between you and me she's not a bad cook. Since you're Mrs. Abramov's friend, we'll charge you the same as her, we won't ill-treat you, you'll live snug as a thug in the jug," and Shchyogolev laughed fruitily.

"Yes, I think the room will suit me," said Fyodor, trying not to look at him. "In fact, I would like to move in on Wednesday."

"Please yourself," said Shchyogolev.

Have you ever happened, reader, to feel that subtle sorrow of parting with an unloved abode? The heart does not break, as it does in parting with dear objects. The humid gaze does not wander around holding back a tear, as if it wished to carry away in it a trembling reflection of the abandoned spot; but in the best corner of our hearts we feel pity for the things which we did not bring to life with our breath, which we hardly noticed and are now leaving forever. This already dead inventory will not be resurrected later in one's memory: the bed will not follow us, shouldering its own self; the reflection in the dresser will not rise from its coffin; only the view from the window will abide for a while, like the faded photograph, fitted into a cemetery cross, of a trim-haired, steady-eyed gentleman in a starched collar. I would like to wish you good-by, but you would not even hear my greeting. Nevertheless, good-by. I lived here exactly two years, thought here about many things, the shadows of my caravan passed over this wallpaper, lilies grew out of the cigarette ash on the carpet—but now the journey is over. The torrents of books have gone back to the ocean of the library. I do not know if I shall ever read the drafts and extracts rammed under the linen in my suitcase, but I do know that I will never look in here again.

Fyodor sat on his suitcase and locked it; went around the room; gave a final check to the drawers, and found nothing: corpses do not steal. A fly climbed up the windowpane, impatiently slipped, half fell and half flew downwards, as if shaking something, and started to crawl again. The house opposite, which he had found in scaffolding the April before last, was evidently in need of repairs again now: prepared boards were stacked by the sidewalk. He carried his things out, went to say good-by to the landlady, for the first and last time shaking her hand, which turned out to be dry, strong and cold, gave her back the keys and left. The distance from the old residence to the new was about the same as, somewhere in Russia, that from Pushkin Avenue to Gogol Street.

Chapter Three

EVERY morning just after eight he was guided out of his slumber by the same sound behind the thin wall, two feet from his temple. It was the clean, round-bottomed ring of a tumbler being replaced on a glass shelf; after which the landlord's daughter cleared her throat. Then came the spasmodic *trk-trk* of a revolving cylinder, then the sound of flushed water, choking, groaning and abruptly ceasing, then the bizarre internal whine of a bath tap that finally turned into the rustle of a shower. A slip-bolt clacked and footsteps receded past his door. From an opposite direction came other footsteps, dark and heavy, with a slight shuffle: that was Marianna Nikolavna hurrying to the kitchen to get some coffee for her daughter. One could hear the gas at first refusing with noisy bursts to catch light; subdued, it flared and hissed steadily. The first footsteps returned, now heeled; in the kitchen a fast, angrily agitated conversation started up. Just as some people speak with a southern or Moscow pronunciation so did mother and daughter invariably speak to one another in the accents of a quarrel. Their voices were similar, both swarthy and smooth, but one more coarse and somehow cramped, the other freer and purer. In the rumble of the mother's there was a pleading, even a guilty pleading; in the daughter's increasingly short replies there rang hostility. To the accompaniment of this indistinct morning storm Fyodor Konstantinovich would again fall peacefully asleep.

Through his patchily thinning slumber he made out the sounds of cleaning; the wall would suddenly collapse on him: that meant a mop handle that had been insecurely leaning against his door. Once a week the janitor's wife, fat, heavily breathing, reeking of stale sweat, came with a vacuum cleaner, and then all hell broke loose, the world was shattered to bits, a hellish grinding pervaded one's very soul, destroying it, and drove Fyodor out of his bed, out of his room and out of the house. But usually, around ten o'clock, Marianna Nikolavna took her turn in the bathroom and after her came, hawking up phlegm as he went, Ivan Borisovich. He flushed the toilet as many as five times but did not use the bath, contenting himself with the murmur of the little washbasin. By half past ten everything in the house was quiet: Marianna Nikolavna had gone away to do her shopping, Shchyogolev on his shady affairs. Fyodor Konstantinovich descended into a blissful abyss where the warm remnants of his slumber mingled with a feeling of happiness, both from the previous day and still to come.

Quite often now he began the day with a poem. Lying supine with the first satisfyingly tasty, large and long-lasting cigarette between his parched lips, he again after a break of almost ten years was composing that particular kind of poem of which a gift is made in the evening so as to be reflected in the wave that has carried it out. He compared the structure of these verses with that of the others. The words of the others had been forgotten. Only here and there among the erased letters had rhymes been preserved, rich ones interspersed with poor ones: kiss-bliss, wind in–linden–leaves–grieves. During that sixteenth summer of his life he had first taken up the serious writing of poetry; before that, except for entomological doggerel, there had been nothing. But a certain atmosphere of composition had been long known and familiar to him: at home, everyone did some scribbling—Tanya wrote in a little album with a little key to it; Mother wrote touchingly unpretentious prose-poems about the beauty of the native weald; Father and Uncle Oleg made up occasional verses—and these occasions were not infrequent; and Aunt Ksenya—she wrote poems only in French, temperamental and "musical" ones, with a complete disregard for the subtleties of syllabic verse; her outpourings were very popular in St. Petersburg society, particularly the long poem "La Femme et la Panthère," and also a translation of Apukhtin's "A Pair of Bays"—one stanza of which went:

Le gros grec d'Odessa, le juif de Varsovie,
Le jeune lieutenant, le général âgé,
Tous ils cherchaient en elle un peu de folle vie,
Et sur son sein rêvait leur amour passager.

Finally there had been one "real" poet, Mother's cousin, Prince Volkhovskoy, who had published on velvety paper an exquisitely printed, thick, expensive volume of languorous poems *Auroras and Stars,* all in Italian viny vignettes, with a portrait photograph of the author in the front and a monstrous list of misprints at the back. The verses were broken up into departments: Nocturnes, Autumn Motifs, The Chords of Love. Most of them were emblazoned with a motto and under all there was the exact date and place: *Sorrento*, *Ai-Todor*, or *In the Train*. I do not remember anything of these pieces except the oft-repeated word "transport": which even then sounded to me like a means of moving from one place to another.

My father took little interest in poetry, making an exception only for Pushkin: he knew him as some people know the liturgy, and liked to declaim him while out walking. I sometimes think that an echo of Pushkin's "The Prophet" still vibrates to this day in some resonantly receptive Asian gully. He also quoted, I remember, the incomparable "Butterfly" by Fet, and Tyutchev's "Now the dim-blue shadows mingle"; but that which our kinsfolk liked, the watery, easily memorized poesy of the end of the last century, avidly waiting to be set to music as a cure for verbal anemia, he ignored utterly. As to avant-garde verse, he considered it rubbish—and in his presence I did not publicize my own enthusiasms in this sphere. Once when with a smile of irony already prepared he leafed through the books of poets scattered on my desk and as luck would have it happened on the worst item by the best of them (that famous poem by Blok where there appears an impossible, unbearable *dzhentelmen* representing Edgar Poe, and where *kovyor*, carpet, is made to rhyme with the English "Sir" transliterated as *syor*), I was so annoyed that I quickly pushed Severyanin's *The Thunder-Bubbling Cup* into his hand so that he could better unburden his soul upon it. In general I considered that if he would forget for the nonce the kind of poetry I was silly enough to call "classicism" and tried without prejudice to grasp what it was I loved so much, he would have understood the new charm that had appeared in the features of Russian poetry, a charm that I sensed even in its most absurd manifestations. But when today I tote up what has remained to me of this new poetry I see that very little has survived, and what has is precisely a natural continuation of Pushkin, while the motley husk, the wretched sham, the masks of mediocrity and the stilts of talent—everything that my love once forgave or saw in a special light (and that seemed to my father to be the true face of innovation—"the mug of modernism" as he expressed it), is now so old-fashioned, so forgotten as even Karamzin's verses are not forgotten; and when on someone else's shelf I come across this or that collection of poems which had once lived with me as brother, I feel in them only what my father then felt without actually knowing them. His mistake was not that he ran down all "modern poetry" indiscriminately, but that he refused to detect in it the long, life-giving ray of his favorite poet.

I met her in June 1916. She was twenty-three. Her husband, a distant relative of ours, was at the front. She lived in a small villa inside the boundaries of our estate and often used to visit us. Because of her I almost forgot butterflies and completely overlooked the revolution. In the winter of 1917 she went away to Novorossisk—and it was only in Berlin that I accidentally heard about her terrible death. She was a thin little thing, with chestnut hair combed high, a gay look in her big black eyes, dimples on her pale cheeks, and a tender mouth which she made up out of a flacon of fragrant ruby-red liquid by putting the glass stopper to her lips. In all her ways there was something I found lovable to the point of tears, something indefinable at the time, but now appearing to me as a kind of pathetic insouciance. She was not intelligent, she was poorly educated and banal, that is, your exact opposite . . . no, no, I do not mean at all that I loved her more than you, or that those assignations were happier than my evening meetings with you . . . but all her shortcomings were concealed in such a tide of fascination, tenderness and grace, such enchantment flowed from her most fleeting, irresponsible word, that I was prepared to look at her and listen to her eternally—but what would happen now if she were resurrected—I don't know, you should not ask stupid questions. In the evenings I used to see her home. Those walks will come in handy sometime. In her bedroom there was a little picture of the Tsar's family and a Turgenevian odor of heliotrope. I used to return long after midnight (my tutor, fortunately, had gone back to England), and I shall never forget that feeling of lightness, pride, rapture and wild night hunger (I particularly yearned for curds-and-whey with black bread) as I walked along our faithfully and even fawningly soughing avenue toward the dark house (only Mother had a light on) and heard the barking of the watchdogs. It was then also that my versificatory illness began.

At times I would be sitting at lunch, seeing nothing, my lips moving—and to my neighbor who had asked for the sugar bowl I would pass my glass or a napkin ring. Despite my inexperienced desire to transpose into verse the murmur of love filling me (well do I remember Uncle Oleg saying that if he were to publish a volume of poetry he would certainly call it *Heart Murmur*), I had already rigged up my own, albeit poor and primitive, wordsmithy; thus, in selecting adjectives, I was already aware that ones like "innumerable" or "intangible" would simply and conveniently fill the yawning gap, which was longing to sing, from the caesura to the word closing the line ("For we shall dream innumerable dreams"); and again that for this last word one could take an additional adjective, of only two syllables, so as to combine it with the long centerpiece ("Of loveliness intangible and tender"), a melodic formula which, by the way, has had a quite disastrous effect on Russian, as well as on French poetry. I knew that handy adjectives of the amphibrachic type (a trisyllable that one visualizes in the shape of a sofa with three cushions—the middle one dented) were legion in Russian—and how many such "dejécted," "enchánted" and "rebéllious" I wasted; that we had also plenty of trochees ("ténder"), but far fewer dactyls ("sórrowful"), and these somehow all stood in profile; that finally anapaestic and iambic adjectives were on the rare side, and in addition always rather dull and inflexible, like "incompléte" or "forlórn." I knew further that great long ones like "incomprehénsible" and "infinitésimal" would come into the tetrameter bringing with them their own orchestras, and that the combination "unwanted and misunderstood" gave a certain moiré quality to the line; look at it this way—it is an amphibrach, and that way—an iamb. A little later Andrey Bely's monumental research on "half stresses" (the "comp" and the "ble" in the line "Incomprehensible desires") hypnotized me with its system of graphically marking off and calculating these scuds, so that I immediately reread all my old tetrameters from this new point of view and was terribly pained by the paucity of modulations. When plotted, their diagrams proved to be plain and gappy, showing none of those rectangles and trapeziums that Bely had found for the tetrameters of great poets; whereupon for the space of almost a whole year—an evil and sinful year—I tried to write with the aim of producing the most complicated and rich scud-scheme possible:

> In miserable meditations,
> And aromatically dark,
> Full of interconverted patience,
> Sighs the semidenuded park.

and so on for half-a-dozen strophes: the tongue stumbled but one's honor was saved. When graphically expressed by joining the "half-stresses" ("ra," "med," "ar," "cal," etc.), in the verses and from one verse to another, this monster's rhythmic structure gave rise to something in the nature of that wobbly tower of coffeepots, baskets, trays and vases which a circus clown balances on a stick, until he runs into the barrier of the arena when everything slowly leans over the nearest spectators (screaming horribly) but on falling turns out to be safely strung on a cord.

As a result, probably, of the weak motive power of my little lyrical rollers, verbs and other parts of speech interested me less. Not so with questions of meter and rhythm. Overcoming a natural preference for iambics, I dangled after ternary meters; later on, departures from meter fascinated me. That was the time when Balmont in his poem beginning "I will be reckless, I will be daring" launched that artificial iambic tetrameter with the bump of an extra syllable after the second foot, in which, as far as I know, not a single good poem was ever written. I would give this prancing hunchback a sunset to carry or a boat and was amazed that the former faded and the latter sank. Things went easier with the dreamy stutter of Blok's rhythms, but as soon as I began to use them my verse was imperceptibly infiltrated by stylized medievalizing—blue page-boys, monks, princesses—similar to the way that in a German tale the shadow of Bonaparte visits the antiquary Stolz at night to look for the ghost of its tricorn.

As my hunt for them progressed, rhymes settled down into a practical system somewhat on the order of a card index. They were distributed in little families—rhyme-clusters, rhymescapes. *Letuchiy* (flying) immediately grouped *tuchi* (clouds) over the *kruchi* (steeps) of the *zhguchey* (burning) desert and of *neminuchey* (inevitable) fate. *Nebosklon* (sky) let the muse onto the *balkon* (balcony) and showed her a *klyon* (maple). *Tsvety* (flowers) and *ty* (thou) summoned *mechty* (fancies) in the midst of *temnoty* (darkness). *Svechi, plechi, vstrechi,* and *rechi* (tapers, shoulders, meetings, and speeches) created the old-world atmosphere of a ball at the Congress of Vienna or on the town governor's birthday. *Glaza* (eyes) shone blue in the company of *biryuza* (turquoise), *groza* (thunderstorm), and *strekoza* (dragonfly), and it was better not to get involved in the series. *Derevya* (trees) found themselves dully paired with *kochevya* (nomad encampments) as happens in the game in which one has to collect cards with the names of cities, with only two representing Sweden (but a dozen in the case of France!). *Veter* (wind) had no mate, except for a not very attractive setter running about in the distance, but by shifting into the genitive, one could get words ending in "meter" to perform (*vetra-geometra*). There were also certain treasured freaks, rhymes to which, like rare stamps in an album, were represented by blanks. Thus it took me a long time to discover that *ametistovyy* (amethystine) could be rhymed with *perelistyvay* (turn the pages), with *neistovyy* (furioso), and with the genitive case of an utterly unsuitable *pristav* (police constable). In short, it was a beautifully labeled collection that I had always close to hand.

I do not doubt that even then, at the time of that ugly, crippling school (which I would hardly have bothered with at all were I a typical poet who never fell for the blandishments of harmonious prose) I nevertheless knew true inspiration. The agitation which seized me, swiftly covered me with an icy sheet, squeezed my joints and jerked at my fingers. The lunatic wandering of my thought which by unknown means found the door in a thousand leading into the noisy night of the garden, the expansion and contraction of the heart, now as vast as the starry sky and then as small as a droplet of mercury, the opening arms of a kind of inner embracement, classicism's sacred thrill, mutterings, tears—all this was genuine. But at that moment, in a hasty and clumsy attempt to resolve the agitation, I clutched at the first hackneyed words available, at their ready-made linkages, so that as soon as I had embarked on what I thought to be creation, on what should have been the expression, the living connection between my divine excitement and my human world, everything expired in a fatal gust of words, whereas I continued to rotate epithets and adjust rhymes without noticing the split, the debasement and the betrayal—like a man relating his dream (like any dream infinitely free and complex, but clotting like blood upon waking up), who unnoticed by himself and his listeners rounds it out, cleans it up and dresses it in the fashion of hackneyed reality, and if he begins thus: "I dreamt that I was sitting in my room," monstrously vulgarizes the dream's devices by taking it for granted that the room had been furnished exactly the same as his room in real life.

Farewell forever: on a winter day, with large snowflakes falling since morning, drifting anyhow—vertically, slantwise, even upwards. Her big arctics and tiny muff. She was taking away with her absolutely everything—including the park where they used to meet in summer. There remained only his rhymed inventory plus the briefcase under his arm, the shabby briefcase of an upper-former who had skipped school. An odd constraint, the desire to say something important, silence, vague insignificant words. Love, to put it simply, repeats at the last parting the musical theme of shyness that precedes its first avowal. The reticulate touch of her salty lips through the veil. At the station there was vile animal bustle: this was the time when the black and white seeds of the flower of happiness, sunshine and freedom were being liberally sown. Now it has grown up. Russia is populated with sunflowers. This is the largest, most fat-faced and stupidest of flowers.

Poems: about parting, about death, about the past. It is impossible to define (but it seems this happened abroad) the exact period of change in my attitude to writing poetry, when I became sick of the workshop, the classification of words and the collection of rhymes. But how excruciatingly difficult it was to break, scatter and forget all that: Faulty habits clung firmly, words accustomed to go together did not want to be uncoupled. In themselves they were neither bad nor good, but their combination in groups, the mutual guarantee of rhymes, the rank-grown rhythms—all this made them foul, hideous and dead. To consider himself a mediocrity was hardly any better than believing he was a genius: Fyodor doubted the first and conceded the second, but more important, strove not to surrender to the fiendish despair of a blank sheet. Since there were things he wanted to express just as naturally and unrestrainedly as the lungs want to expand, hence words suitable for breathing ought to exist. The oft repeated complaints of poets that, alas, no words are available, that words are pale corpses, that words are incapable of expressing our thingummy-bob feelings (and to prove it a torrent of trochaic hexameters is set loose) seemed to him just as senseless as the staid conviction of the eldest inhabitant of a mountain hamlet that yonder mountain has never been climbed by anyone and never will be; one fine, cold morning a long lean Englishman appears—and cheerfully scrambles up to the top.

The first feeling of liberation stirred in him when he was working on the little volume *Poems*, published two years ago now. It had remained in his consciousness as a pleasant exercise. One or two out of those fifty octaves, it was true, he was now ashamed of—for example that one about the bicycle, or the dentist—but on the other hand, there were some vivid and genuine bits: the lost and found ball, for instance, had come out very nicely, and the rhythm of its last two lines still continued to sing in his ear with the same inspired expressiveness as before. He had published the book at his own expense (having sold an accidental survivor of his former wealth, a flat, gold cigarette case with the date of a distant summer night scratched on it—oh that creak of her wicket gate wet with dew!) and out of the total of five hundred copies printed, four hundred and twenty-nine still lay, dusty and uncut, forming a neat mesa in the distributor's warehouse. Nineteen had been presented to different people, and one he had kept himself. Sometimes he wondered about the exact identity of the fifty-one who had bought his book. He imagined a roomful of these people (like a meeting of stockholders—"readers of Godunov-Cherdyntsev") and they were all alike, with thoughtful eyes and a small white volume in their affectionate hands. He learned for sure the fate of only one copy: it had been bought two years ago by Zina Mertz.

He lay and smoked, and gently composed, reveling in the womblike warmth of the bed, the quietness of the flat and the lazy passage of time: Marianna Nikolavna would not be returning for a while and dinner was not earlier than one fifteen. During the past three months the room had been completely domesticated and its movement in space now coincided exactly with that of his life. The ring of a hammer, the hiss of a pump, the roar of an engine being checked, German bursts of German voices—all this humdrum complex of noises coming every morning from left of the yard, where there were garages and car workshops, had long since become familiar and harmless—a barely noticeable pattern in the stillness and not a violation of it. He could touch the little table by the window with his toe, if he stretched it from under the army blanket, and with a sideways projection of his arm he could reach the wardrobe by the left wall (which, by the way, sometimes for no reason, suddenly opened with the officious look of some fool of an actor who has come onto the stage at the wrong time). On the table stood the Leshino photograph, a bottle of ink, a lamp beneath cloudy glass and a saucer with traces of jam on it; reviews were lying around, the Soviet *Krasnaya Nov'*, and the émigré *Sovremennye Zapiski*, and a little volume of verse by Koncheyev, *Communication*, which had only just come out. Collapsed on the rug by his couch were yesterday's paper and an émigré edition of *Dead Souls*. None of this did he see for the moment, but it was all there: a small society of objects schooled to become invisible and in this finding their purpose, which they could only fulfil through the constancy of their miscellaneousness. His euphoria was all-pervading—a pulsating mist that suddenly began to speak with a human voice. Nothing in the world could be better than these moments. Love only what is fanciful and rare; what from the distance of a dream steals through; what knaves condemn to death and fools can't bear. To fiction be as to your country true. Now is our time. Stray dogs and cripples are alone awake. Mild is the summer night. A car speeds by: Forever that last car has taken the last banker out of sight. Near that streetlight veined lime-leaves masquerade in chrysoprase with a translucent gleam. Beyond that gate lies Baghdad's crooked shade, and yon star sheds on Pulkovo its beam. Oh, swear to me—

From the hall came the jangling peal of the telephone. By tacit consent Fyodor attended to it when the others were out. And what if I don't get up now? The ringing went on and on, with brief pauses to catch its breath. It did not wish to die; it had to be killed. Unable to hold out, with a curse Fyodor gained the hall phantom-fast. A Russian voice asked irritably who was speaking. Fyodor recognized it instantly: it was an unknown person—by the whim of chance a fellow countryman—who already the day before had got the wrong number and now again, because of the similarity of the numbers, had blundered into the wrong connection. "For Christ's sake go away," said Fyodor and hung up with disgusted haste. He visited the bathroom for a moment, drank a cup of cold coffee in the kitchen, and dashed back into bed. What shall I call you? Half-Mnemo*syne*? There's a half-shim*mer* in your surname too. In dark Berlin, it is so strange to me to roam, oh, my half-fantasy, with you. A bench stands under the translucent tree. Shivers and sobs reanimate you there, and all life's wonder in your gaze I see, and see the pale fair radiance of your hair. In honor of your lips when they kiss mine I might devise a metaphor some time: Tibetan mountain-snows, their glancing shine, and a hot spring near flowers touched with rime. Our poor nocturnal property—that wet asphaltic gloss, that fence and that street light—upon the ace of fancy let us set to win a world of beauty from the night. Those are not clouds—but star-high mountain spurs; not lamplit blinds—but camplight on a tent! O swear to me that while the heartblood stirs, you will be true to what we shall invent.

At midday the peck of a key (now we switch to the prose-rhythm of Bely) was heard, and the lock reacted in character, clacking: that was Marianna (stopgap) Nikolavna home from the market; with a ponderous step and a sickening swish of her mackintosh she carried a thirty-pound netful of shopping past his door and into the kitchen. Muse of Russian prose-rhythm! Say farewell forever to the cabbage dactylics of the author of *Moscow*. All feeling of comfort was now gone. Of the morning capaciousness of time nothing remained. The bed had turned into a parody of a bed. In the sounds of dinner being prepared in the kitchen there was an unpleasant reproach, and the perspective of washing and shaving seemed as flat and impossible as the perspective of the early Italians. And with this, too, you will have to part some day.

A quarter past twelve, twenty past twelve, half past . . . He allowed himself one last cigarette in the tenacious although already tedious warmth of the bed. The anachronism of his pillow became more and more obvious. Without finishing his cigarette he got up and passed immediately from a world of many interesting dimensions into one that was cramped and demanding, with a different pressure, which instantly caused his body to tire and his head to ache; into a world of cold water: the hot was not running today.

A poetic hangover, dejection, the "sad animal" . . . The day before he had forgotten to rinse his safety razor, between its teeth there was stony foam, the blade had rusted—and he had no other. A pale self-portrait looked out of the mirror with the serious eyes of all self-portraits. On a tenderly itchy spot to one side of his chin, among the hairs which had grown up overnight (how many yards of them shall I cut off in my life?), there had appeared a yellow-headed pimple which instantly became the hub of Fyodor's existence, a rallying point for all the unpleasant feelings now trekking in from different parts of his being. He squeezed it out—although he knew it would later swell up three times as big. How awful all this was. Through the cold shaving-soap foam pierced the little red eye: *L'oeil regardait Caïn.* Meanwhile the blade had no effect on the hairs, and the feel of the bristles when he checked them with his fingers produced a sense of hellish hopelessness. Drops of blood dew appeared in the vicinity of his Adam's apple but the hairs were still there. The Steppe of Despair. On top of everything else the bathroom was on the darkish side and even if he had put on the light the immortelle-like yellowness of daytime electricity would have been no help at all. Finishing his shave anyhow, he squeamishly climbed into the bath and groaned under the icy impact of the shower; then he made a mistake with the towels and thought miserably that he would be smelling all day of Marianna Nikolavna. The skin of his face smarted, revoltingly chafish, with one particularly hot little ember on the side of his chin. Suddenly the door handle of the bathroom was jerked vigorously (that was Shchyogolev returning). Fyodor Konstantinovich waited for the footfalls to recede, and then popped back into his room.

Soon afterwards he entered the dining room. Marianna Nikolavna was ladling out the soup. He kissed her rough hand. Her daughter, who was just back from work, came to the table with slow steps, worn out and seemingly dazed by her office; she sat down with graceful languor—a cigarette in her long fingers, powder on her lashes, a turquoise silk jumper, short-cut fair hair brushed back from the temple, sullenness, silence, ash. Shchyogolev gulped down a dram of vodka, tucked his napkin into his collar and began to slop up his soup, looking over his spoon affably but cautiously at his stepdaughter. She was slowly mixing a white exclamation mark of sour cream into her borshch, but then, shrugging her shoulders, she pushed her plate away. Marianna Nikolavna, who had been gloomily watching her, threw her napkin on the table and left the dining room.

"Come on, eat, Aïda," said Shchyogolev, thrusting out his wet lips. Without a word of reply, as if he was not there—only the nostrils of her narrow nose quivered—she turned in her chair, easily and naturally twisted her long body, obtained an ashtray from the sideboard behind her, placed it by her plate and flicked some ash into it. Marianna Nikolavna, with a hurt look beglooming her ample crudely madeup face, returned from the kitchen. The daughter placed her left elbow on the table and slightly leaning on it slowly began her soup.

"Well, Fyodor Konstantinovich," began Shchyogolev, having satisfied his first hunger, "it seems matters are coming to a head! A complete break with England, and Hinchuk walloped! You know it's already beginning to smell of something serious. You remember, only the other day I said Koverda's shot was the first signal! War! You have to be very, very naïve to deny it's inevitable. Judge for yourself, in the Far East, Japan cannot put up with . . ."

And Shchyogolev launched on a discussion of politics. Like many unpaid windbags he thought that he could combine the reports he read in the papers by paid windbags into an orderly scheme, upon following which a logical and sober mind (in this case his mind) could with no effort explain and foresee a multitude of world events. The names of countries and of their leading representatives became in his hands something in the nature of labels for more or less full but essentially identical vessels, whose contents he poured this way and that. France was AFRAID of something or other and therefore would never ALLOW it. England was AIMING at something. This statesman CRAVED a rapprochement, while that one wanted to increase his PRESTIGE. Someone was PLOTTING and someone was

STRIVING for something. In short, the world Shchyogolev created came out as some kind of collection of limited, humorless, faceless and abstract bullies, and the more brains, cunning and circumspection he found in their mutual activities the more stupid, vulgar and simple his world became. It used to be quite awesome when he came across another similar lover of political prognoses. For example, there was a Colonel Kasatkin, who used to come sometimes to dinner, and then Shchyogolev's England clashed not with another Shchyogolev country but with Kasatkin's England, equally nonexistent, so that in a certain sense international wars turned into civil wars, although the warring sides existed on different levels which could never come into contact with one another. At present, while listening to his landlord, Fyodor was amazed by the family likeness between the countries mentioned by Shchyogolev and the various parts of Shchyogolev's own body: thus "France" corresponded to his warningly raised eyebrows; some kind of "limitrophes" to the hairs in his nostrils, some "Polish corridor" or other went along his esophagus; "Danzig" was the click of his teeth; and Russia was Shchyogolev's bottom.

He talked all through the next two courses (goulash, kissel) and after that, picking his teeth with a broken match, went to take a nap. Marianna Nikolavna busied herself with the dishes before doing the same. Her daughter, having not uttered a single word, went back to her office.

Fyodor had only just managed to clear the bedclothes from the couch before a pupil arrived, the son of an émigré dentist, a fat, pale youth in horn-rimmed spectacles, with a fountain pen in his breast pocket. Attending, as he did, a Berlin high school, the poor boy was so steeped in the local habitus that even in English he made the same ineradicable mistakes as any skittle-headed German would have made. There was no force on earth, for example, which could have stopped him using the past continuous instead of the simple past, and this endowed every of his accidental activities of the day before with a kind of idiotic permanence. Equally stubbornly he handled the English "also" like the German "*also*," and in overcoming the thorny ending of the word "clothes" he invariably added a superfluous sibilant syllable ("clothes-zes"), as if skidding after having cleared an obstacle. At the same time he expressed himself fairly freely in English and had only sought the aid of a coach because he wanted to get the highest mark in the final examination. He was self-satisfied, discursive, obtuse and germanically ignorant; i.e., he treated everything he did not know with skepticism. Firmly believing that the humorous side of things had long since been worked out in the proper place for it (the back page of a Berlin illustrated weekly), he never laughed, or limited himself to a condescending snicker. The only thing that could just barely amuse him was a story about some ingenious financial operation. His whole philosophy of life had been reduced to the simplest proposition: the poor man is unhappy, the rich man is happy. This legalized happiness was playfully put together to the accompaniment of first-class dance music, out of various items of technical luxury. For the lesson he always did his best to come a little before the hour and tried to leave a little after it.

Hurrying to his next trial, Fyodor left together with him, and the latter, accompanying him as far as the corner, endeavored to collect a few more English expressions gratis, but Fyodor, with dry glee, lapsed into Russian. They parted at the crossroads. It was a windy and shabby crossroads, not quite grown to the rank of a square although there was a church, and a public garden, and a corner pharmacy, and a public convenience with thujas around it, and even a triangular island with a kiosk, at which tram conductors regaled themselves with milk. A multitude of streets diverging in all directions, jumping out from behind corners and skirting the above-mentioned places of prayer and refreshment, turned it all into one of those schematic little pictures on which are depicted for the edification of beginning motorists all the elements of the city, all the possibilities for them to collide. To the right one saw the gates of a tram depot with three beautiful birches standing out against its cement background, and if, say, some absentminded tramdriver forgot to pause by the kiosk three yards before the lawful tram stop (a woman with parcels invariably making fussily to get off and being held back by everybody) in order to throw the switch with the point of his iron rod (alas, such absentmindedness almost never occurred), the tram would have solemnly turned in under the glass dome where it spent the night and was serviced. The church which loomed to the left was encircled with a low belt of ivy; in the parterre surrounding it grew several dark bushes of rhododendron with purple flowers, and at night one used to see a mysterious man here with a mysterious lantern looking for earthworms on the turf—for his birds? for fishing? Opposite the church across the street, beneath the radiance of a lawn-sprinkler that waltzed on one spot with the ghost of a rainbow in its dewy arms, was the green oblong lawn of the public garden, with young trees along either side (a silver fir among them) and a pi-shaped walk, in whose shadiest corner there was a sandpit for children; but *we* touch this kind of rich sand only when we are burying someone we know. Behind the garden there was an abandoned soccer field, along which Fyodor walked toward the Kurfürstendamm. The green of the lindens, the black of the asphalt, the truck tires leaning against the railings by the shop for motorcar accessories, the beaming young bride on a poster displaying a packet of margarine, the blue of a tavern sign, the gray of house fronts getting older as they got closer to the avenue—all this flickered by him for the hundredth time. As always, when a few steps from the Kurfürstendamm, he saw his bus sweep across the vista in front of him: the stop was immediately around the corner, but Fyodor did not get there in time and was forced to wait for the next one. Over the entrance to a cinema a black giant cut out of cardboard had been erected, with turned-out feet, the blotch of a mustache on his white face beneath a bowler hat, and a bent cane in his hand. In wicker armchairs on the terrace of a neighboring café businessmen sprawled in identical poses with their hands identically gabled in front of them, all very similar to one another as regards snouts and ties but probably varied in the extent of their solvency; and by the curb stood a small car with a heavily damaged wing, broken windows and a bloody handkerchief on the running board; a half-a-dozen people still loafed around, gaping at it. Everything was sun mottled; a puny old man with a dyed little beard and wearing cloth spats sat sunning himself on a green bench, with his back to the traffic, while opposite him across the sidewalk, an elderly, rosy-faced beggar woman with legs cut off at the pelvis was set down like a bust at the foot of a wall and was selling paradoxical shoelaces. Between the houses could be seen a vacant lot and on it something was modestly and mysteriously blooming; beyond it the continuous slaty-black backs of houses that seemed to have turned to leave, carried strange, attractive and seemingly completely autonomous whitish designs, reminding one not quite of the canals on Mars and not quite of something very distant and half-forgotten, like an accidental expression from a once-heard fairy tale or old scenery for some unknown play.

Down the helical stairs of the bus that drew up came a pair of charming silk legs: we know of course that this has been worn threadbare by the efforts of a thousand male writers, but nevertheless down they came, these legs—and deceived: the face was revolting. Fyodor climbed aboard, and the conductor, on the open top deck, smote its plated side with his palm to tell the driver he could move on. Along this side and along the toothpaste advertisement upon it swished the tips of soft maple twigs—and it would have been pleasant to look down from above on the gliding street ennobled by perspective, if it were not for the everlasting, chilly thought: there he is, a special, rare and as yet undescribed and unnamed variant of man, and he is occupied with God knows what, rushing from lesson to lesson, wasting his youth on a boring and empty task, on the mediocre teaching of foreign languages—when he has his own language, out of which he can make anything he likes—a midge, a mammoth, a thousand different clouds. What he should be really teaching was that mysterious and refined thing which he alone—out of ten thousand, a hundred thousand, perhaps even a million men—knew how to teach: for example—multi-level thinking: you look at a person and you see him as clearly as if he were fashioned of glass and you were the glass blower, while at the same time without in the least impinging upon that clarity you notice some trifle on the side—such as the similarity of the telephone receiver's shadow to a huge, slightly crushed ant, and (all this simultaneously) the convergence is joined by a third thought—the memory of a sunny evening at a Russian small railway station; i.e., images having no rational connection with the conversation you are carrying on while your mind runs around the outside of your own words and along the inside of those of your interlocutor. Or: a piercing pity—for the tin box in a waste patch, for the cigarette card from the series *National Costumes* trampled in the mud, for the poor, stray word repeated by the kind-hearted, weak, loving creature who has just been scolded for nothing—for all the trash of life which by means of a momentary alchemic distillation—the "royal experiment"—is turned into something valuable and eternal. Or else: the constant feeling that our days here are only pocket money, farthings clinking in the dark, and that somewhere is stocked the real wealth, from which life should know how to get dividends in the shape of dreams, tears of happiness, distant mountains. All this and much more (beginning with the very rare and painful so-called "sense of the starry sky," mentioned it seems in only one treatise [Parker's *Travels of the Spirit*], and ending with professional subtleties in the sphere of serious literature), he would have been able to teach, and teach well, to anyone who wanted it, but no one wanted it—and no one could, but it was a pity, he would have charged a hundred marks an hour, the same as certain professors of music. And at the same time he found it amusing to refute himself: all this was nonsense, the shadows of nonsense, presumptuous dreams. I am simply a poor young Russian selling the surplus from a gentleman's upbringing, while scribbling verses in my spare time, that's the total of my little immortality. But even this shade of multifaceted thought, this play of the mind with its own self, had no prospective pupils.

The bus rolled on—and presently he arrived at his destination—the place of a lone and lonesome young woman, very attractive in spite of her freckles, always wearing a black dress opened at the neck and with lips like sealing-wax on a letter in which there was nothing. She continually looked at Fyodor with pensive curiosity, not only taking no interest in the remarkable novel by Stevenson which he had been reading with her for the past three months (and before that they had read Kipling at the same rate), but also not understanding a single sentence, and noting down words as you would note down the address of someone you knew you would never visit. Even now—or more exactly, precisely now and with greater agitation than before, Fyodor (although in love with another who was incomparable in fascination and intelligence) wondered what would happen if he placed his palm on this slightly trembling little hand with the sharp fingernails, lying so invitingly close—and because he knew what would happen then his heart suddenly began to thump and his lips immediately went dry; at this point, however, he was involuntarily sobered by a certain intonation of hers, her little laugh, the smell of that certain scent which somehow was always used by the very women who liked him, although to him this dullish, sweetish-brown smell was unbearable. She was a worthless, cunning woman with a sluggish soul; but even now, when the lesson was over and he had gone out into the street, he was seized by a vague feeling of annoyance; he could imagine much better than he had just been able to, in her presence, how gaily and yieldingly her compact little body would probably have responded to everything, and with painful vividness he saw in an imaginary mirror his hand on her back and her smooth auburn head thrown back, and then the mirror significantly emptied and he experienced that most trivial of all feelings on earth: the stab of a missed opportunity.

No, that was not so—he had missed nothing. The sole joy of these unrealizable embraces was their ease of evocation. During the past ten years of lonely and restrained youth, living on a cliff where there was always a bit of snow and from where it was a long way down to the little brewery town at the foot of the mountain, he had become accustomed to the thought that between the deceit of casual love and the sweetness of its temptation there was a void, a gap in life, an absence of any real action on his part, so that on occasion, when he looked at a passing girl, he imagined simultaneously both the stupendous possibility of happiness and repugnance for its inevitable imperfection—charging this one instant with a romantic image, but diminishing its triptych by the middle section. He knew therefore that their reading of Stevenson would never be interrupted by a Dantean pause, knew that if such a break should take place he would not experience a thing, except a devastating chill because the demands of the imagination were unfulfillable, and because the vacuousness of a gaze, forgiven for the sake of beautiful, moist eyes, inevitably corresponded to a defect as yet concealed—the vacuous expression of breasts, which it was impossible to forgive. But sometimes he envied the simple love life of other men and the way they probably had of whistling while taking off their shoes.

Crossing Wittenberg Square where, as in a color film, roses were quivering in the breeze around an antique flight of stairs which led down to an underground station, he walked toward the Russian bookshop: between lessons there was a chink of spare time. As always happened when he came to this street (beginning under the auspices of a huge department store that sold all forms of local bad taste, and ending after several crossroads in burgherish calm, with poplar shadows on the asphalt, all chalked over by hopscotchers) he met an elderly, morbidly embittered St. Petersburg writer who wore an overcoat in summer to hide the shabbiness of his suit, a dreadfully skinny man with bulging dark brown eyes, wrinkles of fastidious distaste around his apish mouth, and one long, curved hair growing out of a big black pore on his broad nose—a detail which attracted Fyodor Konstantinovich's attention much more than the conversation of this clever schemer, who embarked immediately he met anyone upon something in the nature of a fable, a long farfetched anecdote of yore, which turned out to be merely a prelude to some amusing gossip about a mutual acquaintance. Fyodor had barely got rid of him when he caught sight of two more writers, a good-naturedly gloomy Muscovite whose carriage and aspect were somewhat reminiscent of the Napoleon of the island period, and a satirical poet from the Berlin Russian-émigré paper, a frail little man with a kindly wit and a quiet, hoarse voice. These two, like their predecessor, invariably turned up in this region, which they used for leisurely walks, rich in encounters, so that it seemed as if on this German street there had encroached the vagabond phantom of a Russian boulevard, or as if on the contrary a street in Russia, with several natives taking the air, swarmed with the pale ghosts of innumerable foreigners flickering among those natives like a familiar and barely noticeable hallucination. They chatted about the writer just encountered, and Fyodor sailed on. After a few steps he noticed

Koncheyev reading on the stroll the feuilleton at the bottom of the Paris Russian-émigré paper, with a marvelous angelic smile on his round face. The engineer Kern came out of a Russian food shop, cautiously thrusting a small parcel into the briefcase pressed against his chest, and on a cross street (like the confluence of people in a dream or in the last chapter of Turgenev's *Smoke*) he caught a glimpse of Marianna Nikolavna Shchyogolev with some other lady, mustachioed and very stout, who perhaps was Mme. Abramov. Immediately after that Alexander Yakovlevich Chernyshevski cut across the street—no, a mistake—a stranger not even very like him.

Fyodor Konstantinovich reached the bookshop. In the window he could see, among the zigzags, cogs and numerals of Soviet cover designs (this was the time when the fashion there was to have titles like *Third Love, The Sixth Sense* and *Point Seventeen*), several new émigré publications: a corpulent new romance by General Kachurin, *The Red Princess,* Koncheyev's *Communication,* the pure white paperbacks of two venerable novelists, an anthology of recitable poetry published in Riga, the minute, palm-sized volume of a young poetess, a handbook *What a Driver Should Know,* and the last work of Dr. Utin, *The Foundations of a Happy Marriage.* There were also several old St. Petersburg engravings—in one of which a mirror-like transposition had put the rostral column on the wrong side of the neighboring buildings.

The owner of the shop was not there: he had gone to the dentist's and his place was being taken by a rather accidental young lady reading a Russian translation of Kellerman's *The Tunnel* in a fairly uncomfortable pose in the corner. Fyodor Konstantinovich approached the table where the émigré periodicals were displayed. He unfolded the literary number of the Paris Russian *News* and with a chill of sudden excitement he saw that the feuilleton by Christopher Mortus was devoted to *Communication.* "What if he demolishes it?" Fyodor managed to think with a mad hope, already, however, hearing in his ears not the melody of detraction but the sweeping roar of deafening praise. He greedily began to read.

"I do not remember who said—perhaps Rozanov said it somewhere," began Mortus stealthily; and citing first this unauthentic quotation and then some thought expressed by somebody in a Paris café after someone's lecture, he began to narrow these artificial circles around Koncheyev's *Communication;* but even so, to the very end he never touched the center, but only directed now and then a mesmeric gesture toward it from the circumference—and again revolved. The result was something in the nature of those black spirals on cardboard circles which are everlastingly spinning in the windows of Berlin ice-cream parlors in a crazy effort to turn into bull's-eyes.

It was a venomously disdainful "dressing down" without a single remark to the point, without a single example—and not so much the critic's words as his whole manner made a pitiful and dubious phantom out of a book which Mortus could not fail to have read with delight and from which he avoided quoting in order not to damage himself with the disparity between what he wrote and what he was writing about; the whole review seemed to be a séance for the summoning of a spirit which is announced in advance to be, if not a fraud, at least a delusion of the senses. "These poems," ended Mortus, "induce in the reader an indefinite but insuperable repulsion. People friendly to Koncheyev's talent will probably think them enchanting. We shall not quarrel—perhaps this is really so. But in our difficult times with their new responsibilities, when the very air is imbued with a subtle moral *angoisse* (an awareness of which is the infallible mark of 'genuineness' in a contemporary poet), abstract and melodious little pieces about dreamy visions are incapable of seducing anyone. And in truth it is with a kind of joyous relief that one passes from them to any kind of 'human document,' to what one can read 'between the words' in certain Soviet writers (granted even without talent), to an artless and sorrowful confession, to a private letter dictated by emotion and despair."

At first Fyodor Konstantinovich felt an acute almost physical pleasure from this article, but it immediately dispersed and was replaced by a queer sensation, as if he had been taking part in a sly, evil business. He recalled Koncheyev's smile of a moment ago—over these very lines, of course—and it occurred to him that a similar smile might apply to him, Godunov-Cherdyntsev, whom envy had leagued with the critic. Here he recalled that Koncheyev himself in his critical reviews had more than once—from the heights and in fact just as unscrupulously—stung Mortus (who was, by the way, in private life, a woman of middle age, the mother of a family, who in her youth had published excellent poems in the St. Petersburg review *Apollo* and who now lived modestly two steps from the grave of Marie Bashkirtsev, suffering from an incurable eye illness which endowed Mortus' every line with a kind of tragic value). And when Fyodor realized the infinitely flattering hostility of this article he felt disappointed that no one wrote about *him* like that.

He also looked through a little illustrated weekly published by Russian émigrés in Warsaw and found a review on the same subject, but of a completely different cut. It was a *critique-bouffe.* The local Valentin Linyov, who from issue to issue used to pour out his formless, reckless, and not altogether grammatical literary impressions, was famous not only for not being able to make sense of the book he reviewed but also for not having, apparently, read it to the end. Jauntily using the author as a springboard, carried away by his own paraphrase, extracting isolated phrases in support of his incorrect conclusions, misunderstanding the initial pages and thereafter energetically pursuing a false trail, he would make his way to the penultimate chapter in the blissful state of a passenger who still does not know (and in his case never finds out) that he has boarded the wrong train. It invariably happened that having leafed blindly through a long novel or a short story (size played no part in it) he would provide the book with his own ending—usually exactly opposite to the author's intention. In other words, if, say, Gogol had been a contemporary and Linyov were writing about him, Linyov would remain firmly of the innocent conviction that Hlestakov was indeed the inspector-general. But when, as now, he wrote about poetry, he artlessly employed the device of so-called "inter-quotational footbridges." His discussion of Koncheyev's book boiled down to his answering for the author a kind of implied album questionnaire (Your favorite flower? Favorite hero? Which virtue do you prize most?): "The poet," Linyov wrote of Koncheyev, "likes [there followed a string of quotations, forcibly distorted by their combination and the demands of the accusative case]. He dreads [more bleeding stumps of verse]. He finds solace in—[*même jeu*]; but on the other hand [three-quarters of a line turned by means of quotes into a flat statement]; at times it seems to him that"—and here Linyov inadvertently extricated something more or less whole:

> Days of ripening vines! In the avenues, blue-shaded statues.
> The fair heavens that lean on the motherland's shoulders of snow.

—and it was as if the voice of a violin had suddenly drowned the hum of a patriarchal cretin.

On another table, a little farther, Soviet editions were laid out, and one could bend over the morass of Moscow magazines, over a hell of boredom, and even try to make out the agonizing constriction of capitalized abbreviations, carried like doomed cattle all over Russia and horribly recalling the lettering on freight cars (the banging of their buffers, the clanking, the hunchbacked greaser with a lantern, the piercing melancholy of godforsaken stations, the shudder of Russian rails, infinitely long-distance trains). Between *The Star* and *The Red Lamp* (trembling in railway smoke) lay an edition of the Soviet chess magazine *8 × 8*. As Fyodor leafed through it, rejoicing over the human language of the problem diagrams, he noticed a small article with the picture of a thin-bearded old man, glowering over his spectacles; the article was headed "Chernyshevski and Chess." He thought that this might amuse Alexander Yakovlevich and partly for this reason and partly because in general he liked chess problems he took the magazine; the girl, tearing herself away from Kellerman, "couldn't say" how much it cost, but knowing that Fyodor was anyway in debt to the shop she indifferently let him go. He went away with the pleasant feeling that he would have some fun at home. Being not only an excellent solver of problems but also being gifted to the highest degree with the ability to compose them, he found therein not only a rest from his literary labors but certain mysterious lessons. As a writer he derived something from the very sterility of these exercises.

A chess composer does not necessarily have to play well. Fyodor was a very indifferent player and played unwillingly. He was fatigued and infuriated by the disharmony between the lack of stamina of his chess thought in the process of the contest and that exclamation-mark-rating brilliance for which it strove. For him the construction of a problem differed from playing in about the same way as a verified sonnet does from the polemics of publicists. The making of such a problem began far from the board (as the making of verse began far from paper) with the body in a horizontal position on the sofa (i.e., when the body becomes a distant, dark blue line: its own horizon) when suddenly, from an inner impulse which was indistinguishable from poetic inspiration, he envisioned a bizarre method of embodying this or that refined idea for a problem (say, the combination of two themes, the Indian and the Bristol—or something completely new). For some time he delighted with closed eyes in the abstract purity of a plan realized only in his mind's eye; then he hastily opened his Morocco board and the box of weighty pieces, set them out roughly, on the run, and it immediately became clear that the idea so purely embodied in his brain would demand, here on the board—in order to free it of its thick, carved shell—inconceivable labors, a maximum of mental strain, endless trials and worries, and most of all—that consistent resourcefulness out of which, in the chess sense, truth is constructed. Pondering the alternatives, thus and thus excluding cumbrous constructions, the blots and blanks of support pawns, struggling with duals, he achieved the utmost accuracy of expression, the utmost economy of harmonious forces. If he had not been certain (as he also was in the case of literary creation) that the realization of the scheme already existed in some other world, from which he transferred it into this one, then the complex and prolonged work on the board would have been an intolerable burden to the mind, since it would have to concede, together with the possibility of realization, the possibility of its impossibility. Little by little the pieces and squares began to come to life and exchange impressions. The crude might of the queen was transformed into refined power, restrained and directed by a system of sparkling levers; the pawns grew cleverer; the knights stepped forth with a Spanish caracole. Everything had acquired sense and at the same time everything was concealed. Every creator is a plotter; and all the pieces impersonating his ideas on the board were here as conspirators and sorcerers. Only in the final instant was their secret spectacularly exposed.

One or two more refining touches, one more verification—and the problem was ready. The key to it, White's first move, was masked by its apparent absurdity—but it was precisely by the distance between this and the dazzling denouement that one of the problem's chief merits was measured; and in the way that one piece, as if greased with oil, went smoothly behind another after slipping across the whole field and creeping up under its arm, constituted an almost physical pleasure, the titillating sensation of an ideal fit. Now on the board there shone, like a constellation, a ravishing work of art, a planetarium of thought. Everything here cheered the chess player's eye: the wit of the threats and defenses, the grace of their interlocked movement, the purity of the mates (so many bullets for exactly so many hearts); every polished piece seemed to be made especially for its square; but perhaps the most fascinating of all was the fine fabric of deceit, the abundance of insidious tries (the refutation of which had its own accessory beauty), and of false trails carefully prepared for the reader.

The third lesson that Friday was with Vasiliev. The editor of the Berlin émigré daily had established relations with an obscure English periodical and now contributed a weekly article to it on the situation in Soviet Russia. Having a smattering of the language, he wrote his article out in rough, with gaps and Russian phrases interspersed, and demanded from Fyodor a literal translation of the usual phrases found in leaders: you're only young once, wonders never cease, this is a lion and not a dog (Krïlov), troubles never come singly, Peter's been paid without robbing Paul, jack of all trades, master of none, you can't make a silk purse out of a sow's ear, necessity is the mother of invention, it's only a lover's tiff, hark at the pot calling the kettle black, birds of a feather flock together, the poor man always gets the blame, it's no use crying over spilt milk, we need Reform, not reforms. And very often there occurred the expression "it produced the impression of an exploding bomb." Fyodor's task consisted in dictating from Vasiliev's rough copy Vasiliev's article in its corrected form direct into the typewriter—this seemed extraordinarily practical to Vasiliev, but actually the dictation was monstrously dragged out as a result of the agonizing pauses. But oddly enough, the method of using old saws and fables turned out to be a condensed way of conveying something of the "*moralités*" characteristic of all conscious manifestations of the Soviet authorities: reading through the finished article which had seemed rubbish as he dictated it, Fyodor detected under the clumsy translation and the author's journalistic effects the movement of a logical and forceful idea, which progressed steadily toward its goal—and calmly produced a mate in the corner.

Accompanying him afterwards to the door, Vasiliev with a sudden fierce knitting of his bristly brows said quickly:

"Well, did you see what they have done to Koncheyev? I can imagine how it affected him, what a blow, what a flop."

"He couldn't care less, I know that," replied Fyodor, and an expression of momentary disappointment appeared on Vasiliev's face.

"Oh, he's just putting it on," he retorted resourcefully, cheering up again. "In reality he's sure to be stunned."

"I don't think so," said Fyodor.

"In any case I'm sincerely grieved for him," ended Vasiliev, with the look of one who had no wish at all to part with his grief.

Somewhat weary but glad of the fact that his working day was over, Fyodor Konstantinovich boarded a tram and opened his magazine (again that glimpse of Chernyshevski's inclined face—all I know about him is that he was "a syringe of sulphuric acid," as Rozanov, I think, says somewhere, and that he wrote the novel *What to Do?*, which blends in my mind with another social writer's *Whose Fault?*). He became absorbed in an examination of the problems and soon satisfied himself that if it had not been for two end-games of genius by an old Russian master plus several interesting reprints from foreign publications, this *8* × *8* would not have been worth buying. The conscientious student exercises of the young Soviet composers were not so much "problems" as "tasks": cumbrously they treated of this or that mechanical theme (some kind of "pinning" and "unpinning") without a hint of poetry; these were chess comic strips, nothing more, and the shoving and jostling pieces did their clumsy work with proletarian seriousness, reconciling themselves to the presence of double solutions in the flat variants and to the agglomeration of police pawns.

Having missed his stop he still managed to jump off at the public garden, turning at once on his heels as a man usually does after abruptly leaving a tram, and went by the church along Agamemnonstrasse. It was early evening, the sky was cloudless and the motionless and quiet sunshine endowed every object with a peaceful, lyrical air of festivity. A bicycle, leaned against a yellow-lit wall, was slightly bent outwards, like one of the side horses of a troika, but even more perfect in shape was its transparent shadow on the wall. An elderly, stoutish gentleman, waggling his rear, was hurrying to tennis, wearing a fancy shirt and city trousers and carrying three gray balls in a net, and beside him walking swiftly on rubber soles was a German girl of the sporting sort, with an orange face and golden hair. Behind the brightly painted pumps a radio was singing in a gas station, while above its pavilion vertical yellow letters stood against the light blue of the sky—the name of a car firm—and on the second letter, on the "*E*" (a pity that it was not on the first, on the "*B*"—would have made an alphabetic vignette) sat a live blackbird, with a yellow—for economy's sake—beak, singing louder than the radio. The house in which Fyodor lived was a corner one and stuck out like a huge red ship, carrying a complex and glassy turreted structure on its bow, as if a dull, sedate architect had suddenly gone mad and made a sally into the sky. On all the little balconies which girdled the house in tier after tier there was something green blossoming, and only the Shchyogolevs' was untidily empty, with an orphaned pot on the parapet and a corpse hung out in moth-eaten furs to air.

Right at the very beginning of his stay in this flat Fyodor, supposing that he would need complete peace in the evenings, had reserved himself the right to have supper in his room. On the table among his books there now awaited him two gray sandwiches with a glossy mosaic of sausage, a cup of stale tea and a plate of pink kissel (from the morning). Chewing and sipping, he again opened 8 × 8 (he was again glared at by a butting N. G. Ch.) and began to enjoy quietly a study in which the few white pieces seemed to be hanging over an abyss and yet won the day. Then he found a charming four-mover by an American master, the beauty of which consisted not only of the cleverly hidden mating device but also of the fact that in reply to a tempting but incorrect attack, Black, by drawing in and blocking his own pieces, managed to construct just in time a hermetic stalemate. Then in one of the Soviet productions (P. Mitrofanov, Tver) a beautiful example turned up of how to come a cropper: Black had NINE pawns—the ninth having evidently been added at the last minute, in order to cure a cook, as if a writer had hastily changed "he will surely be told" in the proofs to the more correct "he will doubtless be told" without noticing that this was immediately followed by: "of her doubtful reputation."

Suddenly he felt a bitter pang—why had everything in Russia become so shoddy, so crabbed and gray, how could she have been so befooled and befuddled? Or had the old urge "toward the light" concealed a fatal flaw, which in the course of progress toward the objective had grown more and more evident, until it was revealed that this "light" was burning in the window of a prison overseer, and that was all? When had this strange dependence sprung up between the sharpening of thirst and the muddying of the source? In the forties? in the sixties? and "what to do" now? Ought one not to reject any longing for one's homeland, for any homeland besides that which is with me, within me, which is stuck like the silver sand of the sea to the skin of my soles, lives in my eyes, my blood, gives depth and distance to the background of life's every hope? Some day, interrupting my writing, I will look through the window and see a Russian autumn.

Some friends of the Shchyogolevs, gone to Denmark for the summer, had recently left Boris Ivanovich a radio. One could hear him diddling with it, strangling squeakers and creakers, moving ghostly furniture. An odd pastime!

The room meanwhile had grown dark; above the blackened

outlines of the houses beyond the yard, where the windows were already alight, the sky had an ultramarine shade and in the black wires between black chimneys there shone a star—which, like any star, could only properly be seen by switching one's vision, so that all the rest moved away out of focus. He propped his cheek on his fist and sat there at the table, looking through the window. In the distance a large clock (whose position he was always promising himself to define, but always forgot, the more so since it was never audible under the layer of daytime sounds) slowly chimed nine o'clock. It was time to go and meet Zina.

They usually met on the other side of the railway bridge, on a quiet street in the vicinity of Grunewald, where the massifs of the houses (dark crossword puzzles, in which not everything was yet filled in by yellow light) were interrupted by waste plots, kitchen gardens and coal-houses ("the ciphers and sighs of the darkness"—a line of Koncheyev's), where there was, by the way, a remarkable fence made out of another one which had been dismantled somewhere else (perhaps in another town) and which had previously surrounded the camp of a wandering circus, but the boards had now been placed in senseless order, as if nailed together by a blind man, so that the circus beasts once painted on them, and reshuffled during transit, had disintegrated into their component parts—here there was the leg of a zebra, there a tiger's back, and some animal's haunch appeared next to another creature's reversed paw: life's promise of a life to come had been kept with respect to the fence, but the rupture of the earthly images on it destroyed the earthly value of immortality; at night, however, little could be made out of it, while the exaggerated shadows of the leaves (nearby there was a streetlight) lay on the boards quite logically, in perfect order—this served as a kind of compensation, the more so since it was impossible to transfer them to another place, with the boards, having broken up and mixed the pattern: they could only be transferred *in toto*, together with the whole night.

Waiting for her arrival. She was always late—and always came by another road than he. Thus it transpired that even Berlin could be mysterious. Within the linden's bloom the streetlight winks. A dark and honeyed hush envelops us. Across the curb one's passing shadow slinks: across a stump a sable ripples thus. The night sky melts to peach beyond that gate. There water gleams, there Venice vaguely shows. Look at that street—it runs to China straight, and yonder star above the Volga glows! Oh, swear to me to put in dreams your trust, and to believe in fantasy alone, and never let your soul in prison rust, nor stretch your arm and say: a wall of stone.

She always unexpectedly appeared out of the darkness, like a shadow leaving its kindred element. At first her ankles would catch the light: she moved them close together as if she walked along a slender rope. Her summer dress was short, of night's own color, the color of the streetlights and the shadows, of tree trunks and of shining pavement—paler than her bare arms and darker than her face. This kind of blank verse Blok dedicated to Georgi Chulkov. Fyodor kissed her on her soft lips, she leaned her head for a moment on his collarbone and then, quickly freeing herself, walked beside him, at first with such sorrow on her face as if during their twenty hours of separation an unheard-of disaster had taken place, but then little by little she came to herself and now smiled—smiled as she never did during the day. What was it about her that fascinated him most of all? Her perfect understanding, the absolute pitch of her instinct for everything that he himself loved? In talking to her one could get along without any bridges, and he would barely have time to notice some amusing feature of the night before she would point it out. And not only was Zina cleverly and elegantly made to measure for him by a very painstaking fate, but both of them, forming a single shadow, were made to the measure of something not quite comprehensible, but wonderful and benevolent and continuously surrounding them.

When he had first moved in with the Shchyogolevs and seen her for the first time he had had the feeling that he already knew a great deal about her, that even her name had been long familiar to him, and certain characteristics of her life, but until he spoke to her he was unable to make out whence and how he knew it. At first he saw her only at dinner and he watched her carefully, studying her every movement. She hardly spoke to him, although by certain signs—not so much by the pupils of her eyes as by their luster that seemed slanted at him—he felt that she was noticing every glance of his and that all her movements were restricted by the lightest shrouds of that very impression she was producing on him; and because it seemed completely impossible to him that he should have any part in her life, he suffered when he detected something particularly enchanting in her and was glad and relieved when he glimpsed some flaw in her beauty. Her pale hair which radiantly and imperceptibly merged into the sunny air around her head, the light blue vein on her temple, another on her long, tender neck, her delicate hand, her sharp elbow, the narrowness of her hips, the weakness of her shoulders and the peculiar forward slant of her graceful body, as if the floor over which, gathering speed like a skater, she hastened, was always gently sloping away toward the haven of the chair or table on which lay the object she sought—all this was perceived by him with agonizing distinctness and then, during the day, was repeated an infinity of times in his memory, returning ever more lazily, pallidly and jerkily, losing life and dwindling as a result of the automatic repetitions of the disintegrating image to a mere sketch broken and blurred, in which nothing of the original life subsisted; but as soon as he saw her again, all this subconscious work directed at the destruction of her image, whose power he feared more and more, went by the board, and beauty again flared forth—her nearness, her frightening accessibility to his gaze, the reconstituted union of all the details. If, during those days, he had had to answer before some pretersensuous court (remember how Goethe said, pointing with his cane at the starry sky: "There is my conscience!") he would scarcely have decided to say that he loved her—for he had long since realized that he was incapable of giving his entire soul to anyone or anything: its working capital was too necessary to him for his own private affairs; but on the other hand, when he looked at her he immediately reached (in order to fall off again a minute later) such heights of tenderness, passion and pity as are reached by few loves. And at night, especially after long periods of mental work, half coming out of sleep not by the way of reason as it were, but through the back door of delirium, with a mad, long-drawn-out rapture, he felt her presence in the room on a camp-bed hastily and carelessly prepared by a property man, two paces away from him, but while he nursed his excitement and reveled in the temptation, in the shortness of the distance, in the heavenly possibilities, which, incidentally, had nothing of the flesh (or rather, had some blissful replacement for the flesh, expressed in semi-dreamlike terms), he was enticed back into the oblivion of sleep whence he hopelessly retreated, thinking he still continued to hold his prize. Actually she never appeared in his dreams, remaining content to delegate various representatives of hers and confidantes, who bore no resemblance to her but who produced sensations that made a fool of him—to which the bluish dawn was a witness.

And then, waking completely to the sounds of the morning, he immediately landed in the very thick of the happiness sucking at his heart, and it was good to be alive, and there glimmered in the mist some exquisite event which was just about to happen. But on trying to imagine Zina all he saw was a faint sketch which her voice behind the wall was incapable of igniting with life. And an hour or two later he met her at table and everything was renewed, and he again understood that without her there would not be any morning mist of happiness.

One evening, a fortnight after he had moved in, she knocked on his door and with a haughtily resolute step, and an almost contemptous expression on her face, entered, holding in her hand a small volume hidden in a pink cover. "I have a request," she said briskly and curtly. "Will you sign this for me?" Fyodor took the book—and recognized in it a pleasantly worn, pleasantly softened up by two years of use (this was something quite new to him) copy of his collection of poems. He began very slowly to unstopper his bottle of ink—although at other times, when he wanted to write, the cork would pop out as that in a bottle of champagne; meanwhile, Zina, watching his fingers fumbling the cork, added hastily: "Only your name, please, only your name." F. Godunov-Cherdyntsev signed his name and was about to put the date, but thought better of it, fearing she might detect in this some vulgar emphasis. "That's fine, thank you," she said and went out, blowing on the page.

The next day but one was Sunday, and around four it suddenly became clear that she was alone at home; he was reading in his room; she was in the dining room and kept making short expeditions from time to time into her own room across the hall, whistling as she went, and in her light crisp footfalls there was a topographical enigma since a door from the dining room led straight into her room. But we are reading and we will keep on reading. "Longer, longer, and for as long as possible, shall I be in a strange country. And although my thoughts, my name, my works will belong to Russia, I myself, my mortal organism, will be removed from it" (and at the same time, on his walks in Switzerland, the man who could write *thus,* used to strike dead with his cane the lizards running across his path—"the devil's brood"—as he said with the squeamishness of a Ukrainian and the hatred of a fanatic). An unimaginable return! The régime; what do I care! Under a monarchy—flags and drums, under a republic—flags and elections. . . . Again she went by. No, reading was out—too excited, too full of the feeling that another in his place would have sauntered out and addressed her with casual savoir-faire; but when he imagined himself sailing out and butting into the dining room and not knowing what to say, he began to wish that she would soon go out or that the Shchyogolevs would come home. And at the very moment when he decided to stop listening and give his undivided attention to Gogol, Fyodor quickly got up and went into the dining room.

She was sitting by the door to the balcony and with her gleaming lips half parted was aiming a thread at a needle. Through the open door one could see the little sterile balcony and hear the tinny ringing and clicking of leaping raindrops—it was a heavy, warm, April shower.

"Sorry, I didn't know you were here," said mendacious Fyodor. "I only wanted to say something about that book of mine: it's not the real thing, the poems are bad, I mean, they're not all bad, but generally speaking. Those I've been publishing these last two years in the *Gazeta* are much better."

"I liked very much the one you recited at that evening of poetry," she said. "The one about the swallow that cried out."

"Oh, were you there? Yes. But I have even better ones, I assure you."

She suddenly jumped up from her chair, threw her darning on the seat, and with her arms dangling, leaned forward, taking quick small gliding steps, she sped into her room and returned with some newspaper clippings—his and Koncheyev's poems.

"But I don't think I have everything here," she remarked.

"I didn't know that such things happened," said Fyodor and added awkwardly: "Now I'll ask them to make little holes around them with a perforator—you know, like coupons, so that you can tear them out more easily."

She continued to busy herself with a stocking stretched over a wooden mushroom and without lifting her eyes, but smiling quickly and slyly, she said:

"I also know that you used to live at seven Tannenberg Street, I often went there."

"You did?" said Fyodor, amazed.

"I used to know Lorentz's wife in St. Petersburg—she gave me drawing lessons."

"How queer," said Fyodor.

"Romanov is now in Munich," she continued. "A most objectionable character, but I always liked his things."

They talked about Romanov and about his pictures. He had reached full maturity. Museums were buying his stuff. Having passed through everything, loaded with rich experience, he had returned to an expressive harmony of line. You know his "Footballer"? There's a reproduction in this magazine, here it is. The pale, sweaty, tensely distorted face of a player depicted from top to toe preparing at full speed to shoot with terrible force at the goal. Tousled red hair, a burst of mud on his temple, the taut muscles of his bare neck. A wrinkled, soaking wet, violet singlet, clinging in spots to his body, comes down low over his spattered shorts, and is crossed with the wonderful diagonal of a mighty crease. He is in the act of hooking the ball sideways; one raised hand with wide-splayed fingers is a participant in the general tension and surge. But most important, of course, are the legs: a glistening white thigh, an enormous scarred knee, boots swollen with dark mud, thick and shapeless, but nevertheless marked by an extraordinarily precise and powerful grace. The stocking has slipped down one vigorously twisted calf, one foot is buried in rich mud, the other is about to kick—and how!—the hideous, tar-black ball—and all this against a dark gray background saturated with rain and snow. Looking at this picture one could *already* hear the whiz of the leather missile, *already* see the goalkeeper's desperate dive.

"And I know something else," said Zina. "You were supposed to help me with a translation, Charski told you about it, but for some reason you didn't turn up."

"How queer," repeated Fyodor.

There was a bang in the hall—that was Marianna Nikolavna returning—and Zina deliberately got up, gathered the cuttings together and went to her room—only later did Fyodor understand why she considered it necessary to act that way, but at the moment it seemed to him like discourtesy—and when Mrs. Shchyogolev came into the dining room the result was as if he had been stealing sugar out of the sideboard.

One evening a few days later he overheard an angry conversation from his room—the gist of which was that guests were due to arrive and that it was time for Zina to go downstairs with the key. He heard her go, and after a brief inner struggle, he thought himself up a walk—say to the slot machine by the public garden for a postage stamp. To complete the illusion, he put on a hat, although he practically never wore one. The minute light went out while he was on his way down but immediately there was a click and it went on again: that was she downstairs who had pressed the button. He found her standing by the glass door, playing with the key looped on her finger, the whole of her brightly illuminated, everything glistened—the turquoise knit of her jumper, her fingernails and the even little hairs on her forearm.

"It's unlocked," she said, but he stopped, and both of them began to look through the glass at the dark, mobile night, at the gas lamp, at the shadow of the railings.

"It doesn't look as if they're coming," she muttered, softly clinking the keys.

"Have you been waiting long?" he asked. "If you like I'll take a turn," and at that moment the light went out. "If you like I'll stay here all night." he added in the darkness.

She laughed, and then sighed abruptly, as if fed up with waiting. Through the glass the ashen light from the street fell on both of them and the shadow of the iron design on the door undulated over her and continued obliquely over him, like a shoulder-belt, while a prismatic rainbow lay on the wall. And, as often happened with him—though it was deeper this time than ever before—Fyodor suddenly felt—in this glassy darkness—the strangeness of life, the strangeness of its magic, as if a corner of it had been turned back for an instant and he had glimpsed its unusual lining. Close to his face there was her soft cinereous cheek cut across by a shadow, and when Zina suddenly, with mysterious bewilderment and a mercurial sparkle in her eyes, turned toward him and the shadow lay across her lips, oddly changing her, he took advantage of the absolute freedom in this world of shadows to take her by her ghostly elbows; but she slipped out of the pattern and with a quick jab of her finger restored the light.

"Why?" he asked.

"I'll explain it some other time," replied Zina, not taking her eyes off him.

"Tomorrow," said Fyodor.

"All right, tomorrow. Only I want to warn you that there is not going to be any conversation between you and me at home. That's final and for good."

"Then let's . . ." he began, but at this point stocky Colonel Kasatkin and his tall, faded wife loomed on the other side of the door.

"A very good evening to you, my pretty," said the colonel, cleaving the night at a single stroke. Fyodor went out into the street.

The next day he contrived to catch her on the corner as she returned from work. They arranged to meet after supper by a bench which he had spied out the night before.

"Well, why?" he asked when they had sat down.

"For five reasons," she said. "In the first place because I'm not a German girl, in the second place because only last Wednesday I broke up with my fiancé, in the third place because it would be—well, pointless, in the fourth place because you don't know me at all, and in the fifth place . . ." She fell silent, and Fyodor cautiously kissed her burning, melting, sorrowing lips. "That's why," she said, her fingers running over his and strongly compressing them.

Thereforth they met every evening. Marianna Nikolavna, who never dared to ask her about anything (the very hint of a question would draw forth the familiar storm), guessed that her daughter was meeting someone, the more so since she knew of the mysterious fiancé. He was a strange, sickly, unbalanced person (that, at least, is how Fyodor imagined him from Zina's description—and, of course, those *described* people are usually endowed with one basic characteristic: they never smile) whom she had met when she was sixteen, three years before, he being twelve years older than she, and in this seniority there was also something dark, unpleasant and embittered. Then again, according to her account, their meetings had taken place without any sentiments of love being expressed, and because she never made reference to even a single kiss, the impression was given that this had been simply an endless succession of tedious conversations. She resolutely refused to reveal his name or even his type of work (although she gave him to understand that he had been, in a sense, a man of genius) and Fyodor was secretly grateful to her for this, realizing that a ghost with neither name nor environment would fade out more easily—but neverthless he experienced pangs of disgusting jealousy which he strove not to probe, but this jealousy was always present just around the corner, and the thought that somewhere, somewhen, for all he knew, he might meet the anxious, mournful eyes of this gentleman, caused everything around him to assume nocturnal habits of life, like nature during an eclipse. Zina swore that she had never loved him, that from lack of will-power she had been dragging out a tired romance with him and would have continued to do so had it not been for Fyodor coming along; but he was unable to discern any particular lack of will-power in her, rather he noticed a mixture of feminine shyness and unfeminine resoluteness in everything. Despite the complexity of her mind, a most convincing simplicity was natural to her, so that she could permit herself much that others would be unable to get away with, and the very speed of their coming together seemed to Fyodor completely natural in the sharp light of her directness.

At home she behaved in such a way that it was monstrous to imagine an evening rendezvous with this alien, sullen young lady; but it was not pretense, rather it was also an idiosyncratic form of directness. When he once jokingly stopped her in the little corridor she paled with anger and did not come to meet him that evening, and later she forced him to swear on oath that he would never do that again. Very soon he understood why this was so: the domestic situation was of such a low-grade variety that with it as a background the fugitive touching of hands between a boarder and the landlord's daughter would have been turned simply into "goings on."

Zina's father, Oscar Grigorievich Mertz, had died of angina pectoris in Berlin four years ago, and immediately after his death Marianna Nikolavna had married a man whom Mertz would not have allowed over his threshold, one of those cocky and corny Russians who, when the occasion presents itself, savor the word "Yid" as if it were a fat fig. But whenever good Shchyogolev was away, there quite simply appeared in the house one of his fishy business friends, a skinny Baltic baron with whom Marianna Nikolavna deceived him—and Fyodor, who had happened to see the baron once or twice, could not help wondering with a shudder of disgust what they could find in one another, and, if they found anything, what procedure did they adopt, this elderly, fleshy woman with a toad's face and this old skeleton with decaying teeth.

If it was sometimes agonizing to know that Zina was alone in the flat and that their agreement prevented him talking to her, it was agonizing in a totally different way when Shchyogolev remained alone at home. No lover of solitude, Boris Ivanovich would soon begin to get bored, and from his room Fyodor would hear the rustling growth of this boredom, as if the flat were slowly being overgrown with burdocks—which had now grown up to his door. He would pray to fate that something might distract Shchyogolev, but (until he got the radio) salvation was not forthcoming.

Inevitably came the ominous, tactful knock and Boris Ivanovich, horribly smiling, squeezed sideways into the room. "Were you asleep? Did I disturb you?" he would ask, seeing Fyodor flat on his back on the sofa, and then, ingressing entirely, he would shut the door tightly behind him and sit by Fyodor's feet, sighing. "It's deadly dull, deadly dull," he would say, and would launch upon some pet subject. In the realm of literature he had a high opinion of *L'homme qui assassina* by Claude Farrère, and in the realm of philosophy he had studied the *Protocols of the Sages of Zion*. He could discuss these two books for hours and it seemed that he had read nothing else in his life. He was generous with stories of judicial practice in the provinces and with Jewish anecdotes. Instead of "we had some champagne and set out" he expressed himself as follows: "We cracked a bottle of fizz—and hup." As with most babblers, his reminiscences always contained some extraordinary conversationalist who told him endless things of interest ("I've never met another as clever as he in all my life," he would remark somewhat uncivilly)—and since it was impossible to imagine Boris Ivanovich in the role of a silent listener, one had to allow that this was a special form of split personality.

Once, when he had noticed some written-up sheets of paper on Fyodor's desk, he said, adopting a new heartfelt tone of voice: "Ah, if only I had a tick or two, what a novel I'd whip off! From real life. Imagine this kind of thing: an old dog—but still in his prime, fiery, thirsting for happiness—gets to know a widow, and she has a daughter, still quite a little girl—you know what I mean—when nothing is formed yet but already she has a way of walking that drives you out of your mind—A slip of a girl, very fair, pale, with blue under the eyes—and of course she doesn't even look at the old goat. What to do? Well, not long thinking, he ups and marries the widow. Okay. They settle down the three of them. Here you can go on indefinitely—the temptation, the eternal torment, the itch, the mad hopes. And the upshot—a miscalculation. Time flies, he gets older, she blossoms out—and not a sausage. Just walks by and scorches you with a look of contempt. Eh? D'you feel here a kind of Dostoevskian tragedy? That story, you see, happened to a great friend of mine, once upon a time in fairyland when Old King Cole was a merry old soul," and Boris Ivanovich, turning his dark eyes away, pursed his lips and emitted a melancholy, bursting sound.

"My better half," he said on another occasion, "was for twenty years the wife of a kike and got mixed up with a whole rabble of Jew in-laws. I had to expend quite a bit of effort to get rid of that stink. Zina [he alternately called his stepdaughter either this or Aïda, depending on his mood], thank God, doesn't have anything specific—you should see her cousin, one of these fat little brunettes, you know, with a fuzzy upperlip. In fact, it has occurred to me that my Marianna, when she was Madam Mertz, might have had other interests—one can't help being drawn to one's own people, you know. Let her tell you herself how she suffocated in that atmosphere, what relatives she acquired—oh, my Gott—all gabbling at table and she pouring out the tea. And to think that her mother was a lady-in-waiting of the Empress and that she herself had gone to the Smolny School for young ladies—and then she went and married a yid—to this very day she can't explain how it happened: he was rich, she says, and she was stupid, they met in Nice, she eloped to Rome with him—in the open air, you know, it all looked different—well, but when afterwards the little clan closed upon her, she saw she was stuck."

Zina told it quite differently. In her version the image of her father took on something of Proust's Swann. His marriage to her mother and their subsequent life were tinted with a romantic haze. Judging by her words and judging also by the photographs of him, he had been a refined, noble, intelligent and kindly man—even in these stiff St. Petersburg cabinet pictures with a gold stamped signature on the thick cardboard, which she showed Fyodor at night under a streetlamp, the old-fashioned luxuriance of his blond mustache and the height of his collars did nothing to spoil his delicate features and direct, laughing gaze. She told him about his scented handkerchief, and his passion for trotting races and music, and that time in his youth when he had routed a visiting grand master of chess, and the way he recited Homer by heart: in talking of him she selected things that might touch Fyodor's imagination, since it seemed to her she detected something sluggish and bored in his reaction to her reminiscences of her father, that is to the most precious thing she had to show him. He himself noticed this strangely delayed responsiveness of his. Zina had one quality which embarrassed him: her home life had developed in her a morbidly acute pride, so that even when talking to Fyodor she referred to her race with challenging emphasis, as if stressing the fact that she took for granted (a fact which its stressing denied) that he regarded Jews, not only without the hostility present to a greater or lesser degree in the majority of Russians, but did so without the chilly smile of forced goodwill. In the beginning she drew these strings so taut that he, who in general did not give a damn about the classification of people according to race, or racial interrelations, began to feel a bit awkward for her, and on the other hand, under the influence of her burning, watchful pride, he became aware of a kind of personal shame for listening silently to Shchyogolev's loathesome rot and to his trick of garbling Russian, in imitation of a farcical Jewish accent as when he said, for instance, to a wet guest who had left traces on the carpet: "Oy, vat a mudnik!"

For a certain time after her father's death their former friends and relatives from his side had automatically continued to visit her mother and her; but little by little they thinned out and fell away, and only one old couple for a long time continued to come, feeling sorry for Marianna Nikolavna, feeling sorry for the past and trying to ignore Shchyogolev's retreating to his bedroom with a cup of tea and a newspaper. But Zina had continued to preserve her connection with the world her mother had betrayed, and on visits to these former family friends she changed extraordinarily, grew softer and kinder (she herself remarked upon this), as she sat at the tea table among the quiet conversations of old people about illnesses, weddings and Russian literature.

At home she was unhappy and this unhappiness she despised. She also despised her work, even though her boss was a Jew—however, a German Jew, i.e., first of all a German, so that she had no qualms about abusing him in Fyodor's presence. So vividly, so bitterly and with such revulsion did she tell him about that lawyer's office, where she had already been working for two years, that he saw and smelled everything as if he himself were there every day. The atmosphere of her office reminded him somehow of Dickens (in a German paraphrase, it is true)—a semi-insane world of gloomy lean men and repulsive chubby ones, subterfuge, black shadows, nightmare snouts, dust, stench and women's tears. It began with a dark, steep, incredibly dilapidated staircase which was fully matched by the sinister decrepitude of the office premises, a state of affairs not true only of the chief barrister's office with its overstuffed armchairs and giant glass-topped-table furnishings. The main office, large, plain, with bare, shuddering windows, was choked with an accumulation of dirty, dusty furniture—especially dreadful was the sofa, of a dull purple color with protruding springs, a horrible, obscene object dumped here after gradually passing through the offices of all three directors—Traum, Baum and Käsebier. The innumerable shelves blocking every inch of wall were crammed with grim blue folders that stuck out their long labels, along which from time to time crawled a hungry, litigious bedbug. By the windows worked four typists: one was a hunchback who spent her salary on clothes; the second was a slender, flighty little thing whose father, a butcher, had been killed with a meat hook by his hot-tempered son; the third was a defenseless young girl who was slowly collecting a trousseau, and the fourth was a married woman, a buxom blonde, whose soul was little more than a replica of her apartment and who recounted movingly how after a day of SPIRITUAL LABOR she felt such a thirst for the relaxation of physical work that upon coming home she would throw open all the windows and joyously set about the washing. The office manager, Hamekke (a fat, coarse animal with smelly feet and a perpetually oozing furuncle on the nape, who liked to recall how in his sergeant days he had made clumsy recruits clean the barrack-room floor with toothbrushes), used to persecute the latter two with particular pleasure—one because the loss of her job for her would have meant not getting married, the other because she forthwith began to cry—those abundant, noisy tears which were so easy to provoke afforded him wholesome pleasure. Hardly literate, but gifted with an iron grip, immediately able to grasp the most unsavory aspect of any case, he was highly prized by his employers, Traum, Baum and Käsebier (a complete German idyll, with little tables amid the greenery and a wonderful view). Baum was rarely to be seen; the office maidens found that he dressed marvelously, and in truth his suit was as rigid as on a marble statue, with everlastingly creased pants and a white collar attached to a colored shirt. Käsebier cringed before his prosperous clients (for that matter all three of them cringed), but when he grew angry with Zina he accused her of putting on airs. The boss, Traum, was a shortish man with hair distributed in such a way as to conceal his bald spot, with a profile like the outside of a half-moon, tiny hands and a shapeless body, more wide than it was fat. He loved himself with a passionate and completely reciprocated love, was married to a rich, elderly widow, and having something of the actor in his nature, strove to do everything in style, spending thousands for show and haggling with his secretary over a nickel; he demanded of his employees that they refer to his wife as "*die gnädige Frau*" ("the missus telephoned," "the missus left a message") and plumed himself on a sublime ignorance of what went on at the office, although in fact he knew everything through Hamekke, right down to the last blot. In his capacity as one of the legal consultants to the French Embassy he often traveled to Paris, and since his outstanding characteristic was a tremendously smooth effrontery in the pursual of advantages, he energetically struck up useful acquaintances while there, shamelessly asking for recommendations, badgering, foisting himself upon people without feeling the snubs—his skin was like the armor on a peba. In order to gain popularity in France he wrote little books in German on French themes (*Three Portraits* for example—the Empress Eugénie, Briand and Sarah Bernhardt), and in the course of their preparation, the collecting of materials turned into the collecting of connections. These hastily compiled works, in the terrible *style moderne* of the German republic (and essentially yielding little to the works of Ludwig and the Zweigs), were dictated by him to his secretary between business, when he suddenly feigned a flow of inspiration, which flow, incidentally, always coincided with a stretch of leisure time. Some French professor into whose friendship he had insinuated himself once answered a most tender epistle of his with (for a Frenchman) extremely blunt criticism: "You write the name Deschanel at times with an *accent aigu* and at others without it. Since a certain uniformity is necessary here it would be good if you were to take a firm decision as to which system you wish to adhere to, and then stick to it. If for any reason you should desire to write this name correctly, then write it without an *accent*." Traum at once responded with a rapturously grateful letter, continuing at the same time to ask for favors. Oh, how well he could round out and sweeten his letters, what Teutonic warblings and whistlings there were in the endless modulation of his openings and conclusions, what courtesies: "*Vous avez bien voulu bien vouloir. . . .*"

His secretary, Dora Wittgenstein, who had worked for him for fourteen years, shared a small musty office with Zina. This aging woman with bags under her eyes, smelling of carrion through her cheap eau de cologne, who worked for any number of hours and who had dried up in the service of Traum, resembled an unfortunate, worn-out horse whose whole muscular system had been displaced, leaving only a few iron tendons. She was little educated, organized her life according to two or three generally accepted concepts and in her dealings with French was guided by certain private rules of her own. When Traum was writing his periodic "book" he would call her to his house on Sundays, haggle over her payment and keep her for extra time; and sometimes she would proudly inform Zina that his chauffeur had driven her home—or at least as far as the tram stop.

Zina had to work not only at translations but also, as did all the other typists, at copying out the long applications presented at court. Frequently she also had to take down in shorthand, in the presence of a client, the circumstances of his case, very often dealing with divorce. These cases were all fairly sordid—lumps of all sorts of muck and stupidity stuck together. A person from Kottbus, divorcing a wife who, according to him, was abnormal, accused her of consorting with a great Dane; the chief witness was the janitress, who through the door had allegedly heard the wife talking to the hound and expressing delight concerning certain details of its organism.

"To you it's only funny," said Zina crossly, "but honestly I can't go on, I can't, and I would abandon all this scum right away if I didn't know that another office would have the same scum, or worse. This worn-out feeling in the evening is something phenomenal, it baffles any description. What am I good for now? My spine aches so much from that typewriter that I feel like howling. And the main thing is that this will never end, because if it came to an end there'd be nothing to eat—Mother can't do anything, she can't even work as a cook because she'd only sob in her employer's kitchen and break the dishes, and her filthy husband only knows how to go bankrupt—in my opinion he was already bankrupt when he was born. You've no idea how I hate him, he's a swine, a swine, a swine. . . ."

"One could make ham out of him" said Fyodor. "I also had a fairly hard day. I wanted to write a poem for you, but somehow it hasn't quite cleared up yet."

"My darling, my joy," she exclaimed, "can all this be true—this fence and that blurry star? When I was little I didn't like drawing anything that didn't finish, so I didn't draw fences because they don't finish on paper; you can't imagine a fence that finishes, but I always did something complete, a pyramid, or a house on a hill."

"And I liked horizons most of all, and diminishing dashes beneath it—to represent the wake of the sun setting beyond the sea. And the greatest childhood torment of all was an unsharpened or broken crayon pencil."

"But then the sharpened ones. . . . Do you remember the white one? Always the longest—not like the red and blue ones—because it didn't do much work, do you remember?"

"But how much it wanted to please! The drama of the albino. *L'inutile beauté*. Anyhow, later I let it have its fill. Precisely because it drew the invisible and one could imagine lots of things. In general there await us unlimited possibilities. Only no angels, or if there must be an angel, then with a huge chest cavity, and wings like a hybrid between a bird of paradise and a condor, and talons to carry the young soul away—not 'embraced' as Lermontov has it."

"Yes, I also think that we can't end here. I can't imagine that we could cease to exist. In any case I wouldn't like to turn into anything."

"Into diffused light? What do you think of that? Not too good, I'd say. I am convinced that extraordinary surprises await us. It's a pity one can't imagine what one can't compare to anything. Genius is an African who dreams up snow. Do you know what it was that most amazed the very first Russian pilgrims when they were crossing Europe?"

"The music?"

"No, the fountains in the cities, the wet statues."

"It sometimes annoys me that you have no feeling for music. My father had such an ear that sometimes he would lie on the sofa and hum a whole opera, from beginning to end. Once he was lying like that and someone came into the next room and began talking to Mother—and he said to me: 'That voice belongs to so-and-so, I saw him twenty years ago in Carlsbad and he promised to come and see me one day.' That's what his ear was like."

"And I met Lishnevski today and he mentioned a friend of his who complained that Carlsbad was no longer what it used to be. Those were the days! he said: you stand with your mug of water and there next to you is King Edward . . . handsome, imposing man . . . suit of real English cloth. . . . Now why are you offended? What's the matter?"

"Never mind. There are some things you'll never understand."

"Don't say that. Why is your skin hot here and cold there? You are not cold? Better take a look at that moth by the lamp."

"I saw it long ago."

"Do you want me to tell you why moths fly toward the light? No one knows that."

"And you know?"

"It always seems to me that in a minute I'll guess if I just think hard enough. My father used to say that it resembled most of all a loss of equilibrium, as when learning to ride a bike you are lured by a ditch. Light in comparison with darkness is a void. Look at it circling! But there's something deeper here—in a minute I'll get it."

"I'm sorry that you didn't write your book after all. Oh, I have a thousand plans for you. I have such a clear feeling that one day you'll really lash out. Write something huge to make everyone gasp."

"I'll write," said Fyodor Konstantinovich jokingly, "a biography of Chernyshevski."

"Anything you like. But it must be quite, quite genuine. I don't need to tell you how much I like your poems, but they are never quite up to your measure, all the words are one size smaller than your real words."

"Or a novel. It's queer, I seem to remember my future works, although I don't even know what they will be about. I'll recall them completely and write them. Tell me, by the way, how do you tend to see it: are we going to meet all our lives like this, side by side on a bench?"

"Oh no," she replied in a musically dreamy voice. "In the winter we'll go to a dance, and this summer, when I have my holiday, I'll go to the sea for two weeks and send you a postcard of the breakers."

"I'll also go to the sea for two weeks."

"I don't think so. And then don't forget that we must meet sometime in the Tiergarten in the rosarium, where the statue of the princess is with the stone fan."

"Pleasant prospects," said Fyodor.

But a few days later he happened to come across that same copy of *8 × 8*; he leafed through it, looking for unfinished bits, and when all the problems turned out to be solved, he ran his eyes over the two-column extract from Chernyshevski's youthful diary; he glanced through it, smiled, and began to read it over with interest. The drolly circumstantial style, the meticulously inserted adverbs, the passion for semicolons, the bogging down of thought in midsentence and the clumsy attempts to extricate it (whereupon it got stuck at once elsewhere, and the author had to start worrying it out all over again), the drubbing-in, rubbing-in tone of each word, the knight-moves of sense in the trivial commentary on his minutest actions, the viscid ineptitude of these actions (as if some workshop glue had got onto the man's hands, and both were left), the seriousness, the limpness, the honesty, the poverty—all this pleased Fyodor so much, he was so amazed and tickled by the fact that an author with such a mental and verbal style was considered to have influenced the literary destiny of Russia, that on the very next morning he signed out the complete works of Chernyshevski from the state library. And as he read, his astonishment grew, and this feeling contained a peculiar kind of bliss.

When, a week later, he accepted a telephone invitation from Alexandra Yakovlevna ("Why does one never see you? Tell me, are you free tonight?"), he did not take *8 × 8* with him to show to his friends: this little magazine now had a sentimental value for him, the memory of an encounter. Among the guests there he found the engineer Kern and a capacious, very smooth-cheeked and taciturn gentleman with a fat, old-fashioned face, by the name of Goryainov, who was well known for the fact that being able to imitate beautifully (by stretching his mouth wide, making moist ruminant sounds, and speaking in falsetto) a certain unfortunate, cranky journalist with a poor reputation, he had grown so accustomed to this image (which thus had its revenge on him) that not only did he also pull down the corners of his mouth when imitating other of his acquaintances, but even began to look like it himself in normal conversation. Alexander Chernyshevski, grown thinner and quieter after his illness—this being the price of redeeming his health for a while—seemed that evening quite lively again, and even his familiar tic had returned; but Yasha's ghost no longer sat in the corner, leaning on his elbow among disarrayed books.

"Are you still pleased with your lodgings?" asked Alexandra Yakovlevna. "Well, I'm very glad. You don't flirt with the daughter? No? Apropos, I remembered the other day that at one time Mertz and I had some common acquaintances—he was a wonderful man, a gentleman in all senses of the word—but I don't think she cares very much to admit her origins. She does admit them? Well, I don't know. I suspect you don't quite understand these matters."

"In any case she's a girl with character," said the engineer Kern. "I once saw her at a meeting of the dance committee. She looked down her nose at everything."

"And what's her nose like?" asked Alexandra Yakovlevna.

"You know, to tell you the truth I didn't look at it very carefully, and in the final analysis all girls aspire to be beauties. Let's not be catty."

Goryainov, who sat with his hands clasped on his stomach, was silent except that occasionally he lifted his fleshy chin with a bizarre jerk and shrilly cleared his throat, as if calling to someone. "Yes, thank you, I would indeed," he said with a bow whenever he was offered jam or a glass of tea, and if he wished to impart something to his neighbor he did not turn toward him but moved his head closer, still looking ahead, and having imparted it or asked a question, slowly moved away again. In a conversation with him there were strange gaps because he did not back your speeches in any way and did not look at you, but would let the brown gaze of his small, elephant eyes stray around the room, and would convulsively clear his throat. When he spoke of himself it was always in a gloomily humorous vein. His whole appearance evoked for some reason such obsolete associations as, for example: department of the interior, cold vegetable soup, glossy rubbers, stylized snow falling outside the window, stolidity, Stolypin, statist.

"Well, my friend," said Chernyshevski vaguely, moving to a seat by Fyodor, "what have you got to say for yourself? You don't look too well."

"You remember," said Fyodor, "once about three years ago you gave me the happy advice to describe the life of your renowned namesake?"

"Absolutely not," said Alexander Yakovlevich.

"A pity—because now I'm thinking of getting down to it."

"Oh, really? Are you serious?"

"Quite serious," said Fyodor.

"But how did such a wild thought get into your head?" chimed in Mme. Chernyshevski. "Why, you ought to write—I don't know—say, the life of Batyushkov or Delvig, something in the orbit of Pushkin—but what's the point of Chernyshevski?"

"Firing practice," said Fyodor.

"An answer which is, to say the least, enigmatic," remarked the engineer Kern, and the rimless glass of his pince-nez gleamed as he attempted to crack a nut with his palms. Dragging them by one leg, Goryainov passed him the crackers.

"Why not," said Alexander Yakovlevich, coming out of a brief spell of musing, "I begin to like the idea. In our terrible times when individualism is trampled underfoot and thought is stifled it must be a great joy for a writer to immerse himself in the bright era of the sixties. I welcome it."

"Yes, but it's so distant from him!" said Mme. Chernyshevski. "There's no continuity, no tradition. Frankly speaking, I myself wouldn't be very interested in resuscitating everything that I felt in this connection when I was a college student in Russia."

"My uncle," said Kern, cracking a nut, "was thrown out of school for reading *What to Do?*"

"And what is your opinion?" said Alexandra Yakovlevna addressing Goryainov.

Goryainov spread his hands. "I don't have any particular one," he said in a thin voice, as if mimicking someone. "I've never read Chernyshevski, but when I come to think of it. . . A most boring, Lord forgive me, figure!"

Alexander Yakovlevich leaned back slightly in his armchair, blinking, twitching, his face alternately lighting up in a smile and then fading again, and said:

"Nevertheless I welcome Fyodor Konstantinovich's idea. Of course a lot strikes us today as both comic and boring. But in that era there is something sacred, something eternal. Utilitarianism, the negation of art and so on—all this is merely an accidental wrapping, under which it is impossible not to distinguish its basic features: reverence for the whole human race, the cult of freedom, ideas of equality—equality of rights. It was an era of great emancipations, the peasants from the landowners, the citizen from the state, women from domestic bondage. And don't forget that not only were the best principles of the Russian liberation movement born then—a thirst for knowledge, steadfastness of spirit, heroic self-sacrifice—but also it was precisely in this era, fed by it in one way or another, that such giants as Turgenev, Nekrasov, Tolstoy and Dostoevsky were developing. Moreover it goes without saying that Nikolai Gavrilovich Chernyshevski himself was a man with a vast, versatile mind, with enormous, creative willpower, and the fact that he endured dreadful sufferings for the sake of his ideology, for the sake of humanity, for the sake of Russia, more than redeems a certain harshness and rigidity in his critical views. Moreover I maintain that he was a superb critic—penetrating, honest, brave. . . . No, no, it's wonderful, you must certainly write it!"

The engineer Kern had already been on his feet for some time, walking about the room, shaking his head and bursting to say something.

"What are we talking about?" he suddenly exclaimed, taking hold of the back of a chair. "Who cares what Chernyshevski thought of Pushkin? Rousseau was a lousy botanist, and I wouldn't have been treated by Dr. Chekhov for anything in the world. Chernyshevski was first of all a learned economist and that's how he should be regarded—and with all my respect for Fyodor Konstantinovich's poetic talents, I am somewhat doubtful that he is capable of appreciating the merits and demerits of his man's *Commentaries on John Stuart Mill.*"

"Your comparison is absolutely wrong," said Alexandra Yakovlevna. "It's ridiculous! Chekhov didn't leave the slightest trace in medicine, Rousseau's musical compositions are mere curiosities, but in this case no history of Russian literature can omit Chernyshevski. But there's something else I don't understand," she continued swiftly. "What interest does Fyodor Konstantinovich have in writing about people and times to which his whole mentality is completely alien? Of course I don't know what his approach will be. But if he, let's speak plainly, wants to show up the progressive critics then it's not worth the effort: Volynski and Eichenwald did this long ago."

"Oh, come, come," said Alexander Yakovlevich, "*das kommt nicht in Frage.* A young writer has become interested in one of the most important epochs in Russian history and is about to write a literary biography of one of its major figures. I don't see anything strange in that. It's not very difficult to get to know the subject, he'll find more than enough books, and the rest all depends on talent. You say approach, approach. But granted a talented approach to a given subject, sarcasm is *a priori* excluded, is irrelevant. That's how it seems to me at least."

"Did you see how Koncheyev was attacked last week?" asked the engineer Kern, and the conversation took another turn.

Out on the street when Fyodor was saying good-by to Goryainov the latter retained his hand in his own large, soft hand and said puckering up his eyes: "Let me tell you, my lad, you're quite a joker. Recently there died the social-democrat Belenki—a kind of perpetual émigré, so to speak: he was exiled by both the Tsar and the proletariat, so that whenever he indulged in his reminiscences he would begin: *"U nas v Zheneve,* chez nous à Genève. . . ." Perhaps you'll write about him as well?"

"I don't understand?" said Fyodor half-questioningly.

"No, but on the other hand I understood perfectly. You are as much preparing to write about Chernyshevski as I am about Belenki, but then you made a fool of your audience and stirred up an interesting argument. All the best, good night," and he left with his slow, heavy gait, leaning on a cane and holding one shoulder slightly higher than the other.

The way of life to which he had become addicted while studying his father's activities was now renewed for Fyodor. It was one of those repetitions, one of those thematic "voices" with which, according to all the rules of harmony, destiny enriches the life of observant men. But now, taught by experience, he did not allow himself his former slovenliness in the use of sources and provided even the smallest note with an exact label of its origin. In front of the national library, near a stone pool, pigeons strolled cooing among the daisies on the lawn. The books to be taken out arrived in a little wagon along sloping rails at the bottom of the apparently small premises, where they awaited distribution, and where there seemed to be only a few books lying around on the shelves when in fact there was an accumulation of thousands.

Fyodor would embrace his portion, struggling with its disintegrating weight, and walk to the bus stop. From the very beginning the image of his planned book had appeared to him extraordinarily distinctly in tone and outline, he had the feeling that for every detail he ran to earth there was already a place prepared and that even the work of hunting up material was already bathed in the light of the forthcoming book, just as the sea throws a blue light on a fishing boat, and the boat itself together with this light is reflected in the water. "You see," he explained to Zina, "I want to keep everything as it were on the very brink of parody. You know those idiotic '*biographies romancées*' where Byron is coolly slipped a dream extracted from one of his own poems? And there must be on the other hand an abyss of seriousness, and I must make my way along this narrow ridge between my own truth and a caricature of it. And most essentially, there must be a single uninterrupted progression of thought. I must peel my apple in a single strip, without removing the knife."

As he studied his subject he saw that in order to completely soak himself in it he would have to extend his field of activity two decades in either direction. Thus an amusing feature of the age was revealed to him—essentially trifling, but proving to be a valuable guideline: during fifty years of utilitarian criticism, from Belinski to Mihailovski, there was not a single molder of opinion who did not take the opportunity to jeer at the poems of Fet. And into what metaphysical monsters turned sometimes the most sober judgments of these materialists on this or that subject, as if the Word, Logos, were avenging itself on them for being slighted! Belinski, that likable ignoramus, who loved lilies and oleanders, who decorated his window with cacti (as did Emma Bovary), who kept five kopecks, a cork and a button in the empty box discarded by Hegel and who died of consumption with a speech to the Russian people on his bloodstained lips, startled Fyodor's imagination with such pearls of realistic thought as, for example: "In nature everything is beautful, excepting only those ugly phenomena which nature herself has left unfinished and hidden in the darkness of the earth or water (molluscs, worms, infusoria, and so on)." Similarly, in Mihailovski it was easy to discover a metaphor floating belly upwards as for example: "[Dostoevski] struggled like a fish against the ice, ending up at times in the most humiliating positions"; this *humiliated fish* rewarded one for working through all the writings of the "reporter on contemporary issues." From here there was a direct transition to the fighting lexicon of the present day, to the style of Steklov speaking of Chernyshevski's times ("The plebeian writer who nestled in the pores of Russian life . . . branded routine opinions with the battering ram of his ideas"), or to the idiom of Lenin who in his polemical heat attained the heights of absurdity: ("Here there is no fig leaf . . . and the idealist stretches out his hand directly to the agnostic"). Russian prose, what crimes are committed in thy name! A contemporary critic wrote about Gogol: "His people are deformed grotesques, his characters, Chinese-lantern shadows, the events he depicts, impossible and ridiculous," and this fully corresponded to the opinions held by Skabichevski and Mihailovski about Chekhov—opinions that, like a fuse lit at the time, have now blown these critics to bits.

He read Pomyalovski (honesty in the role of tragic passion) and found there this lexical fruit salad: "little raspberry-red lips like cherries." He read Nekrasov, and sensing a certain urban-journalist defect in his (frequently enchanting) poetry, he found an apparent explanation for the vulgarisms in his pedestrian *Russian Women* ("How jolly, furthermore, To share your every thought in common With someone you adore") in the discovery that despite his walks in the country he confused gadflies with bumblebees and wasps ([over the flock] "a restless swarm of bumblebees" and ten lines lower down: the horses under the smoke of a bonfire "seek shelter from the wasps"). He read Herzen and was again better able to understand the flaw (a false glib glitter) in his generalizations when he noticed that this author, having a poor knowledge of English (witnessed by his surviving autobiographical reference, which begins with the amusing Gallicism "I am born"), had confused the sounds of two English words "beggar" and "bugger" and from this had made a brilliant deduction concerning the English respect for wealth.

Such a method of evaluation, taken to its extreme, would be even sillier than approaching writers and critics as exponents of general ideas. What is the significance of Suhoshchokov's Pushkin's not liking Baudelaire, and is it fair to condemn Lermontov's prose because he twice refers to some impossible "crocodile" (once in a serious and once in a joking comparison)? Fyodor stopped in time, thus preventing the pleasant feeling that he had discovered an easily applicable criterion from being impaired by its abuse.

He read a great deal—more than he had ever read. Studying the short stories and novels of the men of the sixties he was surprised by their insistence on the various ways their characters saluted one another. Meditating over the thralldom of Russian thought, that eternal tributary to this or that Golden Horde, he was carried away by weird comparisons. Thus, in paragraph 146 of the censorship code for 1826, in which authors were enjoined to "uphold chaste morals and not to replace them solely by beauty of the imagination," one had only to replace "chaste" by "civic" or some such word in order to get the private censorship code of the radical critics; and similarly, when the reactionary Bulgarin informed the government in a confidential letter of his readiness to color the characters in the novel he was writing to suit the censor, one could not help thinking of the later fawning that even such authors as Turgenev indulged in before the Court of Progressive Public Opinion; and the radical Shchedrin, using a cart shaft to fight with and ridiculing Dostoevski's sickness, or Antonovich, who called that author "a whipped and expiring animal," were little different from right-winger Burenin, who persecuted the unfortunate poet Nadson. In the writings of another radical critic, Zaytsev, it was comical to find, forty years before Freud, the theory that "all these aesthetic feelings and similar illusions 'elevating us' are only modifications of the sexual instinct . . ."; this was the same Zaytsev who called Lermontov a "disillusioned idiot," bred silkworms in leisured exile at Locarno (they never cocooned), and often crashed down the stairs from shortsightedness.

Fyodor tried to sort out the mishmash of philosophical ideas of the time, and it seemed to him that in the very roll call of names, in their burlesque consonance, there was manifested a kind of sin against thought, a mockery of it, a blemish of the age, when some extravagantly praised Kant, others *Kont* (Comte), others again Hegel or Schlegel. And on the other hand he began to comprehend by degrees that such uncompromising radicals as Chernyshevski, with all their ludicrous and ghastly blunders, were, no matter how you looked at it, real heroes in their struggle with the governmental order of things (which was even more noxious and more vulgar than was their own fatuity in the realm of literary criticism), and that other oppositionists, the liberals or the Slavophiles, who risked less, were by the same token worth less than these iron squabblers.

He sincerely admired the way Chernyshevski, an enemy of capital punishment, made deadly fun of the poet Zhukovski's infamously benign and meanly sublime proposal to surround executions with a mystic secrecy (since, in public, he said, the condemned man brazenly puts on a bold face, thus bringing the law into disrepute) so that those attending the hanging would not see but would only hear solemn church hymns from behind a curtain, for an execution should be moving. And while reading this Fyodor recalled his father saying that innate in every man is the feeling of something insuperably abnormal about the death penalty, something like the uncanny reversal of action in a looking glass that makes everyone left-handed: not for nothing is everything reversed for the executioner: the horse-collar is put on upside down when the robber Razin is taken to the scaffold; wine is poured for the headsman not with a natural turn of the wrist but backhandedly; and if, according to the Swabian code, an insulted actor was permitted to seek satisfaction by striking the *shadow* of the offender, in China it was precisely an actor—a shadow—who fulfilled the duties of the executioner, all responsibility being as it were lifted from the world of men and transformed into the inside-out one of mirrors.

He clearly sensed a deception on a governmental scale in the actions of the "Tsar-Liberator," who very soon got bored with all this business of granting freedoms; for it was the Tsar's boredom that gave the chief hue to reaction. After the manifesto the police fired into the people at the station of Bezdna—and Fyodor's epigrammatic vein was tickled by the tasteless temptation to regard the further fate of Russia's rulers as the run between the stations Bezdna (Bottomless) and Dno (Bottom).

Gradually, as a result of all these raids on the past of Russian thought, he developed a new yearning for Russia that was less physical than before, a dangerous desire (with which he successfully struggled) to confess something to her and to convince her of something. And while piling up knowledge, while extracting his finished creation out of this mountain, he remembered something else: a pile of stones on an Asian pass; warriors going on a campaign each placed a stone there; on the way back each took a stone from the pile; that which was left represented forever the number of those fallen in battle. Thus in a pile of stones Tamerlane foresaw a monument.

By winter he had already got into the writing of it, having passed imperceptibly from accumulation to creation. Winter, like most memorable winters and like all winters introduced for the sake of a narrational phrase, turned out (they always "turn out" in such cases) to be cold. At his evening trysts with Zina in an empty little café where the counter was painted an indigo color and where dark blue gnomelike lamps, miserably posing as vessels of coziness, glowed on six or seven little tables, he read her what he had written during the day and she listened, her painted lashes lowered, leaning on one elbow, playing with a glove or a cigarette case. Sometimes the proprietor's dog would come up, a fat mongrel bitch with low-hanging bubs, and would place its head on Zina's knee, and beneath the stroking and smiling hand that smoothed back the skin on its silky round forehead, the dog's eyes would take on a Chinese slant, and when she was given a lump of sugar, she would take it, waddle in a leisurely manner into a corner, roll up there and very loudly start crunching. "Wonderful, but I'm not sure you can say it like that in Russian," said Zina sometimes, and after an argument he would correct the expression she had questioned. Chernyshevski she called Chernysh for short and got so used to considering him as belonging to Fyodor, and partly to her, that his actual life in the past appeared to her as something of a plagiarism. Fyodor's idea of composing his biography in the shape of a ring, closed with the clasp of an apocryphal sonnet (so that the result would be not the form of a book, which by its finiteness is opposed to the circular nature of everything in existence, but a continuously curving, and thus infinite, sentence), seemed at first to her to be incapable of embodiment on flat, rectangular paper—and so much the more was she overjoyed when she noticed that nevertheless a circle was being formed. She was completely unconcerned whether or not the author clung assiduously to historical truth—she took that on trust, for if it were not thus it would simply not have been worth writing the book. A deeper truth, on the other hand, for which he alone was responsible and which he alone could find, was for her so important that the least clumsiness or fogginess in his words seemed to be the germ of a falsehood, which had to be immediately exterminated. Gifted with a most flexible memory, which twined like ivy around what she perceived, Zina by repeating such word-combinations as she particularly liked ennobled them with her own secret convolution, and whenever Fyodor for any reason changed a turn of phrase which she had remembered, the ruins of the portico stood for a long time on the golden horizon, reluctant to disappear. There was an extraordinary grace in her responsiveness which imperceptibly served him as a regulator, if not as a guide. And sometimes when at least three customers had gathered, an old lady pianist in pince-nez would sit at the upright piano in the corner and play Offenbach's Barcarolle as a march.

He was already approaching the end of his work (the hero's birth, to be precise) when Zina said it would not hurt him to relax and therefore on Saturday they would go together to a fancy-dress ball at the house of an artist friend of hers. Fyodor was a bad dancer, could not stand German bohemians and moreover refused point-blank to *put fantasy in a uniform*, which is what in effect masked balls do. They compromised on his wearing a half-mask and a dinner jacket that had been made about four years previously and not worn more than four times in the interim. "And I'll go as a—" she began dreamily, but cut herself short. "Only not as a boyar maiden and not as Columbine, I beg you," said Fyodor. "That would be just like me," said she, scornfully. "Oh, I assure you it'll be terribly gay," she added tenderly, to dissipate his gloom. "Why, after all we'll be all alone in the crowd. I so want to go! We'll be the whole night together and no one will know who you are, and I've thought myself up a costume specially for you." He conscientiously imagined her with a naked, tender back and pale bluish arms—but here all kinds of excited bestial faces slipped through illegally, the coarse trash of noisy German revels; bad liquor inflamed his gullet, he belched from the chopped-egg sandwiches; but he again concentrated his thoughts, revolving to the music, on Zina's transparent temple vein. "Of course it'll be gay, of course we'll go," he said with conviction.

It was decided that she should set off at nine and he would follow an hour later. Cramped by the time limit, he did not sit down to work after supper but fiddled around with a new émigré magazine where Koncheyev was twice mentioned fleetingly, and these casual references, which implied the poet's general recognition, were more valuable than even the most favorable review: only six months ago this would have provoked in him what Pushkin's envious Salieri felt, but now he himself was amazed by his own indifference to another's fame. He looked at his watch and slowly began to change. He unearthed his drowsy-looking dinner jacket, and lapsed into thought. Still meditating, he took out a starched shirt, put his evasive collar studs in, climbed into it, shivering from its rigid chill. Again was motionless for a moment, then automatically pulled on his black trousers with a stripe, and remembering that he had made up his mind only that morning to cross out the last of the sentences he had written the previous day, he bent over the already heavily corrected page. As he read the sentence over, he wondered—should he leave it intact after all, made an insertion mark, wrote in an additional adjective, froze over it—and swiftly crossed out the whole sentence. But to leave the paragraph in that condition, i.e., its construction hanging over a precipice with a boarded window and a crumbling porch, was a physical impossibility. He examined his notes for this part and suddenly—his pen stirred and started to fly. When he looked again at his watch it was three in the morning, he had the chills, and everything in the room was dim from tobacco smoke. Simultaneously he heard the click of the American lock. His door was ajar, and as she passed by it through the hall, Zina caught sight of him, pale, with mouth wide open, in an unbuttoned starched shirt with suspenders trailing on the floor, pen in hand and the half-mask on his desk showing black against the whiteness of paper. She locked herself in her room with a bang and everything again grew quiet. "That's a fine mess" said

Fyodor in a low voice. "What have I done?" Thus he never found out what dress Zina had gone in; but the book was finished.

A month later, on a Monday, he took the fair copy to Vasiliev, who as early as last autumn, knowing of his investigations, had half offered to have the *Life of Chernyshevski* published by the house attached to the *Gazeta*. The following Wednesday Fyodor was again there, chatting quietly with old Stupishin, who used to wear bedroom slippers at the office. Suddenly the study door opened and filled with the bulk of Vasiliev, who looked blackly at Fyodor for a moment, and then said impassively: "Be so good as to come in," and moved to one side for him to slip through.

"Well, have you read it?" asked Fyodor as he took a seat across the table.

"I have," replied Vasiliev in a gloomy bass.

"Personally," said Fyodor briskly, "I would like it to come out this spring."

"Here's your manuscript," said Vasiliev suddenly, knitting his brows and handing him the folder. "Take it. There can be no question of my being party to its publication. I assumed that this was a serious work, and it turns out to be a reckless, antisocial, mischievous improvisation. I am amazed at you."

"Well, that's nonsense, you know," said Fyodor.

"No, my dear sir, it's not nonsense," roared Vasiliev, irately fingering the objects on his desk, rolling a rubber stamp, changing the positions of meek books "for review," conjoined accidentally, with no hopes for permanent happiness. "No, my dear sir! There are certain traditions of Russian public life which the honorable writer does not dare to subject to ridicule. I am absolutely indifferent to whether you have talent or not, I only know that to lampoon a man whose works and sufferings have given sustenance to millions of Russian intellectuals is unworthy of any talent. I know that you won't listen to me, but nevertheless [and Vasiliev, grimacing with pain, clutched at his heart] I beg you as a friend not to try to publish this thing, you will wreck your literary career, mark my words, everyone will turn away from you."

"I prefer the backs of their heads," said Fyodor.

That night he was invited to the Chernyshevskis, but Alexandra

Yakovlevna put him off at the last minute: her husband was "down with flu" and "ran a high temperature." Zina had gone to the cinema with someone so that he only met her the next evening. "'Kaput on the first try,' as your stepfather would put it," he said in reply to her question about the manuscript and (as they used to write in the old days) briefly recounted his conversation at the editorial office. Indignation, tenderness toward him, the urge to help him immediately, found expression with her in a burst of enterprising energy. "Oh, *that's* how it is!" she exclaimed. "All right. I'll get the money for publication, that's what I'll do."

"For the baby a meal, for the father a coffin," he said (transposing the words in a line of Nekrasov's poem about the heroic wife who sells her body to get her husband his supper), and another time she would have taken offense at this bold joke.

She borrowed somewhere a hundred and fifty marks and added seventy of her own which she had put away for winter—but this sum was insufficient, and Fyodor decided to write to Uncle Oleg in America, who regularly helped his mother and who also used occasionally to send a few dollars to him. The composition of this letter was put off from day to day, however, just as he put off, in spite of Zina's exhortations, an attempt to get his book printed serially by an émigré literary magazine in Paris, or to interest the publishing house there which had brought out Koncheyev's verses. In her free time she undertook to type the manuscript in the office of a relation of hers and from him she collected another fifty marks. She was angered by Fyodor's inertia—a consequence of his hatred for any practical affairs. He in the meantime occupied himself lightheartedly with composing chess problems, dreamily went about his lessons, and rang up Mme. Chernyshevski daily: Alexander Yakovlevich's flu had changed into an acute inflammation of the kidneys. One day in the Russian bookshop he noticed a tall, portly gentleman with a large-featured face, wearing a black felt hat (a strand of chestnut hair falling from under it) who glanced at him affably and even with a kind of encouragement. Where have I met him? thought Fyodor quickly, trying not to look. The other approached and offered his hand, generously, naïvely, defenselessly spreading it wide, spoke . . . and Fyodor remembered: it was

Busch, who two and a half years ago had read his play at that literary circle. Recently he had published it and now, pushing Fyodor with his hip, nudging him with his elbow, an infantine smile trembling on his noble, always slightly sweaty face, he produced a wallet, from the wallet an envelope and from the envelope a clipping—a pitiful little review which had appeared in the Rigan émigré newspaper.

"Now," he said with awesome weightiness, "this Thing is also coming out in German. Moreover I am now working on a Novel."

Fyodor tried to get away from him, but the latter left the shop with him and suggested they should go together, and since Fyodor was on his way to a lesson, and thus was tied to a definite route, all he could do to try and save himself from Busch was to quicken his step, but this so speeded up his companion's speech that he slowed down again in horror.

"My Novel," said Busch, looking into the distance and stretching aside his hand, with a rattling cuff protruding from the sleeve of his black overcoat, in order to stop Fyodor Konstantinovich (the overcoat, the black hat and the strand of hair gave him the appearance of a hypnotist, a chess maestro or a musician), "my Novel is the tragedy of a philosopher who has discovered the absolute formula. He starts speaking and speaks thus [Busch, like a conjurer, plucked a notebook out of the air and began to read on the move]: 'One has to be a complete ass not to deduct from the fact of the atom the fact that the universe itself is merely an atom, or, it would be truer to say, some kind of trillionth of an atom. This was realized with his intuition already by that genius Blaise Pascal. But let us proceed, Louisa! [At the sound of this name Fyodor started and clearly heard the sounds of the German grenadier march: "Fa-arewell, Louisa! wipe your eyes and don't cry; not every bullet kills a good guy," and this subsequently continued to sound as if passing under the window of Busch's subsequent words.] Exert, my dear, your attention. First, let me give a fanciful example. Let us assume that a certain physicist has managed to track down, out of the absolute-unthinkable sum of atoms out of which the All is composited, that fatal atom with which our reasoning is concerned. We are supposing that he has brought his splitting down to the least essence of that very atom, at which moment the Shadow of a Hand [the physicist's hand!] falls on our universe with catastrophic results, because the universe is but the final fraction of one, I think, central atom, of those it consists of. It's not easy to understand, but if you understand this you will understand everything. Out of the prison of mathematics! The whole is equal to the smallest part of the whole, the sum of the parts is equal to one part of the sum. This is the secret of the world, the formula of absolute-infinity, but having made such a discovery, the human personality can no longer go on walking and talking. Shut your mouth, Louisa!' That's him talking to a cutie, his lady friend," added Busch with good-natured indulgence, shrugging one mighty shoulder.

"If you're interested, I can read it to you from the beginning sometime," he continued. "The theme is colossal. And you, may I ask, what are you doing?"

"I?" said Fyodor with a slight smile. "I have also written a book, a book about the critic Chernyshevski, only I can't find a publisher for it."

"Ah! The popularizator of German materialism—of Hegel's traducers, the grobianistic philosophers! Very honorable. I am more and more convinced that my publisher will take your work with pleasure. He's a comic personality and for him literature is a closed book. But I have the position of adviser to him and he will hear me out. Give me your telephone number. I'll be seeing him tomorrow—and if he agrees in principle, then I'll skim through your manuscript, and I dare to hope that I'll recommend it in the most flattering manner."

What rot, thought Fyodor and therefore was extremely surprised when the next day the kind soul did in fact ring. The publisher turned out to be a plumpish man with a sad nose, reminding him somewhat of Alexander Yakovlevich, with the same red ears and a stipple of black hairs along each side of his polished baldpate. His list of published books was small, but remarkably eclectic: translations of some German psychoanalytic novels done by an uncle of Busch's; *The Poisoner* by Adelaida Svetozarov; a collection of funny stories; an anonymous poem entitled "I"; but among this trash there were two or three genuine books, such as, for example, the wonderful *Stairway to the Clouds* by Hermann Lande and also his *Metamorphoses of Thought.* Busch reacted to the *Life of Chernyshevski* as to a good slap at Marxism (to the delivery of which Fyodor had not given the least thought when writing his work) and at the second meeting the publisher, evidently the nicest of men, promised to publish the book by Easter; i.e., in a month's time. He gave no advance and offered five percent on the first thousand copies, but on the other hand he raised the author's percentage to thirty on the second thousand, which seemed to Fyodor both just and generous. However, he was completely indifferent to this side of the business (and to the fact that the sales of émigré writers seldom reached five hundred copies). Other emotions overwhelmed him. Having shaken the moist hand of radiant Busch he emerged onto the street like a ballerina flying out onto the fluorescent stage. The drizzle seemed a dazzling dew, happiness stood in his throat, rainbow nimbi trembled around the streetlamps, and the book he had written talked to him at the top of its voice, accompanying him the whole time like a torrent on the other side of a wall. He headed for the office where Zina worked; opposite that black building, with benevolent-looking windows inclined toward him, he found the pub where they were to meet.

"Well, what news?" she asked, entering quickly.

"No, he won't take it," said Fyodor watching, with delighted attention, her face cloud as he toyed with his power over it and anticipated the exquisite light he was about to summon.

Chapter Four

Alas! In vain historians pry and probe:
The same wind blows, and in the same live robe
Truth bends her head to fingers curved cupwise;

And with a woman's smile and a child's care
Examines something she is holding there
Concealed by her own shoulder from our eyes.

A SONNET, apparently barring the way, but perhaps, on the contrary, providing a secret link which would explain everything—if only man's mind could withstand that explanation. The soul sinks into a momentary dream—and now, with the peculiar theatrical vividness of those risen from the dead they come out to meet us: Father Gavriil, a long staff in his hand, wearing a silk, garnet-red chasuble, with an embroidered sash across his big stomach; and with him, already illuminated by the sun, an extremely attractive little boy—pink, awkward, delicate. They draw near. Take off your hat, Nikolya. Hair with a russet glint, freckles on his little forehead, and in his eyes the angelic clarity characteristic of nearsighted children. Afterwards (in the quiet of their poor and distant parishes) priests with names derived from Cypress, Paradise, and Golden Fleece recalled his bashful beauty with some surprise: the cherub, alas, proved to be pasted on tough gingerbread which was too hard for many to bite into.

Having greeted us, Nikolya again dons his hat, a gray, downy top hat, and quietly withdraws, very sweet in his homemade little coat and nankeen breeches, while his father, a kindly cleric who dabbles in horticulture, entertains us with talk of Saratov cherries, plums and pears. A whirl of torrid dust veils the picture.

As is invariably noted at the beginning of positively all literary biographies, the little boy was a glutton for books. He excelled in his studies. For his first writing exercise he painstakingly reproduced: "Obey your sovereign, honor him and submit to his laws," and the compressed ball of his index finger thus remained ink-stained forever. Now the thirties are over and the forties have begun.

At the age of sixteen he had a sufficient grasp of languages to read Byron, Eugène Sue and Goethe (being ashamed to the end of his days of his barbarous pronunciation) and already had a command of seminary Latin, owing to his father's being an educated man. Besides this he took Polish with a certain Sokolovski, while a local orange merchant taught him Persian—and also tempted him with the use of tobacco.

Upon entering the Saratov seminary, he showed himself there to be a meek pupil and was never once flogged. He was nicknamed "the little toff," although in fact he was not averse to general fun and games. In the summer he played dibs and took pleasure in bathing; never did he learn to swim, however, nor to fashion sparrows out of clay, nor to make nets for catching tiddlers: the holes came out uneven and the threads got tangled—fish are harder to catch than human souls (but even the souls later escaped through the rents). In winter, in the snowy darkness, a rowdy gang used to tear downhill in a huge, horse-drawn, flat sled while roaring out dactylic hexameters—and the chief of police, in his nightcap, would pull aside his curtain and grin encouragingly, happy that the seminarists' frolics would frighten off any night burglars.

He would have been a priest, like his father, and would have reached, very likely, a high rank—but for the regrettable incident with Major Protopopov. This was a local landowner, a bon vivant, a wencher, a dog lover: it was his son that Father Gavriil too hastily recorded in the parish register as illegitimate; meanwhile, it transpired that the wedding had been celebrated—without fuss, true, but honorably—forty days before the child's birth. Dismissed from his post as member of the consistory, Father Gavriil fell into such a depression that his hair turned gray. "That's how they reward the labors of poor priests," repeated his wife wrathfully—and it was decided to give Nikolya a secular education. What later became of the young Protopopov—did he find out one day that because of him . . . ? Was he seized with a sacred thrill. . . ? Or tiring rapidly of the pleasures of ebullient youth . . . withdrawing. . . ?

Incidentally: the landscape which not long before had with wondrous languor unfolded along the passage of the immortal *brichka;* all that Russian viatic lore, so untrammeled as to bring tears to the eyes; all the humbleness that gazes from the field, from a hillock, from between oblong clouds; that suppliant, expectant beauty which is ready to rush toward you at the slightest sigh and share your tears; in short, the landscape hymned by Gogol passed unnoticed before the eyes of the eighteen-year-old Nikolay Gavrilovich, who with his mother was traveling in a carriage drawn by their own horses from Saratov to St. Petersburg. The whole way he kept reading a book. It goes without saying that he preferred his "war of words" to the "corn ears bowing in the dust."

Here the author remarked that in some of the lines he had already composed there continued without his knowledge a fermentation, a growth, a swelling of the pea, or, more precisely: at one or another point the further development of a given theme became manifest—the theme of the "writing exercises" for example: already during his student days Nikolay Gavrilovich was copying out for his own benefit Feuerbach's "Man is what he eats" (it comes out smoother in German and even better with the help of the spelling now accepted in Russian: *chelovek est' to chto est*). We remark also that the theme of "nearsightedness" develops, too, beginning with the fact that as a child he knew only those faces which he kissed and could see only four out of the seven stars of the Great Bear. His first—copper—spectacles donned at the age of twenty. A teacher's silver spectacles bought for six rubles so as to distinguish his students in the Cadet School. The gold spectacles of a molder of public opinion put on in the days when *The Contemporary* was penetrating to the most fabulous depths of the Russian countryside. Again copper spectacles, bought at a little trading post beyond Lake Baikal, where they also sold felt boots and vodka. The yearning for spectacles in a letter to his sons from Yakutsk territory—requesting lenses for such and such vision (with a line marking the distance at which he could make out writing). Here the theme of spectacles dims for a time. . . . Let us follow another theme—that of "angelic clarity." This is how it develops subsequently: Christ died for mankind because he loved mankind, which I also love, for which I shall also die. "Be a second Savior," his best friend advises him—and how he glows—oh, timid! Oh, weak! (an almost Gogolian exclamation mark appears fleetingly in his student diary). But the "Holy Ghost" must be replaced by "Common Sense." Is not poverty the mother of vice? Christ should first have shod everybody and crowned them with flowers and only then have preached morality. Christ the Second would begin by putting an end to material want (aided here by the machine which we have invented). And strange to say, but . . . something came true—yes, it was as if something came true. His biographers mark his thorny path with evangelical signposts (it is well known that the more leftist the Russian commentator the greater is his weakness for expressions like "the Golgotha of the revolution"). Chernyshevski's passions began when he reached Christ's age. Here the role of Judas was filled by Vsevolod Kostomarov; the role of Peter by the famous poet Nekrasov, who declined to visit the jailed man. Corpulent Herzen, ensconced in London, called Chernyshevski's pillory column "The companion piece of the Cross." And in a famous Nekrasov iambic there was more about the Crucifixion, about the fact that Chernyshevski had been "sent to remind the earthly kings of Christ." Finally, when he was completely dead and they were washing his body, that thinness, that steepness of the ribs, that *dark pallor* of the skin and those long toes vaguely reminded one of his intimates of "The Removal from the Cross"—by Rembrandt, is it? But even this isn't the end of the theme: there is still the posthumous outrage, without which no holy life is complete. Thus the silver wreath with the inscription on its ribbon TO THE APOSTLE OF TRUTH FROM THE INSTITUTIONS OF HIGHER EDUCATION OF THE CITY OF KHARKOV was stolen five years later from the ironworked chapel; moreover the cheerful sacrilegist broke the dark-red glass and scratched his name and the date on the frame with a splinter of it. And then a third theme is ready to unfold—and to unfold quite fantastically if we don't keep an eye on it: the theme of "traveling," which can lead to God knows what—to a tarantass with a gendarme in azure uniform, and even more—to a Yakutsk sled harnessed to half a dozen dogs. Goodness, that Vilyuisk captain of the police is also called Protopopov! But for the time being all is very pacific. The comfortable traveling carriage rolls on, Nikolay's mother Eugenia Egorovna dozes with a handkerchief spread over her face, while her son reclines beside her reading a book—and a hole in the road loses its meaning of hole, becoming merely a typographical unevenness, a jump in the line—and now again the words pass evenly by, the trees pass by and their shadow passes over the pages. And here at last is St. Petersburg.

He liked the blueness and transparency of the Neva—what an abundance of water in the capital, how pure that water was (he quickly ruined his stomach on it); but he particularly liked the orderly distribution of the water, the sensible canals: how nice when you can join this with that and that with this; and derive the idea of good from that of conjunction. In the mornings he would open his window and with a reverence still heightened by the general cultural side of the spectacle, would cross himself facing the shimmering glitter of the cupolas: St. Isaac's, in the process of construction, was all in scaffolding—we'll write a letter to Father about the "fired gold leaf" of the domes, and one to Grandmother about the locomotive. . . . Yes, he had actually seen a train—to which poor Belinski (our hero's predecessor) had so recently looked forward when, with wasted lungs, ghastly, shivering, he had been wont to contemplate for hours through tears of civic joy the construction of the first railway station—that same station, again, on whose platform a few years later the half-demented Pisarev (our hero's successor), wearing a black mask and green gloves, was to slash a handsome rival over the face with a riding crop.

In my work (said the author), ideas and themes continue to grow without my knowledge or consent—some of them fairly crookedly—

and I know what is wrong: "the machine" is getting in the way; I must fish this awkward spillikin out of an already composed sentence. A great relief. The subject is perpetual motion.

The pottering with perpetual motion lasted about five years, until 1853, when—already a schoolteacher and a betrothed man—he burned the letter with diagrams that he had once prepared when he feared he would die (from that fashionable disease, aneurysm) before endowing the world with the blessing of eternal and extremely cheap motion. In the descriptions of his absurd experiments and in his commentaries on them, in this mixture of ignorance and ratiocination, one can already detect that barely perceptible but fatal flaw which gave his later utterances something like a hint of quackery; an imaginary hint, for we must keep in mind that the man was as straight and firm as the trunk of an oak, "the most honest of the honest" (his wife's expression); but such was the fate of Chernyshevski that everything turned against him: no matter what subject he touched there would come to light—insidiously, and with the most taunting inevitability—something that was completely opposed to his conception of it. He, for instance, was for synthesis, for the force of attraction, for the living link (reading a novel he would kiss the page where the author appealed to the reader) and what was the answer he got? Disintegration, solitude, estrangement. He preached soundness and common sense in everything—and as if in response to someone's mocking summons, his destiny was cluttered with blockheads, crackbrains and madmen. For everything he was returned "a negative hundredfold," in Strannolyubski's happy phrase, for everything he was backkicked by his own dialectic, for everything the gods had their revenge on him; for his sober views on the unreal roses of poets, for doing good by means of novel writing, for his belief in knowledge—and what unexpected, what cunning forms this revenge assumed! What if, he muses in 1848, one attached a pencil to a mercury thermometer, so that it moved according to the changes in temperature? Starting with the premise that temperature is something eternal—But excuse me, who is this, who is this making laborious notes in cipher of his laborious speculations? A young inventor, no doubt, with an infallible eye, with an innate ability to fasten, to attach, to solder inert parts together, having them give birth in result to the miracle of movement—and lo! a loom is already humming, or an engine with a tall smokestack and a top-hatted driver is overtaking a thoroughbred trotter. Right here is the chink with the nidus of revenge, since this sensible young man, who—let us not forget—is only concerned with the good of all mankind, has eyes like a mole, while his blind, white hands move on a different plane from his faulty but obstinate and muscular mind. Everything that he touches falls to pieces. It is sad to read in his diary about the appliances of which he tries to make use—scale-arms, bobs, corks, basins—and nothing revolves, or if it does, then according to unwelcome laws, in the reverse direction to what he wants: an eternal motor going in reverse—why, this is an absolute nightmare, the abstraction to end all abstractions, infinity with a minus sign, plus a broken jug into the bargain.

We—consciously—have flown ahead; let us return to that jogtrot, to that rhythm of Nikolay's life to which our ear had already become attuned.

He chose the philological faculty. His mother went to pay her respects to the professors in order to cajole them: her voice would acquire flattering overtones and gradually she would begin to wax tearful and blow her nose. Out of all the St. Petersburg products she was most struck by articles made of crystal. Finally "they" (the respectful pronoun he used in speaking of his mother—that wonderful Russian plural which, as later his own aesthetics, "attempts to express quality by quantity") returned to Saratov. For the road she bought herself an enormous turnip.

At first Nikolay Gavrilovich went to live with a friend, but subsequently he shared an apartment with a cousin and her husband. The plans of these apartments, as of all his other abodes, were drawn by him in his letters. The exact definition of the relations between objects always fascinated him and therefore he loved plans, columns of figures and visual representations of things, the more so since his agonizingly circumstantial style could in no way compensate for the art of literary portrayal, which for him was unattainable. His letters to his relatives are the letters of a model youth: instead of imagination he was prompted by his obliging good nature as to what another would relish. The reverend liked all sorts of events—humorous or horrible incidents—and his son carefully fed him with them over a period of several years. We find mentioned therein Izler's entertainments, his replicas of Carlsbad—*minerashki* (miniature spas) at which venturesome St. Petersburg ladies used to ascend in captive balloons; the tragic case of the rowboat overturned by a steamer on the Neva, one of the victims being a colonel with a large family; the arsenic intended for mice, which got into some flour and poisoned over a hundred people; and of course, of course the new fad, table-turning—all gullibility and fraud in the opinion of both correspondents.

Just as in the somber Siberian years one of his principal epistolary chords was the assurance addressed to his wife and children—always on the same high, but not quite correct note—that he had plenty of money, please don't send money, so in his youth he begs his parents not to worry about him and contrives to live on twenty rubles a month; of this, about two and a half rubles went on white bread and on pastries (he could not bear tea alone, just as he could not bear reading alone; i.e., he invariably used to chew something with a book: over gingerbread biscuits he read *The Pickwick Papers,* over zwiebacks, the *Journal des Débats*), while candles and pens, boot polish and soap came to a ruble: he was, let us note, unclean in his habits, untidy, and at the same time had matured grossly; add to this a bad diet, perpetual colic plus an uneven struggle with the desires of the flesh, ending in a secret compromise —and the result was that he looked sickly, his eyes had dimmed, and of his youthful beauty nothing remained except perhaps that expression of a kind of wonderful helplessness which fugitively lit up his face when a man he respected had treated him well ("he was kind to me—a youth timorous and submissive," he later wrote of the scholar Irinarch Vvedenski, with a pathetic Latin intonation: *animula vagula, blandula . . .*); he himself never doubted his unattractiveness, accepting the thought of it but fighting shy of mirrors: even so, when preparing to make a visit sometimes, especially to his best friends, the Lobodovskis, or wishing to ascertain the cause of a rude stare, he would peer gloomily at his reflection, would see the russety fuzz which looked as if stuck onto his cheeks, count the ripe pimples—and then begin to squeeze them, and at that so brutally that afterwards he did not dare to show himself.

The Lobodovskis! His friend's wedding had produced on our twenty-year-old hero one of those extraordinary impressions, which in the middle of the night cause a youth to sit down in nothing but his underwear to write in his diary. This exciting wedding was celebrated on May 19, 1848; that same day sixteen years later, Chernyshevski's civil execution was carried out. A coincidence of anniversaries, a card index of dates. That is how fate sorts them in anticipation of the researcher's needs; a laudable economy of effort.

He felt joyful at this wedding. What is more, he derived a secondary joy from his basic one ("That means I am able to nourish a pure attachment to a woman")—yes, he was always doing his utmost to turn his heart so that one side was reflected in the glass of reason, or, as his best biographer, Strannolyubski, puts it: "He distilled his feelings in the alembics of logic." But who could have said that he was occupied at that moment with thoughts of love? Many years later in his flowery *Sketches from Life* this same Vasiliy Lobodovski made a careless error when he said that his best man at the wedding, the student "Krushedolin," looked as serious "as if he were subjecting in his mind to an exhaustive analysis certain learned works from England that he had just read."

French romanticism gave us the poetry of love, German romanticism the poetry of friendship. The young Chernyshevski's sentimentality was a concession to an epoch when friendship was magnanimous and moist. Chernyshevski cried willingly and often. "Three tears rolled down," he notes with characteristic accuracy in his diary—and the reader is tormented momentarily with the involuntary thought, can one have an odd number of tears, or is it only the dual nature of the source which makes us demand an even number? "'Remind me not of foolish tears that many times I shed, alas, when my repose oppressive was,'" writes Nikolay Gavrilovich in his diary, addressing his wretched youth, and to the sound of Nekrasov's plebeian rhymery he really does shed a tear: "At this spot in the manuscript there is the trace of a spilled tear," comments his son Mihail in a footnote. The trace of another tear, far hotter, bitterer and more precious, has been preserved on his celebrated letter from the fortress; but Steklov's description of this second tear contains, according to Strannolyubski, certain inaccuracies—which will be discussed later. Then, in the days of his exile and especially in the Vilyuisk dungeon—But hold! the theme of tears is expanding beyond all reason . . . let us return to its point of departure. Now, for example, a funeral is being conducted for a student. In the light blue coffin lies a waxen youth. Another student, Tatarinov (who looked after him when he was ill but who had hardly known him before that) bids him farewell: "He looks long at him, kisses him, and looks again, endlessly . . ." The student Chernyshevski, jotting this down, is himself faint with tenderness; and Strannolyubski, commenting on these lines, suggests a parallel between them and the sorrowful fragment by Gogol, "Nights at a Villa."

But to tell the truth . . . young Chernyshevski's dreams in connection with love and friendship are not distinguished for their refinement—and the more he yields to them the more clearly comes out their fault—their rationality; he was able to bend the silliest daydream into a logical horseshoe. Musing in detail over the fact that Lobodovski, whom he sincerely admires, is developing tuberculosis, and that in consequence Nadezhda Yegorovna will remain a young widow, helpless and destitute, he pursues a particular aim. He needs a dummy image in order to justify his falling in love with her, so he substitutes for it the urge to assist a poor woman, or in other words sets his love upon a utilitarian foundation. For otherwise the palpitations of a fond heart are not to be explained by the limited means of that rough-hewn materialism, to whose blandishments he had already hopelessly succumbed. And then, only yesterday, when Nadezhda Yegorovna "was sitting without a shawl, and of course her 'missionary' [a plain dress] was slit a little at the front and one could see a certain part just below her neck" (a turn of phrase bearing an unusual resemblance to the idiom of literary characters in Zoshchenko's impersonations of Soviet-bred Philistine simpletons), he had asked himself with honest anxiety whether he would have looked at "that part" in the early days after his friend's wedding. And so, gradually burying his friend in his dreams, with a sigh, with an air of unwillingness and as if submitting to a duty, he sees himself deciding to marry the young widow—a melancholy union, a chaste union (and all these dummy images are repeated even more fully in his diary when he subsequently obtains the hand of Olga Sokratovna). The actual beauty of the poor woman was still in doubt, and the method which Chernyshevski selected in order to verify her charms predetermined the whole of his later attitude to the concept of beauty.

At first he established the best specimen of grace in Nadezhda Yegorovna: chance provided him with a living picture in an idyllic vein, albeit somewhat cumbersome. "Vasiliy Petrovich knelt on a chair facing its back; she approached and began to tilt the chair; she tilted it a little and then laid her little face against his chest . . . A candle stood on the tea table . . . and the light fell well enough on her; i.e., a half-light, because she was in her husband's shadow, but clear." Nikolay Gavrilovich looked closely, trying to find something that would not be quite right; he did not find any coarse features, but he still hesitated.

What should one do next? He was constantly comparing her features with the features of other women, but the defectiveness of his eyesight prevented the accumulation of the live specimens essential to a comparison. Willy-nilly he was forced to have recourse to the beauty apprehended and registered by others; i.e., to women's portraits. Thus from the very beginning the concept of art became for him—a myopic materialist (which in itself is an absurd combination)—something subsidiary and applied, and he was now able by experimental means to test something which love had suggested to him: the superiority of Nadezhda Yegorovna's beauty (her husband called her "dearie" and "dolly"), that is Life, to the beauty of all other "female heads," that is Art ("Art"!).

On the Nevski Avenue poetic pictures were exhibited in the windows of Junker's and Daziaro's. Having studied them thoroughly he returned home and noted down his observations. Oh, what a miracle! The comparative method always provided the necessary result. The Calabrian charmer's nose in the engraving was so-so: "Particularly unsuccessful was the glabella as well as the parts lying near the nose, on both sides of its bridge." A week later, still uncertain whether the truth had been sufficiently tested, or else wishing to revel once again in the already familiar compliancy of the experiment, he went once more to the Nevski to see if there were not some new beauty in a shop window. On her knees in a cave, Mary Magdalene was praying before a skull and cross, and of course her face in the light of the lampad was very sweet, but how much better was Nadezhda Yegorovna's semi-illumined face! On a white terrace over the sea were two girls: a graceful blonde was sitting on a stone bench with a young man; they were kissing, while a graceful brunette kept a lookout, holding aside a crimson curtain "which separated the terrace from the remaining parts of the house," as we remark in our diary, for we always like to establish what relation a given detail bears to its speculative environment. Naturally Nadezhda Yegorovna's little neck is far more pleasing. Hence comes an important conclusion: life is more pleasing (and therefore better) than painting, for what is painting, poetry, indeed all art, in its purest form? It is "a crimson sun sinking into an azure sea"; it is picturesque folds in a dress; it is the "rosy nuances which the shallow writer wastes on illuminating his glossy chapters"; it is garlands of flowers, fays, fauns, Phrynae . . . The further it goes the cloudier it gets: the rubbishy idea grows. The luxury of feminine forms now implies luxury in the economic sense. The concept of "fantasy" appears to Nikolay Gavrilovich in the shape of a transparent but ample-breasted Sylphide, corsetless and practically naked, who, playing with a light veil, flies down to the poetically poeticizing poet. A couple of columns, a couple of trees—not quite cypresses and not quite poplars—some kind of urn that holds little attraction for Nikolay Gavrilovich—and the supporter of pure art is sure to applaud. Contemptible fellow! Idle fellow! And indeed, rather than all this trash, how could one not prefer an honest description of contemporary manners, civic indignation, heart-to-heart jingles?

One can safely assume that during those minutes when he was glued to the shop windows his disingenuous master's dissertation, "The Aesthetic Relations of Art to Reality," was composed in its entirety (it is no wonder that he subsequently wrote it right down, straight from the shoulder, in three nights; but it is more of a wonder how, even after a wait of six years, he nonetheless received a master's degree for it).

There were languorous and dim evenings when he lay supine on his dreadful leathern couch—a thing of lumps and rents with an inexhaustible (just pull) supply of horsehair—and "my heart beat somehow wondrously from Michelet's first page, from Guizot's views, from thoughts of Nadezhda Yegorovna, and all this together," and then he would begin to sing off-key, in a ululant voice—he sang "the song of Marguerite," simultaneously thinking of the Lobodovskis' relations with one another— and "gently tears rolled from my eyes." Suddenly he would rise from his couch with the decision to see her immediately; it was, we imagine, an October evening, clouds flew overhead, a sour stench came from the saddlers' and carriage-makers' workshops on the ground floors of houses painted a dreary yellow, and merchants in smocks and sheepskin coats, keys in hand, were already locking up their stores. One bumped into him but he passed quickly by. A ragged lamplighter, his hand-cart rumbling over the cobbles, was bringing lamp oil to a bleary lamp on a wooden post; he wiped the glass with an oily rag and moved on creakily to the next—a long way off. It was beginning to drizzle. Nikolay Gavrilovich flew along with the swift gait of a poor Gogolian character.

At night he was unable to sleep for a long time, tormented by the questions: would Vasiliy Petrovich Lobodovski manage to educate his wife sufficiently so that she might be a helper to him; and in order to stimulate his friend's feelings, should he not send, for example, an anonymous letter which would inflame her husband with jealousy? This already foretells the methods used by the heroes of Chernyshevski's novels. Similar, very carefully calculated but boyishly absurd schemes were thought up by exiled Chernyshevski, old man Chernyshevski, for attaining the most touching objectives. Look how this theme takes advantage of a momentary lack of attention and blossoms out. Halt, roll up again. There is, in fact, no need to go so far ahead. In the student diary one can find the following example of calculation: to print a false manifesto (proclaiming the abolition of conscription) in order to stir up the peasants by a trick; but then he himself abjured it, knowing as a dialectician and a Christian that an inner rot must eat away the whole of a created structure, and that a good end, justifying bad means, will only reveal its fatal kinship with them. Thus politics, literature, painting, even vocal art, were pleasantly entwined with Nikolay Gavrilovich's amorous emotions (we have returned to the point of departure).

How poor he was, how dirty and sloppy, how far removed from the lure of luxury . . . Attention! This was not so much proletarian chastity as the natural disregard with which an ascetic treats the prickle of a permanent hair shirt or the bite of sedentary fleas. Even a hair shirt, however, has at times to be repaired. We are present when the inventive Nikolay Gavrilovich contemplates darning his old trousers: he turned out to have no black thread, so what there was he undertook to soak in ink; an anthology of German verse was lying nearby, open at the beginning of William Tell. As a result of his waving the thread about (in order to dry it), several drops of ink fell on the page; the book did not belong to him. He found a lemon in a paper bag behind the window and attempted to get the blots out, but he only succeeded in dirtying the lemon, plus the windowsill where he had left the pernicious thread. Then he sought the aid of a knife and began to scrape (this book with the punctured poems is now in the Leipzig University library; unfortunately it has not been possible to ascertain how it got there). Ink, indeed, was the natural element of Chernyshevski (he literally bathed in it), who used to smear with it the cracks in his shoes when he was out of shoe polish; or else, in order to disguise a hole in his shoe, he would wrap his foot in a black tie. He broke crockery, soiled and spoiled everything. His love for materiality was not reciprocated. Subsequently, during penal servitude, he turned out to be not only incapable of doing any of a convict's special tasks but also was famous for his inability to do anything at all with his hands (at the same time he was constantly butting in to help his fellow man: "Keep out of what does not concern you, you pillar of virtue," the other convicts used to say gruffly). We have already glimpsed the confusedly hurrying youth being shoved on the street. He rarely grew angry; once, however, not without pride, he noted how he had revenged himself upon a young cabdriver who had caught him a blow with his shaft: wordlessly diving across the sled between the legs of two startled merchants, he tore out a tuft of his hair. In general, however, he was mild and open to insults, but secretly he felt himself capable of "the most desperate, the most crazy" actions. On the side he began dabbling in propaganda by conversing with mujiks, with an occasional Neva ferryman or an alert pastry cook.

Enter the theme of pastry shops. They have seen a good deal in their time. It was there that Pushkin gulped down a glass of lemonade before his duel; there that Sophia Perovski and her companions each took a portion (of what? history did not quite manage to . . .) before proceeding to the Canal Quay to assassinate Alexander II. Our hero's youth had been bewitched by pastry shops, so that later, while on hunger strike in the fortress, he—in *What to Do?*—filled this or that speech with an involuntary howl of gastric lyricism: "Do you have a pastry shop in the vicinity? I wonder if they have ready-made walnut tarts—to my taste they're the best of the tarts, Maria Alexeyevna." But in contradiction to his future recollection, pastry shops and cafés seduced him not at all with their victuals—not with puff pastry made with rancid butter and not even with cherry-jam doughnuts; newspapers, gentlemen, newspapers, that is what they seduced him with! He tried various cafés—choosing such as had the most newspapers, or places where it was simpler and freer. Thus at Wolf's "both last times, instead of his [read: Wolf's] white bread I had coffee with a [read: my] five-kopeck-twist, the last time not hiding"—i.e., the first of these last two times (the punctilious detail of his diary causes an itching in the cerebellum) he hid, not knowing how they would accept pastry brought from outside. The place was warm and quiet and only now and then did a southwest little wind blowing from the newspaper pages cause the candle flames to vacillate ("disturbances have already touched the Russia entrusted to us" as the Tsar put it). "May I have the *Indépendance belge?* Thank you." The candle flames straighten up, it is quiet (but shots ring out on the Boulevard des Capucines, the *révolution* is nearing the Tuileries—and now Louis Philippe takes to flight: along the Avenue de Neuilly, in a fiacre).

And afterwards he was plagued by heartburn. In general he fed on all sorts of odds and ends, being indigent and impractical. Nekrasov's ditty is appropriate here:

Since delicacies tougher
Than tinware I would eat,
Such bellyaches I'd suffer
That death itself seemed sweet.
I'd walk *miles* with that feeling,
I'd read until day broke.
My room had a low ceiling
And goodness how I'd smoke!

Nikolay Gavrilovich, incidentally, did not smoke without reason—it was precisely Zhukov cigarettes that he used for relieving indigestion (and also toothache). His diary, particularly for the summer and autumn of 1849, contains a multitude of most exact references as to how and where he vomited. Besides smoking, he treated himself with rum and water, hot oil, English salts, centaury with bitter-orange leaves, and constantly, conscientiously, with a kind of odd gusto, employed the Roman method—and probably he would ultimately have died of exhaustion if he (graduated as a candidate and retained at the university for advanced work) had not gone to Saratov.

And then in Saratov . . . But no matter how much we should like to lose no time in getting out of this back alley, to which talk of patisseries has led us, and cross over to the sunny side of Nikolay Gavrilovich's life, still (for the sake of a certain hidden continuity) we must hang around here a little longer. Once, in great need, he rushed into a tenement house on the Gorohovaya (there follows a wordy description—with afterthoughts—of the house's location) and was already adjusting his dress when "a girl in red" opened the door. Catching sight of his hand—he had wanted to hold the door—she let out a cry, "as is usually the case." The heavy creak of the door, its loose, rusty hook, the stink, the icy cold—all this is dreadful . . . and yet the queer fellow is quite prepared to debate with himself about true purity, noting with satisfaction that "I didn't even try to discover whether she was good-looking." When dreaming, on the other hand, he looked with a keener eye, and the contingency of sleep was kinder to him than his public destiny—but even here, how delighted he is that when in his dream he thrice kisses the gloved hand of "an extremely fair-haired" lady (the mother of a presupposed pupil sheltering him in his dream, all this in the style of Jean-Jacques), he is unable to reproach himself for a single carnal thought. His memory, too, turned out to be keen-eyed when he recalled that circuitous young yearning for beauty. At the age of fifty in a letter from Siberia he evokes the angelic image of a girl he had once noticed in his youth at an exhibition of Industry and Agriculture: "Now there was a certain aristocratic family walking along," he narrates in his later, Biblically slow style. "She appealed to me, this girl, verily she appealed to me . . . I walked alongside about three paces away and admired her . . . They belonged obviously to the highest society. Everyone saw this from their extraordinarily nice manners [there is a little Dickensian fly in this treacly pathos, as Strannolyubski would remark, but still we must not forget that this is being written by an old man half-crushed by penal servitude, as Steklov would justly put it]. The crowd gave way before them . . . I was quite free to walk at about three paces distance without taking my gaze off that girl [poor satellite!]. And this lasted for an hour or more." (Oddly enough, exhibitions in general, for instance the London one of 1862 and the Paris one of 1889, had a strong effect on his fate; thus Bouvard and Pécuchet, when undertaking a description of the life of the Duke of Angoulême, were amazed by the role played in it . . . by bridges.)

It follows from all this that upon arriving in Saratov he could not help but fall in love with the twenty-year-old daughter of Doctor Sokrat Vasiliev, a gypsyish young lady with earrings hanging from the long lobes of her ears, which were half-concealed by folds of dark hair. A teasing, affected creature, "the cynosure and ornament of provincial balls" (in the words of a nameless contemporary), she seduced and stupefied our clumsy virgin with the rustle of her sky-blue *choux* and the melodiousness of her speech. "Look, what a charming little arm," she would say, stretching it out toward his misted glasses—a bare, dusky arm with a glistening bloom along it. He rubbed himself with attar of roses and shaved bloodily. And what serious compliments he thought up! "You should be living in Paris," he said earnestly, having learned elsewhere that she was a "democrat"; Paris for her, however, meant not the hearth of science but the kingdom of strumpets, so that she was offended.

Before us is "The Diary of my Relations with Her Who now Constitutes my Happiness." The easily carried-away Steklov refers to this unique production (reminding one most of all of an extremely conscientious business report) as "an exultant hymn of love." The maker of the report draws up a project for declaring his love (which is accurately put into effect in February, 1853, and approved without delay) with points for and against marriage (he feared, for example, lest his restive spouse should take it into her head to wear male dress—in the manner of George Sand) and with an estimate of expenses when married, which contains absolutely everything—two stearine candles for the winter evenings, ten kopecks' worth of milk, the theater; and at the same time he notifies his bride that in view of his way of thinking ("I am frightened neither by dirt nor by [setting loose] drunken peasants with clubs, nor by slaughter") sooner or later he is "sure to get caught," and for greater honesty he tells her about the wife of Iskander (Herzen), who being pregnant ("excuse me for going into such details"), upon hearing the news that her husband had been arrested in Italy and sent to Russia, "fell dead." Olga Sokratovna, as Aldanov might have added at this point, would not have fallen dead.

"If some day," he wrote further, "your name is stained by rumor, so that you cannot hope to have any husband . . . I will always be ready at one word from you to become your husband." A chivalrous position, but based on far from chivalrous premises, and this characteristic turn leads us back at once to the familiar path of those earlier quasi fantasies of love, with his detailed thirst for self-sacrifice and the protective coloration of his compassion; which did not prevent him from having his pride smart when his bride warned him that she was not in love with him. His betrothal period had a German touch about it, with Schillerian songs, with a countinghouse of caresses: "I undid at first two and then three buttons on her mantilla . . ." He urgently wanted her to place her foot (in its blunt-toed, gray bottekin stitched with colored silk) on top of his head:

his voluptuousness fed on symbols. Sometimes he read to her from Lermontov or Koltsov; he read poetry in the monotone of a Psalter lector.

But that which occupies the place of honor in the diary and which is particularly important for an understanding of much of Nikolay Gavrilovich's fate is his detailed account of the joke ceremonies with which the Saratov evenings were richly adorned. He could not polka nimbly and was a bad dancer of the *Grossvater*, but on the other hand he loved clowning, for even the penguin is not above a certain playfulness when he surrounds the female he courts with a ring of pebbles. Young people, as the phrase goes, would get together, and setting in motion a device of coquetry fashionable in those days and among that set, Olga Sokratovna would feed one or another of the guests at table from a saucer, like a child, while Nikolay Gavrilovich, miming jealousy, would press a napkin to his heart and threaten to pierce his breast with a fork. In her turn she would pretend to be cross with him. He would then beg forgiveness (all this is horribly unfunny) and kiss the exposed parts of her arms, which she tried to hide, saying: "How dare you!" The penguin assumed "a serious, mournful look, because indeed it was possible that I had said something which would have given offense to another (i.e., a less bold girl) in her place." On holidays he played tricks in the Temple of God, amusing his bride-to-be—but the Marxist commentator (i.e., Steklov) errs in seeing in this "a healthy blasphemousness." As the son of a priest Nikolay felt quite at home in church (thus the young prince who crowns a cat with his father's crown is decidedly not expressing any sympathy with popular government). Even less can one reproach him with mocking the Crusaders because he chalked a cross upon the back of everyone in turn: the mark of Olga Sokratovna's lovesick admirers. And after some more horseplay of the same sort there takes place—let us remember this—a mock duel with sticks.

Now a few years later when he was arrested, the police confiscated this old diary, which was written in an even hand with little striggles and was in a homemade code, with such abbreviations as *weakns! sillns!* (weakness, silliness), *lbrty, =tÿ* (liberty, equality) and *ch-k* (*chelovek*, man,— not Cheka, Lenin's police).

It was deciphered by people who were evidently incompetent, since they made a number of mistakes: for example, they read *dzrya* as *druzya* (friends) instead of *podozreniya* (suspicions), which twisted the sentence "I shall arouse strong suspicions" into "I have strong friends." Chernyshevski grasped at this and began to maintain that the whole diary was the draft of a novel, a writer's invention, since he, he said, "did not then have any influential friends, whereas this was obviously a character with powerful friends in the government." It is not important (although the question is interesting in itself) whether he remembered the actual words in his diary exactly; what is important is that subsequently these words are given a curious alibi in *What to Do?* where their inner "draft" rhythm is fully worked out (for instance in the song of one of the girls at the picnic: "Oh maid, I dwell in gloomy woods, I am an evil friend, and perilous will be my life, and sad will be my end"). Lying in prison and knowing that the dangerous diary was being deciphered, he hastened to send the Senate "examples of my manuscript drafts"; i.e., things which he had written exclusively in order to justify his diary, turning it ex post facto also into some draft for some novel. (Strannolyubski makes the direct supposition that it was this that impelled him to write in jail *What to Do?*—dedicated, by the way, to his wife, and begun on St. Olga's day.) Therefore he could express his indignation over the fact that a judicial meaning was being given to scenes he had invented. "I place myself and others in various positions and develop them quite fancifully . . . One 'I' speaks of the possibility of arrest, another 'I' is beaten with a stick in front of his fiancée." He hoped, recalling this part of his old diary, that the detailed account of all sorts of parlor games would be regarded in itself as "fanciful," since a sedate person would hardly . . . The sad thing was that in official circles he was considered not a sedate person, but precisely a buffoon, and it was in the very buffoonery of his journalist devices in *The Contemporary* that they detected a fiendish infiltration of harmful ideas. And for a complete conclusion of the theme of the Saratov *petits-jeux* let us move on still further, as far as the penal servitude, where their echo still lives in the playlets he composes for his comrades and especially in the novel *The Prologue* (written at the Alexandrov works in 1866), where there are both a student who unfunnily plays the fool, and a young beauty feeding her admirers. If we add to this that the protagonist (Volgin), when talking to his wife of the danger threatening him, refers to a warning he has given her before marriage, then it is impossible not to conclude that here finally we have a late piece of truth inserted by Chernyshevski to prop up his ancient assertion that his diary was merely an author's draft . . . for the very flesh of *The Prologue*, through all the dross of the feeble invention, now seems indeed to be a novelistic continuation of the Saratov jottings.

He was engaged to teach grammar and literature in the gymnasium there and proved to be an extremely popular teacher: in the unwritten classification which the boys applied swiftly and exactly to all the instructors, he was assigned to the type of nervous, absentminded, good-natured fellow who would easily lose his temper but who was also easily led off the subject— to fall at once into the soft paws of the class virtuoso (Fioletov junior in this case): at the critical moment when disaster already seemed inevitable for those who did not know the lesson, and there was only a short time until the caretaker rang his bell, he would ask a saving, delaying question: "Nikolay Gavrilovich, there is something here about the Convention . . ." and forthwith Nikolay Gavrilovich would kindle, would go to the board and crushing the chalk would draw a plan of the hall where the National Convention of 1792–95 held its meetings (he was, as we know, a great expert at plans), and then, becoming more and more animated, he would also point out the places where the members of every party had sat.

During those years in the provinces he evidently behaved rather imprudently, frightening moderate people and God-fearing youths with the harshness of his views and the brashness of his ways. A slightly touched-up story has been preserved to the effect that the coffin had hardly been lowered at his mother's funeral before he lit up a cigarette and went off arm-in-arm with Olga Sokratovna, whom he married ten days later. But the upper-formers were swept away by him; some of them subsequently became attached to him with that rapturous ardor with which the young people of this didactic era clung to the teacher who was on the brink of becoming a leader;

as far as "grammar" was concerned, it must be said in all conscience that his charges never learned to handle commas. Were many of their number there forty years later at his funeral? According to some sources there were two, according to others, none at all. And when the funeral procession was about to stop by the Saratov school building in order to chant a litany, the director sent to inform the priest that this, you know, was undesirable, and accompanied by a stumbling, long-skirted October wind, the procession went by.

Much less successful than his career in Saratov was his teaching after his transfer to St. Petersburg, where for several months during 1854 he taught in the Second Cadet Corps. The cadets behaved rowdily at his lessons. Shouting shrilly at the recreants only served to augment the confusion. You couldn't get very warmed up about Montagnards there! Once during an interval there was some noise in one of the classrooms, the officer on guard went in, barked, and left relative order behind him; in the meantime noise broke out in another classroom which (the interval was now over) Chernyshevski had just entered with his briefcase under his arm. Turning to the officer, he stopped him with a touch of his hand and said with restrained irritation, looking over his glasses: "No, sir, you can't come here now." The officer felt insulted; the teacher refused to apologize and left. Thus began the theme of "officers."

The preoccupation with enlightenment, however, had now been formed in him for the rest of his life, and from 1853 to 1862 his journalistic activities were thoroughly imbued with an aspiration to feed the lean Russian reader with a diet of the most variegated information: the portions were huge, the bread supply inexhaustible, and nuts were provided on Sundays; for while stressing how important were the meat dishes of politics and philosophy, Nikolay Gavrilovich never forgot the sweet either. From his review of Amarantov's *Indoor Magic* it is clear that he had tried out this entertaining physics at home, and to one of the best tricks, namely "carrying water in a sieve," he added his own amendment: like all popularizers, he had a weakness for such *Kunststücke*; nor must we forget that hardly a year had passed since by agreement with his father he had finally abandoned his idea for perpetual motion.

He loved to read almanacs, noting for the general information of the *Contemporary* subscribers (1855): "A guinea is 6 rubles and 47½ kopecks; the North American dollar is 1 silver ruble and 31 kopecks"; or else he would inform them that "telegraph towers between Odessa and Ochakov have been built from donations." A genuine encyclopedist, a kind of Voltaire—with the stress, true, on the first syllable—he unstintingly copied out thousands of pages (he was always ready to embrace the rolled-up carpet of any chance subject and unfold the whole of it before the reader), translated a whole library, cultivated all genres right down to poetry, and dreamed to the end of his life of composing "a critical dictionary of ideas and facts" (which recalls Flaubert's caricature, that "*Dictionnaire des idées reçues*" whose ironic epigraph— "the majority is always right"—Chernyshevski would have adopted in all seriousness). On this subject he writes to his wife from the fortress, telling her with passion, sorrow, bitterness, about all the titanic works which he will still complete. Later, during all the twenty years of his Siberian isolation, he sought solace in this dream; but then, one year before his death, when he learned of Brockhaus's dictionary, he saw in it its realization. Then he yearned to translate it (otherwise "they would stuff it with all sorts of rubbish, such as minor German artists"), deeming that such a work would be the crown of his entire life; it turned out that this, too, had been already undertaken.

In the beginning of his journalistic pursuits, writing on Lessing (who had been born exactly a hundred years before him, and a resemblance to whom he himself admitted), he said: "For such natures there exists a sweeter service than service to one's favorite science—and that is service to the development of one's people." Like Lessing, he was accustomed to develop general ideas on the basis of particular cases. And remembering that Lessing's wife had died in childbirth, he feared for Olga Sokratovna, about whose first pregnancy he wrote to his father in Latin, just as, a hundred years before, Lessing had done.

Let us shed a little light here: on the twenty-first of December, 1853, Nikolay Gavrilovich intimated that according to knowledgeable women his wife had conceived. Her labor was difficult. It was a boy. "My sweety-tweety," cooed Olga Sokratovna over her first-born—very soon, however, becoming disenchanted with little Sasha. The doctors warned them that a second child would kill her. Still, she became pregnant anew—"somehow in expiation of our sins, against my will," he wrote plaintively, in dull anguish, to Nekrasov. . . . No, it was something else, stronger than fear for his wife, that oppressed him. According to some sources, Chernyshevski contemplated suicide during the fifties; he even seems to have drunk—what an awe-inspiring vision: a drunken Chernyshevski! There was no use hiding it—the marriage had turned out unhappy, thrice unhappy, and even in later years, when he had managed with the aid of his reminiscences to "freeze his past into a state of static happiness" (Strannolyubski), nevertheless he still bore the marks of that fateful, deadly heartache—made of pity, jealousy and wounded pride—which a husband of quite a different stamp had experienced and had dealt with in quite a different way: Pushkin.

Both his wife and the infant Victor survived; and in December, 1858, she again almost died, giving birth to a third son, Misha. Amazing times—heroic, prolific, wearing a crinoline—that symbol of fertility.

"They are intelligent, educated, kind, I know it—while I am stupid, uneducated, bad," Olga Sokratovna would say (not without that spasm of the soul termed *nadryv*) in reference to her husband's relatives, the Pypin sisters, who with all their kindness did not spare "this hysteric, this unbalanced wench with her insufferable temper." How she used to fling the plates around! What biographer can stick the pieces together? And that passion for moving . . . Those weird indispositions . . . In her old age, she loved to recall how on a dusty, sunny evening at Pavlovsk, in a phaeton with trotter, she had overtaken Grand Duke Konstantin, suddenly throwing off her blue veil and smiting him with a fiery glance, or how she had deceived her husband with the Polish émigré, Ivan Fyodorovich Savitski, a man renowned for the length of his mustaches: "Raffy [*Kanashka*, a vulgar nickname] knew about it . . . Ivan Fyodorovich and I would be in the alcove, while he went on writing at his desk by the window." One feels very sorry for Raffy; he must have been sorely tormented by the young men who surrounded his wife and were in different stages of amorous intimacy with her. Mme. Chernyshevski's parties were particularly enlivened by a gang of Caucasian students. Nikolay Gavrilovich hardly ever came out to join them in the parlor. Once, on a New Year's Eve, the Georgians, led by the guffawing Gogoberidze, burst into his study, dragged him out, and Olga Sokratovna threw a mantilla over him and forced him to dance.

Yes, one pities him—and nevertheless . . . Well, he could have given her a good thrashing with a strap, sent her to the devil; or even portrayed her with all her sins, wails, wanderings and innumerable betrayals in one of those novels with which he occupied his prison leisure. But no! In *The Prologue* (and partly in *What to Do?*) we are touched by his attempts to rehabilitate his wife. There are no lovers around, only reverential admirers; nor is there that cheap coquetry which led men (whom she called *mushchinki*, an awful diminutive) to think her even more accessible than she really was, and all one finds is the vitality of a witty, beautiful woman. Dissipation becomes emancipation, and respect for her battling husband (some respect she did feel for him, but to no purpose) is made to dominate all her other feelings. In *The Prologue* the student Mironov, in order to mystify a friend, tells him that Volgin's wife is a widow. This so upsets Mme. Volgin that she bursts into tears— and likewise the heroine of *What to Do?*, representing the same woman, pines among giddy clichés for her arrested husband. Volgin leaves the printing office and hurries to the opera house where he carefully scans through a pair of binoculars one side of the auditorium, then the other; whereupon tears of tenderness gush from under the lenses. He came to verify that his wife, sitting in her box, was more attractive and more elegant than anyone else—in exactly the same way as Chernyshevski himself in his youth had compared Nadezhda Lobodovski with "women's heads."

And here we find ourselves again surrounded by the voices of his aesthetics—for the motifs of Chernyshevski's life are now obedient to me—I have tamed its themes, they have become accustomed to my pen; with a smile I let them go: in the course of development they merely describe a circle, like a boomerang or a falcon, in order to end by returning to my hand; and even if any should fly far away, beyond the horizon of my page, I am not perturbed; it will fly back, just as this one has done.

And so: on May 10, 1855, Chernyshevski was defending at the University of St. Petersburg the dissertation with which we are already familiar, "The Relations of Art to Reality," written in three August nights in 1853; i.e., precisely at that time when "the vague, lyrical emotions of his youth that had suggested to him considering art in terms of a pretty girl's portrait, had finally ripened and now produced this pulpy fruit in natural correlation with the apotheosis of his marital passion" (Strannolyubski). It was at this public debate that "the intellectual trend of the sixties" was first proclaimed, as old Shelgunov later recalled, noting with discouraging naïveté that the president of the University, Pletnyov, was not moved by the speech of the young scholar whose genius he failed to perceive.... The audience, on the other hand, was in ecstasy. So many people had piled in that some had to stand in the windows. "They descended like flies on carrion," snorted Turgenev, who must have felt wounded in his capacity of professed aesthete, although he himself was not averse to pleasing the flies.

As often happens with unsound ideas which have not freed themselves of the flesh or have been overgrown by it, one can detect in the "young scholar's" aesthetic notions his own physical style, the very sound of his shrill, didactic voice. "Beauty is life. That which pleases us is beautiful; life pleases us in its good manifestations. . . . Speak of life, and only of life [thus continues this sound, so willingly accepted by the acoustics of the century], and if humans do not live humanely—why, teach them to live, portray for them the lives of exemplary men and well-organized societies." Art is thus a substitute or a verdict, but in no wise the equal of life, just as "an etching is artistically far inferior to the picture" from which it has been taken (a particularly charming thought). "The only thing, however," pronounced the discourser clearly, "in which poetry can stand higher than reality is in the embellishment of events by the addition of accessory effects and by making the character of the personages described correspond with the events in which they take part."

Thus in denouncing "pure art" the men of the sixties, and good Russian people after them right up to the nineties, were denouncing—in result of misinformation—their own false conception of it, for just as twenty years later the social writer Garshin saw "pure art" in the paintings of Semiradski (a rank academician)—or as an ascetic may dream of a feast that would make an epicurean sick—so Chernyshevski, having not the slightest notion of the true nature of art, saw its crown in conventional, slick art (i.e., anti-art), which he combated—lunging at nothing. At the same time one must not forget that the other camp, the camp of the "aesthetes"—the critic Druzhinin with his pedantry and tasteless lambency, or Turgenev with his much too elegant "visions" and misuse of Italy—often provided the enemy with exactly that cloying stuff which it was so easy to condemn.

Nikolay Gavrilovich castigated "pure poetry" wherever he found it—in the most unexpected byways. Criticizing a reference book in the pages of *The Contemporary* (1854), he quoted a list of entries which in his opinion were too long: Labyrinth, Laurel, Lenclos (Ninon de)—and a list of entries which were too short: Laboratory, Lafayette, Linen, Lessing. An eloquent cavil! A motto that fits the whole of his intellectual life! The oleographic billows of "poetry" gave birth (as we have seen) to full-bosomed "luxury"; the "fantastic" took a grim economic turn. "Illuminations . . . Confetti fluttering down to the streets from balloons," he enumerates (the subject is the festivities and gifts occasioned by the christening of Louis Napoleon's son), "colossal bonbonnières descending on parachutes. . . ." And what things the rich have: "Beds of rosewood . . . wardrobes with hinges and sliding mirrors . . . damask hangings . . . And over there the poor toiler. . . ." The link has been found, the antithesis obtained; with tremendous accusatory force and an abundance of articles of furniture, Nikolay Gavrilovich exposes all their immorality. "Is it surprising that the seamstress endowed with good looks little by little slackens her moral principles . . . Is it surprising that, having changed her cheap muslin dress, washed a hundred times, for Alençon lace, and her sleepless nights of work by a bit of gutting candle for other sleepless nights at a public masquerade or at a suburban orgy she . . . whirling . . ." etc. (and, having thought it over, he demolished the poet Nikitin, not because the latter versified badly, but because being an inhabitant of the Voronezh backwoods he had no right whatever to be talking about marble colonnades and sails).

The German pedagogue Kampe, folding his little hands on his stomach, once said: "To spin a pfound of wool is more useful than to write a folume off ferses." We too, with equally stolid seriousness, are annoyed at poets, at healthy fellows who would be better doing nothing, but who busy themselves with cutting trifles "out of very nice colored paper." Get it clear, trickster, get it clear, arabesquer, "the power of art is the power of its commonplaces" and nothing more. What should interest a critic most is the conviction expressed in a writer's work. Volynski and Strannolyubski both note a certain odd inconsistency here (one of those fatal inner contradictions that are revealed all along our hero's path): the dualism of the monist Chernyshevski's aesthetics—where "form" and "content" are distinct, with "content" pre-eminent—or, more exactly, with "form" playing the role of the soul and "content" the role of the body; and the muddle is augmented by the fact that this "soul" consists of mechanical components, since Chernyshevski believed that the value of a work was not a qualitative but a quantitative concept, and that "if someone were to take some miserable, forgotten novel and carefully cull all its flashes of observation, he would collect a fair number of sentences that would not differ in worth from those constituting the pages of works we admire." Even more: "It is sufficient to take a look at the trinkets fabricated in Paris, at those elegant articles of bronze, porcelain and wood, in order to understand how impossible it is nowadays to draw a line between an artistic and an unartistic product" (this elegant bronze explains a lot).

Like words, things also have their cases. Chernyshevski saw everything in the nominative. Actually, of course, any genuinely new trend is a knight's move, a change of shadows, a shift that displaces the mirror. A serious man, moderate, respecting education, art and crafts, a man who has accumulated a profusion of values in the sphere of thought—who perhaps has shown a fully progressive discrimination during the period of their accumulation but now has no desire whatsoever for them to be suddenly subjected to a reconsideration—such a man is much more angered by irrational innovation than by the darkness of antiquated ignorance. Thus Chernyshevski, who like the majority of revolutionaries was a complete bourgeois in his artistic and scientific tastes, was enraged by "the squaring of boots" or "the extraction of cubic roots from boot tops." "All Kazan knew Lobachevski," he wrote to his sons from Siberia in the seventies, "all Kazan was of the unanimous opinion that the man was a complete fool. . . . What on earth is 'the curvature of a ray' or 'curved space'? What is 'geometry without the axiom of parallel lines'? Is it possible to write Russian without verbs? Yes, it is—for a joke. Whispers, timid respiration, trills of nightingale. Written by a certain Fet, a well-known poet in his time. An idiot with few peers. He wrote this seriously, and people laughed at him till their sides ached." (Fet he detested as he also did Tolstoy; in 1856, while buttering up Turgenev—whom he wanted in *The Contemporary*—he wrote him "that no 'Youth's' [Tolstoy's *Childhood and Adolescence*] nor even Fet's poetry . . . can sufficiently vulgarize the public for its not being able to . . ."—there follows a vulgar compliment.)

Once in 1855, when expatiating on Pushkin and wishing to give an example of "a senseless combination of words," he hastily cited a "blue sound" of his own invention—prophetically calling down upon his own head Blok's "blue-ringing hour" that was to chime half a century later. "A scientific analysis shows the absurdity of such combinations," he wrote, unaware of the physiological fact of "colored hearing." "Isn't it all the same," he asked (of the reader in Bakhmuchansk or Novomirgorod, who joyfully agreed with him), "whether we have a blue-finned pike or [as in a Derzhavin poem] a pike with a blue fin [of course the second, *we* would have cried—that way it stands out better, in profile!], for the genuine thinker has no time to worry about such matters, especially if he spends more time in the public square than he does in his study?" The "general outline" is another matter. It was a love of generalities (encyclopedias) and a contemptuous hatred of particularities (monographs) which led him to reproach Darwin for being puerile and Wallace for being inept (". . . all these learned specialties, from the study of butterfly wings to the study of Kaffir dialects"). Chernyshevski had on the contrary a dangerously wide range, a kind of reckless and self-confident "anything-will-do" attitude which casts a doubtful shadow over his own specialized work. "The general interest," however, was given his own interpretation: his premise was that the reader was most of all interested in the "productive" side of things. Reviewing a magazine (in 1855), he praises such items as "The Thermometric Condition of the Earth" and "Russian Coalfields," while decisively rejecting as too special the only article one would want to read, "The Geographical Distribution of the Camel."

Extraordinarily indicative in respect of all this is Chernyshevski's attempt to prove (*The Contemporary* for 1856) that the ternary meter (anapaest, dactyl) is more natural to Russian than the binary one (iamb, trochee). The first (except when it is used in the making of the noble, "sacred"—and therefore hateful—dactylic hexameter) seems more natural to Chernyshevski, "more wholesome," in the way that a bad rider thinks a gallop is "simpler" than trotting. The point, however, was not so much in this as in that "general rule" to which he subjected everything and everyone. Confused by the rhythmic emancipation of Nekrasov's broad-rolling verse and by Koltsov's elementary anapaests ("Why asleep, *muzhichyók*?") Chernyshevski scented something democratic in the ternary meter, something which charmed the heart, something "free" but also didactic, as opposed to the aristocratic air of the iamb: he believed that poets who wished to convince should use the anapaest. However, this was not all: in Nekrasov's ternary verse it happens especially often that one-syllable or two-syllable words occur in the unstressed parts of the feet and lose their accentual individuality, while their collective rhythm on the other hand is heightened: the parts are sacrificed to the whole (as for instance in the anapaestic line "Volga, Vólga, in spríng overflówing" where the first "Volga" occupies the two depressions of the first foot: Volga Vól). All I have just said is nowhere, of course, examined by Chernyshevski himself, but it is curious that in his own verses, produced by him during the Siberian nights, in that terrible ternary meter whose very shoddiness has a tang of madness about it, Chernyshevski unwittingly parodies Nekrasov's device and carries it to absurdity by cramming into the depressions two-syllable words normally accented not on the first syllable (as "Volga") but on the second, and doing it thrice in one line—surely a record: "Remote híll*s*, remote pálms, surprised gírl of the nórth" (verses to his wife, 1875). Let us repeat: all this leaning toward a line created in the image and likeness of definite socio-economic gods was unconscious on Chernyshevski's part, but it is only by making this tendency clear that one can understand the true background of his strange theory. With all this he had no understanding of the real, violinic essence of the anapaest; neither did he understand the iamb, the most flexible of all measures when it comes to transforming stresses into scuds, into those rhythmical deviations from the meter which according to his memories from the seminary seemed to Chernyshevski unlawful; finally he did not understand the rhythm of Russian prose; it is only natural, therefore, that the very method he applied to prove his theory had its revenge on him: in the passages of prose he quoted he divided the number of syllables by the number of stresses and got the result of three, not the two he would have got, he said, had the binary meter been more becoming to the Russian language; but he did not take into account the main thing: the paeons! For in the very passages he quotes, whole pieces of sentences follow the scudded rhythm of blank verse, the most blue-blooded of all meters; i.e., precisely the iamb!

I am afraid that the cobbler who visited Apelles' studio and criticized what he did not understand was a mediocre cobbler. Is all really well from the mathematical point of view in those learned economic works of his, whose analysis demands an almost superhuman curiosity on the part of the investigator? Are they really deep, those commentaries of his on Mill (in which he strove to reconstruct certain theories "in keeping with the new plebeian element in thought and life")? Do all the boots he made really fit? Or is it merely an old man's coquetry which prompts him twenty years later to recall complacently the errors in his logarithmic calculations concerning the effect of certain agricultural improvements on the grain harvest? Sad, all of this, very sad. Our overall impression is that materialists of this type fell into a fatal error: neglecting the nature of the thing itself, they kept applying their most materialistic method merely to the relations between objects, to the void between objects and not to the objects themselves; i.e., they were the naïvest of metaphysicians precisely at that point where they most wanted to be standing on the ground.

Once in his youth there had been an unfortunate morning: he was called on by a book peddler he knew, old, long-nosed Vasiliy Trofimovich, bent like a babajaga beneath the weight of a huge canvas sack full of prohibited and semiprohibited books. Not knowing foreign languages, hardly able to spell out Roman letters and weirdly pronouncing the titles in a thick peasant way, he guessed instinctively the degree of seditiousness of this or that German. That morning he sold Nikolay Gavrilovich (both of them squatting on their haunches beside a pile of books) a still uncut volume of Feuerbach.

In those days Andrey Ivanovich Feuerbach was preferred to Egor Fyodorovich Hegel. *Homo feuerbachi* is a cogitating muscle. Andrey Ivanovich found that man differs from the ape only in his point of view; he could hardly, however, have studied the apes. A half-century after him Lenin refuted the theory that "the earth is the sum of human sensations" with "the earth existed before man did"; and to his trade announcement: "We now turn Kant's unknowable 'thing in itself,' into a 'thing for us,' by means of organic chemistry," he added quite seriously that "since alizarin has existed in coal without our knowledge, then things must exist independently of our cognition." Similarly, Chernyshevski explained: "We see a tree; another man looks at the same object. We see by the reflection in his eyes that his image of the tree looks exactly the same as our tree. Thus we all see objects as they really exist." All this wild rubbish has its own private hilarious twist: the "materialists'" constant appeal to trees is especially amusing because they are all so badly acquainted with nature, particularly with trees. That tangible object which according to Chernyshevski "acts much more strongly than the abstract concept of it" (the Anthropological Principle in Philosophy) is simply beyond their ken. Look what a terrible abstraction resulted, in the final analysis, from "materialism"! Chernyshevski did not know the difference between a plow and the wooden *soha*; he confused beer with Madeira; he was unable to name a single wild flower except the wild rose; and it is characteristic that this deficiency of botanical knowledge was immediately made up by a "generalization" when he maintained with the conviction of an ignoramus that "they [the flowers of the Siberian taiga] are all just the same as those which bloom all over Russia!" There lurks a secret retribution in the fact that he who had constructed his philosophy on a basis of knowing the world was now placed, naked and alone, amidst the bewitched, strangely luxuriant, and still incompletely described nature of northeast Siberia: an elemental, mythological punishment which had not been taken into account by his human judges.

Only a few years earlier the smell of Gogol's Petrushka had been explained away by the fact that everything existing was rational. But the time for hearty Russian Hegelianism was now past. The molders of opinion were incapable of understanding Hegel's vital truth: a truth that was not stagnant, like shallow water, but flowed like blood, through the very process of cognition. The simpleton Feuerbach was much more to Chernyshevski's taste. There is always a danger, however, that one letter will fall out of the cosmic, and this danger was not evaded by Chernyshevski in his article "Communal Ownership," when he began to operate with Hegel's tempting triad, giving such examples as: the gasiformity of the world is the thesis, while the softness of the brain is the synthesis; or, even stupider: a cudgel turning into a carbine. "There lies concealed in the triad," says Strannolyubski, "a vague image of the circumference controlling all life of the mind, and the mind is confined inescapably within it. This is truth's merry-go-round, for truth is always round; consequently, in the development of life's forms a certain pardonable curvature is possible: the hump of truth; but no more."

Chernyshevski's "philosophy" goes back through Feuerbach, to the Encyclopedists. On the other hand, applied Hegelianism, working gradually left, went through that same Feuerbach to join Marx, who in his *Holy Family* expresses himself thus:

> . . . . no great intelligence
> Is needed to distinguish a connection
> Between the teaching of materialism

Regarding inborn tendency to good;
Equality of man's capacities—
Capacities that generally are
Termed mental; the great influence
Exterior circumstances have on man;
Omnipotent experience; sway of habit
And of upbringing; the extreme importance
Of industry; the moral right to pleasure,
And communism.

I have put it into blank verse so it would be less boring.

Steklov is of the opinion that with all his genius, Chernyshevski cannot rank with Marx, in relation to whom he stands as the Barnaul craftsman Polzunov stands to Watt. Marx himself ("that petty bourgeois to the marrow of his bones" according to the testimony of Bakunin, who could not stand Germans) referred once or twice to the "remarkable" writings of Chernyshevski, but he left more than one contemptuous note in the margins of the chief work on economics "*des grossen russischen Gelehrten*" (Marx in general disliked Russians). Chernyshevski repaid him in like coin. Already in the seventies he was treating everything new with negligence, with malevolence. He was particularly fed up with economics, which had ceased to be a weapon for him and by this token took on in his mind the aspect of an empty toy, of "pure science." Lyatski is quite wrong when—with a passion for navigational analogies common to many—he compares the exiled Chernyshevski to a man "watching from a deserted shore the passage of a gigantic ship (Marx's ship) on its way to discover new lands"; the expression is especially unfortunate in view of the fact that Chernyshevski himself, as if anticipating the analogy and wishing to refute it in advance, said of *Das Kapital* (sent to him in 1872): "I glanced through but didn't read it; I tore off the pages one by one and made them into little *ships* [my italics], and launched them on the Vilyui."

Lenin considered Chernyshevski to be "the one truly great writer who managed to remain on a level of unbroken philosophical materialism from the fifties right up until 1888" (he knocked one year off). Once, on a windy day, Krupskaya turned to Lunacharski and said to him with soft sorrow: "There was hardly anyone Vladimir Ilyich liked so much . . . I think he had a great deal in common with Chernyshevski." "Yes, they undoubtedly had much in common," adds Lunacharski, who had tended at first to treat this remark with skepticism. "They had in common both clarity of style and mobility of speech . . . breadth and depth of judgement, revolutionary fire . . . that combination of enormous content with a modest exterior, and finally their joint moral makeup." Steklov calls Chernyshevski's article, "The Anthropological Principle in Philosophy," the "first philosophical manifesto of Russian communism"; it is significant that this first manifesto was a schoolboy's rendering, an infantile assessment of the most difficult moral questions. "The European theory of materialism," says Strannolyubski, rephrasing Volynski somewhat, "took on with Chernyshevski a simplified, muddled, and grotesque form. Passing scornful and impertinent judgment on Schopenhauer, under whose critical fingernail his own saltatory thinking would not have survived for a second, he recognized out of all former thinkers, by a strange association of ideas and according to his mistaken memories, only Spinoza and Aristotle, whom he imagined himself to be continuing."

Chernyshevski hammered unsound syllogisms together; the moment he had gone the syllogisms collapsed and the nails were left sticking out. In eliminating metaphysical dualism he fell into gnoseological dualism, and having lightheartedly taken matter as the first principle, he got hopelessly lost among concepts presupposing something that creates our perception of the external world itself. The professional philosopher Yurkevich had no trouble at all in pulling him to pieces. Yurkevich kept wondering how does Chernyshevski account for the spatial motion of the nerves being transformed into nonspatial sensation? Instead of replying to the poor professor's detailed article, Chernyshevski reprinted exactly a third of it in *The Contemporary* (i.e., as much as was allowed by law) and broke it off in the middle of a word, with no comment. He most definitely did not give a hoot for the opinions of specialists, and he saw no harm in not knowing the details of the subject under examination: details were for him merely the aristocratic element in the nation of our general ideas.

"His head thinks about the problems of humanity . . . while his hand carries out unskilled labor," he wrote of his "socially conscious workman" (and we cannot help recalling those woodcuts in ancient anatomical atlases, where a pleasant-faced youth is depicted nonchalantly leaning against a column and showing the educated world all his viscera). But the political regime that was supposed to appear as the synthesis in the syllogism, where the thesis was the commune, resembled not so much Soviet Russia as the utopias of his day. The world of Fourier, the harmony of the twelve passions, the bliss of collective living, the rose-garlanded workmen—all this could not fail to please Chernyshevski, who was always looking for "coherency." Let us dream of the phalanstery living in a palace: 1,800 souls—and all happy! Music, flags, cakes. The world is run by mathematics and well run at that; the correspondence which Fourier established between our desires and Newton's gravity was particularly captivating; it defined Chernyshevski's attitude to Newton for all his life, and it is pleasant to compare the latter's apple with Fourier's apple costing the commercial traveler a whole fourteen sous in a Paris restaurant, a fact that led Fourier to ponder the basic disorder of the industrial mechanism, just as Marx was led to acquaint himself with economic problems by the question of the wine-making gnomes ("small peasants") in the Moselle Valley: a graceful origination of grandiose ideas.

While defending communal ownership of the land because of its simplifying the organization of associations in Russia, Chernyshevski was prepared to agree to the emancipation of the peasants without land, the ownership of which would have led in the long run to new encumbrances. At this point sparks flash from our pen. The liberation of the serfs! The era of great reforms! No wonder that in a burst of vivid prescience the young Chernyshevski noted in his diary in 1848 (the year somebody dubbed "the vent of the century"): "What if we are indeed living in the times of Cicero and Caesar, when *seculorum novus nascitur ordo*, and there comes a new Messiah, and a new religion, and a new world? . . ."

The fifties are now in full fan. It is permitted to smoke on the streets. One may wear a beard. The overture to *William Tell* is thundered out on every musical occasion. Rumors spread that the capital is being moved to Moscow; that the old calendar is going to be replaced by the new. Under this cover Russia is busily gathering material for Saltikov's primitive but juicy satire. "What is this talk of a new spirit in the air, I'd like to know," said General Zubatov, "only the flunkeys have grown rude, otherwise everything has stayed the way it was." Landowners and notably their wives began to dream terrible dreams not listed in dream books. A new heresy appeared: Nihilism. "A scandalous and immoral doctrine rejecting everything that cannot be palpated," says Dahl with a shudder, in his definition of this strange word (in which "nihil," nothing, corresponds as it were to "material"). Persons in holy orders had a vision: an enormous Chernyshevski strides along the Nevsky Prospect wearing a wide-brimmed hat and carrying a cudgel.

And that first rescript in the name of the Vilno governor, Nazimov! And the Tsar's signature, so handsome, so robust, with two full-blooded, mighty flourishes, which were to be later torn off by a bomb! And the ecstasy of Nikolay Gavrilovich: "The blessing promised to the meek and the peacemakers crowns Alexander the Second with a happiness which no other of Europe's sovereigns has yet known. . . ."

But soon after the provincial committees were formed, Chernyshevski's ardor cooled: he was incensed by the self-seeking of the nobles in most of them. His final disillusionment came in the second half of 1858. The size of the compensation! The smallness of the allotments! The tone of *The Contemporary* became sharp and frank; the expressions "infamous" and "infamy" began pleasantly to enliven the pages of this dullish magazine.

Its director's life was not rich in events. For a long time the public did not know his face. Nowhere was he seen. Already famous, he remained as it were in the wings of his busy, talkative thought.

Always, as was the custom then, in a dressing gown (spotted even behind with candle grease) he sat all day long in his little study with its blue wallpaper—good for the eyes—and its window overlooking the yard (a view of the log-pile covered with snow), at a large desk heaped with books, printer's proofs and cuttings. He worked so feverishly, smoked so much and slept so little that the impression he produced was almost frightening: skinny, nervy, his gaze at once blear and piercing, his hands shaky, his speech jerky and distracted (on the other hand he never suffered from headache and naïvely boasted of this as a mark of a healthy mind). His capacity for work was monstrous, as was, for that matter, that of most Russian critics of the last century. To his secretary Studentski, a former seminarist from Saratov, he dictated a translation of Schlosser's history and in between, while the latter was taking it down, he himself would go on writing an article for *The Contemporary* or would read something, making notes in the margins. He was pestered by callers. Not knowing how to escape from an importunate guest, he would, to his own chagrin, get more and more involved in a conversation. Leaning his elbow on the mantelpiece and fiddling with something, he would talk in a shrill, squeaky voice, but whenever his thoughts wandered, he would drawl and chew monotonously, with an abundance of "well's." He had a peculiar quiet chuckle (causing Leo Tolstoy to break into a sweat), but when he laughed out loud he went off into fits and roared deafeningly (at which Turgenev, hearing these roulades from afar, would take to his heels).

Such methods of knowledge as dialectical materialism curiously resemble the unscrupulous advertisements for patent medicines, which cure all illnesses at once. Still, such an expedient can occasionally help with a cold. There was quite definitively a smack of class arrogance about the attitudes of contemporary wellborn writers toward plebeian Chernyshevski. Turgenev, Grigorovich and Tolstoy called him "the bedbugstinking gentleman" and among themselves jeered at him in all kinds of ways. Once at Turgenev's country place, the first two, together with Botkin and Druzhinin, composed and acted a domestic farce. In a scene where a couch was supposed to catch fire, Turgenev had to come out running with the cry . . . here the common efforts of his friends had persuaded him to utter the unfortunate words which in his youth he had allegedly addressed to a sailor during a fire on board ship: "Save me, save me,

I am my mother's only son." Out of this farce the utterly talentless Grigorovich subsequently concocted his completely mediocre *School of Hospitality*, where he endowed one of the characters, the splenetic writer Chernushin, with the features of Nikolay Gavrilovich: mole's eyes looking oddly askance, thin lips, a flattened, crumpled face, gingery hair fluffed up on the left temple and a euphemistic stench of burnt rum. It is curious that the notorious wail ("Save me," etc.) is attributed here to Chernushin, which gives color to Strannolyubski's idea that there was a kind of mystic link between Turgenev and Chernyshevski. "I have read his disgusting book [the dissertation]" writes the former in a letter to his fellow mockers. "Raca! Raca! Raca! You know that there is nothing in the world more terrible than this Jewish curse."

"This 'raca' or 'raka,'" remarks the biographer superstitiously, "resulted seven years later in Rakeev (the police colonel who arrested the anathematized man), and the letter itself had been written by Turgenev on precisely the 12th of July, Chernyshevski's *birthday* . . ." (it seems to us that Strannolyubski is stretching it a bit).

That same year Turgenev's *Rudin* appeared, but Chernyshevski attacked it (for its caricature of Bakunin) only in 1860, when Turgenev was no longer necessary to *The Contemporary*, which he had left as a result of Dobrolyubov's directing a snake hiss at his "On the Eve." Tolstoy could not tolerate our hero: "One keeps hearing him," he wrote, "hearing that thin, nasty little voice of his saying obtuse, nasty things . . . as he keeps waxing indignant in his corner until someone says 'shut up' and looks him in the eye." "The aristocrats turned into coarse ruffians," remarks Steklov in this connection, "when they talked with inferiors or about people who were inferior to them socially." "The inferior," however, did not remain in debt; knowing how much Turgenev prized every word spoken against Tolstoy, Chernyshevski, in the fifties, freely enlarged upon Tolstoy's *poshlost* (vulgarity) and *hvastovstvo* (bragging)—"the bragging of a thickheaded peacock about a tail which doesn't even cover his vulgar bottom," etc. "You are not some Ostrovski or some Tolstoy," added Nikolay Gavrilovich, "you are an honor to us" (and *Rudin* was already out—had been out for two years).

The other literary reviews picked at him as much as they could. The critic Dudyshkin (in *The National Commentator*) huffily aimed his dudeen at him: "Poetry for you is merely chapters of political economy transposed into verse." His ill-wishers in the mystical camp spoke about Chernyshevski's "evil lure," about his physical resemblance to the Devil (for instance, Prof. Kostomarov). Other journalists, of a plainer cast, like Blagosvetlov (who considered himself a dandy and despite his radicalism had as footboy a real, undyed blackamoor) talked about Chernyshevski's dirty rubbers and German-cum-sexton's style of dress. Nekrasov stood up for the "sensible fellow" (whom he had got for *The Contemporary*) with a limp smile, admitting that he had managed to lay the stamp of monotony on the magazine by stuffing it with mediocre tales denouncing bribe-taking and policemen; but he praised his colleague for his fruitful labors: thanks to him the magazine had 4,700 subscribers in 1858 and three years later—7,000. Nikolay Gavrilovich's relations with Nekrasov were friendly but no more; there is a hint concerning some financial arrangements which displeased him. In 1883, in order to divert the old man, his cousin Pypin suggested that he should write some "portraits of the past." Chernyshevski depicted his first meeting with Nekrasov with the meticulousness and laboriousness already familiar to us (giving a complex plan of all their mutual movements about the room including practically the number of footsteps), a detailism sounding like an insult inflicted on Father Time and his honest work, if one remembers that thirty years had elapsed since these maneuvers took place. He placed Nekrasov the poet above all others (above Pushkin, above Lermontov and Koltsov). *La Traviata* made Lenin weep; similarly, Chernyshevski, who confessed that poetry of the heart was even dearer to him than poetry of ideas, used to burst into tears over those of Nekrasov's verses (even iambic ones!) which expressed everything he himself had experienced, all the torments of his youth, all the phases of his love for his wife. And no wonder: Nekrasov's iambic pentameter enchants us particularly by its hortatory, supplicatory and prophetic force and by a very individual caesura after the second foot, a caesura which in Pushkin, say, is a rudimentary organ insofar as it controls the melody of the line, but which in Nekrasov becomes a genuine organ of breathing, as if it had turned from a partition into a pit, or as if the two-foot part of the line and the three-foot part had moved asunder, leaving after the second foot an interval full of music. As he listened to these hollow-chested verses, to this guttural, sobbing articulation—

Oh, do not say the life you lead is dismal,
And do not call a jailer one half-dead!
Before me Night yawns chilly and abysmal.
The arms of Love before you are outspread.

I know, to you another is now dearer,
It irks you now to spare me and to wait.
Oh, bear with me! My end is drawing nearer,
Let Fate complete what was begun by Fate!

—Chernyshevski could not help thinking that his wife should not hasten to deceive him; could not help identifying the nearness of the end with the shadow of the prison already stretching out toward him. And that was not all: evidently this connection was felt—not in the rational but in the Orphic sense—also by the poet who wrote these lines, for it is precisely their rhythm ("Oh, do not say") that was echoed with a bizarre haunting quality in the poem he subsequently wrote about Chernyshevski:

Oh, do not say he has forgotten caution,
For his own Fate himself he'll be to blame . . .

Thus Nekrasov's sounds were *pleasing* to Chernyshevski; i.e., they happened to satisfy that elementary aesthetic for which he mistook all along his own circumstantial sentimentality. Having described a large circle, having taken in many matters concerning Chernyshevski's attitude to various branches of knowledge, and yet not having impaired for a moment our smooth curve, we have now returned with new forces to his philosophy of art. Now it is time to sum it up.

Like all the rest of our radical critics having a weakness for easy gain, he eschewed courtly compliments to lady writers, and energetically demolished Evdokia Rastopchin or Avdotia Glinka. "An incorrect and careless patter" (as Pushkin puts it) left him unmoved. Both he and Dobrolyubov flayed literary coquettes with gusto—but in real life . . . Well, look what was done to them, look how they were twisted and tortured with peals of laughter (water nymphs laugh thus along streams flowing close to hermitages and other places of salvation) by the daughters of Doctor Vasiliev.

His tastes were eminently solid. He was *épaté* by Hugo. He was impressed by Swinburne (which is not at all strange, come to think of it). In the list of books which he read in the fortress the name of Flaubert is spelled with an "*o*"—and, indeed, he placed him below Zacher-Masoch and Spielhagen. He loved Béranger the way average Frenchmen loved him. "For goodness' sake," exclaims Steklov, "you say that this man was not poetic? Why, do you not know that he would declaim Béranger and Ryleyev with tears of rapture?!" His tastes only congealed in Siberia— and by a strange delicacy of historical fate, Russia did not produce during the twenty years of his banishment a single genuine writer (until Chekhov) whose beginning he had not seen for himself during the active period of his life. From conversations with him in the eighties in Astrakhan it becomes apparent that: "Yes, sir, it is the title of count that made one consider Tolstoy 'a great writer of the Russian land' "; and when bothersome visitors asked him whom he thought the best living writer he named a complete nonentity: Maxim Belinski.

In his youth he noted in his diary: "Political literature is the highest literature." In the fifties when discussing at length Belinski (Vissarion, of course), something the government disapproved of, he followed him in saying that "literature cannot fail to be the handmaiden of one or another ideological trend," and that writers "incapable of being animated by sympathy toward what is being accomplished around us by the force of historical movement . . . will never in any circumstances produce anything great," for "history does not know of any works of art that were created exclusively from the idea of beauty." In the forties Belinski maintained that "George Sand can unconditionally be included in the roll of European poets (in the German sense of *Dichter*), while the juxtaposition of Gogol's name with those of Homer and Shakespeare offends both decency and common sense" and that "not only Cervantes, Walter Scott and Cooper, as artists pre-eminently, but also Swift, Sterne, Voltaire and Rousseau have an incomparably and immeasurably greater significance in the whole history of literature than Gogol." Belinksi was seconded three decades later by Chernyshevski (when, it is true, George Sand had already ascended to the attic, and Cooper had descended to the nursery), who said that "Gogol is a very minor figure in comparison, for example, with Dickens or Fielding or Sterne."

Poor Gogol! His exclamation (like Pushkin's) "Rus!" is willingly repeated by the men of the sixties, but now the troika needs paved highways, for even Russia's *toska* ("yearning") has become utilitarian. Poor Gogol! Esteeming the seminarist in the critic Nadezhdin (who used to write "literature" with three "*t*"s), Chernyshevski found that his influence on Gogol would have been more beneficial than Pushkin's, and regretted that Gogol was not aware of such a thing as a principle. Poor Gogol! Why, that gloomy buffoon Father Matvey had also adjured him to renounce Pushkin. . . .

Lermontov came off luckier. His prose jerked from Belinski (who had a weakness for the conquests of technology) the surprising and most charming comparison of Pechorin to a steam engine, shattering all who were careless enough to get under its wheels. In his poetry the middle-class intellectuals felt something of the socio-lyrical strain that later came to be called "Nadsonism." In this sense Lermontov was the first Nadson of Russian literature. The rhythm, the tone, the pale, tear-diluted idiom of "civic" verse up to and including "as victims you fell in the fateful contest" (the famous revolutionary song of the first years of our century), all of this goes back to such Lermontov lines as:

> Farewell, our dear comrade! Alas, upon earth
> Not long did you dwell, blue-eyed singer!

A plain cross of wood you have earned, and with us
Your memory always shall linger. . . .

Lermontov's real magic, the melting vistas in his poetry, its paradisial picturesqueness and the transparent tang of the celestial in his moist verse—these, of course, were completely inaccessible to the understanding of men of Chernyshevski's stamp.

Now we are approaching his most vulnerable spot; for it has long become customary to measure the degree of flair, intelligence and talent of a Russian critic by his attitude to Pushkin. And this is how it will remain until Russian literary criticism discards its sociological, religious, philosophical and other textbooks, which only help mediocrity to admire itself. Only then will you be free to say what you please: You may then criticize Pushkin for any betrayals of his exigent muse and at the same time preserve both your talent and your honor. Upbraid him for letting one hexameter creep into the pentameters of *Boris Godunov* (ninth scene), for a metrical error in the twenty-first line of "The Feast During the Plague," for repeating the phrase "every minute" (*pominutno*) five times within sixteen lines in "The Blizzard," but for God's sake stop that irrelevant chitchat.

Strannolyubski sagaciously compares the critical utterances of the sixties concerning Pushkin with the attitude to him, three decades earlier, of the chief of police Count Benckendorff or that of the director of the third section, Von Fock. In truth, Chernyshevski's highest praise for a writer, like that of the ruler Nicholas I or the radical Belinski, was: sensible. When Chernyshevski or Pisarev called Pushkin's poetry "rubbish and luxury," they were only repeating Tolmachyov, author of *Military Eloquence*, who in the thirties had termed the same subject: "trifles and baubles." When Chernyshevski said that Pushkin was "only a poor imitator of Byron," he reproduced with monstrous accuracy the definition given by Count Vorontsov (Pushkin's boss in Odessa): "A poor imitator of Lord Byron." Dobrolyubov's favorite idea that "Pushkin lacked a solid, deep education" is in friendly chime with Vorontsov's remark: "One cannot be a genuine poet without constantly working to broaden one's knowledge, and his is insufficient." "To be a genius it is not enough to have manufactured *Eugene Onegin*" wrote the progressive Nadezhdin, comparing Pushkin to a tailor, an inventor of waistcoat patterns, and thus concluding an intellectual pact with the reactionary Count Uvarov, Minister of Education, who remarked on the occasion of Pushkin's death: "To write jingles does not mean yet to achieve a great career."

Chernyshevski equated genius with common sense. If Pushkin was a genius, he argued perplexedly, then how should one interpret the profusion of corrections in his drafts? One can understand some "polishing" in a fair copy but this was the rough work itself. It should have flowed effortless since common sense speaks its mind immediately, for it *knows* what it wants to say. Moreover, as a person ridiculously alien to artistic creation, he supposed that "polishing" took place on paper while the "real work"—i.e., "the task of forming the general plan"—occurred "in the mind"—another sign of that dangerous dualism, that crack in his "materialism," whence more than one snake was to slither and bite him during his life. Pushkin's originality filled him with fears. "Poetic works are good when *everyone* [my italics] says after reading them: yes, this is not only verisimilar, but also it could not be otherwise, for that's how it always is."

Pushkin does not figure in the list of books sent to Chernyshevski at the fortress, and no wonder: despite Pushkin's services ("he invented Russian poetry and taught society to read it"—two statements completely untrue), he was nevertheless above all a writer of witty little verses about women's little feet—and "little feet" in the intonation of the sixties—when the whole of nature had been Philistinized into *travka* (diminutive of "grass") and *pichuzhki* (diminutive of "birds")—already meant something quite different from Pushkin's "*petits pieds,*" something that had now become closer to the mawkish "*Füsschen.*" It seemed particularly astonishing to him (as it did also to Belinski) that Pushkin became so "aloof" toward the end of his life. "An end was put to those friendly relations whose monument has remained the poem 'Arion,'" explains Chernyshevski in passing, but how full of sacred meaning was this casual reference to the forbidden subject of Decembrism for the reader of *The Contemporary* (whom we suddenly imagine as absentmindedly and hungrily biting into an apple—transferring the hunger of his reading to the apple, and again eating the words with his eyes). Therefore Nikolay Gavrilovich must have been more than a little irritated by a stage direction in the penultimate scene of *Boris Godunov,* a stage direction resembling a sly hint and an encroachment upon civic laurels hardly deserved by the author of "vulgar drivel" (see Chernyshevski's remarks on the poem "Stamboul is by the giaours now lauded"): "Pushkin comes surrounded by the people."

"Reading over the most abusive critics," wrote Pushkin during an autumn at Boldino, "I find them so amusing that I don't understand how I could have been angry at them; meseems, if I wanted to laugh at them, I could think of nothing better than just to reprint them with no comment at all." Curiously enough, that is exactly what Chernyshevski did with Professor Yurkevich's article: a grotesque repetition! And now "a revolving speck of dust has got caught in a ray of Pushkin's light, which has penetrated between the blinds of Russian critical thought," to use Strannolyubski's caustic metaphor. We have in mind the following magic gamut of fate: in his Saratov diary Chernyshevski applied two lines from Pushkin's "The Egyptian Nights" to his courtship, completely misquoting the second one, with a characteristic (for him who had no ear) distortion: "I [he] met the challenge of delight / As warfare's challenge met I'd have (instead of "As he would meet in days of war / The challenge of a savage battle"). For this "I'd have," fate—the ally of the muses (and herself an expert in conditional forms), took revenge on him—and with what refined stealth in the evolution of the punishment!

What connection, it seems, could there be between this ill-starred misquotation and Chernyshevski's remark ten years later (in 1862): "If people were able to announce all their ideas concerning public affairs at . . . meetings there would be no need to make magazine articles out of them"? However, at this point Nemesis is already awakening. "Instead of writing, one would speak," continues Chernyshevski, "and if these ideas had to reach everyone who had not taken part in the meeting they could be noted down by a stenographer." And vengeance unfolds: in Siberia, where his only listeners were the larches and the Yakuts, he was haunted by the image of a "platform" and a "lecture hall," in which it was *so* convenient for the public to gather and where the latter would ripple *so* responsively, for, in the final analysis, he, as Pushkin's Improvvisatore (he of the "Egyptian Nights") but a poorer versificator, had chosen for his profession—and later as an unrealizable ideal—variations on a given theme; in the very twilight of his life he composes a work in which he embodies his dream: from Astrakhan, not long before his death, he sends Lavrov his "Evenings at the Princess Starobelski's" for the literary review *Russian Thought* (which did not find it possible to print them), and follows this up with "An Insertion"—addressed straight to the printer:

> In that part where it says that the people have gone from the salon dining room into the salon proper, which has been prepared for them to listen to Vyazovski's fairy tale, and there is a description of the arrangement of the auditorium . . . the distribution of the male and female stenographers into two sections at two tables either is not indicated or else is indicated unsatisfactorily. In my draft this part reads as follows: "Along the sides of the platform stood two tables for the stenographers . . . Vyazovski went up to the stenographers, shook hands with them, and stood chatting with them while the company took their places." The lines in the fair copy whose sense corresponds to the passage quoted from my draft should be replaced now by the following lines: "The men, forming a constricted frame, stood near the stage and along the walls behind the last chairs; the musicians with their stands occupied both sides of the stage. . . . The improvvisatore, greeted by deafening applause rising from all sides. . ."

Sorry, sorry, we've mixed everything up—got hold of an extract from Pushkin's "The Egyptian Nights." Let us restore the situation: "Between the platform and foremost hemicycle of the auditorium [writes Chernyshevski to a nonexistent printer], a little to the right and left of the platform, stood two tables; at the one which was on the left in front of the platform, if you looked from the middle of the hemicycles toward the platform . . ." etc., etc.—with many more words of the same sort, none of them really expressing anything.

"Here is a theme for you," said Charski to the improvvisatore. "The poet himself chooses the subjects for his poems; the multitude has no right to direct his inspiration."

We have been led a long way by the impetus and revolution of the Pushkin theme in Chernyshevski's life; meanwhile a new character—whose name once or twice has already burst impatiently into our discourse—is awaiting his entrance. Now it is just time for him to appear—and here he comes in the tightly buttoned, blue-collared regulation coat of a university student, fairly reeking of *chestnost'* ("progressive principle"), ungainly, with tiny, short-sighted eyes and a scanty Newport Frill (that *barbe en collier* which seemed so symptomatic to Flaubert); he offers his hand jabwise; i.e., thrusting it oddly forward with the thumb turned out, and introduces himself in a catarrhally confidential little bass: Dobrolyubov.

Their first meeting (summer 1856) was recalled almost thirty years later by Chernyshevski (when he also wrote about Nekrasov) with his familiar wealth of detail, essentially sickly and impotent, but supposed to set off the irreproachability of thought in its transactions with time. Friendship joined these two men in a monogrammatic union which a hundred centuries are incompetent to untie (on the contrary: it becomes even faster in the consciousness of posterity). This is not the place to enlarge upon the literary activities of the younger man. Let us merely say that he was uncouthly crude and uncouthly naïve; that in the satirical review *The Whistle* he poked fun at the distinguished Dr. Pirogov while parodying Lermontov (the use of some of Lermontov's lyrical poems as a canvas for journalistic jokes about people and events was in general so widespread that in the long run it turned into a caricature of the very art of parody); let us say also, in Strannolyubski's words, that "from the push given it by Dobrolyubov, literature rolled down an inclined plane, with the inevitable result, once it had rolled to zero, that it was put into inverted commas: the student brought some 'literature'" (meaning propaganda leaflets). What else can one add? Dobrolyubov's humor? Oh, those blessed times when "mosquito" was *in itself* funny, a mosquito settling on someone's nose twice as funny, and a mosquito flying into a governmental office and biting a civil servant caused the listeners to groan and double up with laughter!

Much more engaging than Dobrolyubov's obtuse and ponderous critique (all this pleiade of radical critics in fact wrote with their *feet*) is the frivolous side of his life, that feverish, romantic sportiveness which subsequently supplied Chernyshevski with material for the "love intrigues" of Levitski (in *The Prologue*). Dobrolyubov was extraordinarily prone to falling in love (here we catch a glimpse of him playing assiduously *durachki*, a simple card game, with a much-decorated general whose daughter he courts). He had a German girl in Staraya Russa, a strong, onerous tie. From immoral visits to her, Chernyshevski held him back in the full sense of the word: for a long time they would wrestle, both of them limp, scrawny and sweaty—toppling all over the floor, colliding with the furniture—all the time silent, all you could hear was their wheezing; then, stumbling into one another, they would both search for their spectacles beneath the upturned chairs. At the beginning of 1859, gossip reached Chernyshevski that Dobrolyubov (just like d'Anthès), in order to cover his "intrigue" with Olga Sokratovna, wanted to marry her sister (who already had a fiancé). Both the young women played outrageous tricks on Dobrolyubov; they took him to masked balls dressed as a Capuchin or an ice-cream vendor and confided all their secrets in him. Walks with Olga Sokratovna "completely bemused" him. "I know there is nothing to be gained here," he wrote to a friend, "because not a single conversation goes by without her mentioning that although I am a good man, nevertheless I am too clumsy and almost repulsive. I understand that I should not try to gain anything anyway, since in any case I am fonder of Nikolay Gavrilovich than of her. But at the same time I am powerless to leave her alone." When he heard the gossip, Nikolay Gavrilovich, who entertained no illusions concerning his wife's morals, still felt some resentment: the betrayal was a double one; he and Dobrolyubov had a frank explanation and soon afterwards he sailed to London to "maul Herzen" (as he subsequently expressed it); i.e., to give him a good scolding for his attacks on that same Dobrolyubov in the *Kolokol* (*The Bell*), a liberal periodical published abroad, but of less radical views than the endemic *Contemporary.*

Perhaps, however, the object of this meeting was not only to intercede for his friend: Dobrolyubov's name (especially later, in connection with his death), Chernyshevski very skillfully handled "as a matter of revolutionary tactics." According to certain reports from the past his main object in visiting Herzen was to discuss the publishing of *The Contemporary* abroad: everyone had a premonition that soon it would be closed down. But in general this trip is surrounded with such a haze and has left so few traces in Chernyshevski's writings that one would almost prefer, in spite of the facts, to consider it apocryphal. He who had always been interested in England, he who had nourished his soul on Dickens and his mind on the *Times*—how avidly he should have gulped it down, how many impressions he should have garnered, how insistently he should later have kept turning back to it in memory! Actually, Chernyshevski never spoke of his journey and whenever anyone really pressed him, he would reply briefly: "Well, what's there to talk about—there was fog, the ship rocked, what else could there be?" Thus, life itself (how many times now) refuted his axiom: "The tangible object acts much more strongly than the abstract concept of it."

However that may have been, on the 26th June (New Style?), 1859, Chernyshevski arrived in London (everyone thought that he was in Saratov) and stayed there until the 30th. An oblique ray pierces the fog of these four days: Mme. Tuchkov-Ogaryov walks through a drawing room and into a sunny garden, carrying in her arms her year-old baby girl dressed in a little lace pelerine. In the drawing room (the action takes place in Putney, at Herzen's house) Alexander Ivanovich is walking back and forth (these indoor walks were very much the thing in those days) with a gentleman of medium height whose face is unattractive "but illumined by a wonderful expression of self-abnegation and submissiveness to fate" (which most likely was merely a trick of the memoirist's memory, recalling that face through the prism of a fate which had already been accomplished). Herzen introduced his companion to her. Chernyshevski stroked the infant's hair and said in his quiet voice: "I also have some like this, but I hardly ever see them." (He used to confuse the names of his children: little Victor was in Saratov, where he soon died, for the fate of children does not forgive such slips of the pen—but he sent a kiss to "little Sasha" who had already been brought back to St. Petersburg). "Say how do you do, give us your hand," said Herzen rapidly, and then immediately began to reply to something that had been said by Chernyshevski: "Yes, exactly—that's why they sent them to the Siberian mines"; while Mme. Tuchkov floated into the garden and the oblique ray was extinguished forever.

Diabetes and nephritis added to tuberculosis soon put an end to Dobrolyubov. He was dying in the late autumn of 1861; Chernyshevski paid him a daily call and from there went about his conspiratorial affairs, which were amazingly well concealed from police spies. It is generally considered that he was the author of the proclamation "To the Serfs of Landowners." "There was not much talk," recalls Shelgunov (who wrote the one "To the Soldiers"); and evidently not even Vladislav Kostomarov, who printed these appeals, knew with any certainty about Chernyshevski's authorship. Their style is very reminiscent of Count Rastopchin's corny little placards against Napoleon's invasion: "So this is what it comes to, this thorough-true freedom. . . . And let courts be just and let all be alike before justice. . . . And what's the sense of kicking up a ruction in one village only?" If this was written by Chernyshevski (incidentally, "*bulga*," "ruction," is a Volga word), it was in any case touched up by someone else.

According to information stemming from the People's Freedom organization, Chernyshevski suggested to Sleptsov and his friends in July, 1861, that they form a basic cell of five—the nucleus of an "underground" society. The system consisted in every member forming, moreover, his own cell, and thus knowing only eight people. Only the center knew all the members. All the members were known only to Chernyshevski. This account does not seem free from some stylization.

But let us repeat: he was ideally cautious. After the student disorders of October, 1861, he was put under permanent surveillance, but the agents' work was not distinguished for its subtlety: Nikolay

Gavrilovich had as a cook the wife of the house janitor, a tall, red-cheeked old woman with a somewhat unexpected name: Musa. She was bribed with no trouble—five rubles for coffee, to which she was much addicted. In return Musa used to supply the police with the contents of her employer's wastebasket.

Meanwhile, on November 17, 1861, at twenty-five years of age, Dobrolyubov died. He was buried in the Volkov cemetery "in a simple oak coffin" (the coffin in such cases is always simple) next to Belinski. "Suddenly there stepped forth an energetic, clean-shaven gentleman," recalls a witness (Chernyshevski's appearance was still unfamiliar), and since few people had gathered, and this irritated him, he started to speak of it with detailed irony. While he was speaking, Olga Sokratovna shook with tears, leaning upon the arm of one of those devoted students who were always with her: another, besides his own regulation cap, held the raccoon cap of the "boss," who with his fur coat unbuttoned—in spite of the frost—took out an exercise book and began in an angry, didactic voice to read from it Dobrolyubov's lumpy gray poems about honest principles and approaching death; hoarfrost shone on the birches; and a little to one side, next to the doddering mother of one of the gravediggers, in new felt boots and full of humility, stood an agent of the Secret Police. "Yes," concluded Chernyshevski, "we are not concerned here with the fact that the censorship, by cutting his articles to bits, brought Dobrolyubov to a disease of the kidneys. For his own glory he did enough. For his own sake he had no reason to live longer. For men of such a cast and with such aspirations life has nothing but burning grief to offer. Honest principles—that was his fatal illness," and pointing with his rolled-up notebook to an adjacent, empty place on the other side, Chernyshevski exclaimed: "There is not a man in Russia worthy of occupying that grave!" (There was: it was occupied soon afterwards by Pisarev.)

It is difficult to escape the impression that Chernyshevski, who in his youth had dreamed of being the leader of a national uprising, was now reveling in the rarefied air of danger surrounding him. This significance in the secret life of his country he acquired inevitably, by agreement with his epoch, a family likeness with which he himself realized. Now, it seemed, he needed only a day, only an hour's run of luck in the game of history, one moment of passionate union between chance and destiny, in order to soar. A revolution was expected in 1863, and in the cabinet of the future constitutional government he was listed as prime minister. How he nursed that precious ardor within him! That mysterious "something" which Steklov talks about in spite of his Marxism, and which was extinguished in Siberia (although "learning" and "logic" and even "implacability" remained), undoubtedly existed in Chernyshevski and manifested itself with unusual strength just before his banishment to Siberia. Magnetic and dangerous, it was this that frightened the government far more than any proclamations. "This demented gang is thirsting for blood, for outrages," excitedly said the reports. "Deliver us from Chernyshevski. . . ."

"Desolation . . . Lone mountain ranges . . . A myriad lakes and marshes . . . A shortage of the most essential things . . . Inefficient postmasters . . . [All this] exhausts even the patience of genius." (This is what he had copied into *The Contemporary* from the geographer Selski's book on the Yakutsk province—thinking of certain things, supposing certain things—perhaps having a presentiment.)

In Russia the censorship department arose before literature; its fateful seniority has been always in evidence: and what an urge to give it a tweak! Chernyshevski's activities on *The Contemporary* turned into a voluptuous mockery of the censorship, which unquestionably was one of our country's most remarkable institutions. And right then, at a time when the authorities were fearful, for example, lest "musical notes should conceal antigovernmental writings in code" (and so commissioned well-paid experts to decode them), Chernyshevski, in his magazine, under the cover of elaborate clowning, was frenziedly promulgating Feuerbach. Whenever, in articles about Garibaldi or Cavour (one shrinks from computing the miles of small print this indefatigable man translated from the *Times*), in his commentaries on Italian events, he kept adding in brackets with drilling insistence after practically every other sentence: "Italy," "in Italy," "I am talking about Italy"—the already corrupted reader knew that he meant he was talking about Russia and the peasant question. Or else: Chernyshevski would pretend he was chattering about anything that came to mind, just for the sake of incoherent and vacant prattle—but suddenly, striped and spotted with words, dressed in verbal camouflage, the important idea he wished to convey would slip through. Subsequently the whole gamut of this "buffoonery" was carefully put together by Vladislav Kostomarov for the information of the secret police; the work was mean, but it gave essentially a true picture of "Chernyshevski's special devices."

Another Kostomarov, a professor, says somewhere that Chernyshevski was a first-rate chess player. Actually neither Kostomarov nor Chernyshevski knew much about chess. In his youth, it is true, Nikolay Gavrilovich once bought a set, attempted even to master a handbook, managed more or less to learn the moves, and messed about with it for quite a time (noting this messing about in detail); finally, tiring of this empty pastime, he turned over everything to a friend. Fifteen years later (remembering that Lessing had got to know Mendelssohn over a chessboard) he founded the St. Petersburg Chess Club, which was opened in January, 1862, existed through spring, gradually declining, and would have failed of itself had it not been closed down in connection with the "St. Petersburg fires." It was simply a literary and political circle situated in the so-called Ruadze House. Chernyshevski would come and sit at a table, tapping upon it with a rook (which he called a "castle"), and relate innocuous anecdotes. The radical Serno-Solovievich would arrive–(this is a Turgenevian dash) and strike up a conversation with someone in a secluded corner. It was fairly empty. The drinking fraternity—the minor writers Pomyalovski, Kurochkin, Krol—would vociferate in the bar. The first, by the way, did a little preaching of his own, promoting the idea of communal literary work—"Let's organize," he said, "a society of writer-laborers for investigating various aspects of our social life, such as: beggars, haberdashers, lamplighters, firemen—and pool in a special magazine all the material we get." Chernyshevski derided him and a silly rumor went around to the effect that Pomyalovski had "bashed his mug in." "It's all lies, I respect you too much for that," wrote Pomyalovski to him.

In a large auditorium situated in that same Ruadze House there took place on March 2, 1862, Chernyshevski's first (if you do not count his dissertation defense and the graveside speech in the frost) public address. Officially the proceeds of the evening were to go to needy students; but in actual fact it was in aid of the political prisoners Mihailov and Obruchev, who had recently been arrested. Rubinstein brilliantly performed an extremely stirring march, Professor Pavlov spoke of Russia's millennium—and added ambiguously that if the government stopped at the first step (the emancipation of the peasants) "it would stop on the brink of an abyss—let those with ears to hear, hear." (They heard him; he was immediately expulsed.) Nekrasov read some poor but "powerful" verses dedicated to the memory of Dobrolyubov, and Kurochkin read a translation of Béranger's "The Little Bird" (the captive's languishment and the rapture of sudden freedom); Chernyshevski's speech was also on Dobrolyubov.

Greeted with massive applause (the youth of those days had a way of keeping their palms hollowed while they clapped, so that the result resembled a cannon salvo), he stood for a while, blinking and smiling. Alas, his appearance did not please the ladies eagerly awaiting the *tribune*—whose portrait was unobtainable. An uninteresting, they said, face, haircut *à la moujik*, and for some reason wearing not tails but a short coat with braid and a horrible tie—"a color catastrophe" (Olga Ryzhkov, *A Woman of the Sixties: Memoirs*). Besides that he came somehow unprepared, oratory was new to him, and trying to conceal his agitation he adopted a conversational tone which seemed too modest to his friends and too familiar to his ill-wishers. He began by talking about his briefcase (from which he took a notebook), explaining that the most remarkable part of it was the lock with a small cogwheel: "Look, you give it a turn and the briefcase is locked, and if you want to lock it even more positively, it turns a different way and then comes off and goes in your pocket, and on the spot where it was, here on this plaque, there are carved arabesques: very, very nice." Then in a high, edifying voice he started to read an article by Dobrolyubov that everybody knew, but suddenly broke off and (as in the authorial digressions in *What to Do?*) chummily taking the audience into his confidence, began to explain in great detail that he had not been Dobrolyubov's guide; while speaking, he played ceaselessly with his watch chain—something that stuck in the minds of all the memoirists and was to provide a theme for scoffing journalists; but, when you come to think of it, he might have been fiddling with his watch because there was indeed very little free time left to him (four months in all!). His tone of voice, "négligé with spirit" as they used to say in the seminary, and the complete absence of revolutionary insinuations annoyed his audience; he had no success whatsoever, while Pavlov was almost chaired. The memoirist Nikoladze remarks that as soon as Pavlov had been banished from St. Petersburg, people understood and appreciated Chernyshevski's caution; he himself—subsequently, in his Siberian wilderness, where a live and avid auditorium appeared to him sometimes only in febrile dreams—keenly regretted that lame speech, that fiasco, repining at himself for not having seized that unique opportunity (since he was in any case doomed to ruin!) and not delivering from that lectern in the Ruadze Hall a speech of iron and fire, that very speech which the hero of his novel was about to give, very likely, when upon returning to freedom he took a droshky and cried to the driver: "The Galleries!"

Events went very fast that windy spring. Fires broke out here and there. And suddenly—against this orange-and-black background —a vision. Running and holding on to his hat, Dostoevski sweeps by: where to?

Whit Monday (May 28, 1862), a strong wind is blowing; a conflagration has begun on the Ligovka and then the desperadoes set fire to the Apraxin Market. Dostoevski is running, firemen are galloping "and in pharmacy windows, in gaudy glass globes, upside down are in passing reflected" (as seen by Nekrasov). And over there, thick smoke billows over the Fontanka canal in the direction of Chernyshyov Street, where presently a new, black column arises. . . . Meanwhile Dostoevski has arrived. He has arrived at the heart of the *blackness,* at Chernyshevski's place, and starts to beg him hysterically to *put a stop* to all this. Two aspects are interesting here: the belief in Nikolay Gavrilovich's satanic powers, and the rumors that the arson was being carried out according to the same plan which the Petrashevskians had drawn up as early as 1849.

Secret agents, in tones also not void of mystic horror, reported that during the night at the height of the disaster "laughter was heard coming from Chernyshevski's window." The police endowed him with a devilish resourcefulness and smelled a trick in his every move. Nikolay Gavrilovich's family went to spend the summer at Pavlovsk, a few miles from St. Petersburg, and there, a few days after the fires, on June 10th to be precise (dusk, mosquitoes, music), a certain Lyubetski, adjutant major of the Uhlan regiment of the Guards, a dashing fellow, with a name like a kiss, noticed as he was leaving the "vauxhall" two ladies capering about like mad things, and in the simpleness of his heart taking them for young Camelias (loose women), he "made an attempt to grasp them both by the waist." The four students who were with them surrounded him and threatened him with retribution, announcing that one of the ladies was the wife of the writer Chernyshevski and the other her sister. What, in the opinion of the police, is the husband's design? He tries to get the case to be submitted to the court of the officers' association—not out of considerations of honor but merely for the clandestine purpose of bringing military men and university students together. On July 5th he had to visit the Secret Police Department in connection with his complaint. Potapov, its chief, refused his petition, saying that according to his information the Uhlan was prepared to apologize. Chernyshevski curtly renounced any claims and changing the subject asked: "Tell me, the other day I sent my family off to Saratov and am preparing myself to go there for a rest [*The Contemporary* had already been closed]; but if I should need to take my wife abroad, to a spa—you see she suffers from nervous pains—could I leave without hindrance?" "Of course you could," replied Potapov good-naturedly; and two days later the arrest took place.

All this was preceded by the following event: a "universal exhibition" has just opened in London (the nineteenth century was unusually fond of exhibiting its wealth—a plentiful and tasteless dowry, which the present one has squandered); gathered there were tourists and merchants, correspondents and spies; one day at an enormous banquet Herzen, in a fit of carelessness, in view of everyone handed a certain Vetoshnikov, who was preparing to leave for Russia, a letter to the radical journalist Serno-Solovievich, who was asked to direct Chernyshevski's attention to the announcement made in *The Bell* concerning its willingness to publish *The Contemporary* abroad. The nimble foot of the messenger had hardly had time to touch Russia's sands when he was seized.

Chernyshevski was then living near the church of St. Vladimir (later his Astrakhan addresses were also defined by their proximity to this or that holy building) in a house where, before him, had lived Muravyov (later a cabinet minister), whom he was to depict with such helpless loathing in *The Prologue*. On July 7th two friends had come to see him: Doctor Bokov (who subsequently used to send medical advice to the exile) and Antonovich (a member of "Land and Freedom," who in spite of his close friendship with Chernyshevski did not suspect that the latter was connected with that society). They were sitting in the drawing room, where they were presently joined by Colonel Rakeev, a thickset black-uniformed police officer with an unpleasant, wolfish profile. He sat down with the air of a guest; actually, he had come to arrest Chernyshevski. Again historical patterns come into that odd contact "which thrills the gamester in a historian" (Strannolyubski): this was the same Rakeev who as an embodiment of the government's contemptible scurry had whisked Pushkin's coffin out of the capital into posthumous exile. Having chatted a few minutes for the sake of decorum, Rakeev informed Chernyshevski with a polite smile (which caused Doctor Bokov to "turn chill inside") that he would like to have a word with him alone. "Then let's go to my study," replied the latter and headed for it so precipitately that Rakeev, though not exactly disconcerted—he was too experienced for that—did not consider it possible in his role of guest to follow him with equal speed. But Chernyshevski immediately returned, his Adam's apple convulsively bobbing as he washed something down with cold tea (*swallowed papers* according to Antonovich's sinister guess), and looking over his spectacles, he let his guest enter first. His friends, having nothing better to do (waiting in the drawing room where most of the furniture was shrouded in dust-covers seemed uncommonly bleak), went out for a stroll ("It can't be . . . I can't believe it," Bokov kept repeating), and when they returned to the house, the fourth in Bolshoy Moskovski street, they were alarmed to see that there now stood at the door—in a kind of meek and thus all the more loathsome expectation—a prison carriage. First Bokov went in to say good-by to Chernyshevski, then—Antonovich. Nikolay Gavrilovich was sitting at his desk, playing with a pair of scissors, while the colonel sat next to it, one leg folded over the other; they were chatting—still for the sake of decorum—about the advantages of Pavlovsk over other holiday areas. "And then the company there is so excellent," the colonel was saying with a slight cough.

"What, you too are going without waiting for me?" said Chernyshevski, turning to his apostle. "Unfortunately I have to . . ." replied Antonovich, in deep confusion. "Well, good-by then," said Nikolay Gavrilovich in a joking tone of voice, and lifting his hand high, he lowered it with a swoop into Antonovich's: a type of comradely farewell which subsequently became very widespread among Russian revolutionaries.

"And so," exclaims Strannolyubski at the beginning of the greatest chapter in his incomparable monograph, "Chernyshevski has been seized!" That night the news of the arrest flies around the whole city. Many a breast is swelled with resonant indignation. Many a hand is clenched. . . . But there were not a few gloating sneers: Aha, they've put the ruffian away, removed the "impudent, yowling yokel," as it was expressed by the (slightly cracked, anyway) lady novelist Kokhanovski. Next, Strannolyubski gives a striking description of the complex work which the authorities had to carry out in order to create the evidence "which should have been there but was not," for a very curious situation had arisen: judicially speaking there was nothing to fasten on to and they had to build a scaffolding for the law to climb up and work. So they worked with "dummy quantities," calculating to remove carefully all the dummies only when the emptiness enclosed by the law was filled up by something actual. The case built up against Chernyshevski was a phantom; but it was the phantom of genuine guilt; and then—from outside, artificially, by a roundabout route—they managed to find a certain solution to the problem which almost coincided with the true one.

We have three points: C, K, P. A cathetus is drawn, CK. To offset Chernyshevski, the authorities picked out a retired Uhlan cornet, Vladislav Dmitrievich Kostomarov, who the previous August in

Moscow had been reduced to the ranks for printing seditious publications—a man with a touch of madness and a pinch of Pechorinism about him, and also a verse-maker: he left a scolopendrine trace in literature as the translator of foreign poets. Another cathetus is drawn, KP. The critic Pisarev in the periodical *The Russian Word* writes about these translations, scolding the author for "The magnificent tiara's Coruscation like a pharos" [from Hugo], praising his "simple and heartfelt" rendering of some lines by Burns (which came out as "And first of all, and first of all / Let all men honest be / Let's pray that man be to each man /A brother first of all . . . etc.), and in connection with Kostomarov's report to his readers that Heine died an unrepentant sinner, the critic roguishly advises the "grim denouncer" to "take a good look at his own public activities." Kostomarov's derangement was evidenced in his florid graphomania, in the senseless somnambulistic (even though made-to-order) composition of counterfeit letters studded with French phrases; and finally in his macabre playfulness: he signed his reports to Putilin (a detective): *Feofan Otchenashenko* (Theophanus Ourfatherson) or *Ventseslav Lyutyy* (Wenceslaus the Fiend). And, indeed, he was fiendish in his taciturnity, funest and false, boastful and cringing. Endowed with curious abilities, he could write in a feminine hand —explaining this himself by the fact that he was "visited at the full moon by the spirit of Queen Tamara." The plurality of hands he could imitate in addition to the circumstance (yet one more of destiny's jokes) that his normal handwriting recalled that of Chernyshevski considerably heightened the value of this hypnotic betrayer. For indirect evidence that the appeal proclamation "To the Serfs of Landowners" had been written by Chernyshevski, Kostomarov was given, first, the task of fabricating a note, allegedly from Chernyshevski, containing a request to alter one word in the appeal; and, secondly, of preparing a letter (to "Aleksey Nikolaevich") that would furnish proof of Chernyshevski's active participation in the revolutionary movement. Both the one and the other were then and there concocted by Kostomarov. The forgery of the handwriting is quite evident: at the beginning the forger still took pains but then he seems to have grown bored by the work and to be in a hurry to get it over: to take but the word "I," *ya* (formed in Russian script somewhat like a proofreader's dele). In Chernyshevski's genuine manuscripts it ends with an outgoing stroke which is straight and strong—and even curves a little to the right—while here, in the forgery, this stroke curves with a kind of queer jauntiness to the left, toward the head, as if the *ya* were saluting.

While these preparations went on, Nikolay Gavrilovich was held in the Alekseevski Ravelin of the Peter-and-Paul Fortress, in close proximity to the twenty-two-year-old Pisarev, who had been imprisoned there four days before him: the hypotenuse is drawn, CP, and the fateful triangle CPK is consolidated. At first, life in prison did not oppress Chernyshevski: the absence of importunate visitors even seemed refreshing . . . but the hush of the unknown soon began to chafe him. A "deep" matting swallowed without a trace the steps of the sentries pacing along the corridors. . . . The only sound that came from the outside was a clock's classic striking which vibrated long in one's ears. . . . It was a life whose portrayal demands from a writer an abundance of dots. . . . It was that unkind Russian isolation from which sprang the Russian dream of a kind multitude. By lifting a corner of the green baize curtain the sentry could look through the peephole in the door at the prisoner sitting on his green wooden bed or on a green chair, wearing a dressing gown of frieze and a peaked cap—one was permitted to keep one's own headgear as long as it was not a top hat—which does credit to the government's sense of harmony but creates by the law of negatives a rather tenacious image (as for Pisarev, he sported a fez). He was allowed a goose-quill pen, and one could write on a small green table with a sliding drawer, "whose bottom, like Achilles' heel, had remained unpainted" (Strannolyubski).

Autumn passed. A small rowan tree grew in the prison yard. Prisoner number nine was not fond of walking; at the beginning, however, he went out every day, reasoning (a quirk of thought extremely characteristic for him) that during this time the cell was searched—consequently a refusal to go out for a walk would cause the administration to suspect he was hiding something there; but when he had become convinced that this was not so (by leaving threads here and there as marks), he sat down to write with a light heart: by winter he had finished his translation of Schlosser and had begun to translate Gervinus and T. B. Macaulay. He also wrote one or two things of his own. Let us recall the "Diary"—and from one of our much earlier paragraphs let us pick up the loose ends of some sentences dealing in advance with his writings in the fortress . . . or no—let us go, if you please, even further back, to the "lachrymatory theme," which began to rotate on the initial pages of our mysteriously revolving story.

Before us is Chernyshevski's famous letter to his wife dated December 5, 1862: a yellow diamond among the dust of his numerous works. We examine this harsh-looking and ugly but amazingly legible handwriting, with its resolute strokes at the tails of the words, with loopy *R*'s and *P*'s and the broad, fervent crosses of the "hard signs"—and our lungs dilate with a pure emotion such as we have not experienced for a long time. Strannolyubski justly designates this letter as the beginning of Cherynshevski's brief flowering. All the fire, all the power of will and mind allotted him, everything that was supposed to burst forth at the hour of a national uprising, to burst forth and clutch in its hold, even if only for a short time, the supreme power . . . to jerk violently the bridle and perhaps to crimson the lip of Russia, the rearing steed, with blood—all this now found a sick outlet in his correspondence. One can say, in fact, that here was the aim and crown of all his life's dialectic, which had long been accumulating in muffled depths—these iron, fury-driven epistles to the commission examining his case, which he included in letters to his wife, the exultant rage of his arguments and this chain-rattling megalomania. "Men will remember us with gratitude," he wrote to Olga Sokratovna, and he turned out to be right: it was precisely *this* sound which echoed and spread through all the remaining space of the century, making the hearts of millions of intellectual provincials beat with sincere and noble tenderness. We have already referred to that part of the letter where he talks of his plans for compiling dictionaries. After the words "as was Aristotle" come the words: "I have begun speaking, however, of my thoughts: they are a secret; you must not tell anyone about what I say to you alone." "Here," comments Steklov, "on these two lines a teardrop has fallen and Chernyshevski had to repeat the blurred letters." This is not quite right. The teardrop fell (near the fold of the sheet) *before* the writing of these two lines; Chernyshevski had to rewrite two words, "secret" and "about" (one at the beginning of the first line, the other at the beginning of the second), words which he had started to trace each time on the wet place and which remained therefore unfinished.

Two days afterwards, getting more and more angry and more and more believing in his invulnerability, he began to "maul" his judges. This second letter to his wife can be divided up into points: 1) I told you in connection with the rumors about my possible arrest that I was not mixed up in any affair and that the government would be forced to apologize if it arrested me. 2) I assumed this because I knew they were following me—they boasted that they were doing it very well, and I relied on their boast, for my calculation was that, knowing how I lived and what I did, they would know that their suspicions were groundless. 3) It was a stupid calculation. For I also knew that in our country, people are incapable of doing anything properly. 4) Thus by my arrest they have compromised the government. 5) What can "we" do? Apologize? But what if "he" doesn't accept the apology, but says: You have compromised the government, it is my duty to explain this to the government. 6) Therefore "we" shall postpone the unpleasantness. 7) But the government asks from time to time whether Chernyshevski is guilty—and finally the government will obtain an answer. 8) It is that answer I am waiting for.

"The copy of a rather curious letter from Chernyshevski," added Potapov in pencil. "But he is mistaken: no one will have to apologize."

A few days after that he began to write his novel, *What to Do?*—and by January 15th he had sent the first portion to Pypin; a week later he sent a second, and Pypin handed both to Nekrasov for *The Contemporary*, which had again been permitted (beginning with February). At the same time *The Russian Word* was also allowed after a similar eight-month suspension; and in the impatient expectation of journalistic profit, the dangerous fezzed neighbor had already dipped his pen.

It is gratifying to be able to state that at this juncture some mysterious force resolved to try and save Chernyshevski at least from *this* mess. He was having a particularly hard time—how could one fail to have compassion? On the 28th, because the government, exasperated by his attacks, had refused him permission to see his wife, he began a hunger strike: hunger strikes were then a novelty in Russia and the exponent they found was clumsy. The guards noticed that he was wasting, but the food seemed to be getting eaten. . . . When, however, four days later, struck by the putrid smell in the cell, the warders searched it, they established that the solid food had been hidden among the books while the cabbage soup had been poured into cracks. On Sunday, February 3, at about one P.M., the military doctor attached to the fortress examined the prisoner and found that he was pale, his tongue fairly clear, his pulse a little weak—and on that same day at that same hour Nekrasov, on his way home (corner of Liteynaya and Basseynaya streets) in a hackney sleigh, lost the pink-paper package containing two manuscripts, each threaded through at the corners and entitled *What to Do?* While remembering with the lucidity of despair the whole of his route, he did not recall the fact that when nearing his house he had laid the package beside him in order to take out his purse—and just then the sleigh had turned . . . a crunch as it skidded . . . and *What to Do?* rolled off unnoticed: this was the attempt of the mysterious force—in this case centrifugal—to confiscate the book whose success was destined to have such a disastrous effect upon the fate of its author. But the attempt failed: on the snow near the Maryinski Hospital the pink package was picked up by a poor clerk burdened with a large family. Having plodded home, he donned his spectacles and examined his find . . . he saw that it was the beginning of some kind of literary work and without a tremor, and not burning his sluggish fingers, he put it aside. "Destroy it!" begged a hopeless voice: in vain. A notice of its loss was printed in the Saint Petersburg *Police Gazette*. The clerk carried the package to the indicated address, for which he received the promised reward: fifty silver rubles.

In the meantime his jailers had begun to give Nikolay Gavrilovich appetite-stimulating drops; twice he took them and then, suffering greatly, he announced that he would take no more, for he was refusing to eat not from absence of appetite but from caprice. On the morning of the 6th, "owing to lack of experience in discerning the symptoms of suffering," he ended his hunger strike and had breakfast. On the 12th, Potapov informed the commandant that the commission could not permit Chernyshevski to see his wife until he had completely recovered. The following day the commandant reported that Chernyshevski was well and writing at full blast. Olga Sokratovna came with loud complaints—about her health, about the Pypins, about the shortage of money, and then through her tears began to laugh at the little beard her husband had grown, finally getting even more upset and commencing to embrace him.

"That will do, my dear, that will do," he kept saying quite calmly —using the tepid tone he invariably maintained in his relations with her: actually he loved her passionately, hopelessly. "Neither I nor anyone else can have any grounds for thinking I shall not be set free," he told her in parting, with particular emphasis.

Another month passed. On March 23rd there was the confrontation with Kostomarov. Vladislav Dmitrievich glowered and obviously got tangled up in his own lies. Chernyshevski, with a slight smile of disgust, replied abruptly and contemptuously. His superiority was striking. "And to think," exclaims Steklov, "that at this time he was writing the buoyant *What to Do?*"

Alas! To write *What to Do?* in the fortress was not so much surprising as reckless—even for the very reason that the authorities attached it to his case. In general the history of this novel's appearance is extremely interesting. The censorship permitted it to be published in *The Contemporary,*" reckoning on the fact that a novel which was "something in the highest degree anti-artistic" would be certain to overthrow Chernyshevski's authority, that he would simply be laughed at for it. And indeed, what worth, for example, are the "light" scenes in the novel? "Verochka was supposed to drink half a glass for her wedding, half a glass for her shop and half a glass for the health of Julie [a redeemed Parisian prostitute who is now the girl friend of one of the characters!] She and Julie started a romp, with screams and clamor. . . . They began to wrestle and both fell on the sofa . . . and they no longer wanted to get up, but only continued screaming and laughing and both fell asleep." Sometimes the turn of phrase smacks of folksy barrack lore and sometimes of . . . Zoshchenko: "After tea . . . she went to her room and lay down. So there she is, reading in her comfy bed, but the book sinks away from her eyes and now Vera Pavlovna is thinking, Why is it that somehow I feel lately somewhat dull sometimes?" There are also many charming solecisms—here is a specimen: when one of the characters, a doctor, has pneumonia and calls in a colleague: "For a long time they palpated the sides of one of them."

But nobody laughed. Not even the great Russian writers laughed. Even Herzen, who found it "vilely written," immediately qualified this with: "On the other hand there is much that is good and healthy." Still, he could not resist remarking that the novel ends not simply with a phalanstery but with "a phalanstery in a brothel." For of course the inevitable happened: the eminently pure Chernyshevski (who had never been to a brothel), in his artless aspiration to equip communal love with especially beautiful trappings, involuntarily and unconsciously, out of the simplicity of his imagination, had worked his way through to those very ideals that had been evolved by tradition and routine in houses of ill repute; his gay "evening ball," based on freedom and equality in relations between the sexes (first one and then another couple disappears and returns again), is extremely reminiscent of the concluding dances in *Mme. Tellier's Establishment*.

And nevertheless it is impossible to handle this old magazine (March, 1863), containing the first installment of the novel, without a certain thrill; here also is Nekrasov's poem "Green Noise" ("Endure while you can still endure . . ."), and the derisive dressing down of Aleksey Tolstoy's romance *Prince Serebryanyy*. . . . Instead of the expected sneers, an atmosphere of general, pious worship was created around *What to Do?* It was read the way liturgical books are read—not a single work by Turgenev or Tolstoy produced such a mighty impression. The inspired Russian reader understood the good that the talentless novelist had vainly tried to express. It would seem that, having realized its miscalculation, the government should have interrupted the serialization of *What to Do?* It behaved much more cleverly.

Chernyshevski's neighbor had now also done some writing. He had been receiving *The Contemporary* and on October 8th, he sent *The Russian Word* an article from the fortress, "Thoughts about Russian Novels," at which the Senate informed the Governor-General that this was nothing else but an analysis of Chernyshevski's novel, with praise for this work and a detailed exposition of the materialistic ideas in it. In order to characterize Pisarev it was indicated that he was subject to "dementia melancholica," for which he had been treated: in 1859 he had spent four months in a lunatic asylum.

Just as, in his boyhood, he had arrayed all his notebooks in rainbow covers, so, as a grown man, Pisarev would suddenly abandon some urgent work in order to painstakingly color woodcuts in books, or when going off to the country, would order a red-and-blue summer suit of sarafan calico from his tailor. This professed utilitarian's mental illness was distinguished by a kind of perverted aestheticism. Once at a student gathering he suddenly stood up, gracefully raised his curved arm, as if requesting permission to speak, and in this sculpturesque pose fell down unconscious. Another time, to the alarm of his hostess and fellow guests, he began to undress, throwing off with gay alacrity his velvet jacket, motley vest, checkered trousers—At this point they overpowered him. Amusingly enough there are commentators who call Pisarev an "epicure," referring, for example, to his letters to his mother—unbearable, bilious, teeth-clenching phrases about life being beautiful; or else: to illustrate his "sober realism" they quote his outwardly sensible and clear—but actually completely insane—letter from the fortress to an unknown maiden, with a proposal of marriage: "The woman who agrees to lighten and warm my life will receive from me all the love which was spurned by Raissa when she threw herself at the neck of her handsome eagle."

Now, condemned to a four-year imprisonment for his small part in the general disturbances of the time (which were based in a way on a blind belief in the printed word, especially the secretly printed word), Pisarev wrote about *What to Do?*, reviewing it bit by bit for *The Russian Word* as the installments appeared in *The Contemporary*. Although in the beginning the Senate was puzzled by the novel's being praised for its ideas instead of being ridiculed because of its style, and expressed the fear that the praises might have a deleterious effect on the younger generation, the authorities soon realized how important it was in the present case to obtain by this method a complete picture of Chernyshevski's perniciousness, which Kostomarov had only outlined in the list of his "special devices." "The government," says Strannolyubski "on the one hand permitting Chernyshevski to produce a novel in the fortress and on the other permitting Pisarev, his fellow captive, to produce articles explaining the intentions of this novel, acted with complete awareness, waiting curiously for Chernyshevski to babble himself out and watching what would come of it—in connection with the abundant discharges of his incubator neighbor."

The business went smoothly and promised a great deal, but it was necessary to put pressure on Kostomarov since one or two definite proofs of guilt were needed, while Chernyshevski continued to boil and jeer in great detail, branding the commission as "clowns" and "an incoherent quagmire which is completely stupid." Therefore Kostomarov was taken to Moscow and there the citizen Yakovlev, his former copyist, a drunkard and a rowdy, gave important testimony (for this he received an overcoat which he drank away so noisily in Tver that he was put in a strait-jacket): while doing his copying "on account of the summer weather in a garden pavilion," he allegedly heard Nikolay Gavrilovich and Vladislav Dmitrievich as they were strolling arm-in-arm (a not implausible detail), talking about greetings from well-wishers to the serfs (it is difficult to find one's way in this mixture of truth and promptings). At a second interrogation in the presence of a replenished Kostomarov, Chernyshevski said somewhat unfortunately that he had visited him only once and not found him in; then he added forcefully: "I'll go gray, I'll die, but I will not change my testimony." The testimony of his not being the author of the proclamation is written by him in a trembling hand—trembling with rage rather than fright.

However that may have been, the case was coming to an end. There followed the Senate's "definition": very nobly it found Chernyshevski's unlawful dealings with Herzen unproved (for Herzen's "definition" of the Senate see below, at the end of this paragraph). As for the appeal "To the Serfs of Landowners" . . . here the fruit had already ripened on the espaliers of forgery and bribes: the absolute moral conviction of the senators that Chernyshevski was the author thereof was transformed into judicial proof by the letter to "Aleksey Nikolaevich" (meaning, apparently, A. N. Pleshcheev, a peaceful poet, dubbed by Dostoevski "an all-round blond"—but for some reason no one insisted too much on Pleshcheev's part, if any, in the matter). Thus in Chernyshevski's person they condemned a phantasm closely resembling him; an invented guilt was wonderfully rigged up to look like the real one. The sentence was comparatively light—compared with what one is generally able to devise in this line: he was to be exiled for fourteen years of penal servitude and then to live in Siberia forever. The "definition" went from the "savage ignoramuses" of the Senate to the "gray villains" of the State Council, who completely subscribed to it, and then went on to the sovereign, who confirmed it but reduced the term of penal servitude by half. On May 4, 1864, the sentence was announced to Chernyshevski, and on the 19th, at 8 o'clock in the morning, on Mytninski Square, he was executed.

It was drizzling, umbrellas undulated, the square was beslushed, and everything was wet; gendarmes' uniforms, the darkened wood of the scaffold, the smooth, black pillar with chains, glossy from the rain. Suddenly the prison carriage appeared. From it emerged, with extraordinary celerity, as if they had rolled out, Chernyshevski in an overcoat and two peasant-like executioners; all three walked with swift steps along a line of soldiers to the scaffold. The crowd lurched forward and the gendarmes pressed back the front ranks; restrained cries sounded here and there: "Close the umbrellas!" While an official read the sentence, Chernyshevski, who already knew it, sulkily looked around him; he fingered his beard, adjusted his spectacles and spat several times. When the reader stumbled and barely got out "soshulistic ideas" Chernyshevski smiled and then, recognizing someone in the crowd, nodded, coughed, shifted his stance: from beneath the overcoat his black trousers concertinaed over his rubbers. People standing near could see on his chest an oblong plaque with an inscription in white: STATE CRIMIN (the last syllable had not gone in). At the conclusion of the reading the executioners lowered him to his knees; the elder one, with a backhander, knocked the cap off his long, combed-back, light auburn hair. The face, tapering chinward, its large forehead shining, was now bent down, and with a resounding crack they managed to break an insufficiently incised sword over him. Then they took his hands, which seemed unusually white and weak, and put them in black irons secured to the pillar: he had to stand that way for a quarter of an hour. The rain increased: the younger executioner picked up Chernyshevski's cap and jammed it on his inclined head —and slowly, with difficulty, the chains got in his way—Chernyshevski straightened it. Behind a fence to the left one could see the scaffolding of a house under construction; workmen climbed onto the fence from the other side, one could hear the scrape of their boots; they climbed up, hung there, and abused the criminal from afar. The rain fell; the elder executioner consulted his silver watch. Chernyshevski kept turning his wrists slightly without looking up. Suddenly, out of the better-off part of the crowd, bouquets began to fly. The gendarmes, jumping, tried to intercept them in midair. Roses exploded in the air; fleetingly one was able to see a rare combination: a policeman, wreathed. Bobbed-haired ladies in black burnouses threw racemes of lilac. Meanwhile Chernyshevski was hastily released from his chains and his dead body borne away. No—a slip of the pen; alas, he was alive, he was even cheerful! Students ran beside the carriage with cries of "Farewell, Chernyshevski! *Au revoir*!" He thrust his head out of the window, laughed and shook his finger at the most zealous runners.

"Alas, alive," we exclaimed, for how could one not prefer the death penalty, the convulsions of the hanged man in his hideous cocoon, to that funeral which twenty-five insipid years later fell to Chernyshevski's lot. The paw of oblivion began slowly to gather in his living image as soon as he had been removed to Siberia. Oh yes, oh yes, no doubt students for years sang the song: "Let us drink to him who wrote *What to Do? . . .*" But it was to the past they drank, to past glamour and scandal, to a great shade . . . but who would drink to a tremulous little old man with a tic, making clumsy paper boats for Yakut children somewhere in those fabulous backwoods? We affirm that his book drew out and gathered within itself all the heat of his personality—a heat which is not to be found in its helplessly rational structures but which is concealed as it were between the words (as only bread is hot) and it was inevitably doomed to be dispersed with time (as only bread knows how to go stale and hard). Today, it seems, only Marxists are still capable of being interested by the ghostly ethics contained in this dead little book. To follow easily and freely the categorical imperative of the general good, here is the "rational egoism" which researchers have found in *What to Do?* Let us recall for comic relief Kautski's conjecture that the idea of egoism is connected with the development of commodity production, and Plekhanov's conclusion that Chernyshevski was nevertheless an "idealist," since it comes out in his book that the masses must catch up with the intelligentsia out of calculation—and calculation is an opinion. But the matter is simpler than that: the idea that calculation is the foundation of every action (or heroic accomplishment) leads to absurdity: in itself calculation can be heroic! Anything which comes into the focus of human thinking is spiritualized. Thus the "calculation" of the materialists was ennobled; thus, for those in the know, matter turns into an incorporeal play of mysterious forces. Chernyshevski's ethical structures are in their own way an attempt to construct the same old "perpetual motion" machine, where matter moves other matter. We would very much like this to revolve: egoism-altruism-egoism-altruism . . . but the wheel stops from friction. What to do? Live, read, think. What to do? Work at one's own development in order to achieve the aim of life, which is happiness. What to do? (But Chernyshevski's own fate changed the businesslike question to an ironic exclamation.)

Chernyshevski would have been transferred to a private domicile much sooner if it had not been for the affair of the Karakozovites (adherents of Karakozov, who attempted to assassinate Alexander the Second in 1866): it was made clear at their trial that they had wanted to give Chernyshevski the opportunity of escaping from Siberia and heading a revolutionary movement—or at least publishing a political review in Geneva; and checking the dates, the judges found in *What to Do?* a forecast of the date of the attempt on the Tsar's life. The protagonist Rakhmetov, on his way abroad, "said among other things that three years later he would return to Russia, because, it seemed, not then, but three years later [a highly significant repetition typical of our author], he would be needed in Russia." Meanwhile the last part of the novel was signed on April 4, 1863, and exactly three years later to the day the attempt took place. Thus even figures, Chernyshevski's goldfish, let him down.

Rakhmetov is forgotten today; but in those years he created a whole school of life. With what piety its readers imbibed the sporty, revolutionary element in the novel: Rakhmetov, who "adopted a boxer's diet," followed also a dialectical regime: "Therefore if fruit was served he absolutely ate apples and absolutely did not eat apricots (since the poor did not); oranges he ate in St. Petersburg, but did not eat in the provinces, because you see in St. Petersburg the common people eat them, while in the provinces they do not."

Where did that young, round little face suddenly flit from, with its large, childishly prominent forehead and cheeks like two cups? Who is this girl resembling a hospital nurse, wearing a black dress with a white turn-down collar and a little watch on a cord? It is Sophia Perovski, who is to hang for the assassination of the Tsar in 1881. Coming to Sebastopol in 1872, she toured the surrounding villages on foot in order to become acquainted with the life of the peasants: she was in her period of Rakhmetovism—sleeping on straw, living on milk and gruels. And returning to our initial position we repeat: Sophia Perovski's instantaneous fate is a hundred times more to be envied than the fading glory of a reformer! For as copies of *The Contemporary* with the novel, passing from hand to hand, became more and more tattered, so did Chernyshevski's enchantments fade; and the esteem for him, which had long since turned into a sentimental convention, was no longer able to make hearts glow when he died in 1889. The funeral passed quietly. There were few comments in the newspapers. At the requiem held for him in St. Petersburg the workmen in town clothes, whom the dead man's friends had brought for the sake of atmosphere, were taken by a group of students for plainclothesmen and insulted—which restored a certain equilibrium: was it not the fathers of these workmen who had abused the kneeling Chernyshevski from over the fence?

On the day following that mock execution, at dusk, "with shackles on my feet and a head full of thoughts," Chernyshevski left St.

Petersburg forever. He traveled in a tarantass, and since "to read books on the way" was permitted only beyond Irkutsk, he was extremely bored for the first month and a half of the journey. On July 23rd they brought him at last to the mines of the Nerchin mountain district at Kadaya: ten miles from China, four thousand six hundred from St. Petersburg. He was not made to work much. He lived in a badly caulked cottage and suffered from rheumatism. Two years passed. Suddenly a miracle happened: Olga Sokratovna prepared to join him in Siberia.

During most of his imprisonment in the fortress she, it is said, had been coursing about in the provinces and caring so little about her husband's fate that her relatives even wondered whether she was not deranged. On the eve of the public disgrace she had sped back to St. Petersburg, and on the morning of the 20th had sped off again. We would never have believed her capable of making the trip to Kadaya if we had not known her ability to move easily and hectically from one place to another. How he awaited her! Starting at the beginning of summer in 1866, together with seven-year-old Misha and a Dr. Pavlinov (Dr. Peacock—we are again entering the sphere of beautiful names), she got as far as Irkutsk, where she was held up for two months; there they stayed in a hotel with the enchantingly idiotic name (possibly distorted by biographers but most probably selected with particular care by sly fate) of Hotel de Amour et Co. Dr. Pavlinov was not permitted to go any further: he was replaced by a captain in the gendarmes, Hmelevski (a perfected edition of the dashing Pavlovsk hero), passionate, drunken, and brazen. They arrived on August 23rd. In order to celebrate the meeting of man and wife, one of the exiled Poles, a former cook of Count di Cavour, the Italian statesman of whom Chernyshevski had once written so much and so caustically, baked one of those pastries on which his late master had been wont to stuff himself. But the meeting was not a success: it is amazing how everything bitter and heroic which life manufactured for Chernyshevski was invariably accompanied by a flavoring of vile farce. Hmelevski hovered about and would not leave Olga Sokratovna alone; in her gypsy eyes there lurked something hunted but also enticing—against her will, perhaps. In return for her favors he is even alleged to have offered to arrange her husband's escape, but the latter resolutely refused. In short, the constant presence of this shameless man made things so difficult (and what plans we had made!) that Chernyshevski himself persuaded his wife to set out on the return journey, and this she did on August 27th, having stayed thus, after a three-month journey, only four days—four days, reader!—with the husband whom she was now leaving for seventeen odd years. Nekrasov dedicated *Peasant Children* to her. It is a pity he did not dedicate to her his *Russian Women*.

During the last days of September, Chernyshevski was transferred to Aleksandrovski Zavod, a settlement twenty miles from Kadaya. He spent the winter there in prison, together with some Karakozovites and rebellious Poles. The dungeon was equipped with a Mongolian specialty—"stakes": posts dug vertically into the ground and surrounding the prison in a solid ring. In June of the following year, having completed his probationery term, Chernyshevski was released on parole and took a room in the house of a sexton, a man who looked very much like him: gray purblind eyes, a sparse beard, long, tangled hair. . . . Always a little drunk, always sighing, he would sorrowfully answer the questions of the curious with "The dear fellow keeps writing and writing!" But Chernyshevski stayed there no more than two months. His name was taken in vain at political trials. The half-witted artisan Rozanov testified that the revolutionaries wanted to catch and cage "a bird with royal blood in order to ransom Chernyshevski." Count Shuvalov sent the Irkutsk Governor-General a telegram: THE AIM OF THE EMIGRES IS TO FREE CHERNYSHEVSKI (STOP) PLEASE TAKE ALL POSSIBLE MEASURES IN REGARD TO HIM. Meanwhile the exile Krasovski, who had been transferred at the same time as he, had fled (and perished in the taiga, after having been robbed), so that there was every reason to jail dangerous Chernyshevski once again and to deprive him for a month of the right to correspondence.

Suffering intolerably from drafts, he never removed either his fur-lined dressing gown or his lambskin shapka. He moved about like a leaf blown by the wind, with a nervous stumbling gait, and his shrill voice could be heard now here and now there. His trick of logical reasoning was intensified—"in the manner of his father-in-law's namesake," as Strannolyubski so whimsically puts it. He lived in the "office": a spacious room divided by a partition; along the entire wall in the larger part there ran a low "sleeping shelf," in the nature of a platform; there, as if on a stage (or the way in zoos they exhibit a melancholy beast of prey among its native rocks) stood a bed and a table, which were essentially the natural furnishings of his whole life. He used to get up after midday, would drink tea all day and lie reading the whole time; he would sit down to do some real writing only at midnight, since during the day his immediate neighbors, some nationalist Poles who were completely indifferent to him, would indulge in fiddling and torture him with their unlubricated music: by profession they were wheelwrights. To the other exiles he used to read on winter evenings. They noticed once that although he was calmly and smoothly reading a tangled tale, with lots of "scientific" digressions, he was looking at a blank notebook. A gruesome symbol!

It was then that he wrote a new novel. Still full of the success of *What to Do?* he expected much from it—most of all he expected the money which, printed abroad, the novel was supposed one way or another to bring in for his family. *The Prologue* is extremely autobiographical. When referring to it once, we spoke of its peculiar attempt to rehabilitate Olga Sokratovna; it conceals a similar attempt, in Strannolyubski's opinion, to rehabilitate the author's own person, for, underlining on the one hand Volgin's influence, which reaches the point where "high dignitaries sought his favors through his wife" (because they supposed he had "connections with London"; i.e., with Herzen, of whom the newly fledged liberals were mortally afraid), the author on the other hand insists obstinately on Volgin's suspiciousness, timidity and inactivity: "To wait and wait as long as possible, to wait as quietly as possible." One gets the impression that the stubborn Chernyshevski wants to have the last word in the quarrel, putting firmly on record what he had repeatedly said to his judges: "I must be considered on the basis of my actions and there were no actions and could not have been any."

Concerning the "light" scenes in *The Prologue* we had better keep silent. Through their morbidly circumstantial eroticism one can make out such a throbbing tenderness for his wife that the least quotation from them might appear to be exaggerated derision. Instead let us listen to this pure sound—in his letters to her during those years: "My dearest darling, I thank you for being the light of my life." . . . "I would be even here one of the happiest men in the world if it did not occur to me that this fate, which is very much to my personal advantage, is too hard in its effects on your life, my dear friend." . . . "Will you forgive me the grief to which I have subjected you?"

Chernyshevski's hopes for literary profits were not realized: the émigrés not only misused his name but also pirated his works. And entirely fatal for him were the attempts made to free him, attempts which were in themselves courageous but which seem senseless to us, who can see from the hilltop of time the disparity between the image of a "fettered giant" and the real Chernyshevski whom these efforts by his would-be saviors only enraged: "These gentlemen," he said later, "didn't even know that I can't ride a horse." This inner contradiction resulted in nonsense (a particular shade of nonsense already long known to us). It is said that Ippolit Myshkin, disguised as a gendarme officer, went to Vilyuisk where he demanded of the district police chief that the prisoner be handed over to him, but spoiled the whole business by putting his shoulder knot on the left side instead of the right. Before this, namely in 1871, there was Lopatin's attempt in which everything was absurd: the way he suddenly abandoned the Russian translation of *Das Kapital* that he was making in London, in order to get for Marx, who had learned to read Russian, "*den grossen russischen Gelehrten*"; his journey to Irkutsk in the guise of a member of the Geographical Society (with the Siberian residents taking him for a government inspector incognito); his arrest following a tip-off from Switzerland; his flight and capture; and his letter to the Governor-General of Eastern Siberia in which he told him all about his project with inexplicable frankness. All this only worsened Chernyshevski's situation. Legally his settlement was supposed to begin on August 10, 1870. But only on December 2nd was he moved to another place, to a place which turned out to be far worse than penal servitude—to Vilyuisk.

"Forsaken by God in a dead end of Asia," says Strannolyubski, "in the depths of the Yakutsk region, far to the northeast, Vilyuisk was nothing but a hamlet standing on a huge pile of sand heaped up by the river, and surrounded by a boundless bog overgrown by taiga scrub." The inhabitants (500 people) were: Cossacks, half-wild Yakuts, and a small number of low middle-class citizens (whom Steklov describes very picturesquely: "The local society consisted of a pair of officials, a pair of clerics and a pair of merchants"—as if he were talking about the Ark). There Chernyshevski was lodged in the best house, and the best house turned out to be the jail. The door of his damp cell was lined with black oilcloth; the two windows which anyway were right up against the palisade were barred up. In the absence of any other exiles, he found himself in complete solitude. Despair, helplessness, the consciousness of having been deceived, a dizzy feeling of injustice, the ugly shortcomings of arctic life, all this almost drove him out of his mind. On the morning of July 10, 1872, he suddenly began to break the door lock with a pair of tongs, shaking all over, and mumbling, and crying out: "Has the sovereign or a minister come that the police sergeant dares to lock the door at night?" By winter he had calmed down a bit, but from time to time there were certain reports . . . and here we are granted one of those rare correlations that constitute the researcher's pride.

Once (in 1853), his father had written him (regarding his *A Tentative Lexicon of the Hypatian Chronicle*): "You would do better to write some tale or other . . . tales are still in fashion in good society." Many years afterwards Chernyshevski informs his wife that he has thought up in his prison and wants to set down in writing "an ingenious little tale" wherein he will portray her in the form of two girls: "It will be quite a good little tale [repeating his father's rhythm]. If only you knew how much I have laughed to myself when depicting the various noisy frolics of the younger one, how much I cried with tenderness when depicting the pathetic meditations of the elder!" "At night Chernyshevski," reported his jailers, "sometimes sings, sometimes dances and sometimes weeps and sobs."

The mail went out of Yakutsk once a month. The January number of a St. Petersburg magazine was received only in May. He tried to cure the illness he had developed (goiter) with the aid of a textbook. The exhausting catarrh of the stomach that he had known as a student now returned with new peculiarities. "I am nauseated by the subject of 'peasants' and 'peasant ownership of the land,'" he wrote to his son, who had thought to interest him by sending him some books on economics. The food was repulsive. He ate almost nothing but cooked cereals: straight from the pot—with a silver tablespoon, of which almost a quarter was worn away on the pot's earthenware sides during the twenty years that he himself was wearing away. On warm summer days he would stand for hours with his trousers rolled up in a shallow stream (which could hardly have been beneficial); or, with his head wrapped in a towel against the mosquitoes, which made him look like a Russian peasant woman, he would stroll along forest paths with his plaited mushroom basket, never plunging into the denser wildwood. He would forget his cigarette case under a larch, which he was some time in learning to distinguish from a pine. The flowers which he gathered (whose names he did not know) he wrapped in cigarette paper and sent to his son Misha, who acquired that way "a small herbarium of the Vilyuisk flora": thus did Princess Volkonski in Nekrasov's poem about the Decembrists' wives bequeath her grandchildren "a collection of butterflies, plants of Chita." Once an eagle appeared in his yard . . . "it had come to peck at his liver," remarks Strannolyubski, "but did not recognize Prometheus in him."

The pleasure which he had experienced in his youth from the orderly disposition of the St. Petersburg waters now received a late echo: from nothing to do he dug out canals—and almost flooded one of the Vilyuisk residents' favorite roads. He quenched his thirst for spreading culture by teaching manners to Yakuts, but just as before, the native would remove his cap at a distance of twenty paces and in that position would meekly freeze. The practicality and good sense he used to advocate now dwindled to his advising the water-carrier to substitute a regular yoke of wood for the crook made of hair, which cut his palms; but the Yakut did not change his routine. In the little town where all they did was play cards and have passionate discussions about the price of Chinese cotton, his yearning for activity in public affairs led him to the

Old-Believers, about whose plight Chernyshevski wrote an extraordinarily long and detailed memoir (including even Vilyuisk gossip) and coolly sent it off addressed to the Tsar, with the friendly suggestion he pardon them because they "esteem him as a saint."

He wrote a lot but burned almost everything. He informed his relatives that the results of his "learned work" would undoubtedly be accepted sympathetically; this work was ashes and a mirage. Out of the whole heap of writings which he produced in Siberia, besides *The Prologue*, only two or three stories and a "cycle" of unfinished "novellas" have been preserved. . . . He also wrote poems. In texture they are no different from those versificatory tasks which he had once been given in the seminary, when he had reset a psalm of David in the following manner:

> Upon me lay one duty only—
> To mind my father's flock of sheep,
> And hymns I early started singing
> For to extol the Lord withal.

In 1875 (to Pypin) and again in 1888 (to Lavrov) he sends "an ancient Persian poem": a ghastly thing! In one of the strophes the pronoun "their" is repeated *seven* times ("Their country is barren, Their bodies are fleshless, And through their torn garments their ribs one can tell. Their faces are broad, and their features are flattened; Upon their flat features the soul does not dwell") while in the monstrous chains of the genitive case ("Of howls of the ache of their craving for blood") now, at the parting with literature, under a very low sun, there is evidence of the author's familiar leaning toward congruity, toward links. To Pypin he writes heartrending letters expressing his stubborn desire to thwart the administration and occupy himself with literature: "This thing [*The Academy of Azure Mountains*, signed Denzil Elliot—purporting to be from the English] is of high literary merit. . . . I am patient, but—I hope no one intends to prevent me from working for my family. . . . I am famous in Russian literature for the carelessness of my style. . . . When I want to I can also write in all sorts of good styles."

Weep ye, O! for Lilybaeum;
We with you together weep.
Weep ye, O! for Agrigentum;
Reinforcements we await.

"What is [this] hymn to the Maid of the Skies? An episode from the prose story of Empedocles' grandson . . . And what is the story of Empedocles' grandson? One of the innumerable stories in *The Academy of Azure Mountains*. The Duchess of Cantershire has set off with a company of fashionable friends on a yacht through the Suez Canal to the East Indies in order to visit her tiny kingdom at the foot of the Azure Mountains, near Golconda. There they do what intelligent and good people of fashion do: They tell stories—stories that will follow in the next packages from Denzil Elliot to the editor of *The Messenger of Europe*" (Stasyulevich—who did not print any of this).

One feels dizzy, the letters swim and fade in one's eyes—and here we again pick up the theme of Chernyshevski's spectacles. He asked his relatives to send him new ones, but in spite of his efforts to explain it particularly graphically, he nonetheless made a mess of it, and six months later he received from them number "four and a half instead of five or five and a quarter."

He gave an outlet to his passion for instruction by writing to Sasha about the mathematician Fermat, to Misha about the struggle between Popes and Emperors, and to his wife about medicine, Carlsbad, and Italy. . . . It ended the way it was bound to end: the authorities requested him to stop writing "learned letters." This so offended and shook him that for over six months he did not write any letters at all (the authorities never saw the day when they would get from him those humble petitions which, for instance, Dostoevski used to dispatch from Semipalatinsk to the strong of this world). "There is no news from Papa," wrote Olga Sokratovna to her son in 1879. "I wonder if he, my dear one, is still alive," and she can be forgiven much for this intonation.

Yet one more jackanapes with a name ending in "ski" suddenly pops up as an extra: on March 15, 1881, "your unknown pupil Vitevski," as he recommends himself, but according to police information a tippling doctor at the Stavropol district hospital, sends him a wire to Vilyuisk protesting with completely superfluous heat against an anonymous opinion that Chernyshevski was responsible for the assassination of the Tsar: "Your works are filled with peace and love. You never desired this (i.e., the assassination)." Whether because of these artless words or because of something else, the government softened and in the middle of June it showed its jail tenant a bit of thoughtful kindness: it had the walls of his domicile papered in "*gris perle* with a border," and the ceiling covered with calico, which in toto cost the exchequer 40 rubles and 88 kopecks; i.e., somewhat more than Yakovlev's overcoat and Musa's coffee. And already the following year the haggling over Chernyshevski's ghost was concluded, after negotiations between the Volunteer Security Guards (the secret police) and the executive committee of the underground People's Freedom concerning the preservation of law and order during Alexander the Third's coronation, with the decision that if the latter went off smoothly, Chernyshevski would be freed: thus he was bartered in exchange for tsars—and vice versa (a process that subsequently found its material expression when the Soviet authorities substituted in Saratov his statue for that of Alexander the Second). A year later, in May, a petition was submitted in his sons' names (he, of course, knew nothing of this), in the most florid and tear-jerking style imaginable. The Minister of Justice, Nabokov, made the appropriate report and "His Majesty deigned to permit the transfer of Chernyshevski to Astrakhan."

At the end of February, 1883 (overburdened time was already having difficulty in dragging his destiny), the gendarmes, without a word of the resolution, suddenly took him to Irkutsk. No matter—leaving Vilyuisk was in itself a happy event, and more than once during the summer voyage up the long Lena (revealing such kinship with the Volga in its meanders) the old man broke into a dance, chanting dactylic hexameters. But in September the voyage ended and with it the sensation of freedom. On the very first night Irkutsk appeared as the same kind of casemate in the deepest of provincial backwoods. In the morning he was visited by the chief of the gendarmerie, Keller. Nikolay Gavrilovich sat leaning his elbow on the table and did not respond at once. "The Emperor has pardoned you," said Keller, and repeated it even louder, seeing that the other was apparently half-asleep or beclouded. "Me?" said the old man suddenly, then stood up, placed his hands on the herald's shoulders and, shaking his head, burst into tears. In the evening, feeling as if convalescent after a long illness, but still weak, with a delicious mist permeating his being, he had tea at the Kellers', talking incessantly and telling the latters' children "more or less Persian fairy tales—about asses, roses, robbers . . ." as one of his hearers recalled. Five days later he was taken to Krasnoyarsk, from there to Orenburg—and in the late autumn at between six and seven in the evening he drove with post-horses through Saratov; there, in the yard of an inn by the gendarmery, in the mobile darkness, a wretched little lamp swayed so much in the wind that one simply could not distinguish properly Olga Sokratovna's changeable, young, old, young face wrapped in a woolen kerchief—she had rushed headlong to this unhoped-for meeting; and that same night Chernyshevski (who could tell his thoughts?) was dispatched further.

With great mastery and with the utmost vividness of exposition (it might almost be taken for compassion) Strannolyubski describes his installation in his Astrakhan residence. No one met him with open arms, he was invited by no one, and very soon he understood that all the grandiose plans which had been his only support in exile must now melt away in an inanely lucid and quite imperturbable stillness.

To his Siberian illnesses Astrakhan added yellow fever. He frequently caught cold. He suffered acute palpitations of the heart. He smoked heavily and untidily. But worst of all, he was extremely nervous. He had an odd way of jumping up in the middle of a conversation—an abrupt movement stemming as it were from the day of his arrest, when he had dashed into his study, forestalling the funest Rakeyev. On the street he could be mistaken for a little old artisan: stoop-shouldered, wearing a cheap summer suit and a crumpled cap. "But tell me . . ." "But don't you think . . ." "But . . .": casual busybodies used to bother him with absurd questions. The actor Syroboyarski kept on asking him "Shall I marry or no?" There were two or three last little denunciations which fizzed like damp fireworks. The company he kept consisted of some local

Armenians—grocers and haberdashers. Educated people were surprised by the fact that somehow he did not take much interest in public affairs. "Well, what do you want," he would reply cheerlessly, "what can I make of it all? Why, I haven't even once attended a trial by jury, not once been to a meeting of the zemstvo . . ."

Hair smoothly parted, with uncovered ears too big for her, and with a "bird's nest" just below the crown of her head—here she is again with us (she has brought candy and kittens from Saratov); there is on her long lips that same mocking half-smile, the martyred line of her brows is still sharper, and the sleeves of her dress are now puffed out above the shoulders. She is already past fifty (1833-1918) but her character is still the same, neurotically naughty; her hysterical fits culminate sometimes into convulsions.

During these last six years of his life, poor, old, unwanted Nikolay Gavrilovich translates with machine-like steadiness volume after volume of Georg Weber's *Universal History* for the publisher Soldatenkov—and at the same time, moved by his ancient, irrepressible need to air his opinions, he tries gradually to smuggle through Weber some of his own ideas. He signs his translation "Andreyev"; and in his review of the first volume (in *The Examiner*, February 1884) a critic remarks that this "is a kind of pseudonym, since in Russia there are as many Andreyevs as there are Ivanovs and Petrovs"; this is followed by stinging allusions to the heaviness of the style and by a small reprimand: "There was no need for Mr. Andreyev to dilate in his Foreword on the merits and demerits of Weber, who has long been known to the Russian reader. His textbook came out as early as the fifties and simultaneously three volumes of his *Course of Universal History* in the translation of E. and V. Korsh. . . . He would be well advised not to ignore the works of his predecessors."

E. Korsh, a lover of arch-Russian terminology instead of that accepted by German philosophers, was by now an eighty-year-old man, an assistant of Soldatenkov's, and in this capacity he proofread the "Astrakhan translator," introducing corrections which enraged Chernyshevski, who in letters to the publisher set about "mauling" Evgeniy Fyodorovich according to his old system, at first demanding furiously that the proofreading be given to somebody else "who understands better that there is not another man in Russia who knows the Russian literary language as well as I do," and then, when he had got his own way, employing another device: "Can I really be interested in such trifles? However, if Korsh wants to continue to read the proofs, ask him not to make corrections, they are indeed ridiculous." With no less bitter pleasure he also mauled Zaharyin, who out of the goodness of his heart had spoken to Soldatenkov regarding a monthly payment (of 200 rubles) to Chernyshevski in view of Ogla Sokratovna's extravagance. "You were fooled by the effrontery of a man whose mind has been befuddled by drunkenness," wrote Chernyshevski to Soldatenkov, and setting in motion the whole apparatus of his logic—rusty, creaky but still as wriggly as ever, he at first justified his ire by the fact that he was being taken for a thief who wished to acquire capital, and then explained that his anger was actually only a sham for Olga Sokratovna's sake: "Thanks to the fact that she learned of her extravagance from my letter to you, and I didn't give in to her when she asked me to soften my expression, there were no convulsions." At this point (the end of 1888) another brief review happened along—by now on Weber's tenth volume. The terrible state of his mind, wounded pride, an old man's crotchetiness and the last, hopeless attempts to shout down the silence (a feat even more difficult than Lear's attempt to shout down the storm), all this must be remembered when you read through his spectacles the review on the inside of the pale-pink cover of *The Messenger of Europe:*

> . . . Unfortunately it appears from the Foreword that the Russian translator has remained true to his simple duties as a translator only in the first six volumes, but beginning with the seventh volume he has laid upon himself a new duty . . . "to clean up" Weber. It is hardly possible to be grateful to him for the kind of translation where the author is "refurbished," and such an authoritative author, at that, as Weber.

"It would seem," remarks Strannolyubski here (somewhat mixing his metaphors), "that with this careless kick destiny had given the last suitable touch to the chain of retribution it had forged for him." But that is not so. There remains for our inspection one more—most terrible, most complete, ultimate punishment.

Of all the madmen who tore Chernyshevski's life into shreds, the worst was his son; not the youngest, of course, Mihail (Misha), who lived a quiet life, lovingly working away at tariff questions (he was employed in the railroads department): he had been evolved from his father's "positive number" and was a good son, for at the time (1896–98) when his prodigal brother (which makes a moralistic picture) was publishing his *Fantastic Tales* and a collection of futile poems, he was piously beginning his monumental edition of his late father's works, which he had practically brought to conclusion when he died, in 1924, surrounded by general esteem—ten years after Alexander (Sasha) had died suddenly in sinful Rome, in a small room with a stone floor, declaring his superhuman love for Italian art and crying in the heat of wild inspiration that if people would only listen to him life would be different, different! Created apparently out of everything that his father could not stand, Sasha, hardly out of his boyhood, developed a passion for everything that was weird, chimerical, and incomprehensible to his contemporaries—he lost himself in E.T.A. Hoffmann and Edgar Poe, was fascinated by pure mathematics, and a little later he was one of the first in Russia to appreciate the French "*poètes maudits.*" The father, vegetating in Siberia, was unable to look after the development of his son (who was brought up by the Pypins) and what he learned he interpreted in his own way, the more so since they concealed Sasha's mental disease from him. Gradually, however, the purity of this mathematics began to irritate Chernyshevski—and one can easily imagine with what feelings the youth used to read those long letters from his father, beginning with a deliberately debonair joke and then (like the conversations of that Chekhov character who used to begin so well—"an old alumnus, you know, an incurable idealist . . .") concluding with irate abuse; this passion for mathematics enraged him not only as a manifestation of something nonutilitarian: by jeering at everything modern, Chernyshevski whom life had outdistanced would unburden himself concerning all the innovators, eccentrics and failures of this world.

His kindhearted cousin, Pypin, in January 1875, sends him to Vilyuisk an embellished description of his student son, informing him of what might please the creator of Rakhmetov (Sasha, he wrote, had ordered an eighteen-pound metal ball for gymnastics) and what must be flattering to any father: with restrained tenderness, Pypin, recalling his youthful friendship with Nikolay Gavrilovich (to whom he was much indebted), relates that Sasha is just as clumsy, just as angular as his father was, and also laughs as loud in the same treble tones. . . . Suddenly, in the autumn of 1877, Sasha joined the Nevski infantry regiment, but before he reached the active army (the Russo-Turkish war was in progress) he fell ill with typhus (in his constant misfortunes one is aware of a legacy from his father, who also used to break everything and drop everything). Returning to St. Petersburg he lived alone, giving lessons and publishing articles on the theory of probability. After 1882 his mental ailment was aggravated, and more than once he had to be placed in a nursing-home. He was afraid of space, or more exactly, he was afraid of slipping into a different dimension—and in order to avoid perishing he clung continuously to the safe, solid—with Euclidean pleats—skirt of Pelageya Nikolaevna Fanderflit (née Pypin).

From Chernyshevski, who had now moved to Astrakhan, they continued to hide this. With a kind of sadistic obstinacy, with pedantic callousness matching that of any prosperous bourgeois in Dickens or Balzac, he called his son in his letters "a big ludicrous freak" and an "eccentric pauper" and accused him of a desire "to remain a beggar." Finally Pypin could stand it no longer and explained to his cousin with a certain warmth that although Sasha may not have become "a cold and calculating businessman," he had in compensation "acquired a pure and honorable soul."

And then Sasha came to Astrakhan. Nikolay Gavrilovich saw those radiant, bulging eyes, heard that strange, evasive speech . . . Having entered the service of the oilman Nobel, and being entrusted to accompany a bargeload along the Volga, Sasha, en route, one sultry, oil-soaked, satanic noon, knocked the bookkeeper's cap off, threw the keys into the rainbow water, and went home to Astrakhan. That same summer four of his poems appeared in *The Messenger of Europe*; they show a gleam of talent:

If life's hours appear to you bitter,
Do not rail against life, for it's best
To admit it's your fault you've been born with
An affectionate heart in your breast.
And if you do not wish to acknowledge
Even such a self-evident fault . . .

(Incidentally, let us note the ghost of an additional syllable in "life's hou-urs" matching *zhiz-en'*, instead of *zhizn'* which is extremely characteristic of unbalanced Russian poets of the woebegone sort: a flaw corresponding, it would seem, to something lacking in their lives, something that might have turned life into song. The last line quoted has however an authentic poetic ring.)

The joint domicile of father and son was a joint hell. Chernyshevski drove Sasha to agonizing insomnia with his endless admonitions (as a "materialist" he had the fanatic effrontery to suppose that the main cause of Sasha's disorder was his "pitiful material condition"), and he himself suffered in a way that he had not done even in Siberia. They both breathed easier when that winter Sasha went away—at first to Heidelberg with the family in which he was tutor and then to St. Petersburg "because of the need to get medical advice." Petty, falsely funny misfortunes continued to spatter him. Thus we learn from a letter of his mother's (1888) that while "Sasha was pleased to go out for a stroll, the house in which he was living burned down," and everything that he possessed burned with it; and, by now utterly destitute, he moved to the country house of Strannolyubski (the critic's father?).

In 1889, Chernyshevski received permission to go to Saratov. Whatever emotions this might have awakened in him, these were in any case poisoned by an intolerable family worry: Sasha, who had always had a pathological passion for exhibitions, suddenly undertook a most extravagant and happy trip to the notorious

Exposition universelle in Paris—having at first got stuck in Berlin, where it was necessary to send him money in the consul's name with a request to dispatch him back; but no: when he received the money Sasha made his way to Paris, had his fill "of the wonderful wheel, of the gigantic, filigree tower"—and again was penniless.

Chernyshevski's feverish work on huge masses of Weber (which turned his brain into a forced labor factory and represented in fact the greatest mockery of human thought) did not cover unlooked-for expenditures—and day after day dictating, dictating, dictating, he felt that he could not go on, could not go on turning world history into rubles—and in the meantime he was also tormented by the panicky fear that from Paris, Sasha would come crashing into Saratov. On October 11th, he wrote Sasha that his mother was sending him the money for his return to St. Petersburg, and—for the millionth time—advised him to take any job and do everything that his superiors might tell him to do: "Your ignorant, ridiculous sermons to your superiors cannot be tolerated by any superiors" (thus ends the "theme of writing exercises"). Continuing to twitch and mutter, he sealed the envelope and himself went to the station to mail the letter. Through the town whirled a cruel wind, which on the very first corner chilled the hurrying, angry little old man in his light coat. The following day, despite a fever, he translated *eighteen* pages of close print; on the 13th he wanted to continue, but he was persuaded to desist; on the 14th delirium set in: "*Inga, inc* [nonsense words, then a sigh] I'm quite unsettled . . . Paragraph . . . If some thirty thousand Swedish troops could be sent to Schleswig-Holstein they would easily rout all the Danes' forces and overrun . . . all the islands, except, perhaps Copenhagen, which will resist stubbornly, but in November, in parentheses put the ninth, Copenhagen also surrendered, semicolon; the Swedes turned the whole population of the Danish capital into shining silver, banished the energetic men of the patriotic parties to Egypt . . . Yes, yes, where was I . . . New paragraph . . ." Thus he rambled on for a long time, jumping from an imaginary Weber to some imaginary memoirs of his own, laboriously discoursing about the fact that "the smallest fate of this man has been decided, there is no salvation for him . . . Although microscopic, a tiny particle of pus has been found in his blood, his fate has been decided . . ." Was he talking about himself, was it in himself that he felt this tiny particle that had kept mysteriously impairing all he did and experienced in life? A thinker, a toiler, a lucid mind, populating his utopias with an army of stenographers—he had now lived to see his *delirium* taken down by a secretary. On the night of the 16th he had a stroke—he felt the tongue in his mouth to be somehow thick; after which he soon died. His last words (at 3 A.M. on the 17th) were: "A strange business: in this book there is not a single mention of God." It is a pity that we do not know precisely *which* book he was reading to himself.

Now he lay surrounded by the dead tomes of Weber; a pair of spectacles in their case kept getting into everybody's way.

Sixty-one years had passed since that year of 1828 when the first omnibuses had appeared in Paris and when a Saratov priest had noted down in his prayer book: "July 12th, in the third hour of morning, a son born, Nikolay . . . Christened the morning of the 13th before mass. Godfather: Archpriest Fyod. Stef. Vyazovski . . ." This name was subsequently given by Chernyshevski to the protagonist and narrator of his Siberian novellas—and by a strange coincidence it was thus, or nearly thus (F.V. . . . . ski) that an unknown poet signed, in the magazine *Century* (1909, November), fourteen lines dedicated, according to information which we possess, to the memory of N. G. Chernyshevski—a mediocre but curious sonnet which we here give in full:

What will it say, your far descendant's voice—
Lauding your life or blasting it outright:
That it was dreadful? That another might
Have been less bitter? That it was your choice?

That your high deed prevailed, and did ignite
Your dry work with the poetry of Good,
And crowned the white brow of chained martyrhood
With a closed circle of ethereal light?

Chapter Five

About a fortnight after *The Life of Chernyshevski* appeared it was greeted by the first, artless echo. Valentin Linyov (in a Russian émigré paper published in Warsaw) wrote as follows:

"Boris Cherdyntsev's new book opens with six lines of verse which the author for some reason calls a sonnet (?) and this is followed by a pretentiously capricious description of the well-known Chernyshevski's life.

"Chernyshevski, says the author, was the son of 'a kindly cleric' (but does not mention when and where he was born); he finished the seminary and when his father, having lived a holy life which inspired even Nekrasov, died, his mother sent the young man to study in St. Petersburg, where he immediately, practically on the station, became intimate with the then "molders of opinion," as they were called, Pisarev and Belinski. The youth entered the university and devoted himself to technical inventions, working very hard and having his first romantic adventure with Lyubov' Yegorovna Lobachevski, who infected him with a love for art. After a clash on romantic grounds with some officer or other in Pavlovsk, however, he was forced to return to Saratov, where he proposed to his future bride and soon afterwards married her.

"He returned to Moscow, devoted himself to philosophy, wrote a great deal (the novel *What Are We to Do?*) and became friends with the outstanding writers of his time. Gradually he was drawn into revolutionary work and after one turbulent meeting, where he spoke together with Dobrolyubov and the well-known Professor Pavlov, who was still quite a young man at that time, Chernyshevski was forced to go abroad. For a while he lived in London collaborating with Herzen, but then he returned to Russia and was immediately arrested. Accused of planning the assassination of Alexander the Second, Chernyshevski was sentenced to death and publicly executed.

"This in brief is the story of Chernyshevski's life, and everything would have been all right if the author had not found it necessary to equip his account of it with a host of unnecessary details which obscure the sense, and with all sorts of long digressions on the most diversified themes. And worst of all, having described the scene of the hanging and put an end to his hero, he is not satisfied with this and for the space of still many more unreadable pages he ruminates on what would have happened 'if'—if Chernyshevski, for example, had not been executed but had been exiled to Siberia, like Dostoevski.

"The author writes in a language having little in common with Russian. He loves to invent words. He loves long, tangled sentences, as for example: 'Fate sorts (?) them in anticipation (?) of the researcher's needs (?)'! or else he places solemn but not quite grammatical maxims in the mouths of his characters, like 'The poet himself chooses the subjects for his poems, the multitude has no right to direct his inspiration.'"

Almost simultaneously with this entertaining review appeared that of Christopher Mortus (Paris)—which so aroused Zina's indignation that from that time her eyes glared and her nostrils dilated at the very least mention of this name.

"When speaking of a new young author [wrote Mortus quietly] one usually experiences the feeling of a certain awkwardness: will one not rattle him, will one not injure him by a too 'glancing' remark? It seems to me that in the present instance there are no grounds for such fears. Godunov-Cherdyntsev is a novice, true, but a novice endowed with extreme self-confidence, and to rattle him is probably no easy matter. I do not know whether his book presages any future 'achievements' or not, but if this is a beginning it cannot be called a particularly reassuring one.

"Let me qualify this. Strictly speaking, it is completely unimportant whether Godunov-Cherdyntsev's effort is creditable or not. One man writes well, another badly, and everyone is awaited at the end of the road by the Theme 'which none can evade.' It is a question, I think, of something quite different. That golden time has passed irretrievably when the critic or reader could be interested above all by the 'artistic' quality or exact degree of talent of a book. Our émigré literature—I am speaking of genuine, 'undoubted' literature—people of faultless taste will understand me—has become plainer, more serious, drier—at the expense of art, perhaps, but in compensation producing (in certain poems by Tsypovich and Boris Barski and in the prose of Koridonov . . .) sounds of such sorrow, such music and such 'hopeless,' heavenly charm that in truth it is not worth regretting what Lermontov called 'the dull songs of the earth.'

"In itself the idea of writing a book about an outstanding public figure of the sixties contains nothing reprehensible. One sits down and writes it—fine; it comes out—fine; worse books than that have come out. But the author's general mood, the 'atmosphere' of his thinking fills one with queer and unpleasant misgivings. I will refrain from discussing the question: how appropriate is the appearance of such a book at the present time? After all, no one can forbid a person to write what he pleases! But it seems to me—and I am not alone in feeling this—that at the bottom of Godunov-Cherdyntsev's book there lies something which is in essence profoundly tactless, something jarring and offensive. . . . It is his right, of course (although even this could be questioned), to take this or that attitude toward the 'men of the sixties,' but in 'debunking' them he cannot but awake in any sensitive reader surprise and disgust. How irrelevant all this is! How inopportune! Let me define my meaning. The fact that it is precisely now, precisely today, that this tasteless operation is being performed is in itself an affront to that significant, bitter, palpitating something which is ripening in the catacombs of our era. Oh, of course, the 'men of the sixties,' and in particular Chernyshevski, expressed in their literary judgments much that was mistaken and perhaps ridiculous. Who is not guilty of this sin? And is it such a big sin, after all? But in the general 'intonation' of their criticism there transpired a certain kind of truth—a truth which, no matter how paradoxical it seems, has become close and comprehensible to us precisely today, precisely now. I am talking not of their attacks on bribe-takers nor of the emancipation of women. . . . That, of course, is not the point! I think I shall be properly understood (insofar as another can be understood) if I say that in some final and infallible sense their and our needs coincide. Oh, I know, we are more sensitive, more spiritual, more 'musical' than they were, and our final aim—beneath that resplendent black sky under which life streams on—is not simply 'the commune' or 'the overthrow of the despot.' But to us, as to them, Nekrasov and Lermontov, especially the latter, are closer than Pushkin. I shall take just this simplest of examples because it immediately clarifies our affinity—if not kinship—with them. That chilliness, that foppishness, that 'irresponsible' quality they sensed in a certain part of Pushkin's poetry is perceptible to us, too. One may object that we are more intelligent, more receptive. . . . All right, I agree; but essentially it is not a question of Chernyshevski's 'rationalism' (or Belinski's or Dobrolyubov's, names and dates do not matter), but of the fact that then, as now, spiritually progressive people understood that mere 'art' and the 'lyre' were not a sufficient pabulum. We, their refined and weary grandchildren, also want something that is above all human; we demand the values which are essential to the soul. This 'utilitarianism' is more elevated, perhaps, than theirs, but in some respects it is more urgent even than the one they preached.

"I have digressed from the immediate theme of my article. But then, sometimes, one can express one's opinion with much more exactitude and authenticity by wandering 'around the theme'—in its fertile environs. . . . As a matter of fact, the analysis of *any* book is awkward and pointless, and, moreover, we are interested not in the way an author executed his 'task' nor even in the 'task' itself, but only in the author's attitude toward it.

"And let me add this: are they really so necessary, these excursions into the realm of the past, with their stylized squabbles and artificially vivified way of life? Who wants to know about Chernyshevski's relations with women? In our bitter, tender, ascetic times there is no place for this kind of mischievous research, for this idle literature—which, anyway, is not devoid of a certain arrogant audacity that is bound to repel even the most well-disposed of readers."

After this, reviews poured. Professor Anuchin of Prague University (a well-known public figure, a man of shining moral purity and of great personal courage—the same Professor Anuchin who in 1922, not long before his deportation from Russia, when some revolvered leatherjackets had come to arrest him but became interested in his collection of ancient coins and were slow in taking him away, had calmly said, pointing to his watch: "Gentlemen, history does not wait.") printed a detailed analysis of *The Life of Chernyshevski* in an émigré magazine appearing in Paris.

"Last year [he wrote], a remarkable book came out by Professor Otto Lederer of Bonn University, *Three Despots* (Alexander the Misty, Nicholas the Chill, and Nicholas the Dull). Motivated by a passionate love for the freedom of the human spirit and a burning hatred for its suppressors, Dr. Lederer in certain of his appraisals was unjust—taking no account at all, for instance, of that national Russian fervor which so powerfully gave body to the symbol of the throne; but excessive zeal, and even blindness, in the process of exposing evil is always more understandable and forgivable than the least mockery—no matter how witty it may be—of that which public opinion feels to be objectively good. However, it is precisely this second road, the road of eclectic mordancy, that has been chosen by Mr. Godunov-Cherdyntsev in his interpretation of the life and works of N. G. Chernyshevski.

"The author has undoubtedly acquainted himself throughly and in his own way conscientiously with his subject; undoubtedly, also, he has a talented pen—certain ideas he puts forward, and juxtapositions of ideas, are undoubtedly shrewd; but with all this his book is repellent. Let us try to examine calmly this impression.

"A certain epoch has been taken and one of its representatives chosen. But has the author assimilated the concept of 'epoch'? No. First of all one senses in him absolutely no consciousness of that *classification of time,* without which history turns into an arbitrary gyration of multicolored spots, into some kind of impressionistic picture with a walking figure upside down against a green sky that does not exist in nature. But this device (which destroys, by the way, any scholarly value of the work in question, in spite of its swaggering erudition) does not, nevertheless, constitute the author's chief fault. His chief fault is in the manner in which he portrays Chernyshevski.

"It is completely unimportant that Chernyshevski understood less about questions of poetry than a young esthete of today. It is completely unimportant that in his philosophical conceptions Chernyshevski kept aloof from those transcendental subtleties which please Mr. Godunov-Cherdyntsev. What is important is that, whatever Chernyshevski's views may have been on art and science, they represented the *Weltanschauung* of the most progressive men of his era, and were moreover indissolubly linked with the development of social ideas, with their ardent, beneficial, activating force. It is in this aspect, in this sole true light, that Chernyshevski's system of thought acquires a significance which far transcends the sense of those groundless arguments—unconnected in any way with the epoch of the sixties—which Mr. Godunov-Cherdyntsev uses in venomously ridiculing his hero.

"But he makes fun, not only of his hero: he also makes fun of his reader. How else can one qualify the fact that among the well-known authorities on Chernyshevski a nonexistent authority is cited, to whom the author pretends to appeal? In a certain sense it would be possible if not to forgive then at least to understand scientifically the scoffing at Chernyshevski, if Mr. Godunov-Cherdyntsev were a heated supporter of those whom Chernyshevski attacked. It would at least be a point of view, and reading the book the reader would make a constant adjustment for the author's partisan approach, in that way arriving at the truth. But the pity is that with Mr. Godunov-Cherdyntsev there is nothing to adjust to and the point of view is 'everywhere and nowhere'; not only that, but as soon as the reader, as he descends the course of a sentence, thinks he has at last sailed into a quiet backwater, into a realm of ideas which may be contrary to those of Chernyshevski but are apparently shared by the author—and therefore can serve as a basis for the reader's judgment and guidance—the author gives him an unexpected fillip and knocks the imaginary prop from under him, so that he is once more unaware as to whose side Mr. Godunov-Cherdyntsev is on in his campaign against Chernyshevski—whether he is on the side of the advocates of art for art's sake, or of the government, or of some other of Chernyshevski's enemies whom the reader does not know. As far as jeering at the hero himself is concerned, here the author passes all bounds. There is no detail too repulsive for him to disdain. He will probably reply that all these details are to be found in the 'Diary' of the young Chernyshevski; but there they are in their place, in their proper environment, in the correct order and perspective, among many other thoughts and feelings which are much more valuable. But the author has fished out and put together precisely these, as if someone had tried to restore the image of a person by making an elaborate collection of his combings, fingernail parings, and bodily excretions.

"In other words the author is sneering throughout the whole of his book at the personality of one of the purest and most valorous sons of liberal Russia—not to speak of the passing kicks with which he rewards other progressive Russian thinkers, a respect for whom is in our consciousness an immanent part of their historical essence. In his book, which lies absolutely outside the humanitarian tradition of Russian literature and therefore outside literature in general, there are no factual untruths (if one does not count the fictitious 'Strannolyubski' already mentioned, two or three doubtful details, and a few slips of the pen), but that 'truth' which it contains is worse than the most prejudiced lie, for such a truth goes in direct contradiction to that noble and chaste truth (an absence of which deprives history of what the great Greek called '*tropotos*') which is one of the inalienable treasures of Russian social thought. In our day, thank God, books are not burned by bonfire, but I must confess that if such a custom were still in existence, Mr. Godunov-Cherdyntsev's book could justifiably be considered the first candidate for fueling a public square."

After that Koncheyev had his say in the literary annual *The Tower.* He began by drawing a picture of flight during an invasion or an earthquake, when the escapers carry away with them everything that they can lay hands on, someone being sure to burden himself with a large, framed portrait of some long-forgotten relative. "Just such a portrait [wrote Koncheyev] is for the Russian intelligentsia the image of Chernyshevski, which was spontaneously but accidentally carried away abroad by the émigrés, together with other, more useful things," and this is how Koncheyev explained the stupefaction occasioned by the appearance of Fyodor Konstantinovich's book: "Somebody suddenly confiscated the portrait." Further on, having finished once and for all with considerations of an ideological nature and embarked upon an examination of the book as a work of art, Koncheyev began to praise it in such a way that as he read the review Fyodor felt a burning radiance forming around his face and quicksilver racing through his veins. The article ended with the following: "Alas! Among the emigration one will hardly scrape up a dozen people capable of appreciating the fire and fascination of this fabulously witty composition; and I would maintain that in today's Russia you could not find even one to appreciate it, if I had not happened to know of the existence of two such people, one living on the north bank of the Neva and the other—somewhere in distant Siberian exile."

The monarchist organ *The Throne* devoted to *The Life of Chernyshevski* a few lines in which it pointed out that any sense or value in the unmasking of "one of the ideological mentors of Bolshevism" was completely undermined by "the cheap liberalizing of the author, who goes wholly over to the side of his sorry, but pernicious hero as soon as the long-suffering Russian Tsar finally has him safely tucked away. . . . And in general," added the reviewer, Pyotr Levchenko, "it is high time one ceased writing about so-called cruelties of 'the tsarist regime' with regard to 'pure souls' who are of no interest to anybody. The Red Freemasonry will only rejoice over Count Godunov-Cherdyntsev's work. It is lamentable that the bearer of such a name should engage in hymning 'social ideals' which have long since turned into cheap idols."

The pro-Communist Russian-language daily in Berlin, *Up!* (this was the one which Vasiliev's *Gazeta* invariably termed "the reptile"), had an article devoted to the celebration of the centenary of

Chernyshevski's birth, and concluded thus: "They have also bestirred themselves in our blessed emigration: a certain Godunov-Cherdyntsev with swashbuckling brashness has hurried to concoct a booklet—for which he has dragged in material from all over the place—and has given out his vile slander as *The Life of Chernyshevski.* Some Prague professor or other has hastened to find this work 'talented and conscientious' and everyone chummily joined in. It is dashingly written and in no way differs in its internal style from Vasiliev's leaders about 'The imminent end of Bolshevism.'"

The last dig was particularly amusing in view of the fact that in his *Gazeta* Vasiliev resolutely opposed the slightest reference to Fyodor's book, telling him honestly (although the other had not asked) that had he not been on such friendly terms with him he would have printed a devastating review—"not even a damp spot would have remained" of the author of *The Life of Chernyshevski.* In short, the book found itself surrounded by a good, thundery atmosphere of scandal which helped sales; and at the same time, in spite of the attacks, the name of Godunov-Cherdyntsev immediately came to the fore, rising over the motley storm of critical opinion, in full view of everyone, vividly and firmly. But there was one man whose opinion Fyodor was no longer able to ascertain. Alexander Yakovlevich Chernyshevski had died not long before the book appeared.

When the French thinker Delalande was asked at somebody's funeral why he did not uncover himself (*ne se découvre pas*), he replied: "I am waiting for death to do it first" *(qu'elle se découvre la première).* There is a lack of metaphysical gallantry in this, but death deserves no more. Fear gives birth to sacred awe, sacred awe erects a sacrificial altar, its smoke ascends to the sky, there assumes the shape of wings, and bowing fear addresses a prayer to it. Religion has the same relation to man's heavenly condition that mathematics has to his earthly one: both the one and the other are merely the rules of the game. Belief in God and belief in numbers: local truth and truth of location. I know that death in itself is in no way connected with the topography of the hereafter, for a door is merely the exit from the house and not a part of its surroundings, like a tree or a hill. One has to get out somehow, "but I refuse to see in a door more than a hole, and a carpenter's job" (*Delalande, Discours sur les ombres,* p. 45). And then again: the unfortunate image of a "road" to which the human mind has become accustomed (life as a kind of journey) is a stupid illusion: we are not going anywhere, we are sitting at home. The other world surrounds us always and is not at all at the end of some pilgrimage. In our earthly house, windows are replaced by mirrors; the door, until a given time, is closed; but air comes in through the cracks. "For our stay-at-home senses the most accessible image of our future comprehension of those surroundings which are due to be revealed to us with the disintegration of the body is the liberation of the soul from the eye-sockets of the flesh and our transformation into one complete and free eye, which can simultaneously see in all directions, or to put it differently: a supersensory insight into the world accompanied by our inner participation." (Ibid. p. 64). But all this is only symbols—symbols which become a burden to the mind as soon as it takes a close look at them. . . .

Is it not possible to understand more simply, in a way more satisfying to the spirit without the aid of this elegant atheist and equally without the aid of popular faiths? For religion subsumes a suspicious facility of general access that destroys the value of its revelations. If the poor in spirit enter the heavenly kingdom I can imagine how gay it is there. I have seen enough of them on earth. Who else makes up the population of heaven? Swarms of screaming revivalists, grubby monks, lots of rosy, shortsighted souls of more or less Protestant manufacture—what deathly boredom! I am running a high temperature for the fourth day now, and can no longer read. Strange—I used to think before that Yasha was always near me, that I had learned to communicate with ghosts, but now, when I am perhaps dying, this belief in ghosts seems to me something earthly, linked with the very lowest earthly sensations and not at all the discovery of a heavenly America.

Somehow simpler. Somehow simpler. Somehow at once! One effort—and I'll understand all. The search for God: the longing of any hound for a master; give me a boss and I shall kneel at his enormous feet. All this is earthly. Father, headmaster, rector, president of the board, tsar, God. Numbers, numbers—and one wants so much to find the biggest number, so that all the rest may mean something and climb somewhere. No, that way you end up in padded dead ends—and everything ceases to be interesting.

Of course I am dying. These pincers behind and this steely pain are quite comprehensible. Death steals up from behind and grasps you by the sides. Funny that I have thought of death all my life, and if I have lived, have lived only in the margin of a book I have never been able to read. Now who was it? Oh, years ago in Kiev . . . Goodness, what was his name? Would take out a library book in a language he didn't know, make notes in it and leave it lying about so visitors would think: He knows Portuguese, Aramaic. *Ich habe dasselbe getan.* Happiness, sorrow—exclamation marks *en marge,* while the context is absolutely unknown. A fine affair.

It is terribly painful to leave life's womb. The deathly horror of birth. *L'enfant qui naît ressent les affres de sa mère.* My poor little Yasha! It is very queer that in dying I get further away from him, when the opposite should have been true—ever nearer and nearer. . . . His first word was *muha,* a fly. And immediately afterwards there was a telephone call from the police: to come and identify the body. How will I leave him now? In these rooms . . . He will have nobody to haunt . . . Because *she* would not notice . . . Poor girl. How much? Five thousand eight hundred . . . plus that other money . . . which makes, let me see . . . And afterwards? David might help—but then he might not.

. . . In general, there has been nothing in life except getting ready for an examination—which all the same nobody can get ready for. "Dreadful is death to man and mite alike." Will all my friends go through it? Incredible! *Eine alte Geschichte:* the name of a film Sandra and I went to see the day before his death.

Oh, no. Under no circumstances. She can keep talking about it as much as she pleases. Was it yesterday that she talked about it? Or ages ago? No, they won't be taking me to any hospital. I'll lie here. I've had enough of hospitals. It would mean to go mad again just before the end. No, I'll stay here. How difficult it is to turn one's thoughts over: like logs. I feel much too ill to die.

"What did he write his book about, Sandra? Well, tell me, you should remember! We talked about it once. About some priest—no? Oh, you never . . . anything . . . Bad, difficult . . ."

After this he hardly spoke, having fallen into a twilight condition; Fyodor was admitted to him and forever remembered the white bristle on his sunken cheeks, the dull shade of his bald head, and the hand crusted with gray eczema, stirring like a crawfish on the sheet. The following day he died, but before that he had a moment of lucidity, complaining of pains and then saying (it was darkish in the room because of the lowered blinds): "What nonsense. Of course there is nothing afterwards." He sighed, listened to the trickling and drumming outside the window and repeated with extreme distinctness: "There is nothing. It is as clear as the fact that it is raining."

And meanwhile outside the spring sun was playing on the roof tiles, the sky was dreamy and cloudless, the tenant upstairs was watering the flowers on the edge of her balcony, and the water trickled down with a drumming sound.

In the window of the mortician's on the corner of Kaiserallee there was exhibited as an enticement (just as Cook's exhibits a Pullman model) a miniature crematorium interior: rows of little chairs before a little pulpit, little dolls sitting on them the size of a bent auricular finger, and in front, and somewhat apart, one could recognize the little widow by the square inch of handkerchief she had raised to her face. The German seductivity of this model had always amused Fyodor, so that now it was somewhat disgusting to enter a real crematorium, where from beneath laurels in tubs a real coffin with a real body was lowered to the sounds of heavy-weight organ music into exemplary nether regions, right into the incinerator. Mme. Chernyshevski did not hold a handkerchief but sat motionless and straight, her eyes shimmering through the black crepe veil. The faces of friends and acquaintances bore the guarded expressions usual in such cases: a mobility of the pupils accompanied by a certain tension in the muscles of the neck. The lawyer Charski sincerely blew his nose; Vasiliev, who as a public figure had had a great deal of funeral experience, carefully followed the parson's pauses (Alexander Yakovlevich had turned out at the last minute to be a Protestant). Engineer Kern flashed the lenses of his pince-nez impassively. Goryainov repeatedly freed his fat neck from its collar but did not go so far as to clear his throat; the ladies who had used to visit the Chernyshevskis all sat together; the writers also sat together—Lishnevski, Shahmatov and Shirin; there were many people whom Fyodor did not know—for instance, a prim gentleman with a blond little beard and unusually red lips (a cousin, it seemed, of the dead man), and also some Germans with top hats on their knees, who tactfully sat in the back row.

Upon the conclusion of the service the mourners, according to the scheme of the crematorium's master of ceremonies, were supposed to go up to the widow one at a time and offer words of condolence, but Fyodor resolved to avoid this and went out onto the street. Everything was wet, sunny and somehow nudely bright; on a black football field trimmed with young grass, schoolgirls in shorts were doing calisthenics. Behind the crematorium's shiny, gutta-percha gray dome one could see the turquoise turrets of a mosque, and on the other side of the square gleamed the green cupolas of a white Pskovan-type church, which had recently grown up out of the corner house and thanks to architectural camouflage seemed almost detached. On a terrace by the entrance to the park two badly wrought bronze boxers, also recently erected, had frozen in attitudes that completely disagreed with the reciprocal harmony of pugilism: instead of its collected, crouched, round-muscled grace there were two naked soldiers scrapping in a bathhouse. A kite being flown from an open space behind some trees made a red little rhombus high in the blue sky. With surprise and vexation Fyodor noticed that he was unable to keep his thoughts on the image of the man who had just been reduced to ashes and gone up in smoke; he tried to concentrate, to imagine to himself the recent warmth of their live relationship, but his soul refused to budge and lay there, sleepy eyes shut, content with its cage. The braked line from *King Lear*, consisting entirely of five "nevers"—that was all he could think of. "And so I'll never see him again," he told himself, unoriginally, but this thin goad snapped without displacing his soul. He tried to think about death, but reflected instead that the soft sky, edged on one side with a long cloud like a pale and tender border of fat, would have resembled a slice of ham had the blue been pink. He tried to imagine some kind of extension of Alexander Yakovlevich beyond the corner of life—but at the same time could not help noticing through the window of a cleaning and pressing shop near the Orthodox church, a worker with devilish energy and an excess of steam, as if in hell, torturing a pair of flat trousers. He tried to confess something to Alexander Yakovlevich, and repent at least for the cruel mischievous thoughts he had fleetingly had (concerning the unpleasant surprise he was preparing for him with his book)—and suddenly he recalled a vulgar triviality: how Shchyogolev had once said in some connection or other: "When good friends of mine die, I always think that up there they will do something to improve my destiny here, ho, ho, ho!" He was in a troubled and obscured state of mind which was incomprehensible to him, just as everything was incomprehensible, from the sky to that yellow tram rumbling along the clear track of the Hohenzollerdamm (along which Yasha had once gone to his death), but gradually his annoyance with himself passed and with a kind of relief—as if the responsibility for his soul belonged not to him but to someone who knew what it all meant—he felt that all this skein of random thoughts, like everything else as well—the seams and sleaziness of the spring day, the ruffle of the air, the coarse, variously intercrossing threads of confused sounds—was but the reverse side of a magnificent fabric, on the front of which there gradually formed and became alive images invisible to him.

He found himself by the bronze boxers; in the flower beds around them rippled pale, black-blotched pansies (somewhat similar facially to Charlie Chaplin); he sat on a bench where once or twice at night he had sat with Zina—for of late a kind of restlessness had carried them far beyond the bounds of the dark, quiet lane where they had at first sought shelter. Nearby a woman sat knitting; next to her a small child, entirely clothed in light blue wool, ending above in the pompon of a cap and below in foot straps, was ironing the bench with a toy tank; sparrows twittered in the bushes and from time to time made concerted raids on the turf, on the statues; a sticky smell came from the poplar buds, and far beyond the square the domed crematorium now had a sated, clean-licked look. From a distance Fyodor could see tiny figures dispersing . . . he could even make out someone leading Alexandra Yakolevna to a toy automobile (tomorrow he would have to call on her), and a group of her friends gathering at the tram stop; he saw them concealed for a moment by the immobilized tram and then, with legerdemain magic, they were gone when the shutter was removed.

Fyodor was about to walk home when a lisping voice called him from behind: it belonged to Shirin, author of the novel *The Hoary Abyss* (with an Epigraph from the Book of Job) which had been received very sympathetically by the émigré critics. ("Oh Lord, our Father! Down Broadway in a feverish rustle of dollars, hetaeras and businessmen in spats, shoving, falling and out of breath, were running after the golden calf, which pushed its way, rubbing against walls between the skyscrapers, then turned its emaciated face to the electric sky and howled. In Paris, in a low-class dive, the old man Lachaise, who had once been an aviation pioneer but was now a decrepit vagabond, trampled under his boots an ancient prostitute, Boule de Suif. Oh Lord, why—? Out of a Moscow basement a killer came out, squatted by a kennel and began to coax a shaggy pup: little one, he repeated, little one . . . In London, lords and ladies danced the Jimmie and imbibed cocktails, glancing from time to time at a platform where at the end of the eighteenth ring a huge Negro had laid his fair-haired opponent on the carpet with a knockout. Amid arctic snows the explorer Ericson sat on an empty soapbox and thought gloomily: The pole or not the pole? . . . Ivan Chervyakov carefully trimmed the fringe of his only pair of pants. Oh Lord, why dost Thou permit all this?") Shirin himself was a thickset man with a reddish crew cut, always badly shaved and wearing large spectacles behind which, as in two aquariums, swam two tiny, transparent eyes—which were completely impervious to visual impressions. He was blind like Milton, deaf like Beethoven, and a blockhead to boot. A blissful incapacity for observation (and hence complete uninformedness about the surrounding world—and a complete inability to put a name to anything) is a quality quite frequently met with among the average Russian literati, as if a beneficent fate were at work refusing the blessing of sensory cognition to the untalented so that they will not wantonly mess up the material. It happens, of course, that such a benighted person has some little lamp of his own glimmering inside him—not to speak of those known instances in which, through the caprice of resourceful nature that loves startling adjustments and substitutions, such an inner light is astonishingly bright—enough to make the envy of the ruddiest talent. But even Dostoevski always brings to mind somehow a room in which a lamp burns during the day.

As he walked now across the park with Shirin, Fyodor derived disinterested pleasure from the amusing thought that he had for companion a deaf and blind man with blocked nostrils who regarded this state with complete indifference, although he was not averse at times to sighing naïvely about the intellectual's alienation from nature: recently Lishnevski had related that Shirin had arranged to meet him about some business in the Zoological Garden and when after an hour's conversation Lishnevski had casually drawn his attention to a hyena in its cage, it transpired that Shirin had hardly realized that one keeps animals in a zoological garden, and glancing briefly at the cage had remarked automatically: "Yes, the likes of us don't know much about the animal world," and immediately continued discussing that which particularly disturbed him in life: the activities and composition of the Committee of the Society of Russian Writers in Germany. And now he was in an extreme degree of agitation since "a certain event had come to a head."

Chairman of the Committee was Georgiy Ivanovich Vasiliev, and for this of course there were good reasons: his pre-Soviet reputation, his many years of editorial activity, and most important—that inexorable almost awesome honesty for which his name was famous. On the other hand, his bad temper, polemical harshness, and (despite great public experience) complete ignorance of people, not only did not harm this honesty but on the contrary imparted a certain tang to it. Shirin's dissatisfaction was directed not against him but against the five remaining members of the Committee, first because not one of them (as two-thirds, incidentally, of the whole membership of the society) was a professional writer, and secondly because three of them (including the treasurer and the vice-president) were—if not scoundrels as the partial Shirin maintained—

then at least shade-lovers in their bashful but deft activities. For some time past now a rather comical (in Fyodor's opinion) and absolutely outrageous (in Shirin's terminology) affair had been going on with the Union's funds. Every time a member asked for a loan or a grant (the difference between which was about the same as that between a ninety-nine-year lease and life ownership) one had to track down these funds which at the least attempt to catch up with them became amazingly fluid and ethereal, as if they were always situated equidistantly between three points represented by the treasurer and two members of the Committee. The chase was complicated by the fact that for a long time now Vasiliev had not been on speaking terms with these three members, refusing even to communicate with them in writing, and in recent times had been dispensing loans and grants out of his own pocket, leaving others to get the money from the Union to repay him. In the end the money would be extracted in dribs and drabs, but then it usually turned out that the treasurer had borrowed it from an outsider, so that transactions never caused any change in the phantasmal state of the exchequer. Lately members of the Society who appealed particularly often for aid had begun to grow visibly nervous. A general meeting had been called for next month and Shirin had prepared for it a plan of resolute action.

"There was a time," he said, striding down a path in the park with Fyodor and automatically following its cunningly unobstrusive convolutions, "there was a time when all the people who went on the Committee of our Union were highly respectable, like Podtyagin, Ivan Luzhin, Zilanov, but some died and others are in Paris. Somehow Gurman oozed through into it and then gradually pulled his pals in. For this trio the passive participation of the extremely decent—I'm saying nothing—but completely inert Kern and Goryainov is a convenient cover, a kind of camouflage. And Gurman's strained relations with Georgiy Ivanovich is a guarantee of inactivity on his part also. The ones to blame for all this are us, the members of the Union. If it were not for our idleness, carelessness, lack of organization, indifferent attitude to the Union and flagrant impracticality in social work it would never have happened that Gurman and his chums from year to year elected either themselves or else people congenial to them. It is time to put an end to this. Their list as always will be circulated at the coming elections . . . But we will then put out our own, one hundred percent professional: president—Vasiliev, vice-president—Getz, members of the board: Lishnevski, Shahmatov, Vladimirov, you and I—and then we'll reconstitute the Inspection Committee, the more so since Belenki and Chernyshevski have dropped out."

"Oh no, please," said Fyodor (admiring in passing Shirin's definition of death), "don't count on me. I never went and never will go on any committee."

"Stop it!" exclaimed Shirin, frowning. "That's not fair."

"On the contrary, very fair. And anyway—if I am a member of the Union it's only out of absentmindedness. To tell the truth, Koncheyev is right to stand aside from all this."

"Koncheyev!" said Shirin angrily. "Koncheyev is an absolutely useless handicraftsman working on his own, and is completely devoid of any general interests. But you ought to be interested in the fate of the Union if only because you—excuse my directness—borrow money from it."

"That's just it. You can see for yourself that if I go on the Committee I shan't possibly be able to give handouts to myself."

"Bosh. Why not? It's a completely legal procedure. You will simply get up and go to the lavatory—and so become for a moment, so to speak, an ordinary member, while your colleagues discuss your request. All these are empty excuses that you've just thought up."

"How's your new novel?" asked Fyodor. "Is it nearly finished?"

"We're not talking about my novel now. I ask you very seriously to give your assent. We need young blood. Lishnevski and I have given much thought to this list."

"Under no circumstances," said Fyodor. "I don't want to play the fool."

"Well, if you call your public duty playing the fool . . ."

"If I go on the Committee I shall certainly be playing the fool, so I am refusing precisely out of respect for duty."

"Very sad," said Shirin. "Will we really have to take Rostislav Strannyy instead of you?"

"Of course! Wonderful! I adore Rostislav."

"Actually I had reserved him for the Inspection Committee. There's also Busch, of course . . . But do think it over, please. It's not a trifling matter. We shall have a regular battle with these gangsters. I am preparing a speech that will really make them sit up. Think it over, do, you still have a whole month."

During that month Fyodor's book came out and two or three notices had had time to appear, so that he set off for the general meeting with the pleasant feeling that he would find more than one enemy reader there. It took place as usual in the upper premises of a large café, and when he arrived everybody was already there. A phenomenally dexterous waiter with darting eyes was serving beer and coffee. The members of the Society were seated at little tables. The creative writers formed a close-knit group, and one could already hear the energetic "*psst, psst*" of Shahmatov, who had been served the wrong order. In the back behind a long table sat the Committee: the bulky, extremely gloomy Vasiliev, with Goryainov and engineer Kern on his right, and the three others on his left. Kern, whose main interest was turbines but who had once been on friendly terms with Alexander Blok, and the former official of a former government department, Goryainov, who could recite marvelously "Woe from Wit" as well as Ivan the Terrible's dialogue with the Lithuanian ambassador (when he used to do a splendid imitation of a Polish accent), bore themselves with quiet distinction: they had betrayed long ago their three unrighteous colleagues. Of these, Gurman was a fat man with a bald head half occupied by a coffee-colored birthmark, massive sloping shoulders, and a disdainfully offended expression on his thick, purplish lips. His relationship to literature was limited to a brief and entirely commercial connection with some German publisher of technical guides; the principal theme of his personality, the pith of his existence, was speculation—he was particularly keen on Soviet bills of exchange. Next to him sat a small but sturdily resilient barrister, with a jutting jaw, a rapacious gleam in his right eye (the left one was half-closed by nature), and a whole store of metal in his mouth—an alert, fiery man, something of a swashbuckler in his own way, who was always challenging people to arbitration, and he would talk of this (I called him out, he refused) with the precise severity of a hardened duelist. Gurman's other friend, loose-fleshed, gray-skinned, languid, wearing horn-rimmed spectacles, his whole aspect resembling a peaceful toad that wants only one thing—to be left in complete peace in a damp place—had somewhen somewhere written notes on economic questions, although the evil-tongued Lishnevski denied him even this, swearing that his sole printed effort was a letter in pre-Revolution days to the editor of an Odessa newspaper in which he had indignantly dissociated himself from a villainous namesake, who subsequently turned out to be his relative, then his double, and finally himself, as if there was in action here the irrevocable law of capillary attraction and fusion.

Fyodor sat between the novelists Shahmatov and Vladimirov, by a wide window behind which the night gleamed wetly black, with two-toned (the Berlin imagination did not stretch to any more) illuminated signs—ozone-blue and oporto-red—and rumbling electric trains with rapidly and distinctly lighted insides gliding above the square along a viaduct, against whose archivolts below slow, grinding trams seemed to keep butting without finding a loophole.

Meanwhile the chairman of the board had stood up and proposed the election of a chairman for the meeting. There sounded from various places: "Kraevich, let's have Kraevich . . ." and Professor Kraevich (no relation to the author of the textbook on physics—he was a professor of international law), a mobile, angular old man in a knitted waistcoat and unbuttoned jacket, swept up to the presidium table extraordinarily fast, holding his left hand in his trouser pocket and tossing up his pince-nez on the end of its cord with his right; he sat down between Vasiliev and Gurman (who was slowly and gloomily twisting a cigarette into an amber holder), immediately stood up again, and pronounced the meeting opened.

I wonder, thought Fyodor, glancing sideways at Vladimirov, I wonder if he has read my book? Vladimirov put down his glass and looked at Fyodor, but said nothing. Beneath his jacket he was wearing an English sports sweater with a black-and-orange border along its triangular opening; the receding hair on either side of his forehead exaggerated the latter's dimensions, his large nose was strongly boned, his grayish-yellow teeth glistened unpleasantly beneath his slightly raised lip and his eyes looked out with intelligence and indifference—he had studied, it seemed, at an English university and flaunted a pseudo-British manner. At twenty-nine he was already the author of two novels—outstanding for the force and swiftness of their mirror-like style—which irritated Fyodor perhaps for the very reason that he felt a certain affinity with him. As a conversationalist Vladimirov was singularly unattractive. One blamed him for being derisive, supercilious, cold, incapable of thawing to friendly discussions—but that was also said about Koncheyev and about Fyodor himself, and about anyone whose thoughts lived in their own private house and not in a barrack-room or a pub.

When a secretary had also been elected, Professor Kraevich proposed that all should stand to honor the memory of the two deceased members of the Society; and during this five-second petrification the excommunicated waiter scanned the tables, having forgotten who had ordered the ham sandwich he had just brought in on a tray. Everyone stood as he could. Gurman, for example, his skew-bald head lowered, was holding his hand palm upwards on the table, as if he had just cast the dice and had frozen in astonishment at his loss.

"Allo! Hier!" shouted Shahmatov, who had been waiting anxiously for the moment when with a clatter of relief life would be seated again—and then the waiter quickly raised his index finger (he had remembered), glided over to him, and with a tinkle put the plate down on the imitation marble. Shahmatov immediately began to cut the sandwich, holding his knife and fork crosswise; on the edge of the plate a yellow blob of mustard projected, as is usually the case, a yellow horn. Shahmatov's complaisantly Napoleonic face with its strand of steely-blue hair slanting toward the temple appealed particularly to Fyodor at these gastronomic moments. Next to him, drinking tea with lemon, and himself very lemony, with sadly arched eyebrows, sat the satirist from the *Gazeta*, whose pseudonym, Foma Mur, contained according to his own assertion "a complete French novel (*femme, amour*), a page of English literature (Thomas Moore), and a touch of Jewish skepticism (Thomas the Apostle)." Shirin was sharpening a pencil over an ashtray: he was very much offended at Fyodor for refusing "to figure" in the election list. Of the writers, there were also: Rostislav Strannyy—a rather dreadful person with a bracelet on his hairy wrist; the parchment-pale, raven-haired poetess, Anna Aptekar; a theater critic—a skinny, singularly quiet young man with an elusive something about him recalling a daguerreotype of the Russian forties; and, of course, kindly Busch, his eyes resting paternally on Fyodor, who, with half an ear cocked to the Society president's report, had now transferred his gaze from Busch, Lishnevski, Shirin and the other writers to the general mass of those present, among whom were several journalists, as for instance old Stupishin, whose spoon was working its way through a wedge of mocha cake, many reporters, and—sitting alone and admitted here on God knows what basis—Lyubov Markovna in her timorously gleaming pince-nez; and in general there was a large number of those whom Shirin severely termed "the outside element": the imposing lawyer Charski, holding his fourth cigarette of the night in his white, always trembling hand; a bearded little jobber who had once published an obituary notice in a Bundist paper; a gentle, pale old man, tasting of apple paste, who enthusiastically discharged his duties as the precentor of a church choir; an enormous, enigmatic fat man who lived as a hermit in a pine wood near Berlin, some said in a cave, and had there compiled a collection of Soviet anecdotes; a separate group of rowdies, conceited failures; a pleasant young man of unknown means and position ("a Soviet agent," said Shirin simply and darkly); another lady—someone's former secretary; her husband—the brother of a well-known publisher; and all these people, from the illiterate bum with a heavy, drunken gaze, who wrote denunciatorily mystical verses which not a single newspaper had yet agreed to publish, to the repulsively small, almost portable lawyer, Poshkin, who when talking to people said "I pot" for "I put" and "coshion" for "cushion" as if establishing an alibi for his name; all of these, in Shirin's opinion, damaged the Society's dignity and were liable to immediate expulsion.

"And now," said Vasiliev, after finishing his report, "I bring to the notice of the meeting that I resign as Chairman of the Society and will not stand for re-election."

He sat down. A little chill ran through the assembly. Beneath the burden of sorrow, Gurman closed his heavy lids. An electric train slid bowlike over a bass string.

"Next comes . . ." said Professor Kraevich, raising his pince-nez to his eyes and looking at the agenda, "the treasurer's report. If you please."

Gurman's resilient neighbor, immediately adopting a challenging tone of voice, flashing his good eye and powerfully twisting his valuable-crammed mouth, commenced to read . . . figures were emitted like sparks, metallic words bounced . . . "entered the current year" . . . "debited" . . . "audited" . . . while Shirin, in the meantime, swiftly began to note something on the reverse side of a cigarette pack, added it up, and triumphantly exchanged glances with Lishnevski.

Having read to the end, the treasurer shut his mouth with a click, while some distance off a member of the Auditorial Committee had already risen, a Georgian socialist with a pockmarked face and black hair like a shoe-brush, and briefly enumerated his favorable impressions. After this Shirin asked for the floor and at once there was a whiff of something jolly, alarming, and improper.

He began by seizing on the fact that the expenditure for the New Year's charity dance was inexplicably large; Gurman wanted to reply . . . the chairman, aiming his pencil at Shirin, asked him if he had finished. . . . "Let him speak, no cutting short!" shouted Shahmatov from his seat—and the chairman's pencil, quivering like a serpent's tongue, was aimed at him before returning to Shirin, who, however, bowed and sat down. Gurman rose heavily, carrying his sorrowful burden with disdain and resignation, and began to speak . . . but Shirin soon interrupted him and Kraevich grasped his bell. Gurman finished, after which the treasurer instantly asked for the floor, but Shirin was already up and continuing: "The explanation of the honorable gentleman from the stock exchange . . ." The chairman rang his bell and requested more moderation, threatening to refuse permission to speak. Shirin again bowed and said that he had only one question: in the funds, according to the treasurer's words, there were three thousand and seventy-six marks and fifteen pfennigs—could he see this money right now?

"Bravo," shouted Shahmatov—and the least attractive member of the Union, the mystical poet, guffawed, applauded and almost fell off his chair. The treasurer, paling to a snowy shine, began to speak in a rapid patter . . . While he was speaking and being interrupted by impossible exclamations from the audience, a certain Shuf, lean, clean-shaven, looking somewhat like a Red Indian, left his corner, went up to the committee table unnoticed on his rubber soles, and suddenly slammed his red fist down on it, so that even the bell gave a jump. "You're lying," he bellowed and returned to his seat.

A row was breaking out on all sides when to Shirin's chagrin it transpired that there was yet another faction wishing to seize power—namely the group that was always left out, and that included both the mystic and the Red Indian, as well as the little bearded fellow and several seedy and unbalanced individuals, one of whom suddenly began to read from a piece of paper a list of candidates for election to the committee, all of whom were completely unacceptable. The battle took a new turn, sufficiently tangled, now that there were three warring sides. Such expressions flew about as "black marketeer," "you're not fit to duel" and "you've already been thrashed." Even Busch spoke, trying to drown insulting ejaculations, but because of the natural obscurity of his style no one could understand what he was talking about until, sitting down, he explained that he was fully in agreement with the preceding speaker. Gurman, his nostrils alone expressing sarcasm, busied himself with his cigarette holder. Vasiliev left his seat and retired to a corner, where he pretended to read a newspaper. Lishnevski delivered a crushing speech directed mainly against the board member resembling a peaceful toad, who merely spread his hands and directed a helpless glance at Gurman and the treasurer, both of whom tried not to look at him. Finally, when the poet-mystic stood up, shakily swaying, and with a highly promising smile on his sweaty, leathery face began to speak in verse, the chairman furiously rang his bell and announced an interval, after which the elections were due to be held. Shirin flew over to Vasiliev and commenced to talk to him persuasively, while Fyodor, feeling suddenly bored, found his mackintosh and made his way out onto the street.

He was angry with himself: fancy sacrificing for the sake of this preposterous divertissement the fixed star of his nightly meeting with Zina! The desire to see her at once tortured him with its paradoxical impossibility: if she had not slept six yards from the head of his bed, access to her would have been much easier. A train stretched over the viaduct: the yawn begun by a woman in the lighted window of the first car was completed by another woman—in the last one. Fyodor Konstantinovich strolled toward the tram stop along an oily-black, blaring street. The illuminated sign of a music hall ran up the steps of vertically placed letters, they went out all together, and the light again scrambled up: what Babylonian word would reach up to the sky? . . . a compound name for a trillion tints: diamondimlunalilithlilasafieryviolentviolet and so on—and how many more! Perhaps he should try to phone? He only had a dime in his pocket and he had to decide: to phone meant that in any case he would not be able to take the tram, but to phone for nothing, that is not to get Zina herself (to get her through her mother was not permitted by the code) and then to return on foot would be a bit too galling. I'll risk it. He went into a beerhouse, rang, and everything was over in a twinkle! he got the wrong number, that very number which the anonymous Russian was always trying to get who always got the Shchyogolevs. So what—he would have to hoof it, as Boris Ivanovich would say.

At the next corner his approach automatically triggered off the doll-like mechanism of the prostitutes who always patrolled there. One of them even tried to look like somebody lingering by a shop window, and it was sad to think that these pink corsets on their golden dummies were known to her by heart, by heart. . . . "Sweety," said another with a questioning smile. The night was warm with a dusting of stars. He walked at a swift pace and his bared head felt light from the narcotic night air—and further on when he walked along gardens there came floating to him phantoms of lilacs, the darkness of foliage, and wonderful naked odors spreading on the lawns.

He was hot, and his forehead was burning when finally, quietly clicking the door shut behind him, he found himself in the dark hall. The opaque glass in the upper part of Zina's door resembled a radiant sea: she must be reading in bed, he thought, but while he stood and looked at this mysterious glass she coughed, rustled, and the light went out. What an absurd torture. Go in there, go in . . . Who would know? People like her mother and stepfather sleep with insensible, hundred percent sleep of peasants. Zina's punctiliousness: she would never open at the clinking tap of a fingernail. But she knows I am standing in the dark hall and suffocating. This forbidden room during recent months had become a sickness, a burden, a part of himself, but inflated and sealed off: the pneumothorax of the night.

He stood for another moment—and on tiptoe stole into his room. All in all, French emotions. Fama Mour. Sleep, sleep—the heaviness of spring is utterly untalented. Take oneself in hand: a monastic pun. What next? What exactly are we waiting for? In any case I won't find a better wife. But do I need a wife at all? "Put that lyre away, I've no room to move . . ." No, I would never hear that from her—that's the point.

And a few days later, simply and even somewhat sillily, a solution was indicated to a problem which had seemed so complex that one could not help wondering if there was not a mistake in its construction. Boris Ivanovich, whose affairs during recent years had been getting worse and worse, was most unexpectedly offered by a Berlin firm quite a respectable representative's position in Copenhagen. In two months, by the first of July, he had to move there for at least a year, and perhaps forever if all went well. Marianna Nikolavna who for some reason loved Berlin (familiar haunts, excellent sanitary arrangements—she herself, though, was filthy) felt sad at going away, but when she thought of the improvements in life awaiting her, her grief was dispersed. Thus it was decided that from July Zina would remain alone in Berlin, continuing to work for Traum, until Shchyogolev "had found her a job" in Copenhagen, where Zina would go "at the first summons" (i.e., that is what the Shchyogolevs thought—Zina had decided quite, quite differently). It remained to regulate the question of the apartment. The Shchyogolevs did not want to sell it, so they began to seek somebody to let it to. They found such a person. A young German with a great commercial future, accompanied by his fiancée—a plain, unmade-up, domestically sturdy girl in a green coat—inspected the apartment—dining room, bedroom, kitchen, Fyodor in bed—and was satisfied. However, he was taking the apartment only from August, so that for another month after the Shchyogolevs' departure Zina and the lodger would be able to stay there. They counted the days: fifty, forty-nine, thirty, twenty-five—every one of these numbers had its own face: a beehive, a magpie in a tree, the silhouette of a knight, a young man. Their evening meetings had since spring gone beyond the shores of their initial street (lamp, lime, fence), and now their restless wanderings carried them in ever widening circles into distant and ever new corners of the city. Now it was a bridge over a canal, then a trellised bosket in a park, behind which lights ran past, then an unpaved street between misty wastes where dark vans were standing, then some strange arcades which were impossible to find during the daytime. Change of habits before migration; excitement; a languorous pain in the shoulders.

The newspapers diagnosed the still young summer as being exceptionally hot, and indeed there was a long dotted line of beautiful days, interrupted from time to time by the interjection of a thunderstorm. In the morning, while Zina was wilting from the stinking heat in the office (the sweaty armpits of Hamekke's jacket alone were more than enough . . . and what about the typists' necks melting like wax, what about the sticky blackness of carbon paper?), Fyodor would go to spend the whole day in Grunewald, abandoning his lessons and trying not to think of the long-since-due payment for his room. Never before had he got up at seven, it would have seemed monstrous—but now in life's new light (in which blended somehow the maturing of his gift, a premonition of new labors, and the approach of complete happiness with Zina) he experienced a direct pleasure from the speed and lightness of these early risings, from that burst of motion, from the ideal simplicity of three-second dressing: shirt, trousers and sneakers on bare feet—after which he took a laprobe under his arm, with his swim-trunks wrapped in it, thrust on his way through the hall an orange and a sandwich into his pockets and was already running down the stairs.

A turned-back doormat held the door in a wide-open position while the janitor energetically beat the dust out of another mat by slapping it against the trunk of an innocent lime tree: what have I done to deserve this? The asphalt was still in the dark blue shadow of the houses. On the sidewalk gleamed the first, fresh excrements of a dog. A black hearse, which yesterday had been standing outside a repair shop, rolled cautiously out of a gate and turned down the empty street, and inside it, behind the glass and among artificial white roses, in place of a coffin, lay a bicycle: whose? why? The dairy was already open, but the lazy tobacconist was still asleep. The sun played on various objects along the right side of the street, like a magpie picking out the tiny things that glittered; and at the end of it, where it was crossed by the wide ravine of a railroad, a cloud of locomotive steam suddenly appeared from the right of the bridge, disintegrated against its iron ribs, then immediately loomed white again on the other side and wavily streamed away through the gaps in the trees. Crossing the bridge after this, Fyodor, as usual, was gladdened by the wonderful poetry of railroad banks, by their free and diversified nature: a growth of locusts and sallows, wild grass, bees, butterflies—all this lived in isolation and unconcern in the harsh vicinity of coal dust glistening below between the five streams of rails, and in blissful estrangement from the city coulisses above, from the peeled walls of old houses toasting their tattooed backs in the morning sunshine. Beyond the bridge, near the small public garden, two elderly postal workers, having completed their check of a stamp machine and grown suddenly playful, were stealing up from behind the jasmine, one behind the other, one imitating the other's gestures, toward a third—who with eyes closed was humbly and briefly relaxing on a bench before his working day—in order to tickle his nose with a flower. Where shall I put all these gifts with which the summer morning rewards me—and only me? Save them up for future books? Use them immediately for a practical handbook: *How to Be Happy?* Or getting deeper, to the bottom of things: understand what is concealed behind all this, behind the play, the sparkle, the thick, green greasepaint of the foliage? For there really is something, there is something! And one wants to offer thanks but there is no one to thank. The list of donations already made: 10,000 days—from Person Unknown.

He walked farther, past iron railings, past the deep gardens of bankers' villas with their grotto shadows, boxwood, ivy and lawns pearled with watering—and there among the elms and limes the first pines already appeared, sent out far ahead by the Grunewald pinewoods (or, on the contrary: stragglers behind the regiment?). Whistling loudly and rising (uphill) on the pedals of his three-wheeled bicycle, a baker's roundsman went by; a water-sprayer crawled slowly by with a wet hissing sound—a whale on wheels generously irrigating the asphalt. Someone with a briefcase slammed a vermilion-painted garden gate and set off for some unknown office. Fyodor emerged on his heels onto the boulevard (still the same Hohenzollerdamm at whose beginning they burned poor Alexander Yakovlevich), and there, its lock flashing, the briefcase ran for a tram. Now it was not far to the forest and he quickened his step, already feeling the sun's hot mask on his upturned face. The pickets of a fence flicked by, speckling his vision. On yesterday's vacant lot a small villa was being built, and since the sky was looking in through the gaps of future windows, and since burdocks and sunlight had taken advantage of the slowness of the work to make themselves comfortable within the unfinished white walls, these had acquired the pensive cast of ruins, like the word "sometime," which serves both the past and the future. Toward Fyodor came a young girl with a bottle of milk; she bore some resemblance to Zina—or, rather, contained a particle of that fascination, both special and vague, which he found in many girls, but with particular fullness in Zina, so that they all possessed some mysterious kinship with Zina, about which he alone knew, although he was completely incapable of formulating the indicia of this kinship (outside of which women evoked painful disgust in him)—and now, as he looked back at her and caught her long familiar, golden, fugitive outline that promptly vanished forever, he felt for a moment the impact of a hopeless desire, whose whole charm and richness was in its unquenchability. Oh trite demon of cheap thrills, do not tempt me with the catchword "my type." Not that, not that, but something beyond that. Definition is always finite, but I keep straining for the faraway; I search beyond the barricades (of words, of senses, of the world) for infinity, where all, all the lines meet.

At the end of the boulevard the green edge of the pinewood came into sight, with the gaudy portico of a recently constructed pavilion (in whose atrium was to be found an assortment of rest-rooms—men's, women's and children's), through which— according to the scheme of the local Lenôtres—one had to go in order to enter at first a newly laid-out rock garden, with Alpine flora along geometric paths, which served—still according to that same scheme—as a pleasant threshold to the forest. But Fyodor turned to the left, avoiding the threshold: it was nearer that way. The still wild edge of the pinewood stretched endlessly along an avenue for automobiles, but the next step on the part of the city fathers was inevitable: fence the whole of this free access with endless railings, so that the portico became the entrance of *necessity* (in the most literal, elementary sense). I built this ornamental thing for you but you weren't attracted; so now if you please: it is ornamental and regimental. But (by a mental jump back again: f3–g1) it could hardly have been better when this forest—now retreated, now crowded around the lake (and like us, in our own departure from hairy ancestors, having kept only a marginal vegetation)—used to stretch to the very heart of the present city, and a noisy, princely rabble galloped among its wilds with horns and hounds and beaters.

The forest as I found it was still alive, rich, full of birds. There occurred orioles, pigeons and jays; a crow flew by, its wings panting: *kshoo, kshoo, kshoo*; a redheaded woodpecker was rapping against a pine trunk—and sometimes, I presume, imitating its own rap vocally whereupon it came out particularly loud and convincingly (for the female's benefit); for there is nothing in nature more bewitchingly divine than her ingenious deceptions cropping up in unexpected places: thus a forest grasshopper (starting his little motor but never able to get it going: *tsig-tsig-tsig*—and breaks off), having jumped and landed, immediately readjusts the position of his body by turning in such a way as to make the direction of his dark stripes coincide with those of the fallen needles (or with their shadows!). But careful: I like to recall what my father wrote: "When closely—no matter how closely—observing events in nature we must, in the very process of observation, beware of letting our reason—that garrulous dragoman who always runs ahead—prompt us with explanations which then begin imperceptibly to influence the very course of observation and distort it: thus the shadow of the instrument falls upon the truth."

Give me your hand, dear reader, and let's go into the forest together. Look: first—at these glades with patches of thistle, nettle or willow herb, among which you will find all kinds of junk: sometimes even a ragged mattress with rusty, broken springs; don't disdain it! Here is a dark thicket of small firs where I once discovered a pit which had been carefully dug out before its death by the creature that lay therein, a young, slender-muzzled dog of wolf ancestry, folded into a wonderfully graceful curve, paws to paws. And now come bare hillocks with no undergrowth—merely a carpet of brown needles beneath simplistic pines, which have a hammock stretched between them full of someone's unexacting body—and the wire skeleton of a discarded lampshade is also here, lying on the ground. Further we have a barren, surrounded by locust trees—and there on the gray, burning, sticky sand sits a woman in underwear, her dreadful bare legs stretched out, and darns a stocking, while beside her crawls a child dark-groined from the dust. You can still see from here the thoroughfare and the sparkle of automobile radiators skimming by—but you only have to penetrate a little deeper, and the forest reasserts itself, the pines become nobler, moss creaks underfoot, and some bum is invariably asleep here, a newspaper covering his face: the philosopher prefers moss to roses. Here is the exact spot where a small airplane fell the other day: someone who was taking his girl for a morning ride in the blue got overexuberant, lost control of his joystick, and plunged with a screech and a crackle straight into the pines. I, unfortunately, came too late: they had had time to clear up the wreckage, and two mounted policemen were riding at a walk toward the road—but one could still see the imprint of a daring death beneath the pines, one of which had been shaved from top to bottom by a wing, and the architect Stockschmeisser walking with his dog was explaining to a nurse and child what had happened; but a few days later all traces had disappeared (there was only the yellow wound on the pine tree), and already in complete ignorance an old man and his old woman facing each other—she in her bodice and he in his underpants—were doing uncomplicated gymnastics on the same spot.

Farther on it became very nice: the pines had come into their own, and between their pinkish, scaly trunks the feathery foliage of low rowans and the vigorous greenery of oaks broke the stripiness of the pinewood sun into an animated dapple. In the density of an oak, when you looked from below, the overlapping of shaded and illumined leaves, dark green and bright emerald, seemed to be a jigsaw fitting together of their wavy edges, and on these leaves, now letting the sun caress its yellow-brown silk and now tightly closing its wings, there settled an Angle Wing butterfly with a white bracket on its dark mottled underside; suddenly taking off it alighted on my bare chest, attracted by human sweat. And still higher above my upturned face, the summits and trunks of the pines participated in a complex exchange of shadows, and their leafage reminded me of algae swaying in transparent water. And if I tilted my head back even farther, so that the grass behind (inexpressibly, primevally green from this point of upturned vision) seemed to be growing downward into empty, transparent light, I experienced something similar to what must strike a man who has flown to another planet (with a different gravity, different density and a different stress on the senses)—especially when a family out for a stroll went by upside down, with every step they took becoming a strange, elastic jerk, and a lobbed ball seemed to be falling—ever more slowly—into a dizzy abyss.

If one advanced even further—not to the left where the pinewood stretched endlessly, and not to the right where it was interrupted by a coppice of young birches, freshly and childishly smelling of Russia—the forest again thinned out, lost its undergrowth and straggled down sandy inclines at the foot of which the broad lake rose in pillars of light. The sun changefully illuminated the opposite bank, and when with the onset of a cloud the very air seemed to close, like a great blue eye and then slowly open again, one shore always lagged behind the other in the process of gradually fading and lighting up. There was practically no sandy border on the other side, and the trees descended all together to the dense reeds, while higher up one could find hot, dry slopes overgrown with clover, sorrel and spurge, and fringed with the rich dark green of oaks and beeches, that went trembling down to the damp hollows below, in one of which Yasha Chernyshevski had shot himself.

When in the mornings I entered this world of the forest, whose image I had raised as it were by my own efforts above the level of those artless Sunday impressions (paper trash, a crowd of picnickers) out of which the Berliners' conception of "Grunewald" was composed; when on these hot, summer weekdays I walked over to its southern side, into its depths, to wild secret spots, I felt as much delight as if this was a primeval paradise within two miles from Agamemnonstrasse. Coming to a favorite nook of mine which magically combined a free flow of sunshine with protection by the shrubbery, I would strip to the skin and lie down supine on the rug, placing my unnecessary trunks beneath my head. Thanks to the suntan coating my entire body (so that only my heels, palms and the raylike lines around my eyes kept their natural tint), I felt myself an athlete, a Tarzan, an Adam, anything you like, only not a naked town-dweller. The awkwardness with which nakedness is usually accompanied depends upon the awareness of our defenseless whiteness, which has long since lost all connection with the colors of the surrounding world and for that reason finds itself in artificial disharmony with it. But the sun's impact restores the deficiency, makes us equal in our naked rights with nature, and the brazen body no longer experiences shame. All this sounds like a nudist brochure—but one's own truth is not to blame if it coincides with the truth some poor fellow has borrowed.

The sun bore down. The sun licked me all over with its big, smooth tongue. I gradually felt that I was becoming moltenly transparent, that I was permeated with flame and existed only insofar as it did. As a book is translated into an exotic idiom, so was I translated into sun. The scrawny, chilly, hiemal Fyodor Godunov-Cherdyntsev was now as remote from me as if I had exiled him to the Yakutsk province. He was a pallid copy of me, whereas this aestival one was his magnified bronze replica. My personal I, the one that wrote books, the one that loved words, colors, mental fireworks, Russia, chocolate and Zina—had somehow disintegrated and dissolved; after being made transparent by the strength of the light, it was now assimilated to the shimmering of the summer forest with its satiny pine needles and heavenly-green leaves, with its ants running over the transfigured, most radiant-hued wool of the laprobe, with its birds, smells, hot breath of nettles and spermy odor of sun-warmed grass, with its blue sky where droned a high-flying plane that seemed filmed over with blue dust, the blue essence of the firmament: the plane was bluish, as a fish is wet in water.

One might dissolve completely that way. Fyodor raised himself and sat up. A streamlet of sweat flowed down his clean-shaven chest and fell into the reservoir of his navel. His flat belly had a brown and mother-of-pearl sheen to it. Over the glistening black ringlets of his pubic hair a lost ant scrambled nervously. His shins shone glossily. Pine needles had got stuck between his toes. With his bathing trunks he wiped his short-cropped head, sticky nape and neck. A squirrel with an arched back loped across the turf, from tree to tree, in a wavy and almost clumsy course. The scrub oaks, elder shrubs, pine trunks—everything was dazzlingly spotted, and a small cloud, in no way defiling the face of the summer day, felt its way slowly past the sun.

He got up, took a step—and immediately the weightless paw of a leafy shadow descended upon his left shoulder; it slipped off again at the next step. Fyodor consulted the position of the sun and dragged his rug a yard or so aside to prevent the shade of the leaves from encroaching upon him. To move around naked was astonishing bliss—the freedom around his loins especially pleased him. He walked between the bushes, listening to the vibration of insects and the rustling of the birds. A wren crept like a mouse through the foliage of a small oak; a sand wasp flew by low down, carrying a benumbed caterpillar. The squirrel he had just seen climbed up the bark of a tree with a spasmodic, scrabbly sound. Somewhere in the vicinity sounded girlish voices, and he stopped in a pattern of shadow, which stayed motionless along his arm but palpitated rythmically on his left side, between the ribs. A golden, stumpy little butterfly, equipped with two black commas, alighted on an oak leaf, half opening its slanting wings, and suddenly shot away like a golden fly. And as often happened on these woodland days, especially when he glimpsed familiar butterflies, Fyodor imagined his father's isolation in other forests—gigantic, infinitely distant, in comparison with which this one was but brushwood, a tree stump, rubbish. And yet he experienced something akin to that Asiatic freedom spreading wide on the maps, to the spirit of his father's peregrinations—and here it was most difficult of all to believe that despite the freedom, despite the greenery and the happy, sun-shot dark shade, his father was nonetheless dead.

The voices sounded closer and then receded. A horsefly that had settled unnoticed on his thigh managed to jab him with its blunt proboscis. Moss, turf, sand, each in its own way communicated with the soles of his bare feet, and each in its own way the sun and the shade stroked the hot silk of his body. His senses sharpened by the unrestricted heat were tantalized by the possibility of sylvan encounters, mythical abductions. *Le sanglot dont j'étais encore ivre.* He would have given a year of his life, even a leap-year, for Zina to be here—or any of her corps de ballet.

He again lay flat, then again got up; with a beating heart he listened to sly, vague, vaguely promising noises; then, pulling on only his trunks and hiding laprobe and clothes under a bush, he went off to wander through the woods around the lake.

Here and there, thinly on weekdays, there occurred more or less orange bodies. He avoided looking closely for fear of switching from Pan to Punch. But sometimes, next to a school satchel and beside her shiny bicycle propped against a tree trunk, a lone nymph would sprawl, her legs bared to the crotch and suede-soft to the eye, and her elbows thrown back, with the hair of her armpits glistening in the sun; temptation's arrow had hardly had time to sing out and pierce him before he noticed, a short distance away at three equidistant points, forming a magic triangle (around whose prize?) and strangers to one another, three motionless hunters visible in between the tree trunks: two young fellows (one lying prone, the other on his side) and an elderly man, coatless, with armbands on his shirt-sleeves, sitting solidly on the grass, motionless and eternal, with sad but patient eyes; and it seemed that these three pairs of eyes striking the same spot would finally, with the help of the sun, burn a hole in the black bathing tights of that poor little German girl, who never raised her ointment-smeared lids.

He descended to the sandy shore of the lake and here in the roar of voices the charmed fabric which he himself had so carefully spun completely fell to pieces, and he saw with revulsion the crumpled, twisted, deformed by life's nor'easter, more or less naked or more or less clothed—the latter were the more terrible—bodies of bathers (petty bourgeois, idle workers) stirring on the dirty-gray sand. At the point where the shore road went along the lake's narrow lip, the latter was fenced off by stakes supporting tortured-looking remnants of sagging wire, and the place by these stakes was particularly valued by the beach habitués—partly because trousers could be conveniently hung by their suspenders on them (while underwear was laid on the dusty nettles) and partly because of the vague feeling of security from having a fence at one's back.

Old men's gray legs covered with growths and swollen veins; flat feet; the tawny crust of corns; pink porcine paunches; wet, shivering, pale, hoarse-voiced adolescents; the globes of breasts; voluminous posteriors; flabby thighs; bluish varices; gooseflesh; the pimply shoulder blades of bandy-legged girls; the sturdy necks and buttocks of muscular hooligans; the hopeless, godless vacancy of satisfied faces; romps, guffaws, roisterous splashing—all this formed the apotheosis of that renowned German good-naturedness which can turn so easily at any moment into frenzied hooting. And over all this, especially on Sundays when the crowding was vilest of all, there reigned an unforgettable smell, the smell of dust, of sweat, of aquatic slime, of unclean underwear, of aired and dried poverty, the smell of dried, smoked, potted souls a penny a piece. But the lake itself, with vivid green clumps of trees on the other side and a rippling wake of sunshine in the middle, bore itself with dignity.

Having selected a private little creek among the bulrushes, Fyodor took to the water. Its warm opacity enveloped him, sparks of sunshine danced before his eyes. He swam for a long time, half an hour, five hours, twenty-four, a week, another. Finally, on the twenty-eighth of June around three P.M., he came out on the other shore.

Having made his way out of the lakeside spinach he at once found himself in a grove and from there he climbed onto a hot slope where he quickly dried in the sun. On the right was a ravine overgrown with oakbrush and bramble. And today, just as every time that he came here, Fyodor descended into that hollow which always attracted him, as if he had been somehow guilty of the death of the unknown youth who had shot himself here—precisely here. He reflected that Alexandra Yakovlevna used to come here as well, rummaging purposefully among the bushes with her tiny black-gloved hands. . . . He had not known her then and could not have seen it—but from her account of her multiple pilgrimages he felt it had been exactly like that: the search for something, the rustling of leaves, the prodding umbrella, the radiant eyes, the lips trembling with sobs. He recalled how he had met her this spring—for the last time—after her husband's death, and the strange sensation that overwhelmed him when looking at her lowered face with its unworldly frown, as if he had never really seen her before and was now making out on her face the resemblance to her deceased husband, whose death was expressed on it through some hitherto concealed, funereal blood relationship. A day later she went away to some relatives in Riga, and already her face, the stories about her son, the literary evenings at her house, and Alexander Yakovlevich's mental illness—all this that had served its time—now rolled up of its own accord and came to an end, like a bundle of life tied up crosswise, which will long be kept but which will never again be untied by our lazy, procrastinating, ungrateful hands. He was seized by a panicky desire not to allow it to close and get lost in a corner of his soul's lumber room, a desire to apply all this to himself, to his eternity, to his truth, so as to enable it to sprout up in a new way. There is a way—the only way.

He ascended another slope and there at the top by a path which descended again, sitting on a bench beneath an oak tree, and slowly, pensively tracing the sand with his cane, was a round-shouldered young man in a black suit. How hot he must be, thought the naked Fyodor. The sitter looked up . . . The sun turned and slightly raised his face with a photographer's delicate gesture, a bloodless face with wide-set, myopically gray eyes. Between the corners of his starched collar (the type once called in Russia "dog's delight") a stud gleamed above the slack knot of his tie.

"How sunburned you are," said Koncheyev, "it can hardly be good for you. And where, pray, are your clothes?"

"Over there," said Fyodor, "on the other side, in the woods."

"Someone might steal them," remarked Koncheyev. "It's not for nothing there's a proverb: Freehanded Russian, light-fingered Prussian."

Fyodor sat down and said: "There is no such proverb. By the way, do you know where we two are? Beyond those blackberry bushes, down below, is the place where the Chernyshevski boy, the poet, shot himself."

"Oh, was it here?" said Koncheyev without especial interest. "You know, his Olga recently married a furrier and went off to the United States. Not quite the lancer whom Pushkin's Olga married, but still . . ."

"Aren't you hot?" asked Fyodor.

"Not a bit. I have a weak chest and I always freeze. But of course when one sits next to a naked man one is physically aware that there exist men's outfitters, and one's body feels blind. On the other hand it seems to me that any mental work must be completely impossible for you in such a denuded state."

"A good point," grinned Fyodor. "One seems to live more superficially—on the surface of one's own skin. . . ."

"That's it. All you're concerned with is patrolling your body and trailing the sun. But thought likes curtains and the camera obscura. Sunlight is good in the degree that it heightens the value of shade. A jail with no jailer and a garden with no gardener—that is I think the ideal arrangement. Tell me, did you read what I said about your book?"

"I did," replied Fyodor, watching a little geometrid caterpillar that was checking the number of inches between the two writers. "I did indeed. At first I wanted to write you a letter of thanks—you know, with a touching reference to undeservingness and so on—but then I thought that this would have introduced an intolerable human smell into the domain of free opinion. And besides—if I produced a good book I should thank myself and not you, just as you have to thank yourself and not me for understanding what was good—isn't that true? If we start bowing to one another, then, as soon as one of us stops the other will feel hurt and depart in a huff."

"I didn't expect truisms from you," said Koncheyev with a smile. "Yes, all that is so. Once in my life, only once, I thanked a critic, and he replied: 'Well, as a matter of fact, I really liked your book!' and that 'really' sobered me forever. By the way, I didn't say everything I could have said about you . . . You were so taken to task for nonexistent defects that I no longer wanted to harp on those that were obvious to me. Furthermore, in your next work you will either get rid of them or they will develop into special virtues all your own, the way a speck on an embryo turns into an eye. You are a zoologist, aren't you?"

"In a way—as an amateur. But what are those defects? I wonder if they coincide with the ones I know."

"First, an excessive trust in words. It sometimes happens that your words in order to introduce the necessary thought have to smuggle it in. The sentence may be excellent, but still it is smuggling, and moreover gratuitous smuggling, since the lawful road is open. But your smugglers under the cover of an obscure style, with all sorts of complicated contrivances, import goods that are duty free anyway. Secondly, there is a certain awkardness in the reworking of the sources: You seem to be undecided whether to enforce your style upon past speeches and events or to make their own more salient. I took the trouble to confront one or two passages in your book with the context in the complete edition of Chernyshevski's works, same copy you must have used: I found your cigarette ash between the pages. Thirdly, you sometimes bring up parody to such a degree of naturalness that it actually becomes a genuine serious thought, but on *this* level it suddenly falters, lapsing into a mannerism that is yours and not a parody of a mannerism, although it is precisely the kind of thing you are ridiculing—as if somebody parodying an actor's slovenly reading of Shakespeare had been carried away, had started to thunder in earnest, but had accidentally garbled a line. Fourthly, one observes in one or two of your transitions something mechanical, if not automatic, which suggests you are pursuing *your own* advantage, and taking the course you find easier. In one passage, for example, a mere pun serves as such a transition. Fifthly and finally, you sometimes say things chiefly calculated to prick your contemporaries, but any woman will tell you that nothing gets lost so easily as a hairpin—not to speak of the fact that the least swerve of fashion may make pins obsolete: think how many sharp little objects have been dug up whose exact use not a single archaeologist can tell! The real writer should ignore all readers but one, that of the future, who in his turn is merely the author reflected in time. That, I think, is the sum of my complaints against you and generally speaking they are trivial. They are completely eclipsed by the brilliance of your achievements—about which I could still say a fair bit."

"Oh, that is less interesting," said Fyodor, *who during this tirade* (as Turgenev, Goncharov, Count Salias, Grigorovich and Boborykin used to write) had been nodding his head with an approving *mien*. "You diagnosed my shortcomings very well," he continued, "and they correspond to my own complaints against myself, although, of course, I put them in a different order—some of the points run together while others are subdivided further. But besides the defects you have noted in my book, I am aware of at least three more—they, perhaps, are the most important of all. Only I'll never tell you them—and they won't be there in my next book. Do you want to talk about your poetry now?"

"No thank you, I'd rather not," said Koncheyev fearfully. "I have reasons for thinking that you like my work, but I am organically averse to discussing it. When I was small, before sleep I used to say a long and obscure prayer which my dead mother—a pious and very unhappy woman—had taught me (she, of course, would have said that these two things are incompatible, but even so it's true that happiness doesn't take the veil). I remembered this prayer and kept saying it for years, almost until adolescence, but one day I probed its sense, understood all the words—and as soon as I understood I immediately forgot it, as if I had broken an unrestorable spell. It seems to me that the same thing might happen to my poems—that if I try to rationalize them I shall instantly lose my ability to write them. You, I know, corrupted your poetry long ago with words and meaning—and you will hardly continue writing verse now. You are too rich, too greedy. The Muse's charm lies in her poverty."

"You know, it's odd," said Fyodor, "once, about three years ago, I imagined most vividly a conversation with you on these subjects—and you know it came out somewhat similar! Although, of course, you shamelessly played up to me and all that. The fact that I know you so well without knowing you makes me unbelievably happy, for that means there are unions in the world which don't depend at all on massive friendships, asinine affinities or 'the spirit of the age,' nor on any mystical organizations or associations of poets, where a dozen tightly knit mediocrities 'glow' by their common efforts."

"At all events I want to warn you," said Koncheyev frankly, "not to flatter yourself as regards our similarity: you and I differ in many things, I have different tastes, different habits; your Fet, for instance, I can't stand, and on the other hand I am an ardent admirer of the author of *The Double* and *The Possessed*, whom you are disposed to slight. . . . There is much about you I don't like—your St. Petersburg style, your Gallic taint, your neo-Voltaireanism and weakness for Flaubert—and I find, forgive me, your obscene sporty nudity simply offensive. But then, with these reservations, it would be true probably to say that somewhere—not here but on another plane, of whose angle, by the way, you have an even vaguer idea than I—somewhere on the outskirts of our existence, very far, very mysteriously and inexpressibly, a rather divine bond is growing between us. But perhaps you feel and say all this because I praised your book in print—that also happens, you know."

"Yes, I know. I thought of that myself. Especially since formerly I used to envy your fame. But in all conscience—"

"Fame?" interrupted Koncheyev. "Don't make me laugh. Who knows my poems? A thousand, a thousand five hundred, at the very outside two thousand intelligent expatriates, of whom again ninety percent don't understand them. Two thousand out of three million refugees! That's provincial success, but not fame. In the future, perhaps, I shall recoup, but a great deal of time will have to elapse before the Tungus and the Kalmuk of Pushkin's '*Exegi monumentum*' begin to tear out of each other's hands my 'Communication,' with the Finn looking enviously on."

"But there is a comforting feeling," said Fyodor meditatively. "One can borrow on the strength of the legacy. Doesn't it amuse you to imagine that one day, on this very spot, on this lakeside, beneath this oak tree, a visiting dreamer will come and sit and imagine in his turn that you and I once sat here?"

"And the historian will dryly tell him that we never took a walk together, that we were hardly acquainted and that if we did meet we only talked about routine trifles."

"But nevertheless try! Try to experience that strange, future, retrospective thrill. . . . All the little hairs on the soul stand on end! It would be a good thing in general to put an end to our barbaric perception of time; I find it particularly charming when people talk about the earth freezing in a trillion years and everything disappearing unless our printing shops are moved in good time to a neighboring star. Or the drivel about eternity: so much time has been allotted to the universe that the date of its end should *already* have come, just as it is impossible in a single segment of time to imagine *whole* an egg lying on a road along which an army is endlessly marching. How stupid! Our mistaken feeling of time as a kind of growth is a consequence of our finiteness which, being always on the level of the present, implies its constant rise between the watery abyss of the past and the aerial abyss of the future. Existence is thus an eternal transformation of the future into the past—an essentially phantom process—a mere reflection of the material metamorphoses taking place within us. In these circumstances the attempt to comprehend the world is reduced to an attempt to comprehend that which we ourselves have deliberately made incomprehensible. The absurdity at which searching thought arrives is only a natural, generic sign of its belonging to man, and striving to obtain an answer is the same as demanding of chicken broth that it began to cluck. The theory I find most tempting—that there is no time, that everything is the present situated like a radiance outside our blindness—is just as hopeless a finite hypothesis as all the others. 'You will understand when you are big,' those are really the wisest words that I know. And if one adds to this that nature was seeing double when she created us (oh, this accursed pairing which is impossible to escape: horse-cow, cat-dog, rat-mouse, flea-bug), that symmetry in the structure of live bodies is a consequence of the rotation of worlds (a top that spins for sufficiently long will begin, perhaps, to live, grow and multiply), and that in our straining toward asymmetry, toward inequality, I can detect a howl for genuine freedom, an urge to break out of the circle. . . ."

"*Herrliches Wetter—in der Zeitung steht es aber, dass es morgen bestimmt regnen wird,*" said finally the young German who was sitting beside Fyodor on the bench and who had seemed to him to resemble Koncheyev.

Imagination again—but what a pity! I had even thought up a dead mother for him in order to trap truth. . . . Why can a conversation with him never blossom out into reality, break through to realization? Or is this a realization, and nothing better is needed . . . since a real conversation would be only disillusioning—with the stumps of stuttering, the chaff of hemming and hawing, the debris of small words?

"*Da kommen die Wolken schon,*" continued the Koncheyevoid German, pointing his finger at a full-breasted cloud rising in the west. (A student, most probably. Perhaps with a philosophical or musical vein. Where is Yasha's friend now? He would hardly be likely to come here.)

"*Halb fünf ungefähr,*" he added in response to Fyodor's question, and gathering his cane he left the bench. His dark, stooping figure receded along the shady footpath. (Perhaps a poet? After all, there must be poets in Germany. Puny ones, local ones—but all the same not butchers. Or only a garnish for the meat?)

He was too lazy to swim back to the other side; he followed leisurely the trail that skirted the lake along its northern edge. At the spot where a wide sandy declivity reached the water, with the uncovered roots of apprehensive pines supporting the sliding bank, there were some more people, and down below on a strip of grass lay three naked corpses, white, pink and brown, like a triple sample of the sun's action. Further on, along the bend of the lake, there was a marshy stretch, and the dark almost black soil of the path stuck refreshingly to his bare heels. He went upwards again over a needle-scattered slope, and walked through the speckled forest toward his lair. All was cheerful, sad, sunny, shady—he did not feel like returning home but it was time. For a moment he lay down by an old tree that had seemed to have beckoned to him—"Show you something interesting." A little song sounded among the trees, and presently there came into view, walking at a brisk pace, five nuns—round-faced, wearing black dresses and white coifs—and the little song, half schoolgirlish, half angelic, hovered about them the whole time, while first one and then another bent down on the move to pluck a modest flower (invisible to Fyodor, although he was lying close by) and then straightened up very nimbly, simultaneously drawing level with the others, taking up the rhythm and adding this ghost-flower to a ghostly nosegay with an idyllic gesture (the thumb and index touching for an instant, the other fingers delicately curved)—and it all looked so much like a staged scene—and how much skill there was in everything, what an infinity of grace and art, what a director lurked behind the pines, how well everything was calculated—their walking slightly out of order and then leveling out again, three in front and two behind, and the fact that one of the girls behind giggled briefly (a very cloistral sense of humor) because suddenly one of those in front had, with a touch of expansiveness, almost splashed her hands over a particularly heavenly note, and the way the song dwindled as it receded, while a shoulder continued to stoop and fingers sought a stalk of grass (but the latter, merely swaying, remained to gleam in the sun . . . where had this happened before—what had straightened up and started to sway? . . .)—and now they all departed through the trees on quick feet in button shoes, and some half-naked little boy, pretending to seek a ball in the grass, rudely and automatically repeated a snatch of their song (in what musicians call a "clowning refrain"). How it had been mounted! How much labor had gone into this light, swift scene, into this deft traverse, what muscles there were beneath that heavy-looking, black cloth, which would be exchanged after the intermission for gossamer ballet skirts!

A cloud blocked the sun, the light in the forest drifted and gradually faded. Fyodor walked to the clearing where he had left his clothes. In the hole beneath a bush which always sheltered them so obligingly he now found only a single sneaker; his rug, his shirt and his trousers had vanished. There is a story to the effect that a passenger who inadvertently dropped his glove out of a train window promptly threw out its mate so that at least the person who found them should have a pair. In this case the thief had acted the other way: the old, badly worn sneakers were probably no good to him, but in order to make fun of his victim he had separated the pair. Furthermore, a scrap of newspaper had been left in the sneaker with a penciled inscription: "*Vielen Dank*."

Fyodor wandered all around finding no one and nothing. The shirt was frayed and he did not mind losing it, but he was somewhat grieved about the plaid laprobe (brought all the way from Russia) and the good flannel pants quite recently bought. Together with the trousers had gone twenty marks, obtained two days before for at least partial payment of his room. Also gone were a small pencil, a handkerchief, and a bunch of keys. The latter somehow was worst of all. If nobody happened to be at home, which might easily be the case, it would be impossible to get into the apartment.

The edge of a cloud dazzlingly caught fire, and the sun slipped out. It emitted such hot, blissful strength that forgetting his vexation Fyodor lay down on the moss and began to watch the next snowy colossus draw near, eating up the blue as it advanced: the sun slid into it smoothly, its rim of funeral fire quivering and splitting as it glided through the white cumulus—and then, finding a way out, it first threw out three rays and then expanded, filling the eyes with spotted fire, blackballing them (so that no matter where you looked domino patterns glided past)—and as the light got stronger or died away, all the shadows in the forest breathed and did push-ups.

A small incidental relief was supplied by the fact that thanks to the Shchyogolevs' going away the following day to Denmark there would be an extra set of keys—which meant he could keep quiet about the loss of his bunch. Going away, going away, going away! He imagined what he had constantly been imagining during the past two months—the beginning (tomorrow night!) of his full life with Zina—the release, the slaking—and meanwhile a sun-charged cloud, filling up, growing, with swollen, turquoise veins, with a fiery itch in its thunder-root, rose in all its turgid, unwieldy magnificence and embraced him, the sky and the forest, and to resolve this tension seemed a monstrous joy incapable of being borne by man. A ripple of wind ran over his chest, his excitement slowly subsided, the air grew dark and sultry, it was necessary to hurry home. Once more he searched under the bushes, then shrugged his shoulders, pulled the elastic belt of his trunks tighter—and set out on his way back.

When he left the forest and started to cross a street, the tarry stickiness of the asphalt under his bare foot proved to be a pleasant novelty. It was also interesting to walk on the sidewalk. Dream lightness. An elderly passerby in a black felt hat stopped, looked back after him and made a coarse remark—but immediately, by way of happy compensation, a blind man, sitting with a concertina against a stone wall, mumbled his small request for alms and squeezed out a polygon of music as if there were nothing out of the way (it was odd, though—surely he must have heard that I was barefoot). Two schoolboys shouted at the naked passerby as they rode past clinging to the back of a tram, and then the sparrows returned to the turf between the rails whence they had been frightened by the clattering yellow car. Drops of rain had begun to fall, and it was as if someone were applying a silver coin to different parts of his body. A young policeman detached himself from a newspaper stand and came over to him.

"It's forbidden to walk about the city like that," he said, looking Fyodor in the navel.

"Everything's been stolen," explained Fyodor briefly.

"That mustn't happen," said the policeman.

"Yes, but it happened all the same," said Fyodor nodding (several people had already stopped by them and were following the dialogue with curiosity).

"Whether you've been robbed or not, you can't go about the streets naked," said the policeman, growing angry.

"Quite, but I have to get somehow to the taxi stand—see?"

"You can't in that state."

"Unfortunately I am unable to turn into smoke or grow a suit."

"And I'm telling you you can't walk about like that," said the policeman. ("Unheard-of shamelessness," commented someone's thick voice from the back.)

"In that case," said Fyodor, "it remains for you to fetch me a taxi while I stand here."

"Standing in the nude is also impossible," said the policeman.

"I'll take off my trunks and imitate a statue," suggested Fyodor.

The policeman took out his notebook and so fiercely tore the pencil out of the pencil-hold that he dropped it on the sidewalk. Some workman or other servilely picked it up.

"Name and address," said the policeman, boiling.

"Count Fyodor Godunov-Cherdyntsev," said Fyodor.

"Stop being funny and tell me your name," roared the policeman.

Another one came up, with a higher rank, and inquired what the matter was.

"My clothes were stolen in the forest," said Fyodor patiently and suddenly felt that he was completely wet from the rain. One or two standers-by had run beneath the shelter of an awning and an old woman standing by his elbow put up her umbrella, nearly gouging his eye out.

"Who stole them?" asked the sergeant.

"I don't know and what's more, I don't care," said Fyodor. "Right now I want to go home and you are detaining me."

The rain suddenly grew heavier and swept across the asphalt; the whole of its surface seemed to be covered with jumping little candles. The policemen (all matted and blackened by the damp) probably considered the cloudburst to be an element in which bathing trunks were, if not appropriate, then at least permissible. The younger one again tried to obtain Fyodor's address, but his senior waved his hand, and the two of them, slightly quickening their sedate pace, retreated under the awning of a grocer's shop. The glistening Fyodor Konstantinovich ran through the noisy splashing of the rain, turned a corner, and shot into an automobile.

Arriving home and telling the driver to wait, he pressed the button which until 8 P.M. automatically opened the front door and hurled himself up the stairs. He was let in by Marianna Nikolavna; the hall was full of people and things: Shchyogolev in his shirt-sleeves, two fellows struggling with a box (in which, it seems, was the radio), a comely milliner with a hatbox, a coil of wire, a pile of linen from the laundry . . .

"You're crazy!" cried Marianna Nikolavna.

"For God's sake pay the taxi," said Fyodor, wriggling his cold body through the people and things—and finally, over a barricade of trunks, he crashed his way through to his room.

They had supper all together that evening, and later on were to come the Kasatkins, the Baltic baron, another person or two. . . . At table Fyodor gave an embellished account of his misadventure, and Shchyogolev laughed heartily, while Marianna Nikolavna wanted to know (not without reason) how much cash there had been in the pants. Zina only shrugged her shoulders and with unusual frankness urged Fyodor to help himself to the vodka, obviously fearing that he had caught a chill.

"Well—our last evening!" said Boris Ivanovich, having laughed to his heart's content. "May you prosper, signor. Someone told me the other day that you dashed off a pretty nasty paper on Petrashevski. Very laudable. Listen, Mamma, there's another bottle there, no point in taking it with us, give it to the Kasatkins."

". . . so you're going to remain an orphan [he continued, starting on the Italian salad and devouring it with the utmost sloppiness]. I don't think our Zinaida Oscarovna will look after you too well. Eh, princess?"

". . . Yes, that's how it is, my dear chap, one twist of fate, and the king is mate. I never thought that fortune would smile on me—touch wood, touch wood. Why, only last winter I was wondering what to do: tighten my belt or sell Marianna Nikolavna for scrap? You and I had a year and a half of cohabitation, if you'll excuse the expression, and tomorrow we part—probably forever. Man is fate's plaything. Happy today, pappy tomorrow."

When supper was over and Zina had gone down to let the guests in, Fyodor retreated noiselessly to his room, where everything was animated by rain and wind. He half-closed the casements of his window, but a moment later the night said: "No," and with a kind of wide-eyed insistence, disdaining blows, entered again. "I was so tickled to learn that Tanya has a little girl, and I am terribly glad for her and for you. The other day I wrote Tanya a long, lyrical letter, but I have an uncomfortable feeling that I put the wrong address on it: instead of '122' I put some other number, without thinking, just as I did once before, I don't know why this happens—one writes an address heaps of times, automatically and correctly, and then all of a sudden one hesitates, one looks at it consciously, and one sees you're not sure of it, it seems unfamiliar—very queer . . . You know, like taking a simple word, say 'ceiling' and seeing it as 'sealing' or 'sea-ling' until it becomes completely strange and feral, something like 'iceling' or 'inglice.' I think that *some day* that will happen to the whole of life. In any case wish Tanya from me everything gay, green and Leshino-summery. Tomorrow my landlord and landlady are going away and I am beside myself with joy: *beside myself*—a very pleasant situation, like on a rooftop at night. I'll stay at Agamemnonstrasse another month and then move. I don't know how things will work out. By the way, my Chernyshevski is selling rather well. Who exactly was it told you that Bunin praised it? They already seem ancient history to me now, my exertions over the book, and all those little storms of thought, those cares of the pen— and now I am completely empty, clean, and ready to receive new lodgers. You know, I'm black as a gypsy from the Grunewald sun. Something is beginning to take shape—I think I'll write a classical novel, with 'types,' love, fate, conversations . . ."

The door suddenly opened, Zina half entered and without letting go of the door handle threw something on his desk.

"Pay this to Mamma," she said; she glanced at him through slitted eyes and disappeared.

He unfolded the banknote. Two hundred marks. The amount seemed colossal, but a moment's calculation showed that it would only just suffice for the two past months—eighty plus eighty, and thirty-five for the coming one, from now on without board. But everything grew confused when he began to consider that for the past month he had not been taking lunch, but on the other hand had been receiving bigger suppers; besides that he had contributed during that time ten (or fifteen?) marks, and on the other hand he owed for telephone conversations and for one or two other trifles, such as today's taxi. The solution to the problem was beyond him, it bored him; he thrust the money beneath a dictionary.

". . . and with descriptions of nature. I am very glad that you're reading my thing over again, but now it's time to forget it—it was only an exercise, a tryout, an essay before the school holidays. I have missed you a great deal and perhaps (I repeat, I don't know how it will work out . . .) I'll visit you in Paris. Generally speaking I'd abandon tomorrow this country, oppressive as a headache—where everything is alien and repulsive to me, where a novel about incest or some brash trash, some cloyingly rhetorical, pseudobrutal tale about war is considered the crown of literature; where in fact there is no literature, and hasn't been for a long time; where sticking out of the fog of a most monotonous democratic dampness—also pseudo—you have the same old jackboot and helmet; where our native enforced 'social intent' in literature has been replaced by social opportunity—and so on, and so on . . . I could go on much longer—and it is amusing that fifty years ago every Russian thinker with a suitcase used to scribble exactly the same—an accusation so obvious as to have become even banal. Earlier, on the other hand, in the golden middle of last century, goodness, what transports! 'Little gemütlich Germany'—ach, brick cottages, ach, the kiddies go to school, ach, the peasant doesn't beat his horse with a club! . . . Never mind—he has his own German way of torturing it, in a cozy nook, with red-hot iron. Yes, I would have left long ago, but there are certain personal circumstances (not to mention my wonderful solitude in this country, the wonderful, beneficient contrast between my inner habitus and the terribly cold world around me; you know, in cold countries houses are warmer than in the south, better insulated and heated), but even these personal circumstances are capable of taking such a turn that soon, perhaps, I'll leave the Fetterland and bring them with me. And when will we return to Russia? What idiotic sentimentality, what a rapacious groan must our innocent hope convey to people in Russia. But our nostalgia is not historical—only human— how can one explain this to them? It's easier for me, of course, than for another to live outside Russia, because I know for certain that I shall return—first because I took away the keys to her, and secondly because, no matter when, in a hundred, two hundred years—I shall live there in my books—or at least in some researcher's footnote. There; now you have a historical hope, a literary-historical one . . . 'I lust for immortality—even for its earthly shadow!' Today I am writing you non-stop nonsense (non-stop trains of thought) because I am well and happy—and besides that, all this has something to do in a roundabout way with Tanya's baby.

"The literary review you ask about is called *The Tower*. I don't have it but I think you'll find it in any Russian bookshop. Nothing came from Uncle Oleg. When did he send it? I think you've mixed something up. Well, that's it. Keep well, *je t'embrasse*. Night, rain quietly falling—it has found its nocturnal rhythm, and can now go on for infinity."

He heard the hall fill with departing voices, heard somebody's umbrella fall and the elevator summoned by Zina rumble and come to a halt. All was still again. Fyodor went into the dining room where Shchyogolev sat cracking the last nuts, chewing on one side, and Marianna Nikolavna was clearing the table. Her plump, dark pink face, the glossy wings of her nose, violet eyebrows, apricot hair turning to bristly blue on her fat shaven nape, her azure orb with its mascara-fouled canthus, momentarily immersing its gaze in the dreggy ooze on the bottom of the teapot, her rings, her garnet brooch, the flowery shawl on her shoulders—all this together constituted a crudely but richly daubed picture in a somewhat hackneyed genre. She put on her spectacles and took out a sheet with figures on it when Fyodor asked how much he owed her. At this Shchyogolev raised his eyebrows in surprise: he had been sure that they would not get another penny from their lodger, and being essentially a kindly man he had advised his wife only yesterday not to press Fyodor but to write him a week or two later from Copenhagen with a threat to approach his relatives. After settling up, Fyodor retained three and a half marks out of the two hundred and went off to bed. In the hallway he met Zina returning from below. "Well?" she said, holding her finger on the switch—a half-interrogative, half-urging interjection which meant approximately: "Are you coming this way? I'm putting out the light here, so hurry up." The dimple on her naked arm, pale-silk-clad legs in velvet slippers, lowered face. Darkness.

He went to bed and began to fall asleep to the whisper of the rain. As always on the border between consciousness and sleep all sorts of verbal rejects, sparkling and tinkling, broke in: "The crystal crunching of that Christian night beneath a chrysolitic star" . . . and his thought, listening for a moment, aspired to gather them and use them and began to add of its own: Extinguished, Yasnaya Polyana's light, and Pushkin dead, and Russia far . . . but since this was no good, the stipple of rhymes extended further: "A falling star, a cruising chrysolite, an aviator's avatar . . ." His mind sank lower and lower into a hell of alligator alliterations, into infernal cooperatives of words. Through their nonsensical accumulation a round button on the pillowcase prodded him in the cheek; he turned on his other side and against a dark backdrop naked people ran into the Grunewald lake, and a monogram of light resembling an infusorian glided diagonally to the highest corner of his subpalpebral field of vision. Behind a certain closed door in his brain, holding on to its handle but turning away from it, his mind commenced to discuss with somebody a complicated and important secret, but when the door opened for a minute it turned out that they were talking about chairs, tables, stables. Suddenly in the thickening mist, by reason's last tollgate, came the silver vibration of a telephone bell, and Fyodor rolled over prone, falling . . . The vibration stayed in his fingers, as if a nettle had stung him. In the hall, having already put back the receiver into its black box, stood Zina– she seemed frightened. "That was for you," she said in a low voice. "Your former landlady, Frau Stoboy. She wants you to come over immediately. There's somebody waiting for you at her place. Hurry." He pulled on a pair of flannel trousers and gasping for breath went along the street. At this time of year in Berlin there is something similar to the St. Petersburg white nights: the air was transparently gray, and the houses swam past like a soapy mirage. Some night workers had wrecked the pavement at the corner, and one had to creep through narrow passages between planks, everyone being given at the entrance a small lamp which at the exit was to be left on a hook screwed into a post or else simply on the sidewalk next to some empty milk bottles. Leaving his bottle as well he ran further through the lusterless streets, and the premonition of something incredible, of some impossible superhuman surprise splashed his heart with a snowy mixture of happiness and horror. In the gray murk, blind children wearing dark spectacles came out of a school building in pairs and walked past him; they studied at night (in economically dark schools which in the daytime housed seeing children), and the clergyman accompanying them resembled the Leshino village schoolmaster, Bychkov. Leaning against a lamppost and hanging his tousled head, his scissor-like legs in striped pantaloons splayed wide and his hands stuffed in his pockets, a lean drunkard stood as if just come from the pages of an old Russian satirical rag. There was still light in the Russian bookstore—they were serving books to the night taxicab drivers and through the yellow opacity of the glass he noticed the silhouette of Misha Berezovski who was handing out Petrie's black atlas to someone. Must be hard to work nights! Excitement lashed him again as soon as he reached his former haunts. He was out of breath from running, and the rolled-up laprobe weighed heavy on his arm—he had to hurry, but he could not recall the layout of the streets, and the ashy night confused everything, changing as in a negative image the relationship between dark and light parts, and there was no one to ask, everybody was asleep. Suddenly a poplar loomed and behind it a tall church with a violet-red window divided into harlequin rhombuses of colored light: inside a night service was in progress, and an old lady in mourning with cotton-wool under the bridge of her spectacles hastened to mount the steps. He found his street, but at the end of it a post with a gauntleted hand on it indicated that one had to enter from the other end where the post office was, since at this end a pile of flags had been prepared for tomorrow's festivities. But he was afraid of losing it in the course of a detour and moreover the post office —that would come afterwards—if Mother had not *already* been sent a telegram. He scrambled over boards, boxes and a toy grenadier in curls, and caught sight of the familiar house, and there the workmen had already stretched a red strip of carpet across the sidewalk from door to curb, as it used to be done in front of their house on the Neva Embankment on ball nights. He ran up the stairs and Frau Stoboy immediately let him in. Her cheeks glowed and she wore a white hospital overall—she had formerly practiced medicine. "Only don't get all worked up," she said. "Go to your room and wait there. You must be prepared for anything," she added with a vibrant note in her voice and pushed him into the room which he had thought he would never in his life enter again. He grasped her by the elbow, losing control over himself, but she shook him off. "Somebody has come to see you," said Stoboy, "he's resting . . . Wait a couple of minutes." The door banged shut. The room was exactly as if he had been still living in it: the same swans and lilies on the wallpaper, the same painted ceiling wonderfully ornamented with Tibetan butterflies (there, for example, was *Thecla bieti*). Expectancy, awe, the frost of happiness, the surge of sobs merged into a single blinding agitation as he stood in the middle of the room incapable of movement, listening and looking at the door. He knew *who* would enter in a moment, and was amazed now that he had doubted this return: doubt now seemed to him to be the obtuse obstinacy of one half-witted, the distrust of a barbarian, the self-satisfaction of an ignoramus. His heart was bursting like that of a man before execution, but at the same time this execution was such a joy that life faded before it, and he was unable to understand the disgust he had been wont to experience when, in hastily constructed dreams, he had evoked what was now taking place in real life. Suddenly, the door shuddered (another, remote one had opened somewhere beyond it) and he heard a familiar tread, an indoor Morocco-padded step. Noiselessly but with terrible force the door flew open, and on the threshold stood his father. He was wearing a gold embroidered skullcap and a black Cheviot jacket with breast pockets for cigarette case and magnifying glass; his brown cheeks with their two sharp furrows running down from both sides of his nose were particularly smoothly shaven; hoary hairs gleamed in his dark beard like salt; warmly, shaggily, his eyes laughed out of a network of wrinkles. But Fyodor stood and was unable to take a step. His father said something, but so quietly that it was impossible to make anything out, although one somehow knew it to be connected with his return, unharmed, whole, human, and real. And even so it was terrible to come closer —so terrible that Fyodor felt he would die if the one who had entered should move toward him. Somewhere in the rear rooms sounded the warningly rapturous laughter of his mother, while his father made soft chucking sounds hardly parting his lips, as he used to do when taking a decision or seeking something on the page of a book . . . then he spoke again—and this again meant that everything was all right and simple, that this was the true resurrection, that it could not be otherwise, and also: that he was pleased —pleased with his captures, his return, his son's book about him—and then at last everything grew easy, a light broke through, and his father with confident joy spread out his arms. With a moan and a sob Fyodor stepped toward him, and in the collective sensation of woolen jacket, big hands and the tender prickle of trimmed mustaches there swelled an ecstatically happy, living, enormous, paradisal warmth in which his icy heart melted and dissolved.

At first the superposition of a thingummy on a thingabob and the pale, palpitating stripe that went upwards were utterly incomprehensible, like words in a forgotten language or the parts of a dismantled engine—and this senseless tangle sent a shiver of panic running through him: I have woken up in the grave, on the moon, in the dungeon of dingy non-being. But something in his brain turned, his thoughts settled and hastened to paint over the truth—and he realized that he was looking at the curtain of a half-open window, at a table in front of the window: such is the treaty with reason—the theater of earthly habit, the livery of temporary substance. He lowered his head onto the pillow and tried to overtake a fugitive sense—warm, wonderful, all-explaining—but the new dream he dreamt was an uninspired compilation, stitched together out of remnants of daytime life and fitted to it.

The morning was overcast and cool, with gray-black puddles on the yard's asphalt, and one could hear the nasty flat thumping of carpets being beaten. The Shchyogolevs had finished their packing; Zina had gone off to work and at one o'clock was due to meet her mother for lunch at the Vaterland. Luckily they had not suggested that Fyodor join them—on the contrary, Marianna Nikolavna, as she warmed up some coffee for him in the kitchen where he sat in his dressing gown, disconcerted by the bivouac-like atmosphere in the apartment, warned him that a little Italian salad and some ham had been left in the larder for lunch. It turned out, incidentally, that the luckless person who was getting their number by mistake, had rung up the previous night: this time he had been tremendously agitated, something had happened—something which remained unknown.

For the tenth time Boris Ivanovich transferred from one valise to another a pair of shoes on shoe trees, all clean and shiny—he was unusually meticulous over footwear.

Then they dressed and went out, while Fyodor shaved, carried out long and successful ablutions, and cut his toenails—it was especially pleasant to get under a tight corner, and *clip!*— the parings shot all over the bathroom. The janitor knocked but was unable to enter because the Shchyogolevs had locked the hall door on the American lock, and Fyodor's keys had gone forever. Through the letter-box, clacking the shutter, the mailman threw in the Belgrade newspaper *For Tsar and Church,* to which Boris Ivanovich subscribed, and later someone thrust in (leaving it to stick out boatlike) a leaflet advertising a new hairdresser's. At exactly half past eleven there came a loud barking from the stairs and the agitated descent of the Alsatian which was taken for a walk at this time. With a comb in his hand he went out onto the balcony to see if the weather was clearing up, but although it did not rain, the sky remained hopelessly and wanly white—and one could not believe that yesterday it had been possible to lie in the forest. The Shchyogolevs' bedroom was cluttered up with paper rubbish, and one of the suitcases was open—at the top a pear-shaped object of rubber was lying on a wafer towel. An itinerant mustache came into the yard with cymbals, a drum, a saxophone—completely hung with metallic music, with bright music on his head, and with a monkey in a red jersey—and sang for a long time, tapping his foot and jangling—without managing, however, to drown out the volleying at the carpets on their trestles. Cautiously pushing the door, Fyodor visited Zina's room, where he had never been before, and with the bizarre sensation of a glad moving in he looked for a long time at the briskly ticking alarm clock, at the rose in a glass with its stem all studded with bubbles, at the divan that became a bed at night and at the stockings drying on the radiator. He had a bite to eat, sat down at his desk, dipped his pen, and froze over a blank sheet. The Shchyogolevs returned, the janitor came, Marianna Nikolavna broke a bottle of scent—and he still sat over the glowering sheet and only came to himself when the Shchyogolevs were getting ready to go to the station. There were still two hours until the train's departure, but then the station was a long way off. "I must confess—I like to get there on the cock," said Boris Ivanovich buoyantly as he took hold of his shirt cuff and sleeve in order to climb into his overcoat. Fyodor tried to help him (the other with a polite exclamation, still only halfway in, shied away and suddenly, in the corner, turned into a horrible hunchback), and then went to say good-bye to Marianna Nikolavna, who with an oddly altered expression (as if she were dimming and coaxing her reflection) was in the act of putting on a blue hat with a blue veil before the wardrobe mirror. All at once Fyodor felt strangely sorry for her and after a moment's thought he offered to go to the stand for a taxi. "Yes, please," said Marianna Nikolavna and rushed ponderously to the sofa for her gloves.

There proved to be no cabs at the stand, all had been taken, and he was forced to cross the square and look there. When he finally drove up to the house the Shchyogolevs were already standing below, having carried their suitcases down themselves (the "heavy luggage" had been dispatched the day before).

"Well, God take care of you," said Marianna Nikolavna, and kissed him with gutta-percha lips on the forehead.

"Sarotska, Sarotska, send us a telegramotska!" cried Boris the parodist, waving his hand, and the taxi turned and sped away.

Forever, thought Fyodor with relief and whistling went upstairs.

Only here did he realize that he was unable to enter the apartment. It was particularly galling to raise the brass postal shutter and look through at a bunch of keys lying starwise on the hall floor: Marianna Nikolavna had pushed them back in after locking the door behind her. He went down the stairs much more slowly than he had gone up. Zina, he knew, was planning to go from work to the station: considering that the train would be leaving in about two hours, and that the bus ride would take an hour, she (and the keys) would not be back in less than three hours. The streets were windy and gray: he had no one to go to, and he never went alone into pubs or cafés, he hated them fiercely. In his pocket there were three and a half marks; he bought some cigarettes, and since the gnawing need to see Zina (now, when everything was allowed) was really what was taking away all light and sense from the street, from the sky and the air, he hastened to the corner where the necessary bus stopped. The fact that he was wearing bedroom slippers and an ancient crumpled suit, spotted in front, with trousers a button short on the fly, baggy knees and a patch of his mother's making on the bottom, did not disturb him in the least. His tan and the open collar of his shirt gave him a certain pleasant immunity.

It was some kind of a national holiday. Three kinds of flags were sticking out of the house windows: black-yellow-red, black-white-red, and plain red; each one meant something, and funniest of all, this something was able to excite pride or hatred in someone. There were large flags and small flags, on short poles and on long ones, but none of this exhibitionism of civic excitement made the city any more attractive. On the Tauentzienstrasse the bus was held up by a gloomy procession; policemen in black leggings brought up the rear in a slow truck and among the banners there was one with a Russian inscription containing two mistakes: *serb* instead of *serp* (sickle) and *molt* instead of *molot* (hammer). Suddenly he imagined official festivals in Russia, soldiers in long-skirted overcoats, the cult of firm jaws, a gigantic placard with a vociferous cliché clad in Lenin's jacket and cap, and amidst the thunder of stupidities, the kettledrums of boredom, and slave-pleasing splendors—a little squeak of cheap truth. There it is, eternalized, ever more monstrous in its heartiness, a repetition of the Hodynka coronation festivities with its free candy packages—look at the size of them (now much bigger than the original ones)—and with its superbly organized removal of dead bodies . . . Oh, let everything pass and be forgotten—and again in two hundred years' time an ambitious failure will vent his frustration on the simpletons dreaming of a good life (that is if there does not come *my* kingdom, where everyone keeps to himself and there is no equality and no authorities—but if you don't want it, I don't insist and don't care).

The Potsdam square, always disfigured by city work (oh, those old postcards of it where everything is so spacious, with the droshki drivers looking so happy, and the trains of tight-belted ladies brushing the dust—but with the same fat flower-girls). The pseudo-Parisian character of Unter-den-Linden. The narrowness of the commercial streets beyond it. Bridge, barge, sea gulls. The dead eyes of old hotels of the second, third, hundredth class. A few more minutes of riding, and there was the station.

He caught sight of Zina in a beige georgette dress and a white little hat running up the steps. She was running with her pink elbows pressed to her sides, holding her handbag under her arm—and when he caught up with her and half embraced her, she turned round with that tender, blurry smile, with that happy sadness in her eyes with which she always greeted him when they met alone. "Listen," she said, in a flurried voice, "I'm late, let's run." But he replied that he had already said good-by to them and would wait for her outside.

The low sun settling behind the rooftops seemed to have fallen out of the clouds that covered the rest of the sky (but they were by now quite soft and aloof, as if painted in melting undulations upon a greenish ceiling); there, in that narrow slit, the sky was on fire, and opposite, a window and some metallic letters shone like copper. A porter's long shadow, pushing the shadow of a barrow, sucked in that shadow, but at the turning it protruded again at a sharp angle.

"We'll miss you, Zina," said Marianna Nikolavna, from the window of the carriage. "But in any case take your vacation in August and come over—we'll see if you can't perhaps stay for good."

"I don't think so," said Zina. "Ah yes, I gave you my keys today. Don't take them with you, please."

"I left them in the hall . . . And Boris's are in the desk . . . Never mind: Godunov will let you in," added Marianna Nikolavna appeasingly.

"Well, well. Good luck to it," said Boris Ivanovich from behind his wife's plump shoulder and rolled his eyes. "Ah, Zinka, Zinka, just you come over and you shall ride a bicycle and swill milk—that's the life!"

The train gave a shudder and started to move. Marianna Nikolavna kept waving for a long time. Shchyogolev drew in his head like a tortoise (and having sat down, probably emitted a Russian grunt).

She skipped down the steps—her bag now hung from her fingers, and the last rays of the sun caused a bronze gleam to dance in her eyes as she flew up to Fyodor. They kissed as ardently as if she had just arrived from far off, after a long separation.

"And now let's go and have some supper," she said, taking his arm. "You must be starved."

He nodded. Now how to explain it? Why this strange embarrassment—instead of the exultant, voluble freedom I had been so eagerly looking forward to? It was as if I had grown disused from her, or else was unable to adjust myself and her, the former her, to this freedom.

"What's the matter with you—you seem out of sorts?" she asked observantly after a silence (they were walking toward the bus stop).

"It's sad to part with Boris the Brisk," he replied, trying to see if a joke would resolve his emotional constraint.

"And I think it's yesterday's escapade," said Zina, smiling, and he detected in her tone of voice a high-strung ring, which in its own way corresponded to his own confusion and thus both stressed and augmented it.

"Nonsense. The rain was warm. I feel wonderful."

The bus rolled up, they boarded it. Fyodor paid for two tickets from his palm. Zina said: "I get my wages only tomorrow, so that all I have now is two marks. How much do you have?"

"Very little. Out of your two hundred I was left only three-fifty and more than a half of that I have blowed."

"We have enough for supper, though," said Zina.

"Are you quite sure you like the idea of a restaurant? Because I don't too much."

"Never mind, resign yourself. In general now it's all over with healthy home cooking. I can't even make an omelette. We must think about how to manage things. But for now I know an excellent place."

Several minutes of silence. The streetlamps and shop windows were beginning to light up; the streets had grown pinched and gray from that immature light, but the sky was radiant and wide, and the sunset cloudlets were trimmed with flamingo down.

"Look, the photos are ready."

He took them from her cold fingers. Zina standing in the street before her office, with legs placed tightly together and the shadow of a lime trunk crossing the sidewalk, like a boom lowered in front of her; Zina sitting sideways on a windowsill with a crown of sunshine around her head; Zina at work, badly taken, dark-faced—but to compensate this, her regal typewriter enthroned in the foreground, with a gleam on its carriage lever.

She thrust them back in her bag, took out and put back her monthly tram ticket in its cellophane holder, took out a small mirror, looked into it, baring the filling in her front tooth, replaced the mirror inside, clicked the bag shut, lowered it onto her knees, looked at her shoulder, brushed off a bit of fluff, put on her gloves, turned her head to the window—doing all this in rapid succession, with her features in motion, her eyes blinking and a kind of inner biting and sucking in of her cheeks. But now she sat motionless, looking away, the sinews in her pale neck stretched tight and her white-gloved hands lying on the glossy leather of her handbag.

The *defilé* of the Brandenburg Gate.

Beyond the Potsdam square, just as they were approaching the canal, an elderly lady with prominent cheekbones (where had I seen her?) and with a goggle-eyed, trembling little dog under her arm made a dive for the exit, swaying and struggling with phantoms, and Zina looked up at her with a fleeting, heavenly glance.

"Did you recognize her?" she asked. "That was Lorentz. I think she's mad at me because I never ring her up. Quite a superfluous woman, really."

"There's a smut on your cheek," said Fyodor. "Careful, don't smear it."

Again the handbag, handkerchief, mirror.

"We soon have to get out," she said presently. "What?"

"Nothing. I agree. Let's get out where you like."

"Here," she said two stops later, taking his elbow, sitting again from a jolt, rising finally and fishing out her bag as if from water.

The lights had already taken shape; the sky was quite faint.

A truck went by with a load of young people returning from some civic orgy, waving something or other and shouting something or other. In the middle of a treeless public garden consisting of a large oblong flower-bed rimmed by a footpath, an army of roses was in bloom. The small, open enclosure of a restaurant (six little tables) opposite this garden was separated from the sidewalk by a whitewashed barrier topped with petunias.

Beside them a boar and his sow were feeding, the waiter's black fingernail dipped into the sauce, and yesterday a lip with a sore on it had been pressed to the gold border of my beer glass. . . . The mist of some sorrow had enveloped Zina—her cheeks, her narrowed eyes, her throat pit, her fragile clavicle—and this was somehow enhanced by the pale smoke from her cigarette. The scuffing of passersby seemed to stir up the thickening darkness.

Suddenly, in the frank evening sky, very high . . .

"Look," he said. "What a beauty!"

A brooch with three rubies was gliding over the dark velvet—so high that not even the hum of the engine was audible.

She smiled, parting her lips and looking upwards.

"Tonight?" he asked, also looking upwards.

Only now had he entered into the order of feelings he used to promise himself, when formerly he imagined how they would slip together out of a thralldom that had gradually asserted itself in the course of their meetings, and grown habitual, even though it was based on something artificial, something unworthy, in fact, of the significance it had acquired: now it seemed incomprehensible why on any of those four hundred and fifty-five days she and he had not simply moved out of the Shchyogolev's apartment to dwell together; but at the same time he knew subrationally that this external obstacle was merely a pretext, merely an ostentatious device on the part of fate, which had hastily put up the first barrier to come to hand in order to engage meantime in the important, complicated business that secretly required the very delay in development which had seemed to depend on a natural obstruction.

Pondering now fate's methods (in this white, illuminated little enclosure, in Zina's golden presence and with the participation of the warm, concave darkness immediately behind the carved radiance of the petunias), he finally found a certain thread, a hidden spirit, a chess idea for his as yet hardly planned "novel," to which he had glancingly referred yesterday in the letter to his mother. It was of this that he spoke now, spoke in such a way as if it were really the best and most normal expression of his happiness—which was also expressed in a more accessible edition by such things as the velvetiness of the air, three emerald lime leaves that had got into the lamplight, the icy cold beer, the lunar volcanoes of mashed potato, vague voices, footfalls, the stars among the ruins of clouds. . . .

"Here is what I'd like to do," he said. "Something similar to destiny's work in regard to us. Think how fate started it three and a half odd years ago. . . . The first attempt to bring us together was crude and heavy! That moving of furniture, for example: I see something extravagant in it, a 'no-holds-barred' something, for it was quite a job moving the Lorentzes and all their belongings into the house where I had just rented a room! The idea lacked subtlety: to have us meet through Lorentz's wife. Wishing to speed things up, fate brought in Romanov, who rang me up and invited me to a party at his place. But at this point fate blundered: the medium chosen was wrong, I disliked the man and a reverse result was achieved: because of him I began to avoid an acquaintance with the Lorentzes—so that all this cumbersome construction went to the devil, fate was left with a furniture van on her hands and the expenses were not recovered."

"Watch out," said Zina, "she might take offense at this criticism now and revenge herself."

"Listen further. Fate made a second attempt, simpler this time but promising better success, because I was in need of money and should have grasped at the offer of work—helping an unknown Russian girl to translate some documents; but this also failed. First because the lawyer Charski also turned out to be an unsuitable middleman, and secondly because I hate working on translations into German—so that it again miscarried. Then finally, after this failure, fate decided to take no chances, to install me directly in the place where you lived. As a go-between she chose not the first person to come along, but someone I liked who energetically took the matter in hand and did not allow me to dodge it. At the last minute, true, there occurred a hitch that almost ruined everything: in her haste—or from stinginess—destiny did not produce you at the time of my visit; of course, after talking five minutes to your stepfather—whom fate had been careless enough to let out of his cage—I decided not to take the unattractive room I had glimpsed over his shoulder. And then, at the end of her tether, unable to show me you immediately, fate showed me as a last desperate maneuver your bluish ball dress on the chair—and strange to say, I myself don't know why but the maneuver worked, and I can imagine what a sigh of relief fate must have heaved."

"Only that wasn't my dress, it was my cousin Raissa's—she's very nice but a perfect fright—I think she left it for me to take something off or sew something on."

"Then it was still more ingenious. What resourcefulness! The most enchanting things in nature and art are based on deception. Look, you see—it began with a reckless impetuosity and ended with the finest of finishing touches. Now isn't that the plot for a remarkable novel? What a theme! But it must be built up, curtained, surrounded by dense life—my life, my professional passions and cares."

"Yes, but that will result in an autobiography with mass executions of good acquaintances."

"Well, let's suppose that I so shuffle, twist, mix, rechew and rebelch everything, add such spices of my own and impregnate things so much with myself that nothing remains of the autobiography but dust—the kind of dust, of course, which makes the most orange of skies. And I shan't write it now, I'll be a long time preparing it, years perhaps . . . In any case I'll do something else first—I want to translate something in my own manner from an old French sage—in order to reach a final dictatorship over words, because in my *Chernyshevski* they are still trying to vote."

"That's all marvelous," said Zina. "I like it all immensely. I think you'll be such a writer as has never been before, and Russia will simply pine for you—when she comes to her senses too late. . . . But do you love me?"

"What I am saying is in fact a kind of declaration of love," replied Fyodor.

"A 'kind of' is not enough. You know at times I shall probably be wildly unhappy with you. But on the whole it does not matter, I'm ready to face it."

She smiled, opening her eyes wide and raising her eyebrows, and then she leaned slightly backwards in her chair and began to powder her chin and nose.

"Ah, I must tell you—this is magnificent—he has a famous passage which I think I can say by heart if I go right on, so don't interrupt me, it's an approximate translation: there was once a man . . . he lived as a true Christian; he did much good, sometimes by word, sometimes by deed, and sometimes by silence; he observed the fasts; he drank the water of mountain valleys (that's good, isn't it?); he nurtured the spirit of contemplation and vigilance; he lived a pure, difficult, wise life; but when he sensed the approach of death, instead of thinking about it, instead of tears of repentance and sorrowful partings, instead of monks and a notary in black, he invited guests to a feast, acrobats, actors, poets, a crowd of dancing girls, three magicians, jolly Tollenburg students, a traveler from Taprobana, and in the midst of melodious verses, masks and music he drained a goblet of wine and died, with a carefree smile on his face. . . . Magnificent, isn't it? If I have to die one day that's exactly how I'd like it to be."

"Only minus the dancing girls," said Zina.

"Well, that's only a symbol of gay company. . . . Perhaps, now, we can go?"

"We have to pay," said Zina. "Call him over."

After this they were left with eleven pfennigs, counting the blackened coin which she had picked up a day or two before from the sidewalk: it would bring luck. As they walked down the street he felt a quick tremor along his spine, and again that emotional constraint, but now in a different, languorous form. It was a twenty minutes' slow walk to the house, and the air, the darkness and the honeyed scent of blooming lindens caused a sucking ache at the base of the chest. This scent evanesced in the stretch from linden to linden, being replaced there by a black freshness, and then again, beneath the next canopy, an oppressive and heady cloud would accumulate, and Zina would say, tensing her nostrils: "Ah, smell it," and again the darkness would be drained of savor and again would be heavy with honey. Will it really happen tonight? Will it really happen now? The weight and the threat of bliss. When I walk with you like this, ever so slowly, and hold you by the shoulder, everything slightly sways, my head hums, and I feel like dragging my feet; my left slipper falls off my heel, we crawl, dawdle, dwindle in a mist—now we are almost all melted. . . . And one day we shall recall all this—the lindens, and the shadow on the wall, and a poodle's unclipped claws tapping over the flagstones of the night. And the star, the star. And here is the square and the dark church with the yellow light of its clock. And here, on the corner, the house.

Good-by, my book! Like mortal eyes, imagined ones must close some day. Onegin from his knees will rise—but his creator strolls away. And yet the ear cannot right now part with the music and allow the tale to fade; the chords of fate itself continue to vibrate; and no obstruction for the sage exists where I have put The End: the shadows of my world extend beyond the skyline of the page, blue as tomorrow's morning haze—nor does this terminate the phrase.

The End

ABOUT THE AUTHOR

Vladimir Nabokov was born in St. Petersburg on April 23, 1889. His family fled to Germany in 1919, during the Bolshevik Revolution. Nabokov studied French and Russian literature at Trinity College, Cambridge, from 1919 to 1923, then lived in Berlin (1923–1937) and Paris (1937–1940), where he began writing, mainly in Russian, under the pseudonym Sirin. In 1940 he moved to the United States, where he pursued a brilliant literary career (as a poet, novelist, critic, and translator) while teaching literature at Stanford, Wellesley, Cornell, and Harvard. The monumental success of his novel *Lolita* (1955) enabled him to give up teaching and devote himself fully to his writing. In 1961 he moved to Montreux, Switzerland, where he died in 1977. Recognized as one of this century's master prose stylists in both Russian and English, he translated a number of his original English works–including *Lolita*–into Russian, and collaborated on English translations of his original Russian works.

VINTAGE INTERNATIONAL

___ **The Ark Sakura** by Kobo Abe $8.95 679-72161-4
___ **The Woman in the Dunes** by Kobo Abe $10.00 679-73378-7
___ **Chromos** by Felipe Alfau $11.00 679-73443-0
___ **Locos: A Comedy of Gestures** by Felipe Alfau $8.95 679-72846-5
___ **Dead Babies** by Martin Amis $10.00 679-73449-X
___ **Einstein's Monsters** by Martin Amis $8.95 679-72996-8
___ **London Fields** by Martin Amis $11.00 679-73034-6
___ **Success** by Martin Amis $10.00 679-73448-1
___ **For Every Sin** by Aharon Appelfeld $9.95 679-72758-2
___ **One Day of Life** by Manlio Argueta $9.95 679-73243-8
___ **Collected Poems** by W. H. Auden $16.00 679-73197-0
___ **The Dyer's Hand** by W. H. Auden $12.95 679-72484-2
___ **Forewords and Afterwords** by W. H. Auden $12.95 679-72485-0
___ **Selected Poems** by W. H. Auden $10.95 679-72483-4
___ **Flaubert's Parrot** by Julian Barnes $8.95 679-73136-9
___ **A History of the World in 10½ Chapters** by Julian Barnes $9.95 679-73137-7
___ **A Man for All Seasons** by Robert Bolt $7.95 679-72822-8
___ **The Sheltering Sky** by Paul Bowles $9.95 679-72979-8
___ **The Fall** by Albert Camus $9.00 679-72022-7
___ **The Myth of Sisyphus and Other Essays** by Albert Camus $9.00 679-73373-6
___ **The Plague** by Albert Camus $10.00 679-72021-9
___ **The Stranger** by Albert Camus $7.95 679-72020-0
___ **No Telephone to Heaven** by Michelle Cliff $8.95 679-73942-4
___ **Out of Africa and Shadows on the Grass** by Isak Dinesen $7.95 679-72475-3
___ **Love, Pain, and the Whole Damn Thing** by Doris Dörrie $9.00 679-72992-5
___ **The Assignment** by Friedrich Dürrenmatt $7.95 679-72233-5
___ **Invisible Man** by Ralph Ellison $10.00 679-72313-7
___ **Scandal** by Shusaku Endo $8.95 679-72355-2
___ **Absalom, Absalom!** by William Faulkner $9.95 679-73218-7
___ **As I Lay Dying** by William Faulkner $8.95 679-73225-X
___ **Go Down, Moses** by William Faulkner $9.95 679-73217-9
___ **Light in August** by William Faulkner $9.95 679-73226-8
___ **The Sound and the Fury** by William Faulkner $8.95 679-73224-1
___ **The Good Soldier** by Ford Madox Ford $8.95 679-72218-1
___ **Howards End** by E. M. Forster $8.95 679-72255-6
___ **A Room With a View** by E. M. Forster $7.95 679-72476-1
___ **Christopher Unborn** by Carlos Fuentes $12.95 679-73222-5
___ **The Story of My Wife** by Milán Füst $8.95 679-72217-3
___ **The Story of a Shipwrecked Sailor** by Gabriel García Márquez $7.95 679-72205-X
___ **The Tin Drum** by Günter Grass $9.95 679-72575-X

VINTAGE INTERNATIONAL

	Title	Price	ISBN
___	**Claudius the God** by Robert Graves	$9.95	679-72573-3
___	**I, Claudius** Robert Graves	$8.95	679-72477-X
___	**Aurora's Motive** by Erich Hackl	$7.95	679-72435-4
___	**Dispatches** by Michael Herr	$10.00	679-73525-9
___	**Walter Winchell** by Michael Herr	$9.00	679-73393-0
___	**The Swimming-Pool Library** by Alan Hollinghurst	$8.95	679-72256-4
___	**I Served the King of England** by Bohumil Hrabal	$10.95	679-72786-8
___	**An Artist of the Floating World** by Kazuo Ishiguro	$8.95	679-72266-1
___	**A Pale View of Hills** by Kazuo Ishiguro	$8.95	679-72267-X
___	**The Remains of the Day** by Kazuo Ishiguro	$9.95	679-73172-5
___	**Ulysses** by James Joyce	$14.95	679-72276-9
___	**The Emperor** by Ryszard Kapuściński	$7.95	679-72203-3
___	**China Men** by Maxine Hong Kingston	$9.95	679-72328-5
___	**Tripmaster Monkey** by Maxine Hong Kingston	$9.95	679-72789-2
___	**The Woman Warrior** by Maxine Hong Kingston	$8.95	679-72188-6
___	**Barabbas** by Pär Lagerkvist	$7.95	679-72544-X
___	**The Radiance of the King** by Camara Laye	$9.95	679-72200-9
___	**The Fifth Child** by Doris Lessing	$6.95	679-72182-7
___	**The Drowned and the Saved** by Primo Levi	$8.95	679-72186-X
___	**The Real Life of Alejandro Mayta** by Mario Vargas Llosa	$8.95	679-72478-8
___	**My Traitor's Heart** by Rian Malan	$10.95	679-73215-2
___	**Man's Fate** by André Malraux	$9.95	679-72574-1
___	**Death in Venice and Seven Other Stories** by Thomas Mann	$8.95	679-72206-8
___	**The Captive Mind** by Czeslaw Milosz	$8.95	679-72856-2
___	**Spring Snow** by Yukio Mishima	$10.95	679-72241-6
___	**Runaway Horses** by Yukio Mishima	$10.95	679-72240-8
___	**The Temple of Dawn** by Yukio Mishima	$10.95	679-72242-4
___	**The Decay of the Angel** by Yukio Mishima	$10.95	679-72243-2
___	**Cities of Salt** by Abdelrahman Munif	$12.95	394-75526-X
___	**Ada, or Ardor** by Vladimir Nabokov	$12.95	679-72522-9
___	**Bend Sinister** by Vladimir Nabokov	$9.95	679-72727-2
___	**The Defense** by Vladimir Nabokov	$8.95	679-72722-1
___	**Despair** by Vladimir Nabokov	$7.95	679-72343-9
___	**The Enchanter** by Vladimir Nabokov	$9.00	679-72886-4
___	**The Eye** by Vladimir Nabokov	$8.95	679-72723-X
___	**The Gift** by Vladimir Nabokov	$11.00	679-72725-6
___	**Invitation to a Beheading** by Vladimir Nabokov	$7.95	679-72531-8
___	**King, Queen, Knave** by Vladimir Nabokov	$8.95	679-72340-4
___	**Laughter in the Dark** by Vladimir Nabokov	$8.95	679-72450-8
___	**Lolita** by Vladimir Nabokov	$8.95	679-72316-1
___	**Look at the Harlequins!** by Vladimir Nabokov	$9.95	679-72728-0

VINTAGE INTERNATIONAL

	Title	Price	ISBN
___	**Mary** by Vladimir Nabokov	$6.95	679-72620-9
___	**Pale Fire** by Vladimir Nabokov	$9.95	679-72342-0
___	**Pnin** by Vladimir Nabokov	$7.95	679-72341-2
___	**Speak, Memory** by Vladimir Nabokov	$9.95	679-72339-0
___	**Strong Opinions** by Vladimir Nabokov	$9.95	679-72609-8
___	**Transparent Things** by Vladimir Nabokov	$6.95	679-72541-5
___	**A Bend in the River** by V. S. Naipaul	$7.95	679-72202-5
___	**Guerrillas** by V. S. Naipaul	$10.95	679-73174-1
___	**A Turn in the South** V. S. Naipaul	$9.95	679-72488-5
___	**Black Box** by Amos Oz	$8.95	679-72185-1
___	**The Shawl** by Cynthia Ozick	$7.95	679-72926-7
___	**Dictionary of the Khazars** by Milorad Pavić		
	male edition	$9.95	679-72461-3
	female edition	$9.95	679-72754-X
___	**Swann's Way** by Marcel Proust	$9.95	679-72009-X
___	**Kiss of the Spider Woman** by Manuel Puig	$10.00	679-72449-4
___	**Grey Is the Color of Hope** by Irina Ratushinskaya	$8.95	679-72447-8
___	**Memoirs of an Anti-Semite** by Gregor von Rezzori	$10.95	679-73182-2
___	**The Snows of Yesteryear** by Gregor von Rezzori	$10.95	679-73181-4
___	**The Notebooks of Malte Laurids Brigge** by Rainer Maria Rilke	$10.95	679-73245-4
___	**Selected Poetry** by Rainer Maria Rilke	$11.95	679-72201-7
___	**Shame** by Salman Rushdie	$9.95	679-72204-1
___	**No Exit and 3 Other Plays** by Jean-Paul Sartre	$8.95	679-72516-4
___	**All You Who Sleep Tonight** by Vikram Seth	$9.00	679-73025-7
___	**The Golden Gate** by Vikram Seth	$11.00	679-73457-0
___	**And Quiet Flows the Don** by Mikhail Sholokhov	$10.95	679-72521-0
___	**Ake: The Years of Childhood** by Wole Soyinka	$9.95	679-72540-7
___	**Ìsarà: A Voyage Around "Essay"** by Wole Soyinka	$9.95	679-73246-2
___	**Confessions of Zeno** by Italo Svevo	$9.95	679-72234-3
___	**The Beautiful Mrs. Seidenman** by Andrzej Szczypiorski	$9.95	679-73214-4
___	**Diary of a Mad Old Man** by Junichiro Tanizaki	$10.00	679-73024-9
___	**The Key** by Junichiro Tanizaki	$10.00	679-73023-0
___	**On the Golden Porch** by Tatyana Tolstaya	$8.95	679-72843-0
___	**The Optimist's Daughter** by Eudora Welty	$8.95	679-72883-X
___	**Losing Battles** by Eudora Welty	$8.95	679-72882-1
___	**The Eye of the Story** by Eudora Welty	$8.95	679-73004-4
___	**The Passion** by Jeanette Winterson	$8.95	679-72437-0
___	**Sexing the Cherry** by Jeanette Winterson	$9.00	679-73316-7

Available at your bookstore or call toll-free to order: 1-800-733-3000.
Credit cards only. Prices subject to change.